PRAISE FOR *DAUGHTER OF ROME* AND OTHER NOVELS BY TESSA AFSHAR

"Tessa Afshar has the rare gift of seamlessly blending impeccable historical research and theological depth with lyrical prose and engaging characters. In *Daughter of Rome*, Afshar imagines the multi-textured lives of Priscilla and Aquila, coworkers of the apostle Paul, as they are stretched and shaped through their losses and love. What emerges is a compelling story about their faith and faithfulness—a story that invites our response of faith and faithfulness as well."

SHARON GARLOUGH BROWN, AUTHOR OF *SHADES OF LIGHT* AND THE SENSIBLE SHOES SERIES

"Tessa Afshar's ability to transport readers into the culture and characters of her biblical novels is extraordinary. From the first chapter you'll feel as if you know Priscilla. You might tear up like I did when she meets Aquila and their story unfolds. *Daughter of Rome* is a feast for your imagination as well as balm for your soul."

ROBIN JONES GUNN, BESTSELLING AUTHOR OF *BECOMING US*

THIEF OF CORINTH

"Afshar again shows her amazing talent for packing action and intrigue into the biblical setting for modern readers."

PUBLISHERS WEEKLY, STARRED REVIEW

"Lyrical . . . [with] superb momentum, exhilarating scenes, and moving themes of love and determination. . . . Afshar brings to life the gripping tale of one woman's struggle to choose between rebellion and love."

BOOKLIST

"Afshar's well-drawn characters and lushly detailed setting vividly bring to life the ancient world of the Bible. A solid choice for fans of Francine Rivers and Bodie and Brock Thoene."

LIBRARY JOURNAL

BREAD OF ANGELS

"Afshar continues to demonstrate an exquisite ability to bring the women of the Bible to life, this time shining a light on Lydia, the seller of purple, and skillfully balancing fact with imagination."

ROMANTIC TIMES

"Afshar has created an unforgettable story of dedication, betrayal, and redemption that culminates in a rich testament to God's mercies and miracles."

PUBLISHERS WEEKLY

"With sublime writing and solid research, [Afshar] captures the distinctive experience of living at a time when Christianity was in its fledgling stages."

LIBRARY JOURNAL

"Readers who enjoy Francine Rivers's Lineage of Grace series will love this stand-alone book."

CHRISTIAN MARKET

"With its resourceful, resilient heroine and vibrant narrative, *Bread of Angels* offers an engrossing new look at a mysterious woman of faith."

FOREWORD MAGAZINE

LAND OF SILENCE

"Readers will be moved by Elianna's faith, and Afshar's elegant evocation of biblical life will keep them spellbound. An excellent choice for fans of Francine Rivers's historical fiction and those who read for character."

LIBRARY JOURNAL

"Fans of biblical fiction will enjoy an absorbing and well-researched chariot ride."

PUBLISHERS WEEKLY

"In perhaps her best novel to date, Afshar . . . grants a familiar [biblical] character not only a name, but also a poignant history to which many modern readers can relate. The wit, the romance, and the humanity make Elianna's journey uplifting as well as soul touching."

ROMANTIC TIMES, TOP PICK REVIEW

"Heartache and healing blend beautifully in this gem among Christian fiction."

CBA RETAILERS + RESOURCES

"An impressively crafted, inherently appealing, consistently engaging, and compelling read from first page to last, *Land of Silence* is enthusiastically recommended for community library historical fiction collections."

MIDWEST BOOK REVIEWS

"This captivating story of love, loss, faith, and hope gives a realistic glimpse of what life might have been like in ancient Palestine."

WORLD MAGAZINE

TESSA AFSHAR

Daughter of Rome

Tyndale House Publishers
Carol Stream, Illinois

Visit Tyndale online at www.tyndale.com.

Visit Tessa Afshar at www.tessaafshar.com.

TYNDALE and Tyndale's quill logo are registered trademarks of Tyndale House Publishers, Inc.

Daughter of Rome

Designed by Dean H. Renninger

Edited by Kathryn S. Olson

Published in association with the literary agency of Books & Such Literary Agency, 52 Mission Circle, Suite 122, PMB 170, Santa Rosa, CA 95409

Library of Congress Cataloging-in-Publication Data
Names: Afshar, Tessa, author.
Title: Daughter of Rome / Tessa Afshar.
Description: Carol Stream, Illinois : Tyndale House Publishers, Inc., [2020]
Identifiers: LCCN 2019034281 (print) | LCCN 2019034282 (ebook) | ISBN 9781496428707 (hardcover) | ISBN 9781496428714 (trade paperback) | ISBN 9781496428721 (kindle edition) | ISBN 9781496428738 (epub) | ISBN 9781496428745 (epub)
Subjects: GSAFD: Christian fiction. | Love stories.
Classification: LCC PS3601.F47 D38 2020 (print) | LCC PS3601.F47 (ebook) | DDC 813/.6—dc23
LC record available at https://lccn.loc.gov/2019034281
LC ebook record available at https://lccn.loc.gov/2019034282

Printed in the United States of America

26 25 24 23 22 21
7 6 5 4 3

For Jessie:

Kind. Thoughtful. Funny. Smart. Beautiful.

My lovable bookworm.

You will always be a treasure to my heart.

Also by Tessa Afshar

Bread of Angels

Land of Silence

Pearl in the Sand

Harvest of Rubies

Harvest of Gold

In the Field of Grace

We will tell the next generation
the praiseworthy deeds of the Lord,
his power, and the wonders he has done.

PSALM 78:4

Prologue

HEART SLAMMING AGAINST HER CHEST, stomach roiling like floodwaters, Priscilla stood before the closed door. She had come to this same spot four times already without taking a step within. Today she could not turn back. Time had become the enemy she could not conquer. She had to cross over that threshold.

The wooden slats facing her must have once been painted crimson but had long since faded to a sickly rust color. She raised her hand to knock. Her fingers trembled and she clenched them into a fist. She rested her forehead against the peeling paint. She could not go through with this.

She *had* to go through with this.

Before she could recoil again, she slammed her fist into the wood once. Twice. The third time, she crashed her knuckles against the door so hard, the skin scraped off. She was already bleeding and she had not even taken a step inside.

The door was pulled open by a woman with unkempt gray hair and a fold of loose skin under her chin that shook every time she moved. "I heard you the first time," she said. "No need to knock the door down." She barred the way with her wide body, like a military sentinel, not budging. "What do you want?"

"I am here to . . ." Priscilla stared at her shoes, lost for words. "To see the physician."

The woman said nothing, appraising Priscilla with cold eyes that seemed to calculate the value of her worn tunic and palla, the mantle she wore over her head and shoulders, the delicate earrings with their minute amethyst beads, and her only other piece of jewelry, the chipped glass and silver broach that sat on one shoulder. For a moment Priscilla thought the woman might deny her entry. Relief flooded her mind, followed immediately by terror. What was she supposed to do if the physician refused to help?

"Have you come alone?" the woman said.

"Yes."

"Do you have the coin?"

Priscilla fished for the small purse half-filled with clinking silver, which she had knotted into the ribbons at her waist. Her unsteady hands fumbled with the string, taking too long for the woman's liking.

Without ceremony, she shoved thick fingers into the ribbons, making short work of the knots. Pouring the coins into her palm, the woman counted them carefully before returning them to their purse, which she then tucked into her belt. Turning her body, she finally allowed Priscilla to walk inside.

The cloying scent of incense burning in an iron brazier made Priscilla dizzy. She licked dry lips as she followed her hostess into the courtyard, where she was directed to sit on a dirty bench. To her surprise, Priscilla found that she was not the only occupant of the narrow atrium. Another young woman sat on the bench at the opposite end of the rectangular courtyard. She was clothed in an elegant tunic the color of saffron, her face, like Priscilla's own, half-covered by the curtain of her palla.

Priscilla was not supposed to wear a palla, an article of clothing reserved for wives. That small deceit had been a necessity, protecting her secret.

Needing a distraction from her thoughts, Priscilla glanced over at the other woman. Though she could only see a hint of her profile, something about her regal posture and the silhouette of her face visible through her veil struck Priscilla as familiar. Here sat another soul suffering the consequences of one moment of foolishness, a companion in shame.

Someone screamed in a room above them, making Priscilla jump. The sealed door muted the sound but could not altogether hide the agony of the female whose howls were dwindling to moans. The breath caught in Priscilla's chest. On shaking legs, she pushed herself to the fountain that occupied the middle of the courtyard and leaned into its hot, gray stones to keep from collapsing. She shoved her hand into the water and rinsed her face. The water, as warm as the air, settled wet and heavy on her skin.

A cool breeze wafted in through the wide opening in the ceiling, and Priscilla lifted her head to its caress. It blew harder, making her tunic dance around her legs. From the corner of her eye, she saw the breeze catch the veil covering her silent companion's face, lifting it onto her shoulders. The woman replaced the fabric hastily. But Priscilla had seen enough. She would have recognized that face anywhere.

"Antonia!" she whispered, shocked. "Antonia," she said again, this time louder, lifting an arm in greeting.

Antonia turned her face away, ignoring Priscilla.

Priscilla slumped, dropping her arm. Not that she could blame the young woman. This was no place to be found. Especially not if you were the unmarried niece of the emperor Claudius.

Priscilla could not claim to be the girl's friend. They had barely met. When her father had been alive, he sometimes deigned to take her to gatherings hosted by the nobility of Rome. She had run into Antonia two or three times. Even then, Priscilla had been too unimportant to merit more than a formal introduction. But the aquiline features with their unique cast were hard to forget.

Shoulders drooping, Priscilla returned to the dirty bench and sat, her back sagging against the wall. She wondered what misfortune had brought Antonia to this house of pain. Surely any man would want a girl of such beauty and high connections for his wife. Unlike herself.

She thought of the first time she had seen Appius, with his dark hair and winsome smile as he drew on papyrus, his eyes eating Priscilla with hunger as if she were a ripe plum.

Deprived of social connections and companionship after her father's death two years earlier, she had intended to savor every moment of the feast her brother had allowed her to attend. This fellow guest, whose name she had then not even known, was not going to rob her of enjoying such a rare opportunity.

"What are you doing?" she had asked, wriggling with discomfort under the intensity of his gaze.

"Sketching the most beautiful creature I have ever seen."

Priscilla had rolled her eyes and tried to ignore him. Eventually, unable to bear his scrutiny, she had walked over and stood at his shoulder to examine his art. She burst into laughter when she saw what his drawing had produced.

"That's a bird," she said.

"It's a swan," he clarified, his voice wounded. "A glorious swan."

He had drawn the bird beautifully, she had to give him that. There was something majestic about its pose, long neck turned toward the viewer, beak bright against the black markings of its face.

"You are too lovely to be captured in human form."

Priscilla had pursed her lips as if displeased. But her heart had beat faster, making her flush. "What is that?" she said, pointing to the scarlet crown on the swan's head.

Drawing a finger down the length of a red curl resting on her shoulder, he said, "You have stunning hair. I have never seen its equal. It is lovelier than any crown the goddess Hera ever wore."

Having been teased all her life about her red hair, Priscilla had found his praise a heady wine.

"I am Appius," he had said, bowing his head.

"Prisca."

"Any relation to the famed general?"

He had been sharp enough to pick up the association with her name. "General Priscus was my father," she had acknowledged, forbearing to tell Appius that her mother was no more than a slave the general had carried off from Germania. He had married the red-haired enchantress who brought him no gold or important connections. Those he already had through his own bloodlines, and from his first wife, who had dutifully borne him a son and heir. She had died while trying to bear him another.

What would that father say if he could see her now? He would throw her into the streets. Slit her wrists with his own knife. Anything would be better than this shame. All because a man had drawn the silly likeness of a swan. A few weeks earlier, when after a desperate search she had finally found him, Appius had been drawing another swan. It looked exactly like the one he had sketched of her, but this one had a golden crown, like the young woman who had supposedly inspired it. Wordlessly, Priscilla had dropped the sketch he had made of her, which she always carried on her person like a precious love letter, into the girl's lap. "It's the only thing he can draw," she had said, hoping to spare another woman the pain of discovering his perfidy for herself.

A door slammed above them, and Priscilla turned her head to see the old hostess lead a woman out. She was crying, her body shivering and swaying, her steps unsteady. Their hostess half dragged and half carried her fragile patient down the stairs.

"Sit here," she commanded. "I will bring you something to settle your stomach." She shoved the woman unceremoniously onto a couch before disappearing down a narrow passageway.

Not *woman*, Priscilla amended as she glimpsed her round face. She was hardly more than a child.

Several large spots stained the girl's tunic. Priscilla swallowed hard when she realized they were blood. How was one so young going to survive this nightmare? Without thinking, Priscilla jumped to her feet and approached the girl. "It will be all right," she said. Kneeling by the couch, she stroked the thin, sweat-drenched hair. "You will be fine." She said the words without knowing for certain if they were true. Could this child in the body of a woman emerge from this moment and one day become whole again?

The girl threw herself into Priscilla's arms and wailed. "It hurts!"

Priscilla cradled her. "It will pass. Lean on me. It will pass soon." She hoped she was not making empty promises.

Their hostess returned, bearing an earthenware cup and a threadbare blanket. She gave both to Priscilla. "Make her drink this," she said brusquely, walking to the other side of the courtyard. "He is ready for you," she told Antonia, her voice devoid of the merest hint of warmth.

Without hesitation, Antonia rose to her feet and followed the woman in silence. Priscilla watched her climb the stairs and disappear inside the physician's chamber. She had to admire Antonia's perfect calm, posture tall, as if she were visiting the baths instead of submitting to the butchery of a surgeon. Neither the prospect of pain nor the torture of loss seemed to hold any sway over her. Priscilla wished she could display half as much poise under the circumstance.

She forced herself to return her attention to the child who still clung to her limply. "Here now, my dear. Drink from this cup. You will feel better."

The girl drank a cautious sip and made a face. "Drink all of it," Priscilla said, and gently tipped the cup.

She obeyed, coughing as she came up from the last mouthful. The smell of the potion was vile enough to turn Priscilla's stomach. No wonder the child had gagged. Priscilla settled next to the girl on the couch and wrapped the blanket about the slight body. Within moments, the child was asleep, clinging to Priscilla even as she sank into restless dreams.

Time passed like a cloud, with torturous slowness. No screams escaped the chamber above. Whatever Antonia was enduring, she did it silently. The weight of that silence was crushing. Priscilla tried not to imagine what the hands of the physician were busy doing at that moment. Again, she considered running out the faded-crimson door. Running and never returning.

And then what? After her father's death, her brother had become sole heir to the general's fortune. Volero Priscus had never forgiven their father for sullying the memory of his noble mother by replacing her with an ignorant slave from Magna Germania. Never forgiven the general for covering the slave in fine silks and linens and whelping a child on her.

That child had been a sore Volero could not heal, more thorn than kin. As soon as their father had died, he had thrown out the tutor the general had hired for Priscilla, stripped her of her weekly stipend, and reduced her to a state barely above the slaves in the household.

Her brother's disdain had a tendency to turn into cruelty at the slightest provocation. If he discovered her secret, she had no doubt that her body would soon be floating down the dirty currents of the Tiber.

The river Tiber or the chamber above the stairs. Those were her choices.

Her faithful slave Lollia, who had taken care of her since birth, had unwittingly given her the information she had needed to find this place. She had mentioned a friend who served in the household of Cassius. That woman, Lollia said, had delivered her mistress to this same physician more than once. Lollia had meant to assure Priscilla that she was far from the first Roman girl of good family to find herself in such a quandary. Antonia's presence seemed to confirm that notion.

Yet Lollia, whose half-Jewish ancestry gave her a staunch moral standard, had never intended to suggest that Priscilla should engage the physician's services for herself. She had only meant to comfort Priscilla out of a tempest of despair. In the end, Priscilla had come to this place in secret. No need to add to Lollia's mounting anxiety.

The door to the chamber above crashed open with a deafening boom. Priscilla jumped, tightening her hold on the young girl who rested in her arms. As Antonia emerged, their hostess tried to grasp her arm and help her toward the stairs. With a violent motion, Antonia shook the woman off. She swayed for a moment and placed a flat hand against the wall to steady herself. Her face, marble white, lacked expression. Taking a deep breath, she straightened and began to descend the stairs. Her progress was slow but proud. A sovereign rather than a sinner.

There was something formidable to the implacability that marked her posture. As if she would allow nothing to stand in her way. She passed in front of Priscilla to get to the front door.

"Antonia," Priscilla whispered. "Was it awful?" Her voice broke.

"Don't be an imbecile. It is a physician's visit like any other. And if you say my name one more time, I will knock you so hard, you won't need the services of the surgeon."

Antonia did not linger long enough to drink the stinking potion or recover from the surgeon's iron hooks and blades. She kept walking, hesitating only a moment to drag open the heavy door and disappear into the street.

"Your turn," the woman with the gray hair said, standing over Priscilla, the fold of skin under her chin shaking like a boat sail in the wind.

One

FOUR YEARS LATER

THE INESCAPABLE STENCH of sewage and rotting garbage assaulted Aquila's senses, making him wince. He had been in Rome for a mere two days and had already seen architectural marvels that left the visitor gaping: lavish buildings with intricate mosaics, paved roads as smooth as a youth's face, ingenious aqueducts, and a splendid array of shops, porticos, and gymnasiums. Yet for all its glory, there were few places in Rome that did not stink.

He picked his way carefully as he followed his uncle past a fishmonger's stall and a tavern, while sidestepping a clutch of beggars. Aquila had never seen so many people in one place. It was said that one million people inhabited Rome. The magnitude of such a number was beyond what his mind could grasp. At night, he crawled into bed and pulled his pillow over his head, trying to drown out the noise of carts and wagons that actually swelled in activity between sundown and sunrise. Rome never slept.

His uncle Benyamin, who had visited the city several times and had a passing familiarity with its stone-paved avenues and winding alleyways, was leading the way. They were supposed to meet Rufus at the entrance of the Campi synagogue, located in the northwest corner of the city.

They had left their lodging in the congested neighborhood near Via Appia twenty minutes before. Having entered the ancient part of the city, they were now making their way around Circus Maximus. Aquila studied the Circus, the most famous chariot-racing stadium in the world. It was empty today, save for a few slaves who were clearing horse dung from the huge track.

Benyamin led Aquila down a jumble of narrow roads. He stopped to look around for a moment before taking a decisive right. After a few more turns, he stopped again.

"Are you lost, Uncle?" Aquila hid a smile.

"Of course not. I am merely making sure of my bearings."

"I only ask because we have passed this spot three times. Some people would call that lost. Not me, of course."

"Of course." Benyamin gave him a pointed look. "I am sure you are very wise. In your own eyes."

Aquila grinned. "Well, these eyes detect the Via Tecta coming up to our left. Isn't that what you were looking for?" He pointed to the avenue whose entrance was hidden by several tree trunks. Benyamin, who was considerably shorter, had missed it.

"So it is. Why didn't you notice it sooner?"

The Via Tecta ran parallel to the river. Aquila took in the grand buildings as they walked: theaters, baths, and public memorials. For a moment, he forgot that it was the Sabbath, forgot that a dear friend was awaiting their arrival, and slowed his steps to gaze at his surroundings.

"They will still be here when we come back," Benyamin called from up ahead and Aquila hastened after him. They traveled farther north until they arrived at the Via Flaminia and made their way down a narrow alley toward the Tiber River.

Outside a modest rectangular building, Aquila spied Rufus. He was leaning against the wall, apparently too impatient for their arrival to wait inside. He opened his arms in welcome as soon as he spotted them, his teeth shining white through a short beard.

Benyamin embraced him. "It has been too long, my friend."

"I am relieved you are finally here," Rufus said. "Now I don't have to try and read your letters. I can never make out your crabbed writing. In your last one, I was convinced you wrote that you sold your beard. But I see it is still attached to your face."

Benyamin laughed, stroking the long, full bush of hair growing out of his chin. "Thankfully, you were wrong. It has taken me years of careful grooming to become this handsome." He pointed at Aquila, standing quietly next to him. "You remember my nephew."

Over a decade had passed since Aquila had seen Rufus, son of Simon of Cyrene. It was hard to look at him and not remember the extraordinary fact that this man's father had carried the cross of the Lord for him.

Time had left no trace of its passage on Rufus. His light-brown skin remained free of wrinkles, his tight curls black as ink. His youthful smile shone out like a sunny day.

"No!" he said, raising a thick brow. "This cannot be Aquila. This good-looking fellow with the strapping muscles? The Aquila I remember only came up to here." He held his hand to his chest.

Aquila grinned. "These muscles are a result of too much hard work. Uncle Benyamin shows no mercy."

For a moment they were all silent, remembering why the eldest son of a wealthy merchant had been reduced to a man with calluses on his hands.

Rufus cut through the pained silence. "Well, you are not too big for me. Come here, boy." He enfolded Aquila in his great arms, holding him with a father's affection. Aquila felt an unexpected welter of emotion and blinked his eyes. It had been years since anyone save Uncle Benyamin had shown him such open affection.

"Shall we go in?" Benyamin said, rubbing his hands together. "I am longing to hear the Word of God."

The synagogue was a single-story structure with a wooden door painted sky blue. Aquila had seen far richer and more elegant synagogues in his home province of Pontus, where a large community of Jewish people had lived in relative security for centuries.

Several rows of plaster benches stretched along three sides of the rectangular assembly hall. A simple Torah shrine, an arched nook that housed the sacred Scripture scrolls, sat nestled in the center of the western wall. The tall papyrus cylinder faced the congregation, its elaborate ornamentation the only true luxury that adorned the place. Through a small window, Aquila glimpsed a courtyard, verdant with herbs and flower beds. Beyond it he saw the outline of another building, smaller than the house of assembly. Though not luxurious, everything about the place spoke of careful maintenance. Clean and in good repair, it was obvious that the synagogue at Campi was well loved by its congregation.

Men and women sat together here, though a group of women seemed to have congregated on the last row in the back. He suspected that God fearers, those who were not of Jewish heritage but believed in the Lord, occupied that space.

"Here is my mother," Rufus said, pulling them toward the seats on the front row. "She has been impatient to see you."

Mary had Rufus's lips, full and smiling, and a fluff of tight white curls that peeked out under her palla like clouds. Her eyes, when they landed on Aquila, held kindness.

"Welcome, brothers." She had the merest hint of a lisp, making her words softer. "I hope you are hungry." She spoke in Koine Greek, the language of the working people in the Roman empire, and the tongue that brought the people of many nations together. Even the Hellenist Jews who had spread across the nations of the world did not speak Hebrew to one another, but Greek.

"I heard of Simon's passing," Benyamin said. "God be gracious to you."

Nine months earlier, Simon's unexpected death had shaken his friends and family. One night, he had gone to bed at the usual time and, without a whimper or complaint, had passed into glory before the sun arose.

His eldest son, Alexander, had inherited the house and family business in Cyrene, while Rufus came to Rome to expand their trade. Mary had decided to accompany Rufus into Italia.

"Thank you, Benyamin." She turned to Aquila. "And this is your nephew?"

"Aquila, my older brother's son."

Aquila winced at the words and tried to hold on to his smile. *"Was,"* he said, unable to live with the half lie.

Mary rested her hand on his shoulder for a moment. "He is your father still and always will be. Words and legal documents cannot change that."

Aquila dropped his gaze, turning pale. So Mary already knew of his father's decision. His shame had become public knowledge. His father had disowned him, setting him aside in favor of his younger brother. In the small Christian world, stories spread fast. Spread even across borders and continents.

Rufus wrapped an arm about Aquila's shoulders. "In this company, that is a badge of honor. You may have lost the favor of your father. But your heavenly Father delights in you. It takes courage to stand your ground. Strength to lose everything and still hold to the truth." He half turned as a man walked toward the Torah shrine. "Ah. We are about to begin. Better take our seats."

Aquila expelled a breath. He barely knew these people, and yet his humiliation was out in the open for all to see. It followed him everywhere, the ache of this wound. The knowledge that he was an outcast. Unwanted by his own family.

The familiar order of worship wrapped itself about Aquila, soothing his bruised heart. He focused on the opening prayer and made the right response. He said the *Shema*, his voice melding with others, male and female, accented and pure, the same words binding them together: *Hear, O Israel: the Lord our God, the Lord is one.*

He listened when the readers unfurled the Torah scroll with reverence, seven passages from the Books of the Law, followed by one from the Prophets. The Hebrew was then translated into Greek.

Since Aquila spoke Hebrew fluently, his attention wandered when the translation began. His eyes roamed about the hall, studying the faces of those who worshiped. In the row occupied by the God fearers, his gaze settled on a young woman. Her hair, a bright auburn, stood out in the assembly of dark-haired people. She was no Hebrew, but she did not look Roman either. Her skin was fair, her eyes a startling shade of blue, hard to miss even from this distance. High cheekboned and angular, her face had an arresting quality. He had certainly seen more beautiful women. But few had managed to hold his attention as this one seemed to.

There was a stillness in her face, a depth of reverence as she listened to the words of the Law that he found compelling. The interpreter had reached the Prophets now and was translating the verses from Isaiah:

> Forget the former things;
>   do not dwell on the past.
> See, I am doing a new thing!
>   Now it springs up; do you not perceive it?
> I am making a way in the wilderness
>   and streams in the wasteland.

With a touch of wonder he saw her eyes fill with tears. She drank in the Word like it was life.

Not many people entered worship with this consuming intensity. Esther never had. Aquila was intrigued to find a foreigner thus enthralled with Scripture.

He had to force his mind to return to the worship service as one of the men in the congregation rose up to give the message for the day. But even as Aquila listened, he found his thoughts returning to the Gentile woman.

She was unmarried—he could tell from the absence of the palla, leaving waves of auburn hair flowing around her shoulders and back. He wondered what had drawn her to this Hebrew congregation. Growing impatient with the turn of his wandering focus, he exhaled a slow, annoyed breath.

He had not come to Rome to ogle foreigners. He was here to start a new life. Here to grow in his faith and spread a truth that burned like fire in his belly. Foreign women with red hair had no part in his plan.

Two

As the congregation spoke the prayers, their voices melded into one mellifluous current of sound, washing over Priscilla. This was the sound that had first drawn her to the synagogue over a year ago. She had been walking aimlessly that day, Lollia trailing behind, when the gentle chanting that emanated from within the simple building had brought her feet to a halt.

Though muffled and indistinguishable, something about the words had touched her deeply.

"It's a synagogue," Lollia had whispered with wonder. "A Jewish place of worship." She had been born into slavery and had received little instruction from her Jewish father in the ways of his people. But she knew enough to recognize the prayers.

Without pausing to consider, Priscilla had pushed the door open and walked inside. Standing quietly in a corner, she had been enthralled by the worship, by the words read from mysterious texts and the somber speech in Greek given by a thin man with startlingly white teeth.

Over the years, Lollia had spoken of her father's heritage. The bits and pieces of the fabric of faith she possessed, though incomplete, had always made Priscilla feel an attraction for this God who had a tender spot for a world filled with broken people. Now, for the first time, she was witnessing Jewish worship in person. She felt drawn to its mournful tone, wooed by the sound of hope that wove itself through sorrow.

After the service concluded, several women had approached Priscilla and Lollia, not to censure them for intruding, but to welcome them, as if having two strange women show up on their doorstep was a common occurrence.

Looking back, she liked to think that the Lord had directed her feet that day, had drawn her to this spot and extended an invitation on the wings of his people's prayers. She had accepted that invitation and never looked back.

Alongside her, there were other Romans who worshiped the God of the Hebrews in the Campi synagogue. Like her, they were welcomed into the synagogue for worship, though none of them could fully belong because they were Gentiles. They were not entirely outsiders, either, but lived in a shadowland between.

Priscilla had lived most of her life in that state.

It was sad and familiar at once, this feeling of not quite belonging. It left her hungry for more, hungry to be truly part of these people and their God. The God she had come to see as a wellspring of goodness.

The Lord.

Every Sabbath she came to this place, like one starved coming to a banquet, though never allowed to eat her fill. She was too besmirched for this holy God. He was not likely to ever want someone like her.

She clung to him, and yet felt separated from him by a wall so high, she could never scale it. Sabbaths had become a bittersweet time. The most peaceful day of her week as she basked in the promises of God. But also a day of hungering, yearning for more. For something she could never have: a soul-deep sense of acceptance.

At the conclusion of the service, Mary rushed to her side. "I will not be going with you to visit Sara today. We have guests, and I must go home to attend to the meal."

Priscilla hid the pang of disappointment she felt at the news. Though Mary had only begun to attend the synagogue three months ago, Priscilla had formed a special bond with the older woman. Mary was different from the other women at the synagogue. Often she reached out to Priscilla with a genuine friendliness that seemed to disregard the invisible line that separated the Gentiles from the Jewish congregants.

"I have brought some olives and cheese for you to take to Sara," Mary said, handing her a basket.

Priscilla peeked under the linen towel that lay on top. "That looks delicious."

She bent down to pick up the flask of wine along with the small loaves of barley bread she herself had brought. It had taken her a week of drinking only water to save enough wine to bring to Sara, a widow who had broken her ankle and would be unable to work for several weeks.

It was Mary's example that had taught Priscilla the importance of visiting the needy among them. Unable to hide her disappointment, she said, "I will miss your company."

Mary grinned. "I will pray for you."

Priscilla sighed. Cantankerous on the best of days, Sara's injury had caused her to brim over with even more complaints than usual. "Best you pray for Sara. She needs it more."

Rufus walked over, followed by two men Priscilla had never met. She guessed they must be the guests Mary had mentioned. "Good Shabbat, Priscilla," Rufus said.

"Good week to you, Rufus."

"Benyamin, allow me to introduce Prisca of Rome to you." Rufus used Priscilla's formal name rather than the familiar appellation friends preferred. "Prisca, this is Benyamin and his nephew Aquila, of Pontus."

Priscilla felt the weight of the younger man's gaze resting on her for a moment before he turned his head to stare through a window. He had an arresting face, with hard-edged features that slashed rather than curved and stark eyebrows that sat over deep-set eyes, more gray than green. His sculpted mouth revealed nothing of his feelings, and yet, when he turned his face toward her again, something about his enigmatic expression made her heart beat harder against her chest.

Aquila, Rufus had called him. The word meant "eagle" in Latin. It was a good name for him, she decided. His tanned, high-cheekboned face gave him the look of a bird of prey. Watchful. Clever. Intense.

"Priscilla is on her way to deliver food to one of our widows who is indisposed," Mary explained. "The other women from the synagogue refuse to return to her home after going once. The widow in question can test the patience of angels. But Priscilla, may the Lord bless her, returns again and again."

"Only because you usually accompany me." Priscilla held the basket aloft. "And even when you can't go, you send gifts."

A grumble interrupted them from the vicinity of Benyamin's

belly. Everyone laughed. "I had better feed these men before they wilt at my feet." Mary gave Priscilla a quick kiss on the forehead. "Come and visit me soon. I grow lonely when Rufus goes off to work."

After taking leave of Mary and her guests, Priscilla called on Lollia, and they set off for Sara's apartment. The widow lived on the other side of the city, in the southwestern tip of Rome's suburbs. A long walk from the synagogue.

Mindful of Lollia's aging limbs, Priscilla stuffed the bread inside Mary's basket and wrapped one hand firmly around the handle, leaving the small flask of wine to Lollia. She would have taken that too but knew the servant's pride could not bear it.

"He's a handsome one," Lollia said as they set off on the Via Flaminia.

"Benyamin? I could ask Mary if he is available."

Lollia's lip twitched. "Don't be pert. I meant the nephew, Aquila."

"*Him.* Well, I don't wish to discourage you, dear, but I fear he is too young for a woman of your antiquity."

A sound akin to a chicken's squawk emerged out of Lollia's throat. "I meant for *you*, you ingrate. Would you molder under your brother's thumb for the rest of your life when you could be married and have a home of your own?"

Priscilla's tone hardened. "I will never marry."

"Why not, pray tell? A man would be fortunate to have you for a wife."

Priscilla lengthened her steps with deliberation, making it impossible for Lollia to keep up. This was one topic for which she had no tolerance. Yet for some indecipherable reason, Lollia decided to drag the subject of matrimony into their conversation with annoying regularity.

A few moments later the sound of panting assailed Priscilla's ears, and she slowed to a stop. "I beg your pardon, Lollia," she said, her cheeks flushing. "I should not have made you scramble after me."

"No matter. My tongue is fast. But your feet are faster. We make a good match."

Priscilla grinned. They walked for a while in silent companionship. With no forewarning, a young boy with a dirty face and enormous brown eyes sidled near and began walking next to her.

"I will carry your heavy packages if you give me a piece of bread," he said, forgoing the use of any polite honorifics.

"They are not so burdensome we need your help," Lollia answered, bristling at his arrogance.

Priscilla regarded the boy for a silent moment. If the bones protruding along his shoulders were any indication, the child had known a hungry day or two. Wordlessly, she handed him her basket. His skinny arms wrapped around the sides and held on tight. She wondered if he could manage to see his feet over the bundle inside.

"Need help?" she asked.

He sniffed and shifted the weight against his narrow chest and sped up. Priscilla followed, liking his spirit. Long before they arrived at their destination, she said, "We are close enough. Thank you."

Fishing inside the basket, she pulled out two loaves of barley bread instead of one. "For a job well done. Thank you for your help."

The boy stared at the bread, his tongue licking dry lips. Tucking the loaves inside some invisible pocket within his dirty tunic, he vanished as silently as he had appeared.

"There's thanks for you!" Lollia said, offended.

Priscilla sighed. "He was hungry."

"Well, he didn't have to be rude about it. He could have at least called you mistress."

"He was honest enough to do the work, without making proclamations he did not mean. Now, my dear, try not to argue with Sara today, regardless of how much she goads you."

"Shouldn't you be preaching good manners to *her*?"

"I am too wise to waste my words."

They stopped by a fountain to drink and give Lollia a chance to rest before resuming their walk. Sara's home was on the top floor of a rickety three-story building, not far from the Hill of Amphorae, the place a million Romans discarded their unwanted pottery. The vessels in which wine and grain were transported could be repurposed. But olive oil sank into earthenware, becoming rancid. No amount of washing could get rid of the smell. The Romans broke those amphorae and piled the shards here. It had grown into a veritable hill, reddish brown in color and stinking of putrid oil. On a breezy day, the smell carried all the way into Sara's dark apartment.

The door to the widow's home stood open. "Good Shabbat, Sara," Priscilla called and walked in.

Sara looked like she was waiting for them, seated on a cushion across from the door.

"What's good about it? Is that for me?" She held out veiny hands for the basket, her mouth stamped with a sour expression. Lined and leathery skin made her look older than her forty years.

Sara handed her the basket. "The cheese and bread are from Mary." Lollia placed the wine at the woman's feet and hastily stepped back as if approaching a feral creature.

The widow raised an eyebrow. "And where is Mary? I suppose she could not be bothered to come herself."

"She has guests and is needed at home."

Sara pronounced the Hebrew blessing over the food, her words hurried and careless, missing a few phrases along the way. Without offering anything to her guests, she ripped into the bread and cheese with dirty fingers.

"Is it good?" Priscilla asked, hoping to report a word of praise to Mary.

"I've tasted better," said Sara, without inviting her visitors to sit. Priscilla and Lollia, accustomed to the widow's ways, leaned against the wall. Sara took a sip of wine and shoved a handful of olives in after. With a full mouth she said, "Is this all you brought? You would think a great Roman lady like yourself would be more generous to the poor."

"Now listen, you," Lollia burst out. "Prisca walked all the way here from the synagogue without even stopping to partake of a bite of food herself. She went hungry so you wouldn't."

"Lollia!" Priscilla gave her servant a look of censure.

The sound of a man clearing his throat at the door brought the conversation to a halt. "I beg your pardon," Aquila said from the threshold. "I am looking for Sara. Do I have the right place?"

Lollia's smile broke out like the sun. "Master Aquila! You have come to the right house, indeed. Come and welcome."

"Who are you?" Sara said, mouth gaping.

Rufus walked in behind the young man, huffing a little. "He is with me, Sara. My mother dispatched us to you with hot food. She thought you might enjoy a little meat."

Given how quickly they had arrived, Priscilla suspected that they had come without first taking time to eat. The widow did not seem to appreciate their sacrifice. "Why?" she said, her voice sour with suspicion. "Has it gone bad?"

Laughter bubbled up Priscilla's throat, and she had to cover her mouth with the back of her hand to hold it back. For a moment she locked gazes with Aquila. The lines in the corners of his eyes had deepened, softening the gray irises. Melting them with warmth. Priscilla's mouth turned dry. Abruptly, she forgot the urge to laugh.

"Of course not," Rufus said with dignity. "Was the meat bad the last time she brought it to you?"

Sara waved her hand in the air. "I forget. It was so long ago."

"The last time we ourselves ate lamb, you had a share in it." He motioned to Aquila, who laid a new basket at the widow's feet.

The scent of roasted lamb and rosemary filled the room, making Priscilla feel faint with hunger.

Sara set aside the bread and cheese and delved into the bowl of stew inside the new basket. Her attention thus diverted, she ignored her guests completely as she began to shovel large spoonfuls of stew into her mouth.

"We'd best take our leave. Thank you for your hospitality, Sara." Rufus spoke without a hint of irony, which impressed Priscilla. "My mother will come herself to greet you later this week."

"Tell her to bring fresh fruit next time. My bowels are too slow."

Rufus coughed. For a moment, he seemed robbed of words. Finally he choked out, "Yes. I will," and bolted outside.

The rest of them followed closely, navigating the flights of wobbly stairs with too much speed. They emerged into the sunny street, relieved to be out of the confines of the apartment, not to mention away from Sara's unpredictable tongue.

Rufus turned to Priscilla. "Will you come to my house and

join us for a meal? You must be hungry after walking all this way from Campi."

Priscilla's chin dropped in amazement. It was not lost on her that Aquila was having almost the same reaction. They both stared at Rufus as if he had lost his mind. Although the Jewish members of the synagogue conversed with her, even befriended her, none had ever invited her to share a meal. They would be breaking their dietary laws by sitting at the same table with a Roman and partaking of food.

"Lollia and I would not dream of intruding," she said, wondering if it had somehow slipped Rufus's mind that she was not a Hebrew. Aquila breathed out a long breath at her response, obviously relieved.

"No intrusion. My mother said I was not to return without you, and I for one dare not disobey her. Now, let us set out. Truly, if I do not eat soon, I may swoon at your feet like a bashful maiden, and Aquila would have to carry me all the way across the river to Trastevere. If you will not have mercy on me, be merciful to him."

Priscilla flushed. "I . . . Rufus, I am Roman."

Rufus shrugged. "I, also, am a Roman by citizenship. It provides excellent legal advantages. But it does not fill my stomach, and I am still hungry."

He began to walk, forcing the rest of them to follow. She studied Aquila's stony expression and swallowed a sigh. The visitor from Pontus obviously did not approve of Rufus's cavalier attitude. His disapproval settled in Priscilla's stomach like a stone.

Three

RUFUS'S HOME WAS LOCATED on the other side of the Tiber, in the region called Trastevere. As they covered the long distance heading north, the vistas became more interesting, the buildings larger and more magnificent. But despite his best intentions, Aquila found himself studying the young Roman woman more than the breathtaking sights of Rome.

He recalled the short moment in the widow's apartment when their eyes had met and they had shared a secret spark of amusement. Her lips had softened then, just short of a smile. Inexplicably, he had felt as if he had known her for long years instead of a handful of hours.

He sighed. Why had Rufus insisted that she come along? She added unnecessary complications to what would otherwise have been a peaceful afternoon.

Aquila forced his gaze to shift to the left, where the Tiber flowed, wide and brackish, moodily coiling its way south to the Tyrrhenian Sea.

"There!" Rufus pointed to an arched stone bridge that spanned the width of the river. "Trastevere is just beyond that bridge. I can already taste that lamb stew."

"Uncle Benyamin has probably eaten the whole pot by now," Aquila said. "There is a cavern in that man where there should be a belly. I fear we will get nothing but cold bread and cheese."

"My mother cooks enough to feed one of Caesar's legions. Never fear. And I fancy I can already smell the mouthwatering aroma of that succulent lamb wafting in the air."

Priscilla's sigh was full of yearning. Aquila remembered the servant's words, which he had overheard just as he was about to enter the widow's apartment. *"Prisca walked all the way here from the synagogue without even stopping to partake of a bite of food herself. She went hungry so you wouldn't."*

How many Romans would go to so much trouble on behalf of a Jewish widow?

Even his own people avoided the woman, and for good reason, given his brief glimpse of her. Yet this outsider willingly bore the burden of that prickly creature. He did not understand her. More importantly, he needed to stop trying!

They crossed over Aemilius bridge into Trastevere, an overcrowded neighborhood connected by a dizzying array of alleys and dirt roads. Aquila was grateful Rufus led the way.

Rufus and his mother lived in a less crowded section of Trastevere, where the houses were two or three stories high, and shops occupied the ground level of most buildings. Rufus had rented a two-story house and set up a neat shop on the street level, where he sold the natural hides and dyed leather his family produced.

At the top of the stairs leading to their living quarters, Mary awaited them with a wide smile. Aquila lifted an arm in greeting and took off his sandals before proceeding up the stairs.

"I am sorry to intrude upon you, Mary." Prisca's voice had a hesitant edge as she climbed the steps behind him. "Your son insisted that I come."

Mary gave her a welcoming embrace. "He did so at my behest, I assure you. Now sit and rest while I fetch you some food. We can eat together and leave the men to their own conversation."

Aquila stared. He was being rude, he knew. But he could not help himself. What was Mary thinking, offering to eat with a Gentile? Why had Rufus not foreseen the awkwardness of inviting Prisca for a meal?

Intercepting his gaze, Rufus cleared his throat and whispered something to his mother. She nodded once. "I will take you and Lollia to an alcove where you can eat in comfort," she said to Prisca.

"We have caused you trouble," Prisca said softly. For a Gentile, she had good manners, Aquila would give her that.

He watched as Mary accompanied the women to another room while the men took their seats on the couches that surrounded a table laden with cut fruits and a salad of mixed herbs. The delicate scents of lemon and mint intermingled with that of strawberries, making Aquila forget his censorious thoughts. A moment later, a servant arrived bearing a tray heaped with lamb stew and hot bread. The exquisite smell of fried onions, garlic, and rosemary made Aquila forget everything, save for the meal set before him.

He was halfway through his first bowl when his uncle said, "Thank God I already ate a little before you arrived, or this young lout would have left me nothing."

Aquila looked around, finally becoming more aware of his surroundings than of the incredible sensations on his tongue.

Noticing Mary's lingering absence, he said, "Mary is not really going to eat with that Roman, is she?"

Rufus's brows lowered. "Why not?"

"You jest. She is a Gentile! Unclean. Rufus, you know the Law. If Mary eats with her, she, too, will become unclean."

"Our Lord ate with tax collectors and unrepentant sinners. Surely a Roman is no worse. Should we expect those who hunger and thirst for God to follow our impossible laws, the weight of which our own ancestors could not bear, before we extend them a bit of hospitality?"

Aquila almost choked. This was the kind of reasoning that had enraged his father and made him an enemy of the New Covenant. "That's blasphemy."

Rufus sighed. "Rest easy, my young friend. For your sake, my mother will not allow a morsel to pass her hungry lips while she stays in Prisca's company. But I tell you, I saw Peter himself break bread with Gentiles."

Aquila felt the food stick in his throat. He, too, had heard that story about Peter, the man considered by some in the church to be the greatest apostle. He took a large swallow of his watered wine and leaned back. "I heard he changed his mind. That it was an aberration. A mistake of short duration. He has returned to keeping the Law, as I understand."

Rufus smiled and inclined his head graciously before changing the subject. "We invited Prisca today because we hope to share the message of Christ with her."

Aquila was brought up short. Here he was griping about dietary laws when Rufus had a higher aim. "My apologies," he said.

Rufus swept a hand in the air. "No need. We have much to discuss. I have been awaiting your arrival, you and Benyamin. Since

Mother and I came to Rome, we have attended the synagogue at Campi. I have come to know the congregation, tried to assess what their response might be when we begin to speak to them of the Messiah.

"Around the empire, sharing the gospel in a synagogue has invariably led to division. Some receive our good news with favor and open hearts. Others grow enraged, even violent. We must pray and come to some consensus as to how we should proceed here in Rome. How can we be bold for God and yet avoid disunion?"

Benyamin leaned forward. "Is that why you invited Prisca here? To speak to her in private rather than in the hearing of others who worship at Campi?"

Rufus's expression held an unusual intensity. "I sense the hand of the Lord on this young woman. I believe he will open her heart. For now, we seek to deepen our friendship with her and a few others. You cannot do that if you bar people from your home."

Aquila remembered the profound reverence he had sensed in Prisca while she worshiped. He understood why Rufus thought the Lord was at work in her heart.

He shifted restlessly. Why had he made such an issue of the dietary laws? He swallowed hard. In truth, his outrage had little to do with the Law and everything to do with his absent father. Aquila wanted to prove to him that he was still a devout Jew though he followed Yeshua.

He felt as if someone had doused him with a jar of icy water. He had been so busy pleasing his earthly father that he had forgotten to please his heavenly one. "I am sorry," he said sincerely.

"No harm done, my boy," Rufus said, and plied him with more stew.

Mary joined them and after eating a quick meal, sent for Prisca, who settled on the couch next to their hostess. Aquila noticed that her clothes were worn in places and faded. They were of good quality, but old. She had few jewels, and what she wore had little monetary value. She spoke a cultured Latin and without stumbling switched to an equally cultured Greek to accommodate Mary. Everything about her, including her name, bespoke gentility. Yet he could also see unmistakable signs of poverty.

"What a comfortable house you have, Mary. I don't often have reason to visit Trastevere. This is a very pleasant street," she said.

"We chose this area because one of my cousins lives in an apartment at the end of this road. Indeed, Trastevere is popular with our people. It is also convenient for Rufus's business because of easy access to the river and warehouses."

"Where do you live?" Aquila asked her. "Is Campi close to you?"

"It is not too far. I live in my brother's house in Pincio."

The name sounded familiar. It took Aquila a moment to remember that Pincio was a hilly suburb favored by the wealthy. It was home to vast villas and abundant gardens. He thought it strange that a resident of such an address should wear clothes that were more ragged than his own.

"Do you and Benyamin also live in Trastevere?" she asked.

"We rent lodgings in a neighborhood near Via Appia."

Her eyes widened. He expected her to treat the news with the disparagement it deserved. The southern region around Via Appia, Rome's busiest artery, which connected half the empire to the city, was even more decrepit than parts of Trastevere. Instead, she merely grinned. "That must be exciting. So many interesting people pass along Via Appia."

He liked that unexpected response. Instead of looking down at him, this denizen of Pincio had found something good about his ramshackle surroundings. Forcing himself to shrug with a nonchalance he did not feel, Aquila answered, "It's good for our trade."

"Do you work in leather, like Rufus?"

"We work in leather. But not like Rufus. Rufus and his older brother, Alexander, own sheep. They sell the hides to leatherworkers. My uncle and I buy the prepared leather and make various merchandise, like tents, awnings, and even weatherproof cloaks for those cold and wet winters in the northern parts of the empire."

Without knocking, Lollia appeared at the door. She was one of those slaves who, having been treated more like family than a servant, behaved like an elderly aunt rather than a retainer. "We are going to be late, Priscilla," she said, pointing to the window, drawing everyone's attention to the lengthening shadows cast by the sun.

Prisca scampered to her feet. "Forgive me. We must make our way home."

The words escaped his mouth before Aquila had time to think. "I will escort you."

"There is no need. Lollia is with me."

"If you were my sister, I would not want you walking about the streets of Rome with only Lollia for company. I will come."

She flashed a smile. "Are you sure you will find your way back home? It is a long way, and you are very new to Rome. Perhaps it is Lollia and I who should accompany *you*?"

He felt his stomach tighten into a knot. Everything in him wanted to grin and tease her back. Instead, he said, his tone clipped, "We better not tarry." The sooner he deposited her on her own doorstep, the sooner he could walk away and never see her again.

As they emerged into the weak afternoon sun, he noticed that her hair, which had been a demure shade of red inside, seemed to blaze under the sun, a river of fire hanging down her back. Aquila gulped.

Four

PRISCILLA FOLLOWED AQUILA, impressed that he remembered the way back to Aemilius bridge with its convoluted array of turns. He walked ahead on the edge of the bustling streets, occasionally calling a warning to the women, pointing out obstacles that could prove inconvenient had they had the misfortune of stepping in them. She felt touched by this solicitousness, offered almost without thought, as if he were accustomed to considering the needs of others.

Once they crossed over the bridge, Aquila looked around, clearly lost. "Lead on," he said to Priscilla. She liked the easy way he passed the role of leadership to her. Her brother would have rather pulled his own tooth than admit she knew more than he did on any subject.

"This way is more charming." She pointed straight ahead. "You will have a clear view of the Palatine Hill and the imperial palace."

As they neared the palace, Lollia stopped with a gasp. "Look, Priscilla!" Against a white marble wall, someone had planted a row of dark-pink roses, now blooming in wild profusion, perfuming the air. Roses were Priscilla's weakness. Their scent and fragile loveliness were a reminder of a beloved mother who had often worn them in her hair. Her brother refused to grow them, calling them a waste of good soil.

Although they were running late and she risked a harsh scolding from Volero, she lingered long enough to inhale the scent of a fresh bloom. Closing her eyes for a moment, she let the world and its troubles drift away.

She was brought out of her reverie when something bumped hard against the backs of her knees, sending her headfirst into the bushes. Thorns caught at her hair and scratched the skin of her arms. A strong hand wrapped around her elbow and pulled gently until she was on her feet again.

"Are you trying to smell the roses or become one?" Aquila said, his mouth tipping.

"It was not a voluntary plunge, I assure you." Dusting herself off, Priscilla discovered the agent of her fall: a large black dog, tongue lolling, staring adoringly at Aquila.

Crossing her arms, she raised an eyebrow. "Is he yours?"

"Never met him before."

The dog sat at Aquila's feet, not taking his eyes off the man.

"Then it seems you have made a new friend," Priscilla said.

"Can't help it. Dogs like me." He pointed a finger at her cheek. "Which is more than I can say for rosebushes and you. Your face is bleeding."

Priscilla felt the sting of the scrape on her cheek as soon as Aquila mentioned it. She touched the shallow scratch gingerly and found the blood already dry. She realized her hair was sticking up on one side of her head, and smoothed it down with a self-conscious pat. The indignity of her situation pricked more than the thorns. Straightening her disheveled tunic, she began to walk, leaving the others to follow behind.

"Stop," Aquila said behind her.

She came to a stop and looked at him expectantly.

"Not you. Him." He pointed at the dog, who had sat down again, a nose length from his feet. "He has taken it into his head to follow us."

"He has taken it into his head to follow *you*," Priscilla said, studying the animal's shaggy fur and thin sides. Most Romans loved their dogs and took better care of them than this. He wore no chain or collar, another indication that he was no one's pet. But he seemed at ease in the company of people, his tail wagging with eagerness, mouth open in what could pass for a good-natured smile.

She frowned. "He will tire soon enough. The way to Pincio is hilly and long."

But if the dog felt any weariness, he did not show it. By the time they arrived at the outskirts of Pincio, he still shadowed their steps.

Her brows lowered. "Are you feeding him?"

Aquila held up empty hands. "There have always been dogs on my father's land. I come from a long line of sheepherders. Dogs know I like them. So they like me back."

"I thought you are a worker of leather goods."

His lips lost their smile and became a flat line. "That's what I am now."

"I am sorry. I did not mean to pry," she said.

He shrugged. "No matter." Taking the lead again, he started to walk, the dog close at his heels.

Priscilla was not fooled by the casual words. She had trespassed, somehow, encroaching on a subject that was painful to him. She tamped down the curiosity that clamored for answers and followed him silently for a short distance.

Lollia and she stopped at the corner of the next avenue, while Aquila walked on, so lost in thought, he did not realize they were no longer behind him. "Will you tell him, or shall I?" Lollia said.

Priscilla rolled her eyes. "You there! Aquila! This way," she called, tilting her head to indicate the avenue to her right.

Aquila rubbed the back of his neck and headed back. "I suppose I would provide better protection if I actually stayed at your side."

She smiled. "You have been kind to come this far. My brother's house is just beyond this hill. We are safe enough in this neighborhood. You should go home. It will be dark soon and harder for you to find your way."

Aquila shook his head. "I will see you to your door."

Priscilla's steps lagged. "In truth, that would not be wise. My brother's servants report everything to him. And if he were to hear that a strange man accompanied me home, he would grow . . . agitated."

Aquila stopped. "I see. Does he know of your visits to the synagogue?"

Priscilla shook her head. There was a great deal Volero did not know. She intended to keep it that way.

Aquila considered her in silence. "I can watch you both from a distance to ensure you arrive home. Would that serve?"

Priscilla wanted to tell him that she and Lollia had trekked home by themselves more times than she could count. Since her father's death, no one save Lollia had cared for her safety. Unwilling to throw his show of courtesy back in his face, she thanked him and walked alongside him up the hill.

"You can stop here," she said when they reached the top. "Thank you for accompanying us."

He bent to pet the dog, who licked his hand in appreciation. "I would have done it for anyone," he said, not looking up.

At the door of the house, Lollia paused to look over her shoulder. "I don't think that dog is going to leave Aquila's side."

"More to the point, *Aquila* is not going to leave the dog's side," Priscilla replied.

She thought of the man who had chosen to accompany Rufus to Sara's house, delivering hot food before he had tasted a bite himself. The same man who had traipsed halfway across the city of Rome to ensure she and Lollia were secure from danger. Another long journey still faced him before he could return to the comfort of his own home, and all this for a Gentile with whom he had refused to share a meal. Such a person would not cast out a starving dog.

Though she doubted she would ever see him again, she felt strangely comforted merely knowing there was a man like Aquila in this hard world.

The next morning Volero surprised Priscilla with a visit to her quarters. She stared at him, her comb forgotten midstroke. Her brother never bothered to seek her out. She grew rigid with tension, wondering if someone had seen her with Aquila the previous day and reported it to him. She had been too careless. Now he would rage at her, bent on punishment.

But instead of mentioning her transgression, he merely asked, "Do you remember the tribune, Quintus?"

She let out the breath she had been holding and frowned in confusion. "Father's old friend?"

"Yes. He has been serving in Carthage for some years. Since his return a few months ago, he has been made a senator."

Priscilla put her comb down. Her brother was not in the habit of engaging her in idle conversation. Clearly this volley of information had some aim. She waited in silence, knowing patience was the safest route to take with Volero.

"Quintus asked after your mother."

Priscilla vaguely recalled her mother trying to avoid the unwanted public attentions of a large man with a bad case of dandruff. "I am sure he did."

"He seemed quite sorry to hear she was dead. He asked after you."

"Excellent."

Volero missed the irony in her voice. "I thought so. He invited us to a feast tonight and insisted that you come. It's an outdoor affair. They say Claudius himself will attend."

"The emperor? Don't worry. I would not dream of accepting." She wondered why he had even bothered to mention the invitation to her. He rarely tolerated her presence in public, an attitude his haughty wife ardently supported.

"Of course you must accept."

"I must?"

"And I want you to be agreeable to him, Priscilla. Do you understand me?"

"Agreeable in what way?"

"I mean I want to win his favor. I wish to persuade him to lower his price for a parcel of land I have my eye on. This house is too old for comfort. I want a new villa, and he has the perfect spot for it." He poked his finger painfully into Priscilla's chest. "Charm him. Smile at him. *Whatever* you have to do. I want that land. We will leave early. Be ready by the seventh hour."

Priscilla shot to her feet, too amazed to speak. *Whatever* she had to do? By the time he had made it to the door, she had recuperated enough to mumble, "I have nothing suitable to wear to such an elegant event."

"My wife will lend you something."

For his feast, Quintus had rented a lush garden bordering a man-made lake. Clearly the new senator wished to impress his guests with the abundance of his wealth. A lavishly decorated boat manned by two rows of meticulous slaves waited to ferry passengers around the still water, a welcome luxury on a balmy day.

Priscilla smoothed the folds of her emerald-green tunic after alighting from the carriage. She needed to watch every pleat and fold like a hawk lest she spill something on the fine linen. Her sister-in-law had made it clear that she would not tolerate the slightest damage to her tunic. Priscilla had worn an undergarment of ivory linen, one with a higher neckline than her borrowed clothing, to provide a modest covering under the plunging lines of her sister-in-law's finery. She noted that she was one of the few women present who had bothered with such attempts at propriety and felt, more than ever, like a fish out of water. She wished herself on the other side of Rome. The side that housed her friends from the Campi synagogue.

Quintus was welcoming his guests under the shade of a jasmine arbor, gold rings upon every knuckle glinting in the sun. He had grown more massive with the years, his girth every bit as impressive as the size of his fortune.

His eyes roved when Volero introduced her. "Thank the gods you look nothing like your father! And you possess the same charming shade of hair as your mother." His corpulent hand traveled down a long curl, then wandered lower. Priscilla took a swift sidestep to avoid the shameless groping and found her feet landing squarely on a large object.

"Oomph!" a man exclaimed, hastily moving his foot out of her range. She turned to find a toga-clad man whose head was bald save for a ring of white hair. The scarlet band edging his white garments proclaimed him a senator.

"Pardon!" she croaked.

A young woman, huge brown eyes ringed with curly lashes, stepped from behind the senator. "Do not worry. I just stepped on his toes myself. And for the same reason."

Although she displayed the composure of an older girl, her appearance declared her to be no more than seventeen or eighteen. Priscilla gave her a weak smile. "I hope I did not cause any permanent damage," she said to the senator.

"I have another foot. I can still kick my enemies if need be." He had a kind face, she thought, and plump, white hands that thankfully stayed at his sides. "This is my daughter Pudentiana," he said, motioning to the girl.

"And this is my father, Senator Pudens," she added.

"I am Prisca."

"Daughter of General Priscus?" The senator nodded. "Our paths crossed briefly when I served in Germania. A brave man."

"Thank you."

"And here is my own dear wife, Sabinella." He made room for a tall woman of mature years who shared Pudentiana's exquisite brown eyes.

Sabinella gave a wide smile. "I met your mother years ago. A sweet woman. We had a long discussion about the horrors of travel, in spite of good Roman roads."

Few people talked about her mother without contempt. Sabinella won Priscilla's instant gratitude by her authentic warmth. "My mother loathed any voyage that lasted longer than an hour," she said, "and refused to leave Rome even for short excursions."

"I can't blame her. If it were not for my husband's work, I

would remain in our estate in Antium and never budge. The capital is too crowded for me. But we do not like to leave each other even for a short while." She gave the senator a fond look.

Priscilla wanted to embrace this delightful family and take every one of them back to her brother's house. She had rarely felt so at home with other Romans. But she had to find Volero before her absence offended him. "I should return to my brother," she explained as she stepped away.

"I would not risk it. Your brother is still speaking to Quintus," the senator said.

Priscilla shifted her weight from one foot to the other, trying to determine which would prove worse: Volero's ire or Quintus's roving hands.

As if reading her mind, Pudentiana whispered, "One senator is as good as another, I find. Your brother will not mind you being absent so long as you are with us."

Priscilla bit down a bubble of laughter. The girl had captured Volero's preference for influential people with perfect accuracy. "I hope you are right," she said. "But I fear my brother would insist that I attend Quintus and his fat . . ."

"Fingers?"

There was no covering her laughter this time. "I was going to say *purse*."

"Is my daughter corrupting you?" the senator asked.

"I am trying." Pudentiana linked her arm through the senator's. "Perhaps you would like to join us in a conversation with the new senator, Father? We could use your protection."

Pudens groaned. "Must we?" He glanced at Volero's animated face as he conversed with their host. "I see we must. Come, girls. I shall be your rearguard."

When they arrived at Volero's side, Senator Pudens wagged a friendly finger at him. "And why have you not introduced your delightful sister to us before?"

Volero's face stiffened. "My sister is reserved and not comfortable in unfamiliar company."

"How odd! I detected no reservation in her manner."

Without offering a word of excuse, Quintus reached out boldly to take hold of Priscilla's arm. Moving smoothly, Senator Pudens looped his fingers around her elbow and pulled her to his side. "Hands off, Quintus." Though he was smiling, his voice emerged hard as iron.

A commotion near the lake's shoreline brought the awkward silence to an end.

"The emperor has arrived!" Quintus leapt forward, surprisingly agile for a man of his size. All conversation ceased as guests tried to catch a glimpse of Claudius, who had arrived with a tight circle of companions and several members of the Praetorian Guard. As the band of people around him thinned to make room for Quintus, Priscilla gained a clear view of the man who ruled the empire.

He walked a few steps, his gait made uneven by a limp, reducing him to something less than the Roman ideal of masculine perfection. He was a lean man with ears that stuck out a little too much, a narrow chin and deep lines on his forehead that had been put there, she suspected, more by suffering than age.

He had been one of the few males in his family wily enough to have survived the homicidal tendencies of his nephew Caligula. The young emperor had raped and murdered people of Roman nobility at such a rate, it was a wonder any had survived to continue the line. Claudius's appointment as emperor had astonished many, none perhaps more than himself.

Quintus bellowed his welcome, overcompensating for Claudius's poor hearing. A clutch of birds exploded from the nearby trees in an agitated welter of flapping wings and noise, distressed by the senator's loud greeting. Claudius scratched an ear and said something in a low voice that Priscilla could not hear. Quintus moved, his mass blocking the emperor from view.

Priscilla's gaze wandered into the crowd of people who had arrived with Claudius. She gasped as she recognized a familiar face toward the back. She would know those features with their unforgettable symmetry anywhere, though four years had passed since she last saw them.

Antonia.

No palla covered her elaborately arranged hair, indicating that she remained unmarried. Priscilla felt herself flush and stared at the ground, desperate to quell the rising tide of memories.

"Best go and offer our greetings," Senator Pudens murmured, drawing his daughter and wife forward. Since he had not let go of Priscilla's arm, she was forced to follow, her feet dragging with each step.

Volero grabbed his wife's hand. "Come! We must not lag behind," he declared, giving Priscilla a furious scowl.

Before Priscilla could step away, Pudens maneuvered them to Claudius's side, introducing her to the emperor alongside his wife and daughter.

"It is a relief to see a f-f-f-few young faces!" Claudius said. The famous stammer was not as noticeable as some made out. "These events are often populated by old bores like me. My niece Antonia will be happy to know there are some young women at this affair." He flicked his fingers and Antonia stepped forward. "Here are a couple of charming l-l-l-ladies to keep you company, my dear."

"Thank you, Uncle," Antonia said in a demure voice very unlike the one she had used at the physician's house.

"Have you met my niece?" the emperor asked Priscilla.

"Yes, Caesar."

Antonia gave her a venomous look. "Not that I recall."

Priscilla blinked. Did the woman fear she might reveal her secret? She need not concern herself on that score. Priscilla could say nothing of that day that would not ruin her own life. "I am easy to forget," she said, trying to placate Antonia.

"I hardly think so," Claudius said, looking from one woman to the other. "There can't be more than a handful of women with that shade of hair in all of Rome."

An awkward silence ensued. Priscilla cleared her throat. "Antonia is accustomed to better company than I. We only ever met in passing."

"I see," Claudius said, though Priscilla suspected that his shrewd eyes missed little. She stepped behind Sabinella's tall form, using her as a shield. At least in all the excitement, Quintus had forgotten about her existence and kept his fingers to himself.

"Antonia is very popular with Caesar at the moment," Pudens whispered in her ear. "But she is not appropriate company, I fear. Steer clear of that one."

Priscilla gave a wan smile. The senator need have no worries. She intended to avoid the woman as fervently as Antonia would no doubt avoid her.

Five

"SIT!" Aquila commanded, moving a small chunk of cooked rabbit behind the dog's head. Immediately the dog sat. Aquila gave him the longed-for reward. The dog's tail swept the floor, undulating so fast, he almost elevated into the air. Aquila grinned and ruffled his head. "I told you he is bright."

"That is not at issue." Benyamin set aside his awl and the piece of leather he had been working on for the past hour. "We are not in the green meadows of Pontus anymore. There are no sheep for him to herd here."

"Many people have dogs in Rome. We could use a good guard dog. The same highway that brings hundreds of potential patrons past our store may also bring criminals. We can buy one of those mosaics with the image of a barking dog and put it outside the shop, warning away anyone who has theft on his mind."

As if sensing that he was the topic of discussion, the dog ambled over to Benyamin and pushed his black muzzle into the man's hand. "Off with you," Benyamin cried, trying to ignore the beast. The dog sought Benyamin's hand more insistently, shamelessly seeking attention.

His uncle glared. "If we were in Jerusalem, you would be held in contempt, you scruffy creature, and no one in their right mind would allow you inside their house."

Aquila scratched the dog's neck. "You are fortunate you have found yourself a man of Pontus, for though your master is of the lineage of Abraham, our countrymen appreciate your kind." He nudged his uncle playfully in the shoulder. "Even this old man used to have a dog of his own."

"That was long ago."

"What was his name, that giant monster of yours?"

"Ferox," Benyamin said. Aquila noted his uncle's softened expression as he spoke the name.

"Ferox. That was it! I believe I shall call you Ferox," he said to the mutt who now lay at his feet. "It suits you well." The dog barked as if in agreement. Aquila grinned. Ferox meant "savage." Even he had to admit his new companion did not exactly exude an air of ruthlessness.

"My dog was a noble creature, well trained and powerful. This shaggy mongrel is far from savage. A mouse would probably send him scrambling."

"Ferox it is!" Aquila announced, knowing his uncle was pleased with the choice in spite of his protestations. He settled the dog in a corner of the room and returned to the job of cleaning the storefront they had rented, a tiny shop that had the advantage of sitting close to the famed Via Appia.

Benyamin stretched his back and brushed his apron. "Where are you going to put that dog tonight?"

"In my chamber."

"The one that happens to be my chamber, also?"

"Yes, now that you mention it. He will guard you as well as me. No need to thank me. Consider it a family favor."

Behind the store sat two cramped rooms, which Aquila and Benyamin had set up for their private use. He had to admit that their living arrangements were not ideal for a dog of Ferox's size. But he was determined to give the dog shelter. He could not bear the thought of casting the friendly animal back into the merciless streets of Rome.

He stacked colored squares of leather neatly on a small shelf so that customers could see the variety available to them for special orders. A piece of red leather slipped through his fingers and fell to the ground.

The color reminded him of Priscilla's rich hair. *Priscilla!* When had he taken it into his head to refer to her by her familiar name, as if they enjoyed the intimacy of close friendship?

Unbidden, he remembered her face as she dragged herself out of the rosebushes, her hair awry, cheeks as pink as the petals she had been submerged in. He had gone from alarm to laughter in the span of a moment. Noticing the faint scratch on her face, he had ached to stroke the pale skin grazed by thorns. *Ached.*

He kicked the piece of red leather and it flew to the other side of the cramped chamber. His uncle raised his eyebrows. "Has the leather offended in some way?"

Aquila was saved from answering when an older man stopped to admire the awning they had hung over the entrance of the shop. He wore a fine tunic, and though he sported few jewels, the exquisite quality of each proclaimed him a man of means.

The man fingered the side of the awning, examining the stitching carefully. "Fine workmanship," he said. "My wife wishes to place an awning similar to this in our garden. We don't want to erect a permanent structure there, which might ruin our view. But we do need extra shade in the excessive heat of summer. Is this awning retractable?"

"It is," Aquila said, demonstrating how the awning could be looped around a central pole using a lever so that it furled and unfurled with ease.

The older man watched, fascinated. "We have never found one that is both pleasing to the eye and easy to operate. This is quality work."

After examining the leather samples, the man selected the color and size he wanted and settled on a price. "My estate is in the Esquiline hills to the north," he said, handing a few coins for deposit on his order. "Ask for Senator Pudens. You won't miss it."

"Yes, my lord."

"I expect you will set it up personally?"

"We will, Senator." Aquila gave his new patron precise instructions on a suitable frame before the man took his leave.

When he was out of earshot, Aquila whistled. "Our first senator!"

"The Lord loves senators, too," Benyamin said.

"I myself am not averse to them." Aquila jangled the coins in his hand before putting them away. "He never mentioned his elevated office until he had to, in order for me to know where to deliver his awning. Did you notice? Most men of high status are sure to push their honorifics under your nose as soon as you meet them."

Benyamin shook the heavy hide on his lap, dropping tiny bits of leather onto the floor. "A rare man, then. Perhaps God has a purpose in this meeting."

Priscilla startled awake to the sound of shouting and the noise of scurrying feet. Confused, she sat up in bed and reached for the lamp.

"Lollia!" she called out.

The older woman stirred on her pallet next to Priscilla's bed. "Is it an earthquake? Because unless the world is collapsing on my head, I prefer to keep sleeping."

"There is some disturbance in the house." Priscilla's chamber was not in the main villa, which had been built around a traditional atrium over a hundred years earlier. After her father's death, her brother had demanded that she pack her belongings and move to one of the shacks reserved for the slaves, telling her he needed the extra room for himself and his wife and any children they might have. Though the children had never materialized, Volero's desire for additional room had not diminished.

Priscilla's chamber now sat behind the house proper, enclosed by the ancient perimeter wall that surrounded their land, but farther from the main gate. She wrapped a shawl around her shoulders and sped toward the noise, Lollia following slowly.

"What has happened?" she asked the steward, who stood by the main entrance, his face pale in the light of his burning torch.

He pointed to a terra-cotta planter of geraniums, shattered into several pieces. "Someone tried to sneak in by climbing over the wall. One of the slaves saw him and raised the alarm."

"Was anyone hurt?"

The steward shook his head. "But we haven't managed to capture him yet."

Priscilla raised a brow. "You mean he is still in the house?"

The steward nodded, his mouth a grim line. He could lose his position over such a breach. Without another word, he walked away to supervise the search on the opposite side of the garden.

From the corner of her eye, Priscilla caught a blur of motion and turned, expecting to find one of the house slaves. Her jaw slackened when she spotted a strange man, chest as thick as a tree trunk, rushing her way.

Priscilla froze, heart banging against the wall of her chest. If she remained perfectly still, she reasoned, surely he would swerve past her to get to the wall in order to make his escape. Instead, the man trained his eyes on her face and raced directly toward her.

Without warning, an arm shot out, broad-boned and hard as concrete, reaching for Priscilla. Viselike fingers wrapped around her neck and squeezed until she felt the delicate bones of her throat give way. The pain grew excruciating. Swallowing became impossible. She clawed his wrists, trying to dislodge the implacable hold. It was like trying to fell a tree with her bare fingers. She could not breathe. A rushing sound filled her ears, drowning out all other noise.

Lord, she cried silently, unable to think of another word or a single prayer. Her vision darkened, and the world started to fade. This, then, was death. This raging pain that swallowed mind and body with its torment. Abruptly the ruthless fingers at her throat loosened a notch, enough to allow Priscilla a gasping mouthful of air into burning lungs.

Like a dreamer, she heard the steward shout, his voice close. Several slaves started to run toward them. The intruder swore under his breath. He released his hold on Priscilla, and like a boneless doll, she collapsed to her knees. Groping her neck, she gulped in a lungful of air, then another. As her vision cleared, she saw her attacker vault into a tree that bordered the wall. In the blink of an eye, he had climbed over the wall and into the street beyond.

Lollia huffed to a stop next to Priscilla. In the darkness, she had missed the intruder's savage attack on her young mistress. "What are you doing in the bushes again?" she said.

"Trying not to die." Priscilla's voice emerged hoarse, every syllable making her throat ache.

Lollia stared at her in dawning horror. "What happened? Are you hurt?"

Shivering, Priscilla pushed herself to her feet, rubbing her throbbing throat. "The man was insane. He could have just weaved past me. But he seemed to think I posed some threat and tried to throttle me on his way out."

Her brother did not bother to ask Priscilla if she felt ill after the attack or whether she needed a physician. His only interest was for his house. He strutted around, shouting orders, instructing his men to pursue the intruder. Priscilla doubted they would catch him. The cover of night and the dense trees of Pincio would work to his advantage.

"What an outrage," Volero screamed. "Even here in Pincio the thieves will not let us be. Hire extra men to stand guard at nights," he hissed at the steward. "The gates must be barred by sunset, except by my permission. If anyone is late, they can spend the night in the street."

Her brother, always apprehensive about thieves, would turn the house into a veritable fortress after this night. Priscilla hoped his precautions would keep them safe from further intrusions. It was a miracle she had survived that madman. Truly, the criminals of Rome were growing bolder by the hour. She swallowed past the pain in her throat. She would have a spectacular bruise come morning, and all because she had been standing in the wrong place at the wrong time.

Aquila and Benyamin finished the senator's awning the day before the Sabbath. Aquila had stayed up half the night stitching leather, Ferox dozing at his feet. Benyamin could not see well enough in the light of the lamp to sew, and it fell to Aquila to complete the work once dusk fell. The senator had wanted a quick delivery and had paid for the privilege. Aquila was grateful for the work, though his shoulders felt stiff as they walked up the Esquiline Hill. The awning lay in their cart, pulled by a young donkey they had purchased the day before. Ferox, who could not bear to be parted from his new master, had come along in spite of Benyamin's misgivings.

"We shouldn't bring a whole menagerie to the senator's house," he grumbled.

"The donkey is a necessity and the dog is security."

Ferox approached a large man in soldier's garb, his tail wagging, mouth wearing its customary grin. He did not even bother with a small growl.

Benyamin gave Aquila a long look. "You were saying?"

"If I start bringing along a cage stuffed with lovebirds, then you can grumble. Ferox will prove useful. Wait and see."

The senator's house was a two-story villa featuring arched windows and fluted columns with elegant Doric capitals. The walls had been painted a stately terra-cotta color, set against an ivory portico. Leaving the cart and donkey tied to a post, they met the steward at the door and followed him to the back garden. The awning was to be set up over a copse of white oleanders and scarlet roses.

The free-standing wooden frame for the awning had already been erected as Aquila had directed, and he circled around it to ensure the measurements were accurate.

"Looks good. Let's fetch the awning," he told his uncle.

They hefted the heavy roll of leather between them, grunting as they wound their way back to the garden. The steward fetched a sturdy ladder and left them to their work.

Aquila was about to set the ladder against one side of the frame when he noticed two young women walking down the narrow path toward him. He almost dropped the ladder on his toes when he recognized one of them as Priscilla. No less shocked than he, she came to a sudden stop, her eyes widening.

"Aquila!"

The tall girl walking alongside her looked from one to the other. "You know one another?"

Priscilla nodded. "We have met. Good day to you, Aquila." She turned a fraction, noticing his uncle for the first time. "Peace to you, Benyamin."

"Did they set up an awning in your brother's house, also?" the young woman asked, brown eyes sparkling with curiosity. It was not every day that daughters of the nobility counted Jewish workmen among their acquaintances.

Priscilla gave an awkward shake of her head. "No." Ferox interrupted whatever explanation she might have offered by bounding up to her, yapping a happy greeting as though she were a long-lost friend.

She laughed. "I see you kept him."

"Ferox?" Aquila shrugged. "He is useful."

"You named him Ferox?" She laughed again and bent down to pet the black dog, who embarrassed himself by melting into a puddle at her feet, allowing her to rub his belly. "Are you sure that is a fitting name?"

"That is what *I* said," Benyamin grumbled.

"He will be ferocious when necessary," Aquila said with conviction. "With friends, he is gentle."

The dark-haired girl accompanying Priscilla bent down and drew a cautious hand down Ferox's head. "He is very big."

"And he eats a lot," Benyamin said. "I will have to get a second job merely to feed him. But he is harmless enough."

The girl petted Ferox with more confidence when he lay supine with complete surrender under the attentions of the women. "I wonder if I can convince my father to buy a dog," she said.

"You can convince the senator to buy a tiger if you put your mind to it. Your mother is another matter," Priscilla said.

The girl laughed, her oval face lighting up. "That is the true state of things in this household. My father may be a member of Rome's all-powerful senate. But it is my mother who rules the world."

Aquila heard the conversation with only half an ear. He had lost his equilibrium the moment Priscilla appeared before him, as if sprung from the mists of his imaginings. Despite his best efforts, he had thought so much about her over the past few days that seeing her in the flesh felt something between relief and agony.

Lord, of all the places in Rome, did you have to bring her here today?

He pulled his hand through his hair and tried to focus on the awning. That was his reason for being in this garden. He should not be conversing with a Roman girl who lived in a villa in Pincio. Too many things divided them.

He turned and moved the ladder against the wooden frame,

grabbed one end of the roll of leather, and began to climb. Benyamin held the other end aloft, bearing the weight of it. At the top, Aquila set the edge of the awning upon the crossbeam, shifting his weight on the ladder for a better angle. For a moment, the ladder wobbled.

Priscilla shot to her feet with a gasp. "Have a care!"

He waved a hand. "It's perfectly safe."

She rushed to the base of the ladder. "I will hold it steady," she said, her fingers already grabbing hold of the wooden poles.

He was touched by her show of concern. "You are not planning on falling into the roses again, are you?" he could not resist asking, as she stepped into the bushes to get a better grasp.

"I will make you a proposal," she said, her lips tilting. "I won't pitch into the bushes if you don't fall off the top."

The sun beat down hot and stifling as Priscilla held on to that ladder, refusing to budge even when he warned her that her skin was turning an alarming shade of pink. He had never attached an awning so fast in his life.

Six

THAT EVENING, weary from labor and limp with heat, Aquila settled Ferox on the mat he had prepared for him at the foot of his pallet, then crawled under his threadbare sheet. He barely had time to close his eyes when with a quiet rustle Ferox plopped down at his side. Aquila grunted, rolling to sit up.

"A worthy bedmate for you," his uncle said from the comfort of his pallet on the other side of the chamber.

Aquila ignored the gibe. "Go back to your own mat," he commanded and tried to push the dog off his sheets. Ferox licked his hand and ignored the hint.

"You need a wife in your bed, not a dog." Benyamin smirked.

"I don't need either in my bed." Aquila sighed and, rising, pulled on the dog's leather-and-bronze collar, which he had fashioned himself. "Next time you invade my sanctum, I will put you outside. Don't think I won't."

By the time Aquila lay down again, all semblance of sleep had left him.

"There is something very alluring about Priscilla, do you not agree?" In the faint light of the single lamp that burned in the room, Aquila could see the flash of his uncle's teeth.

"I have seen prettier women," he said, voice stiff.

"And she is godly."

"She is a Gentile!"

"As was Ruth, whose blood flowed in the veins of our Lord. I suppose you would find her too unclean to eat with as well?"

Aquila was silenced. Ruth, the childless widow. The outcast. The great-grandmother of King David. And a forebear of Yeshua of Nazareth. The Lord had certainly welcomed her among his people. Included her. Blessed her.

Chastened, he nodded. "I would eat with Ruth. And I will eat with Priscilla. Satisfied?"

Benyamin raised himself on an elbow. "Dietary laws are not your problem, Nephew. We were speaking of a wife."

"I hope you are not implying that I consider marriage to a Roman."

"You wouldn't consider marriage to anyone. You are entangled in the past, still holding on to Esther. To a dream that never had much substance to begin with. You were betrothed to Esther since you were children. She was more a habit than your heart's desire. You have to let her go."

Aquila hissed through his teeth. "Leave off, Uncle!"

Benyamin threw his hands in the air. "Fine. Sleep with a dog for the rest of your days." He pulled the sheets over his head, and moments later the sound of his snores filled the chamber.

Esther. The very name made Aquila's stomach clench. Benyamin's words rattled about his mind. Had she only been a habit? Had loyalty rather than love made him build a life around her, refusing to think of any other possibility?

His mind flashed back to a gray day three years before, a day that had started with rejoicing. He had just concluded the sale of a new flock of young sheep for his father. Esther and his brother, Lucinus, had joined him in the courtyard for a small celebration.

It was the first year his father had given Aquila the full running of the farm. The ewes had had their best season yet, birthing more healthy lambs than ever before. Aquila had overseen the whole process, changing the ewes' pasture when they became pregnant, adding to their feed, going with little sleep for days when the lambing started in order to give a hand to the mothers that experienced problems.

A few months later, when they were old enough, he had found a buyer and negotiated a fair price for the new flock. Aquila knew that in the long run, an equitable price would benefit their family's business. Gouging the merchants he traded with might win him a bit more silver today, but ultimately, he would lose custom and trust. He had chosen his price with care, making it just, but not too steep.

Lucinus and Esther were congratulating him on his success when his father sauntered in. "What do you call this?" his father asked, waving the receipt from the sale of the sheep.

Aquila tensed as soon as he saw the sour expression on the old man's face. His father had never spoken a single word of praise for his son's achievements. But he did not run short of words when he was displeased.

"You stupid boy! How could you sell my flock for this price?" his father spat. "They practically robbed me, thanks to you." He began walking away, then stopped partway to hurl one final insult before leaving. "Gullible half-wit."

The air left the courtyard. For a moment, Aquila could not

breathe. What had been a merry gathering turned into a mausoleum. Lucinus laid a hand on his arm. "Don't let him distress you."

Esther shook her head. "He never has anything good to say."

Aquila smiled, relieved that she understood how he felt. Here was his true family. These two were the ones who loved him. "It's no matter," he said.

"At least he only calls you stupid once in a while. He calls me useless every day," Lucinus said.

Aquila frowned. "You are not useless, Brother. One day, all of this shall belong to us. You will prove, then, your many talents."

"It shall belong to *you*, dear older brother, as it should."

Shaking his head, Aquila clasped Lucinus on the shoulder. "What is mine is yours, Lucinus. And yours, Esther. We are a family. You would do the same for me."

His future had always been woven with these two. He belonged to them, and they to him. He could not think of his life apart from them.

Esther, clearly, had not suffered from the same allegiance. When on his twentieth birthday the day of their wedding had finally approached, she had given him an ultimatum. Choose her or his faith. He could not have both.

At first, he thought he could sway her. They were meant for each other, after all. But Esther, soft and subdued in her opinions, had put her foot down with a strength that hinted at a will of iron. She would not marry a follower of the Nazarene. Not unless his father accepted his faith.

She delayed their wedding again and again, neither of them willing to be swayed from their convictions.

Six months passed. Then a year. Aquila sent up a storm of prayers. Nothing changed. After two years, Esther broke their betrothal legally. His father did not even protest. The contract was broken and Aquila watched his future crack into pieces. Still, he held on to hope. He waited for a miracle.

He could not have imagined, then, that the worst betrayal was yet to come. The point of that particular knife, plunged in his back by the people he had loved best, still twisted inside him, its ache never leaving. He was living a life poisoned by that wound.

He turned on his thin mattress, feeling the lumps under his back as keenly as the one in his throat. His uncle had the right of it. It was time he let go of these old shades.

God, it seemed, liked irony. Priscilla's brother, who would probably prefer the extraction of a perfectly good fingernail to offering his sister any favors, became the source of a great blessing to her. Had it not been for Volero, she would not have met Senator Pudens and his family. The day after Quintus's feast, the senator coaxed, cajoled, and wheedled her brother into allowing Priscilla to visit his daughter, Pudentiana. Coaxing and cajoling was something the senator was very gifted at, Priscilla soon discovered.

When Volero insisted that Priscilla attend another event sponsored by Quintus, the senator noticed her anxiety and induced a confession from her. By some trick of charm or personal pressure, the very next day Pudens convinced Quintus to sell his land to her brother at an acceptable price.

Having gained his objective, Volero no longer cared if Priscilla attended upon Quintus or not. But he was impressed enough by Pudens that at his insistence he allowed Priscilla to become a regular visitor to the senator's house.

One afternoon, Priscilla was kneeling under the awning Aquila had erected, helping Pudentiana and her younger sister, Praxedis, pull out weeds while their mother idly directed their activities from her seat in the shade.

Pudentiana straightened her back, fanning her face. "Thank the gods for this awning. What a hot year this has been."

Mindful of the man who had erected the structure, Priscilla hoped her friends blamed the reddening of her cheeks on activity. It had been an astonishing shock to find Aquila in this house. Her heart had leapt into her throat at the sight of him, though she could not explain why the man should have such an effect on her.

"Girls," Sabinella called, "will you fetch some refreshments for us, please?"

Priscilla noticed Pudentiana shoot her mother a worried glance. "You should not be left alone here."

"Priscilla can stay with me, then. Go on. Tell the cook to make us a salad with herbs and cheese. And have him fetch a fresh loaf of bread from the bakery."

Sabinella pushed strands of limp hair behind her ear, a pronounced tremor making her fingers unsteady. Priscilla studied the older woman, for the first time noticing the lines of strain around her eyes. "Are you unwell, Sabinella?"

"A little pain. It will pass. Always does."

Priscilla noted the woman's unusual inertia, the rigid way she held her body in the chair, the trembling she could not stop in her fingers. She began to understand the look of concern Pudentiana had given her. This was no passing malady. Her heart sank, for though she had not known Sabinella long, she already felt a deep attachment to her.

"I will pray for you," she said before she could think better of the offer.

Sabinella drew a gentle, unsteady hand down Priscilla's hair. "Thank you, my dear. To what gods do you pray? I myself have offered libations to many. But in recent years, I confess, my faith has abandoned me."

"I pray to the Lord, my lady," Priscilla said. She spoke the words knowing they might close the door of friendship. Still, they were worth saying, for they might open another portal, one far more precious than any human could offer.

"The Lord? I am not familiar with this divinity."

"He is the God worshiped by the Hebrews, my lady. They do not believe in a pantheon of gods, but worship only one, Creator of heaven and earth, and sustainer of all that is in them."

"I suppose that makes life simpler."

Priscilla thought of the convoluted complications of being a Gentile follower of the Lord, always living a little on the outside. "I have not found it simple. But I have found it peaceful." She took Sabinella's hand into her own. "The God I serve makes a way in the deserts of life. He creates streams in the wasteland places of our hearts."

"Then pray for my husband, for I fear when I am gone, my Pudens will find himself in a barren and parched land."

With the Sabbath arrived sweltering heat and gray skies that refused to break into rain. Priscilla and Lollia left the house early, before the heat became unbearable. Priscilla burst into laughter when outside the Campi synagogue, Ferox snapped to attention at the sight of her, barking a few times, before remembering his manners and settling down with the bearing of a dog that knows it belongs. Someone had tied him to a tree and placed a small bowl of water next to him.

She knelt by his side and patted his head. He was already losing a little of that lost, mongrel look, his ribs filling out, his wild fur brushed and clean. Her heart beat faster when she realized that the dog's presence meant his master could not be far. With a sigh, she came to her feet.

Today she was determined to avoid the man. Her heart did not need this entanglement. Not with a Jewish man who refused even to eat in her company.

She settled on the back row, nodding a greeting to familiar faces while Lollia flitted about, conversing with friends.

"You seem very somber today," Mary said, enfolding her in a fond embrace before sitting down next to her. "Will you come to our home after worship? I have roast pork, a favorite among your mother's people, I believe."

Priscilla gave her a horrified look. Mary laughed softly. "I jest. I wanted to remove that scowl from your face. But my invitation is earnest. We have simple lentil stew today. Will you come? I would have sent word earlier, but I know we cannot intrude upon you in your brother's house."

Priscilla squirmed. She suspected that Aquila and his uncle would also be attending, which meant she had to avoid Mary's house at all costs. "They are about to start." She pointed to the man taking his place at the front. The deflection would buy her time to think of a gracious way of refusing.

She tried to settle her mind and focus on the worship. One of the Scriptures assigned for the day was from a prophet named Hosea. The words had a strange effect on her, gathering her scattered thoughts. The reader, a baker with a round belly and a sonorous voice, read the words first in Hebrew, then Greek:

"Therefore, behold, I will allure her,
and bring her into the wilderness,
and speak tenderly to her.
And there I will give her her vineyards
and make the Valley of Achor a door of hope."

Priscilla listened carefully, feeling confused. What was the Valley of Achor? What was this door of hope? The reader continued for a few more verses, the bejeweled roll of Scripture open before him, until he ended with

"And I will have mercy on No Mercy,
and I will say to Not My People, 'You are my people';
and he shall say, 'You are my God.'"

Priscilla strained forward. What had he said? That God would say to those who were *not* his people that they *were* his people? Was that a promise for someone like her? A promise that by some means she could be counted as one who truly belonged to the Lord? Frustrated, she leaned back. Who could answer the questions that burst from her with the force of a geyser?

Her gaze fell on Rufus. With sudden conviction she realized he could solve these puzzles. Rufus would know the meaning of these passages. Mary had provided the perfect opportunity by inviting her to their home. All she had to do was accept the invitation. She could not allow her feelings for Aquila to rob her of this chance.

She expected to be settled in Mary's diminutive alcove again, eating separately from the rest. To her astonishment, they led her to the dining room and served her food alongside everyone else. She stared at her steaming bowl with dismay. "Will I not make you unclean?"

She was surprised that Aquila, who reposed quietly on the couch across from her, was the one to answer. "Among our people, there was a woman named Ruth, a Moabite who married a man of Bethlehem. My uncle reminded me that although an outsider, Ruth is in the lineage of our most revered king. I have noticed something about you, Priscilla, daughter of Priscus. Like Ruth, you are godly." The gray irises flared with a spark of emotion Priscilla could not name. "Like Ruth, you *belong* at this table," he said. "I am only sorry I did not recognize it sooner."

Priscilla felt her throat tighten. *"You* belong *at this table."* The words wound their way into a deep, dry well within her; they flowed into that empty, dark place, and like a balm, they soothed the parched ache in it. Her eyes filled and she dropped her head, trying to hide her tears.

As if sensing that she needed time to pull herself together, Rufus prayed a long blessing over the food.

"May I ask a question?" she said after they had eaten most of their stew and her tears had passed. "Today's reading from Hosea—what did it mean?"

Rufus set his bowl aside and rubbed his hands together. "I was hoping you would ask! The Valley of Achor means 'the valley of trouble.' Our people's faith has proven inconsistent through the ages. We slip away from the Lord. Frequently. And our wanderings bring us much trouble."

Priscilla gave a tight smile. "I know how wandering from the right path can have that effect."

The man of Cyrene gave a rueful smile. "God tells his people that he can turn that place of suffering—that valley of trouble—into a door of hope."

"Hope?"

"It is hard to put to words. Trouble itself can be transformed, you see, in the hands of God. Instead of a place of destruction, pain and heartache can lead to hope."

Priscilla leaned back. "I myself find that my past troubles lead only to regret."

Aquila looked at her. She was shaken to see a pool of compassion in that gaze. "I understand," he said. "The past has a way of sneaking up on the present, making it bitter with old condemnations. When you are alone, it is only the voice of regret that echoes in your heart." He took a deep breath. "But the Lord has not left us alone. He has not abandoned us to our regrets. He has offered us a gate to life, a door of hope.

"And that door . . . is a man."

Seven

PRISCILLA WALKED alongside Aquila in silence. He had insisted on accompanying her and Lollia home again. Ferox ran to and fro between them, acting as if they were his sheep to herd and protect.

She was grateful for Aquila's silence. Her head was too full of all she had heard that afternoon. "Why do they never speak of Yeshua at the synagogue?" she said in a sudden burst of realization. "It is the first time I have heard of him."

Aquila took a deep breath as if preparing for something unpleasant. "My people long for a promised Messiah. A king like David who will free us from our enemies."

"Rome, you mean?"

Aquila shrugged. "Now it is Rome. Centuries ago it was Greece. Down the coils of time, who knows what other master we will long to overthrow. The point is that God promised us a Savior.

"But Yeshua did not come as a potentate or a military general. He did not offer to overthrow Rome. Instead, he offered to overcome sin. He is a spiritual king, not a lord of war."

Priscilla digested his words. "Your people don't accept him as the promised Messiah?"

"Some do. Many don't. There has been a growing division among the Jews over the matter, fomenting violence. We have not spoken of Yeshua openly to the synagogue at Campi, hoping to avoid conflict."

"Surely you will have to speak of him if he is the Savior?"

"We will bear witness to him at the right time, I promise. For now, we share our news with a select few. Those we feel God has already prepared."

Priscilla's eyes widened. "Like me?"

"Like you."

For a moment, she forgot to breathe. Had God chosen her in some way? Prepared her without her knowing? Cared enough to set his gaze on her?

Distracted by her incomprehensible thoughts, her feet lagged, and she fell several steps behind everyone else.

Peripherally, she became aware of the rattle of a cart behind her and moved away from the road, leaving a wide berth for it to pass. Without warning, Ferox began to bark ferociously, doubling back to her. Before she could stop him, he plowed into her with the full force of his body, knocking her sideways into the wall that ran along the edge of the road.

She collapsed against the wide bricks. Only then did she become aware of the cart. It had swerved toward her, its massive wheels clattering loudly in her ears. She gasped and pressed herself against the wall. She heard Aquila shout and Lollia scream with terror.

The wheels rolled by, a finger's breadth from her torso, barely missing her. Ferox ran after the cart for a few steps, barking wildly, before returning to sit by her like a sentinel. Aquila knelt on her other side, his face drained of color. "Are you injured?"

She shook her head. "Just dusty."

Aquila placed a gentle hand behind her shoulders and helped her sit up. Against her flesh, she could feel his fingers trembling.

"My poor girl! I thought you would be crushed before my eyes," Lollia stammered, trying not to cry.

Priscilla gave her a reassuring pat. "I gave you a bad scare, Lollia. I am sorry." She turned to Ferox, who remained still as a statue, his gaze trained on her. "I take back every disparaging remark I ever made against you," she said weakly. "You saved my life."

Aquila shook his head. "I saw the cart too late. The driver must have been swilling wine with a bucket. He veered right into you."

Priscilla wiped her grimy hands against her tunic. "I am still in one piece, I think."

"Rest a moment before trying to rise," Aquila said.

"I am well. Truly." She leaned her weight into her palm to gain leverage, half rising. A small gasp escaped her as pain shot up her wrist. Instinctively, she cradled the injured limb against her chest.

"You are hurt! Let me see."

Her heart did a small flip as Aquila extended her hand softly into his. His examination was at once delicate and thorough as he pressed careful fingers against her palm and wrist, turning it gently one way, then another. "You will have a good bruise. But I don't think it is broken. Just sprained. You may want to bind it up when you arrive home."

Priscilla reclaimed her wrist and managed to rise to her feet. "Ferox certainly redeemed himself. He may have thrown me into a rosebush, but he more than made up for it today. Although, he did choose to save me by barreling me into a wall. I see a pattern emerging."

"Yes. One of you falling on your head all the time." Aquila stepped into the road and craned his neck looking for a sign of the cart and finding none. "Odd how the driver had his hood up in this heat. He never even stopped to see if you were hurt after he mowed you down."

She supposed she should be shaken by how close she had come to dying. Instead, she found herself more distracted by the way Aquila had held her hand, as if she were a piece of spun glass.

Aquila found himself yearning for the Sabbath to come. He wanted to see Priscilla again. He told himself he merely needed to ensure she had recovered from her narrow escape. But he was unsettled by the way his thoughts continued to return to her, caught off guard by the single-mindedness of their direction.

Frustrated that he could not simply walk to her home and inquire after her, he spent the week punching tiny holes in leather using an awl, then slipping his needle through before the holes could close. This was a craft of skill rather than strength, and his long experience with it allowed him to complete the task even though his mind wandered elsewhere most of the time.

He considered Priscilla's habit of referring to the villa in Pincio as her brother's house. Not hers. Not *home*. From what he had seen, the villa, unlike her clothing, was maintained with dignified care. Nothing about that house suggested poverty.

Yet Priscilla's hand, when he had held it in his own, had been callused, its skin roughened by labor. Manual labor, unlike anything someone of her station should be accustomed to doing. Why would the resident of such a house work with her hands?

He tried not to think about how right it had felt to *hold* that hand. How hard to let go of it. A low grunt of frustration escaped him. He was losing his mind, regressing to boyhood.

Once again, he forced his thoughts to return to the mystery of her circumstances. After the accident, he had lingered a good while near the top of the hill to ensure that Priscilla arrived home without further misadventure. As he had waited, an expensive open carriage had exited the back of the house, bearing a fashionable man and woman attired in splendid silks and linens, their bejeweled knuckles and arms shimmering in the sun. He had heard a servant call the man master.

Which made him Priscilla's brother. If so, then how had she come to live in such an impoverished state? The disparity in their situations perplexed him. What brother would allow his own sibling to be so reduced in circumstances when he clearly had the means to help?

He thought of his own brother and his objections plummeted into an ironic heap.

When the Sabbath finally arrived, he was washed and ready to leave the house long before sunrise. He would have been the first person to arrive at the synagogue if his uncle had not delayed him.

"What's your hurry?" Benyamin said, dipping bread into his watered wine. "It will be another late lunch, you mark my words. Mary will send us off on an errand of mercy. Best get some food inside you."

"I'm not hungry."

"Are you feeling sick? I myself did not sleep well last night."

Aquila shoved a hand through his hair. "I slept enough. Have you finished yet?"

When they arrived at the synagogue, his eyes immediately sought the back row. He exhaled and felt his shoulders ease for the first time in seven days.

She was there.

"How is your wrist?" he asked.

"Good as new." She held up her arm, which, except for a few bruises, seemed to be in working order. "Thank you again for helping me. I brought my brave hero a gift." She smiled.

For the fraction of a moment, Aquila assumed she meant *him*. Delight blazed through him. "You did?"

Then she bent to grab a basket into which she had stuffed several packets wrapped in cloth. One was long with knobs at both ends. "For Ferox."

"Ferox!" He choked. "Let me guess," he added, trying to disguise his disappointment. "You bought him a book. In Greek."

She grinned. "He is clever enough to read one. But I thought he might prefer a bone."

"He will be your undying friend for life."

"Until he decides to pitch me into a bush again."

Mary joined them, carrying a large basket. "Elizabeth was up all night. Her baby is teething. I have put together a basket of food and necessities. Will you come with me, Priscilla?"

Aquila reached for the basket, relieving Mary of the weight. "Who is Elizabeth?"

"A young widow. Her husband was killed in a shipwreck off the coast of Malta several months ago. She was pregnant at the time. Her son is eight months old now, and it is hard for her to work with such a young one."

"I would be happy to come with you," Priscilla said. "I have brought a little wine and bread today. I even have a honey cake."

"And I volunteer myself as the mule. That basket weighs as much as a block of Roman concrete." Aquila hefted Mary's basket.

"So long as you don't lighten it by eating what's inside."

"Only a few bites. Consider it transportation tax."

Mary wagged a finger at him, though she left the basket in his care when she went to join a group of women on the opposite side of the room.

After the services concluded, Benyamin went with Rufus to his house while the rest of them visited the young widow, who also lived in Trastevere. To Aquila's disappointment and relief, Priscilla walked alongside Mary, Ferox sticking close to her, while he and Lollia followed behind.

"Does your mistress always visit the poor?" he asked.

"Always. She does not have much. The wine she carries? She drank none all week so that she could save her portion for someone in need. The bread, also, came from her own plate."

Aquila was struck speechless for a moment. She went hungry for the sake of a people she hardly knew. "Why? Why would she do that for Jews?"

Lollia raised an eyebrow. "Can you not guess? She loves the Lord. So she loves what he loves. His people."

Aquila rubbed his temple. His uncle had compared Priscilla to Ruth. Now he saw why. She had the same tender heart that had driven Ruth from her own homeland in order to remain with Naomi. *"Your people shall be my people,"* Ruth had promised her grieving mother-in-law. It seemed that Priscilla had made the same promise to God. His people had become her people.

He felt slightly queasy at the thought of his superior attitude toward her. He had judged her a little beneath him because she was not a daughter of Abraham. Yet he could not remember ever going hungry so that someone less fortunate than himself should eat. Jesus had loved the poor. Loved them with the same selflessness he saw in Priscilla.

What would such a woman become with Christ by her side, his Spirit welling up within her?

"Why is she poor, when her brother appears so wealthy?" he asked Lollia.

Lollia considered for a moment. "That is a question for her to answer. I have already said too much."

They walked through a tightly packed neighborhood, cramped with multistory tenement houses. Aquila studied a tall building to his right and counted quickly. Six stories tall, sitting cheek by jowl with another building of five stories.

They were called *insulae*—Rome's idea of apartments. Their construction was remarkably lightweight given their impressive height and width. The taller building seemed to be supported by long, thin wooden posts, hardly sturdier than a shepherd's staff.

It was well known that one passed under such apartments at one's own risk. The residents were supposed to carry their waste out of the building and dispose of it appropriately. More often than not, they opted to throw it out of their narrow windows. Usually without bothering to see if some innocent happened to be walking below. No wonder there were so many bathhouses in Rome.

Mary led them to a five-story *insula*. Elizabeth's tiny apartment shared the top floor with two other residences. Before entering the building, Aquila had noticed that the top floor was shielded from the rain by nothing more than roofing tiles. A couple of cooing pigeons were walking on those tiles, making them wobble.

Inside Elizabeth's apartment, he could hear every sound as the birds roamed overhead. On a rainy night, Elizabeth would need several large vessels to catch the excess water that would drain into her home through the flimsy roof.

How did the young widow manage daily life without running water or access to outdoor light in her apartment? He could not imagine the noise, trapped smells, and lack of privacy, or the many trips to collect water from the public fountains.

A frazzled Elizabeth bid them to sit, while bouncing a wailing baby in her arms. "He has a fever," she said, her eyes awash in tears. "He hasn't slept all night."

Mary took the babe into her arms and laid an experienced hand against the child's cheek. "This is no teething fever. He burns too hot. How long has he been feverish?"

"Two days. I did not know what to do." Elizabeth wiped tears from blotchy cheeks.

"There, now. I am here. You are not alone anymore. You two—" she pointed to Priscilla and Aquila—"tell Rufus we need a physician. Lollia can remain and help me."

Aquila, happy to be given a useful task, nodded. "Come, Priscilla." In the urgency of the moment, the familiar name sprang from his lips without thought.

They sped to Rufus's house, Aquila adjusting his speed to Priscilla's smaller steps, while Ferox trotted ahead of them.

"There is a Greek physician who lives in this neighborhood," Rufus said when they reached him. "I've heard he is held in high esteem. I will fetch him."

Benyamin came to his feet. "Perhaps I'd best go home. I am not feeling well myself. I will only be in the way here."

Aquila realized with sudden alarm that his uncle looked

unnaturally pale, his skin shiny with sweat. "Uncle!" he exclaimed, stepping toward Benyamin.

"Don't fuss. A strong brew of honeysuckle and I will be as hale as you."

But when he started to walk, Aquila noticed that his gait seemed unsteady. At the top of the steps, he slipped and would have fallen if Aquila had not grabbed hold of him. Aquila swallowed. The arm he held was too hot.

"Fever," Aquila said under his breath.

Eight

"DO YOU WANT THE PHYSICIAN to examine him before visiting Elizabeth's baby?" Rufus asked Aquila.

"Certainly not!" Benyamin answered, looking horrified. "The poor babe needs him more than I. I only need a little rest in my own bed."

Rufus considered his old friend, then nodded. "I will bring the cart for you. You will not walk all the way to the Via Appia."

"Bah! I can walk the length of Rome and back," Benyamin said. But he did not argue as Aquila settled him gently into the cart when it arrived.

"I will come to you as soon as I convey the physician to Elizabeth," Rufus promised before rushing out.

Priscilla turned to Aquila. "May I come? I nursed my father for many weeks when he was ill. And if Benyamin should need a physician, you can fetch one while I stay with him."

Aquila thought for a moment. "Your brother?"

"So long as I arrive home before sunset, when the villa's gates are locked, he will not object."

Aquila was grateful to have her help. He had no experience caring for the sick. The sight of his uncle, usually so sturdy, reduced to wobbly weakness, had shaken him. Benyamin was the only family he had left. He could not imagine life without him. Wordlessly, he hefted Priscilla into the cart next to Benyamin before leaping inside and taking the reins.

Priscilla took charge as soon as they arrived home. When Benyamin was tucked into bed and resting, she rinsed her hands and looked about. Noting that their small dwelling had no garden save for a few pots of mint and thyme, she asked, "Do you keep any medicinal herbs?"

Aquila fetched the wooden chest that contained wool for bandages, bunches of dried herbs, and miniature vials of tinctures and ointments Benyamin insisted on keeping in the house. To Aquila they were a mystery. But Priscilla seemed undaunted by the contents and set a few aside.

"You have silphium. And honeysuckle. That is good."

Once she had boiled water, she steeped the herbs, her manner calm and reassuringly confident. "You are worried?" she asked, looking at him with compassion.

"His fever seems high," Aquila admitted.

She nodded. "I can recommend the physician who tended my father. He is a knowledgeable man, trained in Alexandria." She bit her lip. "He can be expensive."

Aquila waved a hand. "I have some savings."

She gave a relieved smile. "His name is Eratosthenes."

"Poor man. By the time you pronounce that name, half his patients will either be cured or dead."

Priscilla smiled. "I will write down the directions for you. They are even longer than his name." She bit her thumb, her face turning pink. It took him a moment to guess the source of her embarrassment.

He fetched papyrus and ink. "It's all right. I can read." He sensed the stiffness in his voice, the offense he could not hide.

She turned even redder. He forced his rigid shoulders to relax. She was not at fault, after all. To her, he was a simple laborer. Many men in his position were illiterate. "It's all right," he said again, his voice softening. "Remind me to tell you how I put ink in my tutor's shoes."

Her eyes sparkled, turning a deep sapphire blue. "Remind me," she said, "to tell you how I put ants in mine."

It was like a storm breaking. They began to laugh so hard they both had tears in their eyes. Finally he took her note. "I better fetch Eratosthenes."

She wiped the corners of her eyes. "And I better waken Benyamin and give him this brew. It has steeped long enough."

After the momentary relief of laughter, Aquila did not breathe with ease until he returned, Eratosthenes in tow. The physician examined his uncle, who was by now, supine and truly weak. His examination seemed thorough, and he said little until he finished. "This fever has been spreading through Rome," he said. "You should know some have died of it. Your uncle seems strong. He may recover, provided you nurse him properly."

Aquila sank against the wall, his body sagging. It occurred to him that Elizabeth's babe might have been struck by the same malady. "I will nurse him properly. Tell me what to do."

The physician sniffed the bowl containing the potion Priscilla had prepared. "This is good." He handed the bowl back to Priscilla. "I see you remember what I taught you." He gave Aquila a bag of herbs. "This is better. It contains more powerful herbs. Steep a spoonful of this in hot water for thirty minutes. Your uncle should drink five cups of this mixture every day. If you need me, you know where to send for me." He wiped his hands and put away his instruments in a neat bag. "The herbs, light food, and complete rest may restore him."

Rufus arrived just as the physician was leaving. "How is that old rascal?" he asked, his mouth pressed tight with anxiety.

"That old rascal can hear you," Benyamin croaked from his bed.

Rufus grinned. "Not too sick to remain ornery." He sat with Benyamin until he fell asleep.

"I must go now, Aquila," Priscilla said. "Will it be all right if I return in the morning? I can help nurse Benyamin while you work."

Aquila let out a great huff of air. "I did not even have time to grow anxious about our work. The Lord provided for my need before I asked. I accept your gracious offer with thanks. And since Rufus is with my uncle, I will accompany you to Pincio without having to leave my uncle alone."

After the near miss that had almost taken her life, he was not going to take any chances with Priscilla's well-being. Neither was Ferox apparently, since he leapt to his feet as soon as he saw them at the door and charged ahead before they even told him which way to go.

Priscilla fanned herself while Benyamin slept. He had dozed most of the morning, waking up long enough to drink the tincture she had given him, before falling back into a deep sleep. The fever, though not completely abated, seemed to be dissipating.

From where she sat, with the curtain looped on a hook, she could see Aquila at work in the store. Perched on a stool, his head bent over a length of supple leather dyed almost the color of his dark curls, his fingers moved deftly, applying the awl and needle with astonishing precision. From this angle, his nose, sharp in the middle and flared at the edges, more than ever gave him the aspect of an eagle.

Every once in a while, he would look in her direction, a smile breaking out, transforming the reserved lines of his face into something more welcoming.

Aquila, hiding behind his usual guarded mask, was handsome. But Aquila open and friendly became dazzling. Priscilla fidgeted on her cushion, annoyed with her response to the man.

She wished Lollia were here to distract her from the inevitable intimacy of their situation. With Elizabeth's baby sicker even than Benyamin, Mary had needed Lollia's help, and the older woman had left for Trastevere early in the morning.

"You were going to tell me about your tutor," he said into the silence.

She blinked, remembering the conversation that had drawn the confession out of her. "He was the first tutor my father hired for me. I discovered quickly that he was not a pleasant man. He often told me that I was unworthy of his tuition, being a girl. He also had a habit of whacking the back of my hand with willow rods when my answers displeased him.

"One day, I had the bad judgment to point out his error regarding a grammatical point, and he beat me for it. That afternoon, I happened upon an anthill. My mother used to tell me that one could accomplish far more with a bit of honey than a bowl of vinegar. I decided to put her advice to the test. With a bit of honey, I coaxed a jarful of ants out of their nest. When my tutor donned his shoes the next morning, he received an unpleasant surprise. The ants were the biting variety."

Aquila laughed. "I don't think that is quite what your mother intended when she taught you that axiom." He leaned toward her, the leather cloak forgotten. "What did your tutor do?"

"He beat me harder. Fortunately." She smirked.

"Why fortunately?"

"My parents saw the marks and dismissed him. My father had been a general in charge of garrisons of soldiers. If he had ever had any gentleness in him, the soldier's life had obliterated it. But he would not tolerate unjust violence against his children."

In the short years she had known her decorated father, Priscilla had learned to both fear and adore the man. Mostly, she held him in awe. In her childish mind, he had achieved mythical proportions, a being of immense power and occasional demonstrations of absentminded charity toward his only daughter. In the intervening years since his death, she had learned to see him with more clarity: a mortal with failings common to all men.

"Who taught you after that?" Aquila asked, returning to his work.

"My father hired Demodocus, a man of vast knowledge and temperate disposition. I adored him. For five years, he tutored and befriended me. I could have continued for another five, but my brother discharged him when my father died."

Aquila set the awl on his lap and studied her, gray eyes intense. "Why . . . ? Forgive me if I trespass. Why is it that you live in financial strain while your brother lives in comfort?"

Priscilla found herself confiding more than she had intended, probably because Aquila listened with a still and acute concentration, as if every word she said mattered to him.

"My brother is my senior by sixteen years," she explained. "His mother, a great lady from an illustrious Roman family, died in childbirth when Volero was only ten years old. Our father found himself fighting in the wilds of Germania at the time, unable to show up for her funerary rites. Volero has never forgotten that slight."

Aquila glanced up. "Your brother is not proud of the general?"

Priscilla considered the question. "My father cast a long shadow, even while leaving a void by his continuous absence. They never enjoyed a warm relationship, those two. It did not help matters when my father came home from Germania with my mother in tow. She was a simple captive who did not even have the distinction of being a chieftain's daughter. She came to my father barefoot and illiterate. Pretty enough for a slave, but not exactly appropriate for the wife of a well-respected general."

"Your brother objected?"

"Not at first, when she was a mere servant. But she grew quickly in my father's favor. Having natural facility with languages, she learned to speak Latin perfectly, without even a trace of accent, though she never learned to read and write. My father enjoyed her conversation, even after they had been married to each other for fifteen years. My mother could always make him laugh."

"That is a rare gift."

"He found it so. He was not a man given to deep feelings. But I think he *liked* her."

Aquila arched a dark brow. "One hopes for a little more in marriage."

"I certainly would." Priscilla twisted her hands in her lap. "For them it seemed enough; they found contentment with each other."

"Did he marry her right away?"

"No. She had been in my father's possession for a year when Volero fell gravely ill. He was fourteen, a boy of fragile health by all accounts, and my father feared he would die. Thinking that he might lose his only heir, he married my mother, hoping to sire another son. Volero recovered, fortunately. But he never forgave my father for marrying so far beneath him. He had no love for my mother, and even less for me."

"Surely he could not blame you for your father's decisions?"

Priscilla stared into the distance. Volero had not always been the knife-hard man he was today. Once, he had been an impressionable youth, scarred by the cruel barbs of his peers.

"My birth did not make life easy for him," she said. "His friends used to tease him viciously about his barbarian stepmother and redheaded little sister. I became a mark of shame to him. Now, every time he looks at me, I remind him of his father's failings. I become a poor reflection on *him*. He would prefer to hide me altogether if he could. But then, he has had his share of suffering, and in no small part, thanks to my existence."

Something shifted in Aquila's gaze, a final guard melting, replaced by warmth she could feel all the way in her marrow. "Do you always show so much understanding for those who hurt and abuse you? Try to walk in their shoes, so to speak?"

"Sometimes." She wrinkled her nose. "Sometimes I put ants in them."

Aquila threw his head back and laughed. Very softly he said, "I would have been proud to call you my sister."

Priscilla felt an odd battle waging inside her. Part of her wanted to dance with elation, knowing that *this* man could be proud of her. Another part of her, irritating and perverse, found the idea of Aquila as her brother appalling. She did not want him to regard her in that light. For the second time now, he had referred to her as a sister. The thought made her want to weep.

"Can he hurt you? Your brother?" Aquila asked, his voice stony. "Since he is the head of your family, you are under his authority, according to the law."

She shook her head. "I live under my brother's roof. But I don't live under his legal control. My father gave me the gift of my emancipation before his death. He knew, I think, that Volero would be tempted to sell me into slavery or worse if he held such power over me. Rather than giving me a financial inheritance, which Volero would have been able to manipulate, my father gave me legal freedom. A far greater gift for an unmarried woman."

"I knew a father could give the gift of emancipation to a younger son. I did not know it could be done for daughters."

"Due to his military career, my father wielded substantial influence. He found a way."

"I am very relieved to hear it, Priscilla." He flashed another of his melting smiles.

She turned to Benyamin, occupying her hands with the tasks of nursing. Her mind, however, would not be distracted from Aquila as easily.

Impossible. What she wanted from Aquila was impossible.

Thankfully, Benyamin seemed to be improving, though he remained weak. After drinking a full cup of medicinal brew, he fell asleep. Priscilla picked up the half-finished basket she had brought from home and began the soothing motions of weaving the water-softened reeds. Her hands tucked long strands behind the spokes, packing her weave tight.

"That looks good," Aquila said.

She smiled. "Lollia taught me when I was young. It's a useful skill."

Aquila laid the leather cloak on the stool and came to stand by her side. He bent to examine the basket more closely.

"I take that back. This is not good. It is exquisite." He touched the finished base of the basket, his fingers tracing the smooth pattern already emerging. His face bent closer. On his breath, she could smell the scent of cloves and the faint spice of cypress and myrtle in his hair. She gulped a breath. As if becoming abruptly aware of their proximity, Aquila took a hasty step away and scurried back to his perch in the workshop.

For some time, they worked in silence. But the easy camaraderie of the morning had shattered, leaving behind an awkward awareness.

To Priscilla's relief, Benyamin awakened, hungry and well enough to speak.

"How are you faring with that cloak?" he asked Aquila, examining it while Priscilla warmed the rich beef broth Mary had sent over. "Perfect stitching as always," Benyamin commented as he fingered his nephew's workmanship. "But you must be slowing down, Nephew. I expected you to be finished by now. Perhaps it's old age, weakening your big muscles."

"Worry for *you* is slowing me down. What were you thinking, falling ill with all these orders piling up?"

"Thankfully, God, in his wisdom, did not abandon me to your rough-and-tumble care. Instead, he sent me this beautiful creature to minister to me in my hour of need." Benyamin accepted the bowl of broth and warm bread from Priscilla with a satisfied sigh.

She straightened the pillow behind his back and made sure his blanket was tucked around him. Aquila rolled his eyes. "Don't pander to him. With pampering like that, he isn't likely to get out of bed for a month." He wagged a finger at his uncle in mock threat. "We might as well eat with him," he said. "I will get no more work done while he is awake and overflowing with words."

She could tell, even with his gruff words, that Aquila was limp with relief to find his uncle in a jovial mood and strong enough to banter. For the first time in two days the lines of worry on his brow began to smooth out.

They sat next to Benyamin's bed, eating bread and cheese, followed by juicy plums. Benyamin asked after Elizabeth's little boy, who was not out of danger. The fever had proved even stronger for one so young. Benyamin immediately stopped eating so that he could pray for the child. Priscilla listened, moved by the simple words addressed to Yeshua, as if he were present in this modest chamber with them. As if One far greater than they held their concerns tenderly in his hands.

Benyamin fell asleep after the meal, his fragile strength spent. Aquila returned to the storefront, leather cloak back on his lap while Priscilla plied the reeds in her basket. The silence stretched between them, growing strained without Benyamin's good-natured teasing.

Finally, unable to bear the tension, Priscilla said, "I have never been outside Rome. Tell me about life in Pontus." In truth, she longed to ask twenty more questions, having stayed up half the night with curious questions swirling in her mind about this man who had grown up with a tutor, yet lived in a cramped apartment.

Aquila's fingers became still for a moment. "Pontus is an ancient land that lies on the shores of a turquoise sea. My family live to the south, along the foothills of the Paryadres mountains. My father owns farmlands where we grow grain and orchards with cherries so sweet, they burst on your tongue like nectar. But most of his land is used for pasture and the raising of sheep. We have a few workshops dedicated to producing wool and a tannery for hides. The smallest workshop is for leatherworks."

"It sounds beautiful." Priscilla tried to hide her confusion. What he described was a wealthy household. Rural landowners with the magnitude of holdings Aquila described were prospering greatly in an expanding empire that was in constant need of food and clothing. The son of such a household would not need to live so modestly, practically on the edge of Via Appia.

"I see your own story is as convoluted as mine," she said.

"It is." He grew very still. Then with a determined motion, he stepped off the stool and walked toward her. In the doorway, he halted, leaning a shoulder against the wall and crossing his arms over his chest.

"I had a different plan for my life. It did not include Rome or residing in three tiny chambers with my uncle, though I love him dearly. It did not include becoming a worker of leather goods. But I have discovered a strange thing as my cherished dreams have crashed and shattered around my feet.

"The only way to peace is by learning to accept, day by day, the circumstances and tests permitted by God. By the repeated laying down of our own will and the accepting of his as it is presented in the things which happen to us.

"But that lesson came to me at great cost, and I am still learning it."

Nine

AQUILA DREW A DEEP BREATH and held it. He had never told his story to anyone, never unraveled the full humiliation of his loss. Many, including his uncle Benyamin, knew the facts. But none had heard the full account of the events that had culminated in his expulsion from his childhood home.

He was not sure why he wanted to tell the story now. Reveal to *this* woman the ache that had clogged his soul, like a morsel in the throat he could neither swallow nor disgorge.

Perhaps it was the knowledge that all her life she had been treated with disdain—her red hair and Germanic blood, marks of a defilement she could not cleanse. She had never fully belonged to her father's exalted world. She understood what it meant to be unwanted.

Moreover, Priscilla possessed an astonishing kindness; a benevolence that led her to give away what little she had and care for a sick man to whom she had no earthly obligation. A fidelity that made her hold his ladder even though such open support might expose her to criticism and ridicule from cherished friends.

His story would be safe in her work-roughened hands. *He* would be safe in those hands.

"I know what it is to be an outcast in your own home, Priscilla. My father disowned me." He said the stark words simply, without trying to cushion them with excuses.

Her eyes widened. Then compassion replaced shock, and her mouth softened as if with no words it pronounced a benediction over him. He felt his muscles, which had grown knotted with pain, start to unwind.

"I was young when I became a follower of Yeshua, and for a few years, my father took no notice of my growing faith. He cared more for our standing before men than God. So long as I observed the right rules and won the respect of the leaders of our community, he did not care which rabbi I followed. As the eldest son, he entrusted me with the running of his workshops and the administration of his land.

"Then news trickled into Pontus from Jerusalem. Those of us who had claimed the man of Nazareth as the rightful Messiah were accused of blasphemy. My faith now became a public embarrassment. My father demanded that I deny Yeshua."

"Which you would never do," Priscilla said, sounding offended. He was astounded by her understanding. Esther had never grasped the importance of his faith to him. Even after such a short acquaintance, Priscilla knew more about his heart than Esther had after years of companionship.

"Which I would never do," he confirmed.

After his refusal to recant, his father had stripped him bit by bit. Like a knife in a torturer's hand, he had cut away the fabric of his life into small pieces, gouging out one small fragment at a time. First, he had removed Aquila from overseeing their vast farmlands and pastures, reducing him to managing the tanning business. When Aquila still refused to abandon his faith, his father had taken away the tanning business and given him the leather workshop, the smallest of their enterprises.

Every loss had hurt, not because being diminished in worldly importance made him feel small. Rather, each demotion was a reflection of his father's already-stingy regard dissolving, deteriorating. His elder son became a stranger to his heart.

Had Aquila's mother been alive, she might have exerted her softer influence and brought a measure of reconciliation between them. But she had died when her sons were still boys. Where there had once been a mountain of nurturing love, she had left a gaping crater in her absence.

Aquila wiped the film of perspiration that had gathered on his forehead. "I was willing to pay the penalty my father demanded. But his punishment affected another life as much as my own. I had been betrothed since childhood to the daughter of my father's closest friend. Esther and I were supposed to be married when I turned twenty."

Priscilla's brows rose a fraction at that news. He watched the tide of color as it crept from her neck to her cheeks and something in him hummed with satisfaction. She was not indifferent to the news that once he had belonged to another. Why this should please him, he was in no state to ponder. He merely let the perception settle into him like a balm that soothed and relieved an anxious ache.

"Esther delayed our marriage, saying she would not wed me unless I gave up this unseemly obsession with a false prophet." Aquila tipped his head back and stared unseeingly into the dark shadows above. Esther had not developed any signs of religious fervor until Aquila had begun to lose his social standing. Funny how he had never thought of that. "Every time my father demoted me, she delayed the wedding another six months. When my father reduced me to a common laborer—" he brandished his hands, callused and red—"she had enough. She broke our betrothal contract. My father, usually an enthusiast for the binding nature of legal contracts, never even raised a brow."

A small, shocked sound escaped her throat. "She broke your heart?"

"Not then. I still had hope, if you believe it." Aquila pulled his hand through his hair and swallowed hard. "Uncle Benyamin, being a follower of Yeshua himself, was the only member of my family who stood by me through those years. Except for one other: my younger brother, Lucinus. He was my closest companion, the best friend a man could ask for. I trusted him with my life. So I was glad that everything my father stripped from me, he bestowed upon Lucinus. At least my diminishment meant his elevation.

"When my life of ordinary labor did not produce the desired effect, Father gave me one last ultimatum. Repent publicly or leave his house. I tried to reason with him. Assure him of my commitment to the Law of our people. Nothing I said changed his mind. He would not be moved."

"Oh, Aquila!"

"Do you know, the Christ once said that he had come to bring a sword. Not for war. But to divide families. Should I complain that he chose to apply that blade to me? Sometimes following him means severing precious bonds. And finding out in the end that he himself is the most precious bond in life.

"That same day, I packed a chest full of memories and was about to leave the only home I had ever known when my father blocked my path. Without a word, he dropped a document at my feet and left. I broke the seal and my heart with it. To my disbelief, I discovered that he had disavowed me as his son and disowned me of all my inheritance. I never spoke to him after that."

The memory still slashed and stung. He suspected that for the rest of his life he would feel the pain of that moment, the sundering of his bloodlines, like a limb lost in battle. At the same time, it was as if over the months, God had closed the gaping wound, sewed up the bleeding lacerations. In the empty places that longed for his family and the rolling hills that had once been his home, he felt the warmth of God's consolation, deeper than the pain.

Priscilla rose from her seat and walked toward him. She halted a step short, her hands twisted into a knot in front of her. Once again, as he had earlier that morning, he smelled the scent of rose and jasmine which clung to her hair and skin. Once again, he had an overpowering desire to draw her into his arms.

It was a disconcerting sensation. He had never felt so strong a pull for Esther. Esther, to whom he had belonged. He tightened his crossed arms over his chest and leaned harder into the wall.

"I am sorry, Aquila. Did you ever see Esther after that?"

The innocent question severed the tight edge of attraction. He blew out a breath with relief and told himself that his feelings were merely the result of their intimate circumstances. His worry for Benyamin coupled with memories he had buried overlong. "The next day. Benyamin told me that Esther had become betrothed to my brother."

"No!"

"That is precisely what *I* said. Even if she had agreed to such an arrangement, Lucinus never would! Knowing how I felt about her, he would not betray me no matter what my father demanded.

I ran to my old home in search of my brother, only to find him holding hands with Esther."

"Did he ask your forgiveness?"

"Not exactly. As I recall, his first words were 'Congratulate me, Brother!'"

Aquila felt nausea grip his belly as he remembered those words, remembered his brother's gloating eyes and triumphant smirk as he spoke them. What a fool he had been not to see the seed of jealousy that had grown tall, tangling Lucinus's every motive. Fool to have believed in his brother's warm smiles and affectionate expressions.

"He wrapped his arm around Esther's waist and told me, 'You made your bed; now lie in it. The better man won. Now run to your God and stop pestering us.'"

Won?

When had life ever turned into a contest with his brother?

"Did Esther say anything?"

"Only that it was my own fault. Had I been willing to obey my father and retain my rightful place as the eldest son, she would not have broken faith with me."

Priscilla narrowed her eyes. "In other words, if you had remained wealthy and admired by the world, she might have been willing to stay. It sounds like your brother was precisely the right man to be saddled with such a bride."

Aquila nodded, the ghost of a smile touching his lips. "I stayed in Pontus for a few more months, hoping for some manner of reconciliation. At first, I convinced myself that they would come to regret their actions. Eventually it dawned on me that they felt as much contrition as a lion devouring its prey. In the end, I only lingered because I wanted to make one final attempt at salvaging a tiny piece, a crumb of friendship. I didn't want to leave in bitterness."

Priscilla's eyes brimmed. Something in Aquila's chest tightened and squeezed like a physical embrace at that sight. No trace of pity in those tears. Nothing to unman him. Nothing to proclaim him weak. Just a well of compassion and understanding so deep that, for the first time in months, he felt he could breathe without restriction.

"Did you find it?" she asked in a whisper. "Did you find reconciliation?"

"No," he admitted. "On their wedding day, I hid behind an ancient oak outside the entrance to our home, hoping to speak to them. I watched Lucinus accompany Esther as they walked toward me. They looked like the ancient Greek legends come down from Mt. Olympus, dressed in gold-encrusted linen. Lucinus detected me and froze." Aquila stopped, battling the knot in his throat. "My brother looked at me as if I were a mound of dung that might dirty his wedding shoes.

"Noticing the lag in his step, Esther turned and saw me." Again he paused, giving time for his wavering voice to steady. "She stared through me as if I were a stranger to her. As if we had not been lifelong companions who had once known each other's deepest secrets. I had become a mere annoyance to her, and worse: I had become something to be ashamed of."

He drew a hand across his face, trying to wash away the burning humiliation of that moment.

Priscilla took another half step, closing the small gap between them. With an insistent motion, she untucked his hand where it lay hidden in his armpit, and wrapped it in both of hers. "Aquila, I am sorry to say that you are related to some very foolish people.

But fortunately, God had the foresight to separate you from them. If he had not, you would be a wealthy man, married to a silly woman who only wanted you for your position and the comforts of an affluent life. You are not the kind of man who would be happy with such a marriage. God in his mercy rescued you from that desert. He whisked you away halfway across this vast empire so you would be safe.

"Instead of seeing yourself through their eyes, colored by a reproach that you have not earned, you should be celebrating. You were close to making an abominable mistake. Yet here you are, free to choose a life that will bring you happiness."

Aquila, exhausted from retelling the tale that had aggrieved his heart for so long, needed a little time to make sense of Priscilla's words. His mouth tugged upward. A chuckle escaped him. Surprising them both, he started to laugh, mirth rolling out of his depths and flowing into the room, bringing long-sought relief.

Priscilla joined him and the plain chamber, so bare of beautiful objects, became filled with the beauty of joy. Laughter washed over the young man like a cleansing salve, loosening and purging the dark hold of shame.

He became aware of his hand, still wrapped tightly in Priscilla's, and was again shocked by the unexpected sweep of desire that overcame him. He could tug on that hand, one hard pull, and she would tumble against him. His pulse thumped in his temple.

Her eyes widened, turning the deep shade of a bottomless ocean. She took a long step back, then another, releasing his hand.

Aquila turned in a half circle, trying to break the spell, allowing reason to restore the disorder of his mind. On the mattress in the far corner of the room, where Benyamin was supposed to be sleeping, he caught his uncle hastily closing his eyes. But no pretense of slumber could wipe the smirk from the old man's lips.

In the evening, after he had dropped Priscilla off at home and settled Benyamin in for the night, Aquila climbed the narrow outdoor staircase to sit on the roof. Rome lay under a dome of stars that night, glistening in their numberless majesty.

And you know each one by name.

When he had first started to lose his place in his father's house, he had often battled waves of self-pity, resentful that obedience to God had brought him so much heartache. Over the years, he had learned to accept God's will, day by day. Learned to find a measure of peace by repeatedly laying down his own will, even in the midst of his frayed dreams.

Today he felt as though he had been scoured. Released from some of the shame that had made him feel so small.

I have not been in the Valley of Achor without reason, he thought. He studied the fragile starlight, which pierced through the darkness of night. The moment itself turned into a prayer, a confession, a redemption.

I am here because you will use this pain to forge me and shape me and complete me. I am here because you have begun a good work in me, and you are determined to complete it. This is not about the trouble I have known through the years, but about the God who is with me in the trouble. Yeshua. I am yours. Do with me what you will.

Instead of the stars, an image of Priscilla's face flashed before his eyes.

Ten

PRISCILLA SAT on a tattered cushion on the floor of her chamber, knees glued to her chest. The cushion had been repaired so many times that it no longer had enough fabric to cover the holes, and when she moved, a tiny feather floated to the floor.

Her thoughts were full of Aquila.

He had told his story with cutting honesty, exposing what few men had the courage to reveal. Exposing weakness and fear. Exposing shame. Exposing monsters she knew intimately. But they did not belong to a man as good and decent as Aquila.

She relived the feel of his hand in hers, the slight tremor in his fingers as he spoke of his brother and her own overwhelming desire to comfort him as he grieved. That desire had shifted quickly and morphed into a longing that had nothing to do with comfort.

She hissed out a breath as she felt a traitorous tear course down her cheek and wiped it with her palm, only to have another follow in its path.

She should have listened to her own counsel and avoided Aquila. Instead, she had returned, day after day, to help nurse Benyamin. The man who had appeared perfectly robust before the illness had surprised them all by not recovering as quickly as they had hoped.

Though the fever seemed to have abated, the weakness had not, leaving him bedridden for several days and in need of care. Priscilla had returned to the cramped chambers near the Via Appia every day of that week. With the mounting hours spent in Aquila's company, her attraction to him had grown and exploded into something she could no longer extinguish or deny.

Thankfully, Benyamin had fully recovered. But it seemed too late for her. She found herself captured by feelings that would never be returned by any honorable man, least of all one determined to live as a devout Jew.

Another hot tear trailed down her chin. She was becoming like the cushion she sat on, losing bits of herself. Losing her composure. Losing her heart.

She thought of the God who had carried Aquila through so much loss. The God for whom he had been willing to give up everything. The door of hope he had found in the valley of his troubles.

Benyamin had told her about the sheep pens in Israel that often had no door. "During the night, the shepherd has to sleep across that opening to keep the sheep safe. Nothing can have access to the sheep unless it goes through the shepherd first. He is *himself* the door. Yeshua said he was that shepherd to his sheep. And he was that door."

He had raised himself up on an elbow, ignoring the fever-induced weakness that kept him bed-bound. "You can enter into his pen too, Priscilla. He can be your door of hope."

Now, blinded by the salt of her tears and a longing that could never find fulfillment, she considered that invitation. One that would change her life. One that would turn every valley into a door. She might never have Aquila. But perhaps she could have Yeshua. Perhaps he was all she needed.

"Shepherd God, if you have room in your heart for wayward sheep, will you fetch me out of this wilderness and bring me into your pen?" she whispered, her voice cracking. "Help me to draw closer to you, in step with your step. Filled with your hope. Shaped by your love. Help me be yours."

Sabinella's health was slipping. She could no longer hide the severe tremors in the right side of her body or the unsteady gait that often threatened to topple her. Nor could she downplay the fatigue and tingling pain that sometimes reduced her to groaning as she moved. Senator Pudens tried to disguise his escalating anxiety with no success. He watched his wife with a concentration that made Priscilla wonder if he was counting her breaths.

"What do the physicians say?" she asked Pudentiana.

"There has been a parade of them for five years now. None has an answer. She has good months. Then, for no reason, she relapses. With every relapse, she grows weaker. This is the worst she has ever been." Pudentiana bit her lip. "She will come out of it. My mother has the fighting heart of a gladiator."

Priscilla nodded. But she could sense Sabinella's exhaustion. Fighting needed strength, and Sabinella had none left.

The senator's wife often invited Priscilla to their home. Though they had stopped entertaining most of their other acquaintances, she welcomed the young woman's company. "You don't wear me out like others," she admitted. "With you, I don't have to pretend I am well. And your presence is restful. Besides, the girls adore you. It's good to see Pudentiana smile as soon as you enter through the gate."

One afternoon, as they sat in her favorite spot in the garden under the shade of Aquila's awning, she asked without preamble, "Do you still pray to your God?"

"I do, lady."

"And does he answer?"

Priscilla considered her response. "Not always in discernible ways." She thought of Aquila, how it had taken him years to decipher God's goodness at work in the unraveling threads of his life. "Sometimes his answers only become apparent in the long view of things." She cleared her throat, trying to shore up courage. "I have some friends who would pray for you, if you wish."

"By all means. Ask them."

"I mean in person. They would be willing to come here, I am sure."

Sabinella raised a brow. "Here? I am in no state to receive strangers."

Not wishing to offend, Priscilla said no more on the matter. But she grew uneasy with her own silence. She felt certain, though she could not explain why, that Rufus and the other followers of Yeshua were supposed to pray for her ailing friend.

Rufus sucked in a quick breath. "You've never studied the Scriptures before?"

The upper room in Mary's house where they had once again gathered to study and pray had sunk into silence. For weeks now, it had become their regular practice to come together in the cozy upper room in Trastevere and, after the meal, to study and pray. Priscilla's insatiable appetite for learning had found a welcome here.

Every eye trained on her. She felt heat rise up her neck and spread over her face. "Only what I heard at the synagogue over the past year."

Rufus tapped his lips. "I ask because I have known many men who have studied the Law for years and still do not have your grasp."

Benyamin nodded. "Your natural facility for understanding the metaphors of our faith is astounding."

Priscilla felt the flush deepen. "What is so hard to understand? The High Priest is also the sacrifice. The Good Shepherd is also the Lamb of God. The Lamb of God is also the door. The one who provides is himself the offering."

Everyone laughed. Elizabeth, who had started joining them when her son was saved from the jaws of death thanks to Mary's devoted care, scratched her head. "I confess I find it confusing."

Priscilla pressed the young mother's hand. "The more we study, the more I realize it's not so much about understanding or knowledge. Faith is trust. Trusting our future and our past into Yeshua's keeping. Learning that the Christ is the beginning and end of all our needs."

Elizabeth nodded. "When my son was close to death, one evening I thought I might collapse with fear. Mary prayed for me, and as she spoke, I felt his comfort, like a hand resting on my shoulder."

"I too have felt that hand," Priscilla said. "Not a physical touch. But the consolation of knowing that the Christ gives us life and he *is* life. He leads the way, and he *is* the way."

Aquila studied her with an odd intensity. For a brief moment Priscilla thought she caught a hint of approval in the softening cast of his features.

"Do you remember Senator Pudens?" she asked him.

"He is the only Roman senator I have met in person. I remember him well. A good man."

"His wife, Sabinella, has been ill for some years. She seems to be growing worse. I have a strange feeling that we are supposed to pray for her. But she refused the offer when I asked."

"God can change her inclination," Aquila said.

When they had finished praying and the guests were preparing to return home, Priscilla approached Rufus. She had stayed up half the night, struggling to find the courage to make this request, dreading that he might refuse her. Her mouth turned dry.

"Rufus." The entreaty caught in her throat and would not be pushed out. She grabbed hold of her cup and took a gulping swallow. "Rufus," she repeated.

"Yes, my dear?" He regarded her with warm patience.

She cleared her throat. "Rufus?"

"It is good you know my name. Now, why don't you just ask your question?"

She adjusted a corner of her faded tunic that needed no adjustment. "I would like to become a follower of Yeshua. That is . . . May I be baptized?"

Rufus threw his hands in the air and shouted, "Hallelujah!"

The others turned curiously toward them. "Wait," Priscilla said hastily. "I . . . I mean, I have sinned."

"As have the rest of us. That's the point. Remember? The lamb, the sacrifice, the priest? Are you willing to repent?"

"With all my heart."

"Then as I said—" he threw his hands into the air and shouted louder than before—"hallelujah!"

"What are we praising God for?" Aquila asked.

"This little lamb was lost and has been found. We are going to baptize Priscilla!"

Eleven

HIS WORLD HAD TURNED on its head and it was God's fault.

In a way, every follower of Yeshua could say that. Aquila thought of Simon Peter, the most famous apostle of the Lord. Once, he would not have contemplated breaking a single religious rule. God had certainly shaken Peter by sending him off to the house of Cornelius, a Gentile centurion in Caesarea. Peter was not in the habit of visiting Gentiles, not even God-fearing ones like Cornelius. Watching the Holy Spirit poured out on those men and women that day, Peter had realized that Yeshua had unlocked the door he had once thought open only to those who belonged to the lineage of Abraham.

That day, God had upended everything Peter and the followers of Yeshua had believed. With Cornelius's baptism, the door had been opened to outsiders like Priscilla. Aquila had, in time, come to accept this remarkable development in the church. Had come even to harbor a deep joy at the measure of God's mercy that shattered every boundary.

It was one thing to believe that Yeshua welcomed Gentiles. Welcomed them with extraordinary tenderness and grace. Aquila remembered Priscilla rising up out of the waters of the Tiber, made new, made clean. Her face had been transformed in that moment, wet and glowing, going from earthly loveliness to an ethereal beauty he had never seen. She had emerged from those waters luminous with heaven's touch. To his consternation, he had found tears on his face. He had not been the only one.

He could live with that. Give God glory for adding one more to his household of believers.

What he could not live with was the way Priscilla had wormed her way into his thoughts. Esther, whom he had cared for through the comfort of long years, had never consumed him like this. She had cut him, shamed him, with her defection. She had pierced his pride.

Priscilla had ravished his heart.

He had a strong sense that she felt the same. Modest and well-mannered, she never spoke openly of her feelings, of course. But in a dozen small ways—a look that lingered too long, blushes she could not control in his presence, a slightly dazed smile when he spoke to her—she had been unable to hide her attraction for him.

He blamed God.

Had they not been trying to teach her the Way, he would not have been thrown into her company with such regularity. He had hoped that with time the sharpness of his longing would wane. Instead, he found his admiration growing. The sword edge of her intellect combined with a faith as rare as it was passionate, and both fascinated him. He could not seem to get enough of her company. Had he really thought her beauty ordinary once? Now he found her so alluring that sometimes, dry-mouthed and stammering, he stood in her presence like a man struck on the head with a fat length of timber.

He could not go on like this. She burned in his blood, a fever he could not cure.

He tried avoiding her with no success. They were thrown into each other's company at the synagogue and at Rufus's house. As if that were not enough, Benyamin made him accept Priscilla's offer to show him the rows of shops that nestled near the Forum and to acquaint him with the owners who had served the Priscus household for years.

"The personal introduction can lead to new orders," his uncle insisted. "We need her help."

There were many leatherworkers in Rome, and most shopkeepers preferred to work with someone who had an established reputation in the city. Being new arrivals placed Aquila and Benyamin at a disadvantage. Though they had a license to trade in leather, they lacked the long-standing roots of others who had traded in Rome for decades. By vouching for them on behalf of the respected Priscus family, Priscilla could open doors of opportunity they would lack otherwise.

"*You* go with her," he said to Benyamin.

"You have always been better at landing new customers." Benyamin shrugged. "What's the fuss? Just go for a morning and be done."

What could Aquila have said without sounding ungrateful?

He arranged to meet Priscilla and Lollia one morning by the steps of the Temple of Mars in the Forum. Priscilla led him through a parade of shops, as well as market traders, street sellers, and hawkers, most of whom needed leather awnings for their trade.

Bakers, sausage makers, fruit and vegetable sellers, garland weavers, and a hundred other small merchants had set up stalls with their portable tables, their awnings strung up between trees, elegant columns, or poles staked in the ground, depending on what convenient support they could find. As Priscilla introduced him, Aquila passed out small rectangles of papyrus bearing the name and location of his own shop, listing tantalizing prices for popular leather goods.

After three hours of weaving through the chaotic disorder of street sellers and speaking to dozens of merchants, Aquila decided they needed a rest. He purchased three containers of steaming chickpeas and several pastries, added a bag of sweetened almond paste, and the three of them sat on the steps of some public building and ate together.

"These chickpeas are good," Lollia said. "Not as good as Priscilla's. But tasty."

Aquila's brows rose in surprise. "You can cook?"

Priscilla shrugged. "Chickpeas are not difficult."

It continually astounded him to discover fresh evidence of Volero's demeaning treatment of her. Esther's father was not near so wealthy as the Roman, yet he doubted Esther had ever undertaken to lift a pot, let alone use one.

He noticed that Priscilla saved half of everything he had purchased for her and carefully hid it away in the basket she had brought. He wondered if she was saving them for later. Then another thought occurred to him. "What are you doing with those?"

"I am going to visit Sara after this. She will enjoy a treat."

"Surely her ankle is better by now."

She shrugged. "She is having difficulty finding work."

"I'm not surprised," he mumbled under his breath. Louder, he said, "You eat that! Just eat it."

Without waiting to see if she would comply, he walked to the chickpea seller and bought another bag, added a sweet pastry, and gave them to Priscilla. "You can take those to Sara. Finish your own food."

His gut twisted in an odd way when she flashed a happy smile at him. He watched as she tucked into her pastry with relish, and had the satisfaction of knowing that, for once, she wouldn't go half-hungry.

A skinny boy with filthy cheeks seemed to appear out of nowhere and stood staring at them. Priscilla's eyes widened. "I know you! You carried my basket."

The boy nodded. "I will carry it again. Same price."

Priscilla appeared to consider his offer. "I don't need help with my basket today."

The child's face fell, though he tried to hide his disappointment with a careless shrug.

"Tell you what," Priscilla said before he could walk away. "Fetch me a cup of water from the fountain, and you can have a pastry."

In a flash, the boy returned carrying Priscilla's cup. She gave him a sweet pastry, which he gulped down in two giant bites before vanishing with feline grace.

Aquila came to his feet again, intent on buying more pastries for Priscilla, hoping one might actually find its way into her own belly. He had taken a few steps away from the women when in his peripheral vision he saw Priscilla rise to her feet, dusting lingering crumbs from her tunic.

Without warning, a barrel-chested man with greasy dark hair charged toward her. Almost too late, Aquila noticed the glint of metal in his hand. His heart sank as he realized the man was bearing a knife, aimed at Priscilla.

Christ, help me! Aquila prayed and lunged, taking three steps in one. He arrived beside the man just as the point of his knife reached Priscilla's back. Without thinking, he struck a hard blow against the man's wrist. Not expecting resistance, the man's hold loosened, and the knife clattered to the ground without drawing blood.

Aquila shoved Priscilla out of the way and grabbed the neckline of the man's tunic, preventing him from diving for the knife. The assailant was no stranger to street fights, judging by his missing teeth and broken nose. He fought dirty, and he fought rough. Aquila gave thanks for his father, who had given him a full Greek education in his younger years, including wrestling at the local palaestra. He was hopelessly out of practice, however, unlike the ruffian, who clearly knew how to use his fists.

Aquila realized that if he was thrown on his back, the fight would be over. His only advantage was speed. The man secured a shoulder hold on him, but Aquila twisted his upper body and rolled, slithering out of the bruising grip. He ducked, missing an iron-hard fist headed for his nose. The man's body was carried by the momentum of the punch, and Aquila shoved his elbow into the assailant's back, causing him to stumble to one knee.

Before Aquila could try wrestling him to the ground, the man sprang to his feet and took off. Within moments, the serpentine alleyways intersecting the Forum swallowed him, and he disappeared from sight.

Aquila rubbed his sore shoulder. Everything had happened so quickly that no one had had time to help or even raise the alarm. Rome was known for violence, and to some degree, its residents had grown numb to public scuffles. But this daytime attack upon a woman surpassed the normal degree of lawlessness seen even in Rome.

"Are you hurt?" Priscilla ran to him, her voice strained.

"Am *I* hurt?"

"What did he want?"

Aquila straightened his tunic, trying to steady the thunderous beat in his chest. "To kill you." He tilted his head toward the knife that still lay on the ground. Fisting his shaking fingers, he stood, his back as rigid as a slab of granite, trying to resist the desperate desire to drag Priscilla into his arms. To feel her warmth against him. Feel the reassuring thrumming of her heart.

Priscilla gasped and bent to pick up the deadly object, offering it to him for examination. It was a military-issue weapon, no different from thousands like it, well-sharpened and clean. Perhaps the owner had once served in the army or bought it from a former soldier. It was too common a weapon to provide any clues.

"He was trying to rob me in broad daylight!" Priscilla cried. "The depravity of Rome shames us all."

Aquila had gone from heart-pounding fear to icy-cold calm. Something did not add up. If the man had wanted to rob Priscilla, why had he not demanded her purse? Why attack *her* when they were surrounded by more prosperous-looking shoppers? The ruffian had waited for Aquila to step away, then pounced when the women were alone. As if murder was his intent from the start.

Aquila had a sudden recollection of the cart that had plowed into her, almost crushing her. At the time, he had put it down to an odd accident. A drunken driver. Now he questioned his former conclusion.

"Priscilla, that man was no ordinary thief. He tried to kill you."

She snorted. "Few people care if I am alive. But no one wants me dead."

"Do you remember the cart that nearly ran you over on the way to your house?"

Her brow wrinkled. "When Ferox saved me? Of course. But that was an accident."

Aquila stared at her, eyes hot. "Have you experienced other unusual accidents or attacks recently?"

"No," she said, then frowned. "Well . . ."

Aquila felt chilled. "Well?"

"An intruder broke into my brother's house some weeks past. He tried to throttle me just before he escaped over the wall."

"I see. But no one is trying to kill you. No one at all."

The smooth brow pleated again. "I happened to be standing directly in his path."

"He couldn't go around you or knock you down? He had to strangle you in order to escape?"

She gave a weak laugh. "In the heat of the moment, he probably was not thinking clearly. Besides, who would want me dead? I am nobody. And I will have you know, my brother's house is a veritable fortress now. No one can get in unless invited."

Aquila did not argue. No sense in frightening her when he had no proof or solution to this dark mystery. One thing for certain: he had to prevent her from wandering all over the streets of the city alone.

He would ask for Rufus's and Benyamin's help. Between the three of them, they would guard her until they could discover what lay behind these perilous attacks. Before they parted ways, Aquila extracted a reluctant promise from Priscilla that she would stop traveling about with only Lollia for company. For now, he would have to be satisfied with that paltry measure.

Twelve

SOMEONE DRONED on and on in the background. The words of the Law floated about Aquila's head, making no sense. From his place in the front row at the synagogue, he turned his head slightly so that he could gaze at Priscilla more freely.

He had not been able to stop thinking about her since the attack. He drew a hand over his face and swallowed a groan. He had almost lost her. That scene continued replaying in his mind, the tip of the dagger at her back, death breathing against her skin.

He could not bear the thought. Everything in him wanted to get up this instant, to gather her against him and take her home, where he could look after her. Protect her.

He tried to remember why that would be an objectionable idea. In the fog of wanting, the clear reasons for drawing a line in the sand between them had grown muddled. Didn't Boaz marry Ruth? Didn't God bless that marriage?

There. He had said it. *Marriage!*

That was the desire of his heart. He wanted to marry Priscilla.

If Esther walked into the synagogue right now and fell on her knees before him and begged him to take her back, he would have no interest. He wanted one woman. He wanted the daughter of a Roman general.

Once the notion had insinuated itself into his mind, Aquila found he could not dispel it. Benyamin had the right of it. He did not wish to sleep with a dog for the rest of his life. He wanted Priscilla. The woman who loved God with a complete dedication. The woman who had been baptized in Yeshua's name, served in his name, prayed in his name.

They had been born unequal. But God had made them equal in his Son.

Marriage to Priscilla meant that he put to rest any lingering hope he had for reconciliation with his family. He would have to leave Pontus behind forever to have her. To his astonishment, he found no great loss in that possibility. Whatever the cost, he would pay it willingly.

She was worth the price.

He felt calm as soon as he had made that decision. All the sleepless nights and the hours of inner tumult had found their resolution in this one moment. He would marry Priscilla. He would not wait another day. This very afternoon he would settle the matter. He would make her his.

At the house in Trastevere, Aquila barely tasted Mary's perfectly prepared soft-boiled eggs, drizzled in some kind of sweet pine nut sauce. Nor could he swallow one morsel of the leek-and-cheese salad, even though Mary flavored it with his favorite herbs, parsley and coriander. As soon as the meal was finished, he took a long swallow from his cup and approached Priscilla. He could not suppress a wide grin as he stood before her, choosing his words. He must look like a carp on a hook, his mouth hanging open, eyes glassy as he stared at the woman. Lord, she was beautiful!

"Will you come with me to the courtyard, Priscilla?" He had chosen the location because they would have the advantage of being seen for the sake of propriety, without being overheard.

"The courtyard?"

"Please. I want to ask you something in private." He felt a moment of nervous tension. What if she refused him? Then he grinned again, confident that he had not mistaken her feelings toward him. Her head jerked down, indicating her agreement, and she followed him belowstairs.

The scent of roses and mint filled the small atrium. He guided Priscilla to sit on a stone bench and joined her once she had settled her tunic.

"Priscilla." He had not had time to prepare a speech. Forging ahead, he decided the simple truth would serve as well as any well-rehearsed proposal. "If your father were alive, I would seek him first. I thought of approaching your brother, but given his lack of concern for you, I decided it best to ask you directly."

She gave him a quizzical look. "Do you want to make an awning for our home, like you did for Senator Pudens? The family enjoys that awning every day, you know. Especially in the persistent heat of the past few months. But I am afraid I have no influence with Volero. You will have to approach him yourself."

Aquila slashed a hand in the air. "I do not want to speak of awnings."

"Oh."

"I wish to speak of us." He reached for her hand and held it in his own. Everything about that hand was perfect. The way the delicate fingers fit in his palm, the way her work-roughened skin rubbed the calluses in his own. He noticed her fingers were trembling and tightened his hold. "Priscilla, I wish to wed you. My heart aches for you. My thoughts are filled with you. My home is empty for you. Will you be my wife?"

She stared at him as if he had grown a pair of antelope horns on his head. He took it as a sign that she needed further reassurance and rushed on. "I am not wealthy. But you will not go hungry. We can love the Lord and serve him together. My life is yours, Priscilla."

Her skin had turned ivory white. His heart plummeted. He wondered if he had miscalculated her feelings after all. Miscalculated them badly, judging by the way she pulled her hand out of his and scooted backward on the bench until she was sitting at the very edge, as far from him as possible.

"I cannot wed you!" she gasped.

He watched her in narrow-eyed silence and considered her reply. When he had held her hand, he had felt the softening in her, the unintentional response. Nor had he mistaken the initial flush of joy when she first heard his intention to wed her. Her lips had opened with wonder before she had pressed them into a stiff line as if reasoning with herself. "You cannot marry an impoverished Jew?" he asked, his voice hard.

"No! I mean, that is not the reason I cannot wed you."

"Why, then?"

She dropped her eyes and remained frustratingly silent.

Aquila sprang to his feet. "I know you care for me. You love me as I love you. Yet you refuse me. At least have the decency to tell me why."

Still she refused to speak.

His lip curled with disdain. He turned to leave.

"No, wait! Aquila!"

He whirled back. Something flickered over her face that brought him short. *Fear?* He felt the hard edge of anger melting inside him, giving way to patience. To hope. He sat next to her again and took her hand in his once more. "What is it? Tell me."

"Aquila, I cannot marry you, because . . . because you deserve a better wife."

He gave her an uncertain smile. "Then I am doomed to loneliness, for I cannot conceive of a woman better than you."

She drew in a gasp of air as if she were drowning. "You deserve a . . . a pure woman."

It took him a moment to comprehend her meaning. Something inside him shattered as he realized what she had intended him to understand. She had given herself to another man. His skin turned cold.

It was his turn to withdraw his hand from hers and lean back on the bench. "You love another?"

"No." She shook her head in emphasis. "I was young. My life had grown desolate, isolated, after my father's death. I thought I loved a man. The attentions he heaped upon me turned my head. In my foolishness, I believed his empty promises and thought we would marry."

Aquila's heart could not catch up with this new barrage of revelations. He felt cheated somehow. "When?"

"Four years ago. I was sixteen."

A long time, then, though the passing of years did not change the reality that she had given her innocence away in a cheap affair. Part of him felt a sick need to hear every detail, and another part wanted to run out of the courtyard, out of Trastevere, out of Rome, out of his own skin. Run until he left this awful revelation far behind him.

He remembered, with sudden and overwhelming clarity, her kindness to him when he had divulged his own struggle with shame. He gulped in a breath. Out of his depths, past the disappointment and grief that sat like a stone in his gut, he dredged up a few words of grace. "The Lord forgives," he said, though he could not say the same for himself.

"It is worse, you see."

"Worse?" He could not imagine. Worse than this?

She pressed the back of her hand to trembling lips. For a moment he wondered if she would be sick. But she removed her hand and forced herself to go on. "I discovered I was with child."

He sat, frozen, unable to move a muscle. Unable to draw breath.

"When he refused to marry me, I feared my brother would kill me should he discover my shame. So . . . I went to a physician."

Aquila almost toppled off the bench. "A physician?" His voice emerged strained, faint. There was no mistaking her meaning. "Oh, God, help me!" he cried. "My people would stone you for less."

She came to her feet. "And you would pick up the first rock." She was shivering so badly, he thought she might collapse. Placing a hand against the wall, she held herself up. "You should know, Aquila, that I did not go through with it. I left the physician still bearing my child in my womb. But God took the babe from me anyway. I suppose I did not deserve to have him."

A keening sound escaped her. She shoved a fist into her mouth to stop the sobs he knew were desperate for release. Her knees buckled, and time slowed down as he saw her tumble toward the ground. He leapt, capturing her in his arms before she collapsed on the stone floor. He stood uncertain, shifting her against him.

Her head moved fitfully on his arm. "I am sorry," she whispered. "It's all right. You can set me down."

He drew her closer. "You will only collapse again."

Neither spoke as he carried her abovestairs. He could feel the heat of her skin, like a fever. Her limbs trembled with a violence she could not seem to control. He tightened his arms around her. His feet lagged on the steps. Squeezing his eyes shut, he hefted her weight higher against his chest. The air felt heavy and wet. For a moment he could not breathe. He forced his feet to climb again. One, two, three, four . . . every step bringing him closer to the end.

At the landing, Mary noticed them and cried in alarm. "What has happened?"

"She does not feel well," Aquila said, keeping his voice neutral. It was not his place to reveal her secret.

He laid Priscilla on the carpet, her head cushioned on a pillow. Against his will, his fingers lingered on her back for a moment. He had bent close as he laid her down, and their faces almost touched before he jerked back, putting as much distance between them as he could.

"You will care for her?" he asked Mary. "I must go home."

"Home?" Benyamin asked with a frown.

"Home," he said, and unable to force another word out of his frozen lips, he trudged down the stairs and out of the house. Ferox shadowed his steps, his exuberance dampened for once, as though sensing his master's black mood.

He had been willing to give up so much for her. His family, life in Pontus, his intention to marry a woman from among his own people, his desire to live by the letter of the Law. But *this* he could not bear. The weight of her past crushed him and, with it, his dreams.

He felt robbed.

His face flamed as he remembered her words. *"You would pick up the first rock."* He *had* picked up a rock. He hurled it now, bitter with disappointment and determined to put the woman behind him. She was not worthy.

Thirteen

IN THE GLOAMING, the nightmares came, shapeless, nameless, and deadly. Priscilla coiled through the horrors of her dreams, visiting endless visions of terror until, gasping for air, she finally came awake. Soaked in sweat and misery, she sat up. She had no clear memory of the visions that had chased her in her sleep. She only knew that she felt filthy, a polluted and polluting swamp, undeserving of the air she breathed.

She fought the acid taste of vomit rising into her throat as a wave of guilt overwhelmed her. Blindly, Aquila had plunged into that swamp, seeking sweet, clean love, and had instead found himself engulfed by the slime of her past.

Priscilla swallowed as the memory took shape, and her mind threw up an image of Aquila's face the moment he had discovered her secret. His look of horror. Of disgust.

She had been unprepared for his proposal. Her own feelings

had grown and deepened, but she had never considered the possibility that Aquila might feel more than a passing attraction for her. Even if she had had a thousand days to prepare her answer, what else could she have said? He deserved no less than the truth. And the truth had revolted him.

It occurred to her as she sat in the unrelenting dark, listening to Lollia's even breathing in sleep, that she owed the same truth to others.

For months Mary, Rufus, and Benyamin had thought they knew her. They had offered her hospitality, friendship, acceptance. As she had begun to grow in her faith, they had showered her with encouragement, offered her an unending well of admiration.

How she had enjoyed their esteem!

But even as she had reveled in that esteem over the passing weeks, a more honest corner of her heart had felt like a fraud. They admired her because they did not know her. Did not know who she really was or what she had done. She had won their approbation at the cost of the truth.

Time to put an end to false things. To reveal her secrets to these people whom she had grown to love. Her heart cringed at the thought of such exposure, and for a moment, she considered remaining silent. She would lose their precious friendship, she had no doubt. They would abandon her in disgust as Aquila had. His words reverberated in her mind. *"My people would stone you for less."* Her stomach roiled, and she leaned her head back to gather strength. Strength for the truth. She would do what was right in the sight of the Lord.

She had held tight to this part of her life for years, held it in a sealed tomb, never to be opened. She must roll away that dusty stone once more to reveal the skeleton of her past.

With Lollia's help, she planned the time of their final meeting with exquisite care, ensuring Aquila would not be present. Her friends had not seen her since the day Aquila had carried her into the house, dizzy and weak with anguish.

Now she asked her friends to sit in Mary's cheerful living room with its red carpet and soft cushions, explaining that she had something important to share with them.

Before she could start, Benyamin blurted, "I confess, this is a far different outcome from what I expected when my nephew took you belowstairs."

Priscilla gulped. "Outcome?"

"You may think me foolish. I was sure Aquila intended on asking you an important question." He studied Priscilla. "Was I right? Did he ask you a question?"

"He asked," she said softly.

"And you refused him?" His voice rose, indignant. Three faces stared at her, their wide, dark eyes filled with confusion.

"For his own sake, I did." She fought the waves of nausea that never seemed too far away these days and forced herself to speak. Forced herself to confess, leaving nothing out. It was a brutal disclosure, without conceding a hint of mercy.

Lollia wept silently as Priscilla, having gasped out the sorry account of her affair with Appius, reached the part of her tale that she had never even shared with her faithful companion. Her visit to the physician. She avoided any mention of Antonia, finding the weight of her own secrets to be burden enough.

"I quit the physician's house that day, determined to tell my brother the truth and face the consequences." Her voice had grown hoarse, coming out strangled. "If he killed me, I thought, then at least I would die with my babe. One good thing had emerged from my trip to the physician. Having come so close to destroying him, I had learned how much I loved my child.

"Before then, I only saw him as a calamity. The scourge that would lead to my destruction. Afterward, he became real to me. My child. My own to love."

Surely the air had left this room, she thought, gasping. Still, she forced herself to go on. "When I returned home, I found, once again, that I lacked the courage to face Volero's wrath. Every day I delayed the inevitable, knowing my changing body would soon reveal my degradation.

"In my agony, I stopped eating, stopped sleeping. If I had been able to bring myself to confess, I would have borne his punishment once and been done. But fear kept me enslaved. My body began to fall apart under my neglect."

A sob racked through her. Three sets of eyes never shifted from her face. She felt the weight of their regard, a millstone that ground her down. She rushed to finish, to put an end to the pain.

"I lost the babe. It was my own fault. If I had had the sense to take better care of myself, he might have lived. But I lacked the courage to confess my sin to my brother; he might have shown us mercy in the end. Now I shall never know. My child is gone and my innocence with him."

She took a shuddering breath. "That, Benyamin, is why Aquila and I cannot wed. He deserves better than I."

To her utter astonishment, Mary knelt near her and drew her into her arms, her embrace soft, accepting. She stroked her hair, each caress an act of grace. "My poor girl. What you must have endured."

Priscilla sat like a stiff statue under the ministrations of those hands, utterly stunned. Had Mary not heard what she had said?

Benyamin looked like he was trying hard not to weep. "I am sorry, child. My nephew left, I am thinking, after he heard that tale?" He took his long beard into his fist, like a talisman that might offer a measure of reassurance. "He will need time."

Priscilla heaved in a breath and tried to make her voice steady. "Do you want me to leave your house and never return?" She directed the question to Rufus.

"Leave my house?" he rumbled. "I want you to come more often! The courage you lacked to speak to your brother, you have now gained with the help of the Holy Spirit. It is no small thing to entrust that part of your life to the three of us. I am honored that you did."

Thunderstruck, Priscilla slumped against the wall, open-mouthed. *"Honored?"*

"You could have kept your secret to yourself. Aquila would never have betrayed you."

"Aquila is disgusted with me, and he has every right! I do not understand why *you* do not condemn me."

"Did I not tell you, at your baptism, that Yeshua has washed you clean? Made you pure? Set to right your broken past?"

"But *this*! This is no small transgression."

"And he is no small God. Listen, child. You are choosing to see your whole life through the lens of your gravest mistake. To measure yourself by that sin. You have reduced yourself to this one misdeed." Rufus had an odd way of weaving both compassion and strength into the way he gazed at her, his black eyes unwavering.

Priscilla buried her face in her hands, hiding from that gaze.

"Those of us who belong to the Way have a different measure," he said. "We measure our past, and our future, by the Cross. Everything passes through that river of grace. It passes through Yeshua crying, 'Father, forgive them, for they know not what they do.' It passes through the crown of thorns, the welts of whips, the scars of nails. Our lives, our mistakes, our follies, our sins pass through *him* and are returned to us new." He placed gentle fingers under Priscilla's chin and raised it. "Clean. *That* is the measure of who you are now. To deny it is to deny Christ."

Priscilla gaped at him, confounded. She had heard the message of forgiveness before. Heard it a hundred different ways. Somehow, that gift seemed to apply to everyone except her. But as Rufus spoke, it occurred to her that God had meant this forgiveness for *her*.

She had laid bare before Rufus the depth of her sin. Instead of being repulsed, he settled next to her, his face a mirror of mercy. In that face, she thought she found a reflection of the Christ himself. This was how *he* looked at her.

"My father carried Yeshua's cross for him, you know. The whips had shredded his back, and he had grown too weak to bear the weight of it himself. Father had been standing on the side of the street, watching the procession to Golgotha, when the soldiers grabbed him and put the crossbeam on his back instead.

"My father used to say that he was never the same man, after. Because for one infinitesimal moment, he came closer to Yeshua than anyone in that crowd. Close enough to touch him. To have his blood stain his skin. To gaze into his eyes.

"He said he had never known love until that moment, when the Messiah looked upon him. And he knew without a single word passing between them, that it was for him that this man suffered.

"And for *you*, Priscilla. Give him your past. This is the day of new beginnings."

For the first time since she had lost her babe, Priscilla experienced the balm of mercy. Tasted the elixir of grace. The costly grace of the Cross, which had the power to refashion worlds and more than enough power to lap up the sins of her youth. In the recesses of her mind, she saw a shadowy vision of Yeshua standing before her, his holy brow bloodied by a barbed crown, offering her a forgiveness she had never dared hope for.

Remaining hidden behind the cover of a jutting wall, Aquila observed the two women emerge from the house. He followed them with his eyes until he became certain that they would not notice him shadowing their steps before he slipped into the street. They plodded in silence, their feet swallowing the pavement with rapid, purposeful strides.

Neither Rufus nor his manservant were available to keep an eye on Priscilla today, and Uncle Benyamin had insisted on the need to complete a tent. Which left only Aquila.

In the first days following his painful proposal, he had stewed with an unreasoning outrage, as if Priscilla had betrayed him somehow. As if her seedy affair had not taken place four years before he had ever laid eyes on her.

That outrage had dissipated, leaving behind an occasional spark of lukewarm anger. Mostly what he felt now was choking disappointment, coupled with a leaden sorrow that clung to him night and day. The disappointment simmered hot, erupting into resentment when he remembered how thoroughly he had trusted her. And how she had broken that trust long before they even met.

And yet here he found himself shadowing her steps, not letting her out of his sight. He scowled and called himself a few names, none of them complimentary. But he did not stop his pursuit. Aquila could not dispel the notion that some dark force intended Priscilla harm. In truth, though her mere presence pained him, he could not bear the thought of her being hurt.

So much for being free of her.

Bile swished in his gut as Aquila kept her in his sight, her bright hair an easy beacon to track. His steps never slowed. Like a wrathful angel, he watched over her, even as he swallowed the bitter taste of broken hopes.

"What do you have in there?" Pudentiana asked as Priscilla placed her basket on the floor of her chamber.

"I am visiting a young widow and her baby boy after I leave your house. They have very little and sometimes go hungry." She had finished weaving the basket the night before and stuffed it with a wide array of gifts, which she had come upon unexpectedly. Her sister-in-law had intended to discard a bundle of old sheets and blankets. Priscilla had gathered them and, after washing and carefully mending several holes, had put the lot in the basket, along with a few apples and three pale carrots. She lifted the corner of the blanket covering the basket and showed Pudentiana its contents.

Pudentiana peered into the basket for a moment. "Wait here!" she said, then rushed out of the room. When she returned, she was carrying a tray heaped with fruits, cheese, a sack of almonds, and three bulky loaves of bread which the Romans called *quadratus* because it was scored into eight pieces using four slashes of a knife before being baked.

Priscilla giggled. "It's good you are tall or you would not be able to see over that tower."

"This is for your widow."

"Oh, Pudentiana, you are generous! Elizabeth will be dumbstruck to receive this food, though I cannot take it all. Lollia refuses to admit it, but she is no longer able to carry a heavy load, and this is too much for me alone."

Pudentiana set the tray on a marble table. "Then I shall come with you." She bit her lip. "Unless Elizabeth would be offended by my presence."

"I am certain she would welcome you. Your mother, however, may be harder to convince. Elizabeth lives in Trastevere."

"Well, we will just have to assure her that Trastevere is as safe as the Esquiline hills these days."

Priscilla laughed. "There are not enough words in Latin to convince your mother of such an outrageous claim."

To their delight, Sabinella, sensing her daughter's determination, consented to the arrangement so long as they agreed to take along two muscular manservants as escorts into Trastevere. Priscilla approved heartily of the plan. It meant the men could carry the heavy baskets. Besides, since the strange incident at the Forum, and Aquila's insistence that someone was plotting her demise, she grew anxious walking about the streets of Rome without masculine accompaniment. Not that she believed Aquila's outrageous hypothesis. No one could possibly want to go to the trouble of killing her. She had neither money nor influence. Having almost been stabbed in broad daylight, however, had taught her caution.

The women sauntered at a leisurely pace ahead of the guards, walking toward the Aemilius bridge. "Your mother assures me she feels well. But how is she truly?" Priscilla asked her friend.

Pudentiana winced. "She grows weaker every day. Father is wild with anxiety. She refuses to see any physicians, and she will not tolerate mention of new potions. I think she has given up."

They walked in heavy silence the rest of the way. Priscilla grew even more convinced that they had to pray for Sabinella. How was she to sway the older woman from her staunch refusal to receive strangers into her home?

Lollia, who had helped tend to the baby for over a week and grown fond of the child, rushed to relieve Elizabeth of the cooing boy the moment they stepped over the threshold. Priscilla set down her bundle and introduced Pudentiana to their hostess.

"Welcome." Elizabeth wiped her hands on the side of her tunic and then froze as she took in the overflowing baskets. "All this for me?"

"You can thank Pudentiana for that."

Elizabeth picked up the bag of nuts and a fat cucumber and inhaled the scent of the still-warm *quadratus*. Her eyes welled up. "So much! So much!"

Pudentiana, who had probably never stepped into such an impoverished *insula*, with its chipped roof tiles and damp walls, gulped a breath and, for the first time since Priscilla had met her, seemed lost for words.

Lollia dumped the baby into the girl's long arms. "He is too skinny. Thanks to you, he is going to gain a bit of flesh."

Pudentiana instinctively wrapped the boy in a protective embrace. He grinned at her, displaying the entire bank of his gums and five tiny white teeth. Charmed, she sank to the floor, the babe on her lap, trying to tease another smile out of him.

The sound of footsteps outside made Priscilla turn to the door. She rushed forward when she spied Mary, a fluff of white hair escaping from under her palla, her mouth widening with surprised delight at the sight of Priscilla. Before she could greet her friend, Priscilla skidded to a stop when she saw who stood behind Mary, carrying a wide basket.

Aquila.

His face grew still when he spotted her. Whatever emotions welled up in him at the sight of her, he covered quickly under a veil of civility. She had seen him in the synagogue over the past few weeks, of course, sitting on the far side of the assembly hall. They had avoided each other with scrupulous care, slithering in the opposite direction every time they came near one another.

Since the day of Aquila's ill-fated proposal, she had refused Mary's invitations for lunch at her house, knowing her presence would be a painful intrusion on Aquila. This was the first time they had found themselves in close quarters since that day.

Pudentiana, unaware of the underlying tensions between them, lifted an arm in greeting. "Aquila, is it not? We do so enjoy your awning. My father has determined to hire you to make an identical one for the other side of the garden."

Aquila bent his head in acknowledgment. "I shall look forward to the senator's visit."

Priscilla introduced Mary to her friend. For a few moments, they were lost in Elizabeth's joy as she went from basket to basket, admiring their contents with tearful gratitude.

"I hope you are all hungry. I have brought enough fig rolls to feed a village in Gaul," Mary said. "Shall we pray before we eat?" she suggested and before anyone had time to respond, simply began. After the traditional blessing of the bread and words of thanksgiving, the prayer turned into a heartfelt intercession for Elizabeth and her babe. She then asked God to bestow his provision and favor on those in the chamber, naming each individually.

As the prayer lengthened, Priscilla found herself distracted by the many currents flowing through the sparse room: Pudentiana's unblinking scrutiny, Elizabeth's disbelieving gratitude, the baby's childish glee, Mary's rolling waves of faith.

Aquila prayed next, his deep voice at once calm and powerful. To her surprise, he chose to intercede for Pudens and his family. As often with Aquila, his prayers emerged short, simple, and gripping. Pudentiana's eyes were swimming by the time he finished.

For a moment, Priscilla was caught again in that extraordinary web that made her feel attached to Aquila, somehow connected as if she could hear his thoughts. His eyes turned to her and lingered. She sensed a wave of anguish pass through him, similar to the anguish she herself felt. Then the thread was broken; he crossed his arms and leaned away.

She knew if not for his obligation to see Mary home safely, he would have left the place immediately. She did for him what he could not do for himself. She signaled Pudentiana and they took their leave.

The young woman was full of questions on the way home. Could she return to see Elizabeth and the baby? Could she accompany Priscilla to visit others who needed help? Did her friends always pray like that? And then, just as Priscilla was asking God why he had allowed her to run into Aquila, opening the wound of his rejection afresh, the girl said, "Would Aquila pray like that for my mother, do you think?"

"Oh, Pudentiana, I am sure he would. All my friends from the synagogue would be willing to intercede for her. Indeed, I offered as much to your mother. Though she refused me, she may not refuse you. We will come to pray for her as soon as you can convince her."

Pudentiana chewed the corner of her lip. "She can be stubborn."

"She can. But after today, I am thinking she is no match for you. I never thought she would allow you to come to Trastevere. Yet here we are."

Pudentiana gazed ahead thoughtfully. "It may take a little time. I think I can wear her down, though."

Priscilla laughed. "You are the woman to do it."

Fourteen

AQUILA GRITTED HIS TEETH. It was hard enough to see her in the synagogue week after week. To force himself to ignore her. To avoid thinking of her. But in all the great expanse that was Rome, with its one million inhabitants and coiling warren of streets, God had to lead him into the one house where she would be. He wanted to punch a wall.

Seeing her in Elizabeth's tiny room, surrounded by the evidence of her generosity and kindness, he could almost forget her past. That tempting face with its soft lips could cause him to set aside, once and for all, the words that still haunted him. *"You deserve a pure woman."*

He growled. Mary, too wise to remark on his obvious foul temper went to fetch a batch of sweet cakes for Benyamin. Aquila clenched his fists. He felt at war with his own heart and with heaven.

For a moment in that damp *insula*, Priscilla had wormed her way into his soul, and he had felt that familiar knowledge as if he had known her all his life. As if she *belonged* with him.

Weeks had gone by since that disastrous day when she had

revealed her awful story. He should have taken a giant step away from her and left her in the hands of God. He should have recovered his senses by now. Instead, he felt like he had lost a treasure he had not known he possessed.

Rufus emerged from one of the chambers above and headed directly for him. "Is all well, Aquila?"

Aquila's scowl deepened. "Of course. What could be wrong?"

"I ask because—" he waved his fingers in the air—"your face looks like you just swallowed a beehive."

Aquila shrugged. "I am merely waiting for Mary."

"My mother said you ran into Priscilla."

"Hmmm."

"How did she seem? She has not been to our home for many weeks. I wonder why that might be."

Aquila shrugged again and tightened his arms about his chest. "How should I know?"

"I thought that perhaps it had to do with your proposal."

Aquila choked. "My proposal?"

Rufus nodded enthusiastically. "You remember? When you asked her to wed you? Here, in the courtyard."

"You *know*?" Aquila pressed the bridge of his nose. What had possessed the woman to publicly announce what had been a private matter between the two of them?

"Not because she divulged it, if that's what you are thinking. Benyamin guessed as much and told us. Only, the matter did not seem to go as we had all hoped."

"Nor I," Aquila could not resist blurting sourly.

"Because of her past? Her sin?"

"What?" He straightened slowly and gaped at Rufus. "You know about that, too?"

"Oh yes. She told us everything."

"Everything?" Aquila rested his shoulder on the doorframe once more. "She is more brazen than I realized."

Rufus's voice hardened. "She has more *humility* than you assumed. She told us her story because she did not want to presume on our hospitality. Not without us knowing the worst about her. It was no easy thing, that confession, Aquila. As you know, revealing our hearts to one another can be brutally hard."

Aquila felt himself flush. "At least you understand why I avoid her."

"I do not."

"How can you say that?" Aquila barked. "Knowing what she has done? *Intended* to do? I *loved* her! As you obviously know, I had resolved to bind my life to hers. Am I to pretend all is well now?"

Rufus laid a hand on his shoulder. "Come. Walk with me a little way." Aquila felt the warmth of that hand seep through him, calming him. He followed Rufus's footsteps and allowed himself to be drawn down on the bench where he had proposed to Priscilla. The memory of it shattered his veneer of calm. He felt his throat clench.

"Do you love her still?" Rufus asked, his voice gentle, as if that question did not cut in a hundred different ways.

Aquila wanted to deny it. But he could not lie. "I won't forever," he said. "I will overcome this unwise attachment."

"Why is it unwise?" He held up his hand in a gesture of peace before Aquila could explode into a long list of objections. "Have you heard of Rahab?"

The abrupt change of topic threw Aquila for a moment and he gaped. His quick mind made the connection fast enough, in spite of the turmoil in his heart. He rolled his eyes.

Rufus went on, undeterred. "She was a harlot. A woman besmirched. An enemy of our people. Yet the son of Nahshon, the leader of the tribe of Judah, married her. Chose her to be the mother of his son."

"That was because she demonstrated her faith by risking her own neck to save our spies in Jericho," Aquila said hotly. "It was a unique circumstance. An exception. You can't expect me to pattern my life after an oddity in our history."

"That oddity was in Yeshua's lineage. Her presence there is no happenstance, Aquila. It is not an anomaly. It is a lesson of grace. A truth for all men and women to live by. Because Rahab did not *remain* a harlot. She repented and became a woman of God. And by that repentance and by that life of faith, she entered into the kingdom of God.

"Priscilla is such a woman. That makes her worthy in God's eyes. And it certainly makes her worthy of you." Rufus stretched his legs, taking up most of the room on the bench. "Whether you are worthy of *her* remains to be seen."

Aquila sat stupefied, feeling as if Rufus had slapped him. He had been so focused on Priscilla's transgression, he had forgotten all the reasons she had won his heart in the first place. She was no less faithful than Rahab in her care for God's people. She loved the Lord with the same abandon as Rahab must have loved. She was kind, uncomplaining, forgiving. Her mind was brilliant, but she remained humble. She could make him laugh one minute and melt his heart the next.

He had tried to cram all that beauty into death's sarcophagus, sealing it under the slab of her sin. If Rufus was right, then her faith and life of repentance had broken the seal on that slab. Christ had shattered it.

He shoved his fingers into his hair. Could he set aside her past? Touch her without remembering that someone else had touched her first?

Rufus bent toward him until his face filled Aquila's vision. "Son, a marriage between you would be a marriage of equals. Christ follower to Christ follower. Lover of God to lover of God. Forgiveness to forgiveness. You are both clever and would not be content with less. You both know what it means to be rejected by your families. That wound has softened Priscilla's heart. I worry that it might have hardened yours. Made you harsher in your judgments.

"Marriage to Priscilla could be a union of joy. But only you can make it so, Aquila. If you leave behind your condemnation of her past, then you could experience an uncommon marriage. A marriage worthy of the name of Christ, which you both bear.

"If you cannot forgive her transgression, then you have greater problems than a broken heart." Rufus tapped Aquila's arm with affection, rose nimbly, and departed as if he had not just delivered a blistering lesson. As if he had not turned Aquila's whole life on its head.

Aquila walked away in a haze, barely taking note which way he went. Halfway across the Aemilius bridge he came to a stop and, gripping the stone's edge with shaking hands, gazed into the river's opaque waters. The previous week, the heavens had opened and poured down rain enough to swell the Tiber, making the waters roil and churn in dark eddies. He sympathized. His thoughts churned as violently.

Rufus's voice reverberated in his mind. *"That wound has softened Priscilla's heart. I worry that it might have hardened yours. Made you harsher in your judgments."* Had he become harsh? In his quest to prove himself to his father, had he become implacable like the man he had never been able to truly please? His father had always expected more. A little better than Aquila could offer. A touch more success than he could deliver. Even before he had become a follower of the Way, his father had shown the hard side of his judgment to Aquila.

Had Aquila turned into *that* man, his eyes seeing every mar, critical of every imperfection?

He could forgive Priscilla in a detached, religious way. Or at least acknowledge that Jesus would wish to forgive her. But could he forgive her to such a degree that her past failings did not rob her of worth in his own sight? Make her lesser, somehow? Too damaged for him?

Rufus had said, *"Whether you are worthy of* her *remains to be seen."* Those words had shaken Aquila. He had thought her culpable of the worst sin possible. But in God's sight, was his own unbending condemnation just as grave a sin?

Equal in faith. Equal in sin.

Except for this: her sin had made her softer. More compassionate. Out of her past failures flowed an unending river of mercy. Grace for the broken. Had he not tasted of it himself when he had told her of *his* shame?

Her sin, once repented, had been transformed by God into something beautiful. It was, he realized, one of the things he loved about her—that deep-rooted compassion that seemed to accept everyone just as they were.

Several years before, Aquila had visited a glassmaker's workshop. The master craftsman, dark skin glistening with sweat from his proximity to a blazing furnace, had begun with sand, which he had melted with a bit of salt. Then he had extracted the resultant material, still molten, and using a blowpipe, had inflated it into a delicate vase with exquisite walls you could glimpse the world through. What had begun as ordinary sand had, after passing through a conflagration and the ministrations of a master's touch, turned into a splendid work of art.

In the hand of God, Priscilla had become like that vase. The impure sands of her past had been transformed into beauty. She was a new creation.

Aquila saw himself with new eyes and realized he had become like a man who chose to smash that vase into the ground, walking over the shattered pieces as if they had been returned to sand.

He had been a fool. He had rejected what God had redeemed. Changed.

Tears of regret burned his eyes and clogged his throat. Regret for having hurt this precious woman with the stone of his judgment.

A boulder pressed him down as he acknowledged the sobering reality of his own failure. Guilt that weighed a mountain. He poured out half-uttered words of repentance as he doubled over, gasping into the frothing river, until finally the weight of his sin started to glide, to move in slow increments, from him onto Christ's shoulders. Whether he lingered there for hours or mere moments, he could never recall.

In time, he turned toward home, walking slowly at first and then running, long legs pumping, muscles contracting, joints pivoting as he wove through the crowds and spoke to God. He admitted his transgressions, holding nothing back, and felt a lightening of the bitterness he had been carrying inside since his proposal. He began to feel peaceful for the first time in weeks. Clear-headed.

By the time he walked into his chamber, he wore a grin the size of a Roman galley. And he knew what he had to do.

"Why are you in such good humor?" Benyamin asked.

Aquila tapped his uncle on the cheek. "You are a handsome old man, you know. I am off to the baths."

He made his way to the Antonine baths, a short walk from home, and returned scrubbed, his hair trimmed neatly, his face cleanly shaven like a Roman gentleman. He still had a few pieces of luxurious clothing left from his days of living as the scion of a wealthy household. Grabbing a light linen tunic with thin purple embroidery, he topped it with a long cloak made of featherlight wool, dyed midnight blue, and added jeweled clasps to attach the cloak to his shoulders.

Benyamin whistled at the sight of him. "Where are you going, now? Visiting Claudius in his palace?"

"That's tomorrow. Where is that agate ring from my grandfather?" He did not wear rings anymore, finding them a hindrance in his work. But for his purpose today, he wanted to look as impressive by Roman standards as he could.

"In your box." Benyamin scratched his beard. "Do you have a fever?"

"A very high one." Ferox followed him as he turned to leave. "No," he said firmly to the dog. "You can't come today. I have to do this by myself."

As he stepped onto the narrow lane that led to the Via Appia, he noticed the smile on his uncle's face. It shone with the brilliance of the lampstand in the Campi synagogue.

"I wish to visit Prisca," he said to the servant guarding the entrance of the house. Instead of welcoming him inside, the guard fetched the steward. The steward slipped out to the street and kept the gate firmly shut behind him.

"She does not receive uninvited guests," the man said.

"I think you will find that she will receive me. Tell her Aquila is here."

"Aquila who?"

Aquila narrowed his eyes. "Aquila, son of Philip of Pontus."

"Never heard of him."

Aquila laid a hand against the wall and leaned his face into the steward's. "Call your master to the door. I will speak to him."

The steward hesitated.

"Now! Fetch Volero Priscus at once," Aquila growled. He would get nowhere if he could not even step over the threshold. The man drew a hasty step back, withdrew inside, and forgot to close the gate.

Fifteen

LOLLIA SCRAMBLED into Priscilla's chamber, panting. "Come! Hurry!"

Priscilla placed the basket she had been weaving on the floor. "What is it?"

Lollia grabbed her hand and pulled. "Hurry, I say!"

Something of the woman's urgency transferred into Priscilla and she jumped to her feet. "What has happened?"

"Aquila is here. Speaking to your brother."

Priscilla's blood ran cold. "No! No no no no no . . ." She drew no breath between the words as she rushed behind Lollia. This spelled disaster. It spelled catastrophe. It spelled bloodshed.

"Where are they?" she cried.

"By the gate."

Priscilla picked up speed and whipped past Lollia. Halfway to the courtyard, she heard Aquila's voice, clear and strong. "I have come to ask your sister to marry me."

Someone must have hit her on the head with the fat end of a

spear. She could not have heard rightly. Her legs froze, refusing to move.

"Who are you to make such a request?" Volero said, his voice pitched high with indignation.

"I beg your pardon, Volero Priscus. Did I sound like I was making a request? I was not. I was merely informing you to be polite."

"How dare you? I will have you thrown out of my house this instant."

"With pleasure. This is not a place I care to linger. Call Priscilla and we will leave you in peace."

"I do not bestow my permission! She is not allowed to marry anyone. I forbid it. That cow has no right to—" Volero's voice ended in an abrupt squeak.

"Watch your tongue when you speak of your sister," Aquila said so softly that Priscilla had to hold her breath to hear him. "There is no one on this earth I treasure more, and if you get out of my way, I intend to tell her so myself."

Priscilla clapped her hands over her mouth and squeezed her eyes shut.

The sounds of a scuffle filled the courtyard. "Priscilla!" Aquila shouted above the din. "Priscilla!"

"Go!" Lollia cried, shoving her forward.

Priscilla came to herself. Galvanized by the urgency in Aquila's voice, she sprinted forward. He was struggling against two of Volero's servants, who between them had, despite their prodigious size, not yet managed to secure him.

"Aquila!" she cried.

As if the sight of her gave him renewed strength, Aquila wrenched hard, slithering out of the arms that seized him, leaving behind his cloak.

He fell to his knees before her. "Priscilla, I have been a fool, and I am more contrite than I can say. No time for long speeches. I love you! Please, marry me. Be my wife. And say yes quickly before your brother sets his men upon me again."

A blubbering sound issued from her throat. "Yes!" she gasped, hardly able to believe the unreal scene unfolding before her.

Aquila rose to his feet and enfolded her hand in his. "I will tell you how happy you have made me as soon as we are away from this place."

"I forbid this lunacy," Volero barked. "I will not have this . . . person . . . for a brother-in-law."

"Dear Volero, you need not worry. You never had me for a sister. Not truly. By that same token, you shall not have Aquila for a brother-in-law. I, however, will have him for my husband."

Aquila beamed like a torch.

Volero raised a hand of command. Before he could order his servants to detain them, Priscilla laid her fingertips on his shoulder. "Volero, Volero. You will do no good here. You know Father gave me my emancipation before he died. The law has bound your hands and freed mine. Come. Let us part as friends."

Volero snarled. "Go, then, and never return. I don't want to see your face again. It is good to be rid of you at last. Leave and take nothing."

Aquila took her hand. "We don't need anything from him. Come."

Priscilla gave his fingers a reassuring squeeze but refused to budge. "Our father gave Lollia to me. She is no more yours than I am. She will come with us. And I will take my mother's belongings, which Father left to me. There are no treasures there worthy of your concern, Volero. But they matter to me. What is mine, I will keep."

He gave her a black look. "What do I care? Take your rubbish." He motioned to his servants, and they dispersed.

"You will ever be in my heart, Volero," she said before he could turn away. "My only brother. I love you more than you know. If ever you need me, send to Senator Pudens, and he will know how to find me."

"*Need* you?" Volero spat. "I would sooner need a rat."

They walked to the Via Appia in a daze. "I can't believe you actually came for me," Priscilla said.

She felt stunned. The same man who had spurned her, shunned her, avoided her, had now by some miracle come to claim her. He had pursued her into the lion's den of her brother's house and fallen at her feet. This felt like a dream. Any moment now she would wake in her narrow bed and find herself alone.

Aquila, who held her bundle under one arm and her hand in a secure grip, tightened his hold. "I should have come sooner. I have so many pardons to ask of you, my love."

Mindful of Lollia strolling alongside them, her face nearly split with a satisfied smile, Priscilla swallowed the questions that bubbled out of her.

Her eyes widened in sudden realization. "I have no place to live."

"Rufus and Mary will no doubt welcome you and Lollia into their home." He gave her a sidelong look that made her stomach flutter. "It won't be for long," he said with confidence. "We will be married soon."

She hid a smile. "It will be weeks and weeks. I have to weave my wedding tunic by my own hand according to Roman tradition, and I am a very slow weaver."

"Two weeks."

She shook her head. "Only if you want to see your bride in a short tunic that does not cover her knees."

Priscilla's bundle slipped from under Aquila's arm and crashed to the ground. A slow flush spread over his cheeks as he bent to retrieve it. "I could live with that," he said when he straightened.

She choked and neither of them said another word until they reached his lodgings.

"Uncle, would you like to take Lollia to visit Mary?" Aquila said as soon as they entered.

Benyamin sprang to his feet, dropping the tent he had been stitching, his head swiveling from Aquila to Priscilla.

Lollia sat on the stool he had just vacated and puffed out her cheeks. "I only just arrived. I am too old to go traipsing around again before I have had a very long rest."

Benyamin cleared his throat. "I will give you a ride in the cart, Lollia. You won't have to take a step."

She came to her feet. "Fine. But I have waited a long time for this. It is cruel to make me miss it."

"Uncle, please tell Mary that Priscilla and I will come later," Aquila added, following behind them. "Lollia will explain."

"Explain what? I am missing all the good bits."

Priscilla chuckled. "Go on with you."

Aquila shut and barred the door, ensuring no customers would be able to wander in. Without a word, he hauled Priscilla into his arms and held her for a long, aching moment. "I thought we would never be alone."

"What made you come for me?" Her face was half-buried against his chest.

He took a short step away, his hands lingering on her arms. "I have been in misery. I thought I could walk away from you. But every day, I found that I longed for you more than before." He drew her to sit next to him on the cushions that lined the wall.

"You never showed it." She could not keep a note of accusation from seeping into her voice.

"I was determined to overcome my feelings. I thought Benyamin might cast me out of this house, I had grown so ill-tempered. Then Rufus, may the Lord bless him, censured me and brought me back to my senses."

"What did he say?"

"I don't remember all his words. But I do know that by the time he finished, I realized I had been the world's greatest idiot." He took her hand into his. "Priscilla, you are everything I want. Kind, gentle, loyal, trustworthy, generous. Forgive me, love. I allowed the past to blind me to who you truly are."

She stared at her feet. Though overwhelmed with joy, part of her could not truly trust the transformation in Aquila's feelings. "You seem a changed man."

He caressed her palm with his thumb. "Seeing you at Elizabeth's *insula*, I felt again that odd sense of belonging I only have with you. As if I have come home. All the while," he added, his voice apologetic, "in the background of my heart, a storm of judgment brewed, pointing fingers. But the winds and waves of it could not shake this certainty: I am yours and you are mine. Then Rufus showed me how appalling my rejection of you truly was." He shook his head in self-disgust.

He grinned, trying to lighten the heaviness that lay between them. "To the man who abused you I owe perhaps the greatest debt."

"To . . . Appius?" she stuttered.

"If he had not been such a dolt, he would have married you. And then where would I be?"

"Don't sweep my sin under a carpet of jests. It goes too deep. If we do not settle it, it will always come between us. I know you abhor what I did," Priscilla said, trying to keep her voice even. This had been why she had once resolved never to marry. She knew that regardless of anyone's good intentions, the past could always spread like rot into the beams of the present and destroy it.

"Priscilla. My Priscilla. I have already settled it. I dropped the stone, beloved. Look in my hand and you will only find mercy."

"Why?" she asked.

"Because you are worth more than all your sins. Because I cannot remember your misdeeds without my own mocking me." He drew her to him. "Come. Will you not trust me? Give me your heart and your future, and I will give you mine."

He pulled her tighter into the circle of his arms, and this time, he kissed her, a slow, smoldering kiss that stole her breath away. She had been with Appius three times. Never, not even when he was at his most charming, had Appius kissed her like this. With Aquila's first kiss, she learned more about passion than in all the stolen moments with Appius.

Aquila's touch was a weaving of boundaries and desire, as if she was worth the cost of waiting. Because he treated her like she was altogether clean, she felt clean. Almost.

"You're shaking," he said, pulling her tightly against him.

Priscilla felt like she had been through an earthquake. And come out intact, standing on solid ground. "I give you my heart and my future," she whispered, her lips moving on his.

His eyes closed and he let out a breath. Tangling his hand into her hair, he drew her closer still, until there was no room between them. His arm cradled her back, and he kissed her one more time, until her bones dissolved.

He pulled back abruptly. "Two weeks."

She nodded. In truth, she had no breath for words.

He slipped a ring on her finger, the seal and symbol of their betrothal. It twirled loosely and nearly fell on the ground. "I should have bought something dainty for you. This was my grandfather's."

She closed her fingers around it. "Then I will treasure it all the more. Aquila . . . forgive me. I bring you no dowry."

He kissed the top of her head. "You bring me yourself. It is more than enough."

Priscilla and Lollia moved into a room under the eaves of Mary's roof. After years of living in Volero's unwelcoming house, Priscilla felt like she had taken residence with devoted kin. The household became a welter of happy activity, preparing for the wedding.

As promised, the bride to be began weaving her tunic, a simple white linen garment. Mary, tasked with picking up the traditional yellow veil, could not resist the purchase of a long white undertunic while she was at the market.

"Aquila bid me to ensure your tunic was long enough in time for the wedding," she said, her eyes twinkling.

Aquila and Benyamin did their best to ready their cramped home for two more occupants. They had decided that Lollia would sleep in the shop, Benyamin remain in his present chamber, while Priscilla and Aquila moved into the more diminutive chamber in the farthest part of the house. They would have to share their room with leather supplies and cooking implements. It would be a tight fit. To Priscilla, it sounded like a slice of heaven.

Every night Aquila would come to visit her. If work allowed, he arrived in time for supper and prayers, though often he came too late to eat. No matter how tired from his long day of work, he made the trek from the Via Appia merely to see her for a short while. She had never felt so cherished as when his exhausted eyes would light up at the sight of her, and he would smile his ravishing smile and take her hand in his. In those moments, she knew she had come home. And she knew it was the Lord who had given her this extravagant gift.

In the Valley of Achor, she had found a door of hope. His name was Yeshua. And walking through that door, she had discovered more fulfilment and joy than she thought this world had to offer.

Priscilla had made an odd decision, by Roman standards, in choosing to marry a Jewish man of working class. Senator Pudens and his family, she hoped, would not be so offended by her choice, or by the fact that she had disobeyed her brother, that they would refuse to welcome her company again. It was a painful possibility. Many patrician families would shun her for less.

She wrote Sabinella a short letter, praying that God would protect these cherished friendships. Within an hour of sending it, she received a reply in the form of a huffing slave boy. "My mistress bids you come."

Pudentiana met her at the gate of the house, where she had obviously been waiting for her arrival. She gave Priscilla a fierce embrace. "My mother read your letter to us. Oh, Priscilla! He *is* handsome, I will grant you. But it will mean a hard life. Are you sure?"

"I am sure."

"Come. My mother is impatient to see you. She is in bed today."

Priscilla knelt by the older woman's bed, her chest tightening at the sight of the skeletal figure huddled among the sheets. She winced as she noted fresh lines of pain in that dear face. Reaching out, she kissed Sabinella's trembling fingers.

The older woman patted her head. "Tell me what happened."

Priscilla had never shared with any of them her true state in Volero's house. They had guessed, to some extent, by the manner of her dress and Volero's lack of regard in public, that he was not as affectionate as one would wish in a sibling. Now, as she described life in his home, Sabinella hissed. "He should be ashamed, your brother."

"I hold no grudge against him. But you can see why I do not feel I owe him the obligations of a sister. My father gave me my freedom. Volero has no hold over me, either by law, duty, or natural inclination."

"I understand your feelings regarding your brother. Yet to marry this leatherworker places you in a difficult position. My husband tells me your Aquila is talented and honest. Good qualities in a man, certainly. But in a husband, Priscilla? You will become a plebeian. Work with your hands, have no servants to ease your labors. You will eke out an arduous living without the pleasures of wealth that are due to someone of your station."

Priscilla held up her hands, red and callused already from years of work. "I am accustomed to hard work, my lady. Only now, I shall do it alongside one I love dearly and know the joy of being loved in return."

Sabinella shook her head. "Your brother has much to answer for."

"My years of solitude and hardship were not wasted, for they brought me to God." She went on to tell Sabinella her tale of finding comfort in the synagogue and of the friends whose kindness had changed her life. She painted her faith with a broad brush, knowing that too many details would baffle her friends and perhaps even turn them away. Silently she cautioned herself to choose her words with care rather than enthusiasm.

"My daughter will not stop speaking of the day you took her to the widow's house," Sabinella said. "She informs me that the prayers of your friends filled her with unwavering peace."

Priscilla nodded once, her eyes widening. She wondered if God had finally opened a door of opportunity.

"Aquila prayed for our family without being asked," Pudentiana added. "You can see why Priscilla has chosen to wed him. He is caring and thoughtful, more so than the young men born to Roman senators and legates, many of whom I have had the pleasure of meeting."

Priscilla gave her friend a grateful smile. "They can pray for you, too, dear lady. Today, if you will allow it."

Pudentiana added the force of her pleas. "Say yes, Mother. Please!"

Sabinella sighed. "For you, then, Daughter. Though I expect nothing will happen and you will only find yourself disappointed."

Sixteen

THE CHAMBER SEEMED layered in shadows, dark moving against dark, giving the space a sense of inscrutable menace. His forehead furrowed and shining with sweat, the senator slumped on a chair by his wife's bed. She lay on the sheets, her skin an odd shade of gray. One side of her body spasmed and trembled, the uncontrollable movements sapping her of strength she could ill afford to expend.

Aquila asked for a few more lamps, placing them in the shadowed corners until the chamber became bathed in soft light. He knelt down by Sabinella. "Lady, there is a God who created the earth and the heavens. He knows the tears you have shed, and he has sent us to intercede for you."

"I know not this God of whom you speak," Sabinella said, her tone apologetic.

Aquila liked her honesty. "I do not know Caesar Claudius. But he is still emperor. We will come to the Lord on your behalf."

"You seem confident," she said. "The gods, I find, are capricious at best and fickle when it comes to extending their help."

"I know only one God, and he is steadfast. I am confident

because I approach him not as a stranger, but as a son. He is always glad to welcome us into his presence. I will tell you one more truth with confidence. You are loved by him."

Sabinella's mouth tipped to one side. "That's a pretty speech."

"I have more," Aquila said with an answering smile. "Do not worry. I will save them for another day. For now, may we pray?"

And that was what they did. With the ease of long familiarity, they slipped into the hallowed in-between place which is prayer, one foot firmly in the world and the other on a higher plane. They spoke to God, they walked with Yeshua, they heard from the Spirit. They were filled, once more, with the wonder of the Father, who loved them and rejoiced over them.

They prayed as those who are a glorious crown on Christ's brow, an outward sign of his victory, his power, and his kingship. In the world, they were merchants and workers of leather. Ordinary men and women. In the light of heaven, they had become warriors, princes, and queens wielding a sword that only God could craft.

When they had finished, Aquila looked toward Sabinella. With disappointment he saw that her body still shook and convulsed. Then he raised his eyes further and saw her face.

It was transformed.

Where there had been a wide current of anxiety that her courage could not quite hide, there was now peace. An utter calm. God had not healed her body. But he had healed her heart.

"Did you put the petals on the bed as I asked?" Aquila said to his uncle.

"Lots of them. Roses, as you wanted. They smell very . . . vegetative."

"No thorns?"

"Just the petals, as per your instructions."

Aquila stopped in the act of putting on his sandals. "Have we washed the dishes left over from last night's supper? I don't remember. I don't want her to come home to a mess."

"All clean and put away."

"I think my tunic must have shrunk when the washerwoman laundered it. It feels tight," he said, pulling down the neckline of his linen tunic.

Benyamin sighed. "It looks fine."

"Where is my cloak?"

"Folded over your arm."

"Ah, yes. It feels very light. It has probably shrunk as well. I am as ready as I am going to be."

"You might consider putting on your other shoe." Benyamin pointed at his bare foot.

Aquila groaned and bent to slip on the forgotten shoe. Ferox bounded forward, his tongue extended, ready for a lick. "No!" Aquila cried. "Put that weapon away this instant. It is my wedding day, and I am not going to my bride with the smell of dog on my face." Ferox sat abruptly and closed his mouth.

They had decided to travel to Trastevere in the cart since Benyamin was moving in with Rufus and Mary for a couple of weeks, leaving Priscilla and Aquila time to adjust to living as man and wife. They would use the cart to bring Priscilla and her meager belongings home at the end of the festivities.

Ferox homed in on the cart as soon as they headed toward it, jumping into the back, and sitting as if he were an honored guest.

"Out, beast!" Aquila pointed a finger to the door. "You are not invited to the wedding."

Ferox looked back at him with a wounded expression. Aquila fought a pang of guilt. Priscilla would likely laugh if he showed up with the dog in tow. But he wanted her to have everything perfect on this day. Ferox, in his excitement at seeing her, would probably try to knock her into the bushes.

"Out!" he said again more firmly, and Ferox vaulted to the ground obediently. Aquila comforted himself with the fact that he had left the beast enough food and drink to last a week.

"You had better let me drive," Benyamin said gently. "Sit back, close your eyes, and I will navigate."

Aquila's lips twitched. "Have I been that bad?"

"You have no idea. We have to wed you off and fast, before you lose what little wits you have left."

Aquila would never remember that drive, which passed in a haze, or recall walking into Rufus's house or speaking to any of the guests. His first memory of his wedding was the sight of Priscilla waiting for him in the courtyard under a wooden arch covered in flowers, Rufus by her side. She was garbed in white, her simple dress cinched high at the waist, a yellow veil draped modestly over her hair, held in place by a circlet of autumnal flowers and late-blooming roses.

He had never seen anything so beautiful. If so many eyes had not been glued to them, he would have pulled her to him and kissed her. Maybe for an hour, straight. Instead, he bent his lips to her ear so only she could hear him. "I can't wait to make you mine." He had the satisfaction of seeing her blush as pink as the flowers woven through her hair.

Rufus read the story of Adam. "Before God created marriage, he had to create a bride," he said. "The Lord put Adam to sleep, a sleep as deep as death. He cut Adam's flesh, opened his side, extracted his bone in order to make a bride for him."

He waved a hand toward Aquila. "Today Aquila gazes upon his Eve. Priscilla is now bone of his bone and flesh of his flesh.

"We celebrate with joy the union between this man and woman, a joining that only God could have fashioned by his grace. But we celebrate another astounding reality. Because as besotted as Aquila is with his bride, it is nothing compared to how our God feels toward us.

"Yeshua, when he walked among us, called himself the bridegroom. Like Adam, to win us, to have us, he too had to be put to the sleep of death. His side had to be pierced, his flesh had to be sacrificed. We who were dead in spirit, came to life out of his death, born from Christ as Eve was born from Adam. And we are now bone of his bone, flesh of his flesh."

Mary stepped forward then, acting as the matron of honor, and taking Priscilla's right hand, placed it into Aquila's. Aquila felt his bride's fingers nestled in his palm, warm and strong. Strong enough to build a life on. In her crisp Latin, Priscilla pronounced the words that made her his wife: "Wherever you go, I, your wife, will also go."

Finally he was allowed to kiss her in full view of their guests. He drew her into his arms and kissed her on the mouth, his touch chaste. He held her for a beat longer, his eyes promising more, before letting her go.

Pudens and his daughters were among the guests. "You honor us by your presence, Senator," Aquila said. "How is the lady Sabinella?"

"She has slept well since your visit, which is a mercy. I have not seen her so at rest for months." Pudens adjusted the heavy folds of his toga. "On a different subject, in the absence of family, I feel called to speak in place of Priscilla's father today.

"I have been married a long time. Happily married, unlike

many of my acquaintance. I have learned one thing. Some women know how to love with their whole being. They know how to turn a house into a haven. A place of joy and peace. Priscilla is one of them. Love her well, young man."

The words had the weight of a sacred charge, one laid on Aquila for the rest of his life. If he had learned nothing else in the past months, he had learned this: love was fragile. Loving well required hard work, both moral and emotional. He bowed his head to the senator, signaling both his assent and his commitment.

Priscilla would have been touched by how hard Aquila and Benyamin had worked to make the small apartment a welcoming home for her if she had not been so anxious. Part of her had been longing for this moment, to be finally alone with Aquila without a thousand interruptions. Another part, far larger, dreaded what was to come. She worried that he might be disappointed. That bitterness might creep in between them when her bridegroom, by virtue of circumstances, would be forced to remember Appius.

"I saved the best for last," Aquila said, proudly leading her to the narrow chamber that now belonged to them. She heard him hiss under his breath.

The pallet, which he must have made up carefully before setting out to Rufus's house, had become a heap of crumpled sheets. Among the folds, she detected a flash of scarlet, then another. "Rose petals," she said, picking one up and smelling it. In the corner, as far from the bed as possible, she saw Ferox curled in a large ball, as if trying to disappear into himself, one red petal stuck to his black nose, another hanging from his mouth. As she watched, his tongue flashed out and lapped up the delicate petal.

"Traitor!" Aquila cried.

Ferox whimpered, casting pathetic eyes at Priscilla. She dissolved into laughter. Aquila gave her a reproachful glance. "It's no laughing matter." He pointed to the dog. "Away, you creature. I will deal with you later." Ferox, tail tucked between long, skinny legs, bolted to the next chamber. "I meant this to be a warm welcome for you," Aquila huffed.

She gave in to another wave of hilarity. "It is."

Aquila came a pace closer. Before she knew what he was about, his hand flashed out and she landed against his chest, laughter forgotten. He lowered his mouth to hers. She felt again that hot, bewildering gale of emotions she had experienced when he had kissed her the first time, the night they had become betrothed. Felt dizzy and lost in the kiss as it deepened. He grasped the yellow palla and with one motion swept aside the veil and wreath of flowers that held it in place, dropping both to the floor. His fingers slid to the back of her head, gently undoing the loops and twirls until her hair fell loose down her back and shoulders.

"I have been dreaming of seeing you like this," he said and swung her up into his arms to lay her on the ruined pallet.

It was fitting that her wedding bed should not be pristine. Should be tumbled and used. Like *her*. The thought came sudden and piercing. She froze. Would he regret marrying her when his passion cooled? Her body, melting just a moment before under his restless fingers, became unyielding.

"Priscilla?" Aquila pulled away. He traced a finger down her cheek. "What is it?"

She stared at him mutely.

"You don't like this?" His lips trailed down the side of her neck. "Or this?" They trailed a little lower.

She grew more rigid. He lifted his head, tiny lines of worry gathering at the corners of his eyes. In the darkening room, the irises had grown huge and charcoal colored. He eased himself away on an elbow. She became aware, in the uncanny way they had at times of reading each other without words, that she was making him doubt himself. Doubt his own ability as a man.

The breath leaked out of her. "I like it," she assured him. "All of it."

"Then what is it?"

She licked dry lips. "I . . . worry that you will . . . find me disappointing."

He sifted through her words, trying to decipher their meaning. "You worry I will find you . . . *tainted*?

Her throat clogged. That word. It was perfect for her, wasn't it? She nodded.

"You fear I will leave you?"

She thought about that. "I know you won't. You are the man who couldn't leave a dog on the side of a road. You wouldn't walk away from me. Not physically. But I fear you might take back your heart."

He cradled her cheek in his hand. "One day you will believe that I will never stop loving you. Never abandon you. Until then, you have to trust me, one kiss at a time." He took her lips in a searing kiss. "One touch at a time." He caressed her, fingers roving against the thin linen of her tunic. "One embrace at a time." His arms came about her, drawing her closer. "You will trust me, one day, when I tell you that you are my beloved, more precious to me than my life. And the past has no power to change that."

When he kissed her again, murmuring words of love and need against her skin, she resisted the shame that tried to reclaim her.

She kissed him back, shyly offering herself to this tender man who had wooed and won her.

Their time together, undergirded by a foundation of love, was full of promise. But she knew that she had held a corner of herself back from him, shielded a part of herself that could not entirely relax in his arms. In the melting heat of intimacy with her husband, Priscilla became aware that there were layers of shame that clung to her so deep and hidden, they had proven inaccessible to the grace offered by both God and her husband. Layers that crippled her body's ability to respond fully.

As she lay sleepless in Aquila's arms, she could only hope that with the passage of months, she might one day feel free in her husband's arms, meeting yearning with yearning, passion with passion, holding nothing back.

A week after the wedding, a messenger brought a letter from Senator Pudens. Priscilla read the short missive twice and frowned.

"Bad news?" Aquila asked.

"I am not certain. It sounds cryptic. He apologizes for intruding on us so close to our wedding and invites us to supper tomorrow."

Aquila set down his cup. "That seems harmless enough. He wouldn't invite us to supper if he had unpleasant news to share."

"Sabinella has not been receiving visitors. The evening we prayed for her was an exception. And Pudens wouldn't interrupt our time alone for a casual supper. This dinner makes no sense." She crinkled the papyrus in her hand. "I fear Sabinella's condition may have deteriorated. What if she is near the end and wants to say good-bye?"

Aquila took her in his arms. "We don't know that. Let's not think the worst. Tomorrow we will discover what it all means."

Priscilla leaned into Aquila. His mere presence, solid and somehow unshakable, gave her comfort. Still, she could not dismiss a lingering cloud of anxiety, which had hung over her even after they had prayed.

For once, Priscilla walked faster than her husband, climbing the hilly roads into the Esquiline with the determination of a soldier on the march. Pudens himself welcomed them, his face wreathed in a wide smile. She felt her shoulders loosening at the sight of his beaming face.

"I want you to see something," he said. He took her hand and led her to the garden, where Sabinella was sitting under the leather awning. The old Sabinella. The one with flesh on her bones and color in her cheeks. She stood, her movements more fluid than they had been in months, holding a hand out to Priscilla.

The fingers stretching toward her still trembled, but not with the devastating violence of recent weeks. Priscilla sprinted to the older woman and stood uncertainly, before Sabinella pulled her into a warm embrace.

Priscilla's eyes welled. She had expected death and had instead found life. Limp with relief, she sagged against Aquila, who had come up behind her. "I don't understand," she said.

Sabinella drew her down next to her on the bench while the senator and Aquila occupied another.

"I am not healed," Sabinella said, holing out her trembling fingers. "But it is as if time has reversed, and the disease has returned to its early days." She smiled at Aquila. "After you prayed, something shifted inside me. I felt an utter absence of fear. I would call it peace, except the word is not adequate. A calm beyond anything I have known, even when I enjoyed full health. I ate a good meal and managed to hold it down. Then I slept, another small miracle.

"I thought the peacc was the only gift of your prayer. But with every day, I grew a little stronger, until I became like this. Your God lifted the hand of death from me." She reached for Pudens's hand. "For some reason, the disease itself remains, though much diminished. More of an annoyance than an illness. I feel like I have been brought into an oasis. Given strength and life.

"Your God did this for me. Tell me: how can I repay him?"

Silence filled the arbor. That question had blown open a holy portal; it invited one whose breath had made the heavens and the earth to partake of their exchange. Exhilaration swelled through Priscilla. She sensed that something had shifted in the axis of the world, and the Kingdom of God had drawn near. "Ask him to draw near to you," she murmured.

Seventeen

"THAT'S THE THIRD SENATOR THIS WEEK," Aquila said, writing the latest order on a sheet of papyrus to ensure he wouldn't forget the details. "They are all sending their stewards over, thanks to Pudens."

Benyamin examined the tip of his awl. "That makes thirteen large orders for the next month, plus the demands of daily trade. We can't keep up. We need to hire someone. It will cut into our profits, but we have no choice."

Priscilla, who was working on a heavy basket in the corner of the workshop, snapped her head up. "I could help. I have watched you and Benyamin work and I know I can learn. Especially smaller pieces like the round cloaks."

Their work did not demand physical strength as much as proficiency. A woman could do it as well as a man. But Aquila did not want his wife to feel forced into the trade. "Do you really want to?"

She nodded eagerly. "It will be a family venture."

He smiled. He had worried, when she had first moved in, that she might feel uncomfortable living with two men who were accustomed to their bachelor ways. Instead, the four of them had quickly grown past the initial awkwardness of their cramped quarters and become deeply attached to each other. Perhaps the most profound change came in Lollia.

The first afternoon Lollia had returned from Rufus's house, before she had a chance to stow her meager belongings, Priscilla and Aquila had turned her right around and marched her out.

"Where are you taking me?" she had wailed.

"You will see," Priscilla had said, blue eyes shimmering with joy.

They came to a stop beneath the overhang at the magistrate's door. Before stepping inside, Priscilla said, "Lollia, I could never free you while we lived under my brother's roof. The only protection I could offer you was to keep you as my slave. By law, he had no power over you as long as I owned you. Now that I am married to Aquila, my brother is no longer a threat."

"We are here to give you your freedom," Aquila said quietly.

"You shall not remain a slave," Priscilla added. "From now on, you will live with us as a member of the family." They had made their promise official, paying the magistrate to draw up a certificate of manumission. Lollia had walked out, clutching that certificate, tears blinding her aged eyes. She belonged to them in a different way now. Not out of obligation or law, but by the unbreakable ties of love.

It had been one of the unexpected joys of his marriage, this sudden expansion of belonging. It wasn't merely that he had married Priscilla. They had welded their small worlds together and created not only a happy couple, but a tight-knit family.

He had noticed that anything Priscilla did with and for that family made her glow with happiness. "Benyamin could teach you to work with the leather," he said. "He taught me everything I know."

His uncle grinned. "Not too old to still teach you new tricks, young man."

Aquila nodded acknowledgment. "True enough."

"Don't forget me. I can learn too," Lollia piped up.

Benyamin raised a thick brow. "I charge for my tuition, you know. An extra bowl of stew every evening."

Lollia shrugged. "You already have an extra bowl of stew every evening."

Aquila studied the pile of orders before him. The rapid expansion of their business was causing a few problems that Priscilla and Lollia's added help would not solve. They had purchased more leather from Rufus, and their supplies were taking over every surface. Ferox had started to look haunted, crying to be let out at all hours. Aquila himself felt the oppression of his shrinking world and knew they needed a new home. One large enough to suit the demands of their growing trade.

There was another reason he wanted to move. The senator and his family were starting to grow in their faith. They were like a painter's blank wall, with no prior knowledge of God. Unlike Priscilla, whose year at the synagogue had laid strong foundations of faith, they knew nothing and required patient tutelage. They had tried coming to Rufus's home once, but although they found the people there welcoming, it felt foreign to them, as if they had to become un-Roman in order to follow Yeshua.

Understanding their discomfort, Priscilla had arranged to meet them at the senator's villa. The slaves and servants in the Pudens household were invited to join in these gatherings, and their numbers were growing by the day. Every night they could, Aquila and Priscilla went to the Esquiline to teach this precious community about God. The past few months had blurred into a whirlwind of constant motion and joyous growth.

But Aquila knew he could not keep this pace up. He could not keep losing hours traipsing up and down the hills of Rome while new orders mounted. If he had a larger house, one more conveniently located, he could open his own home, saving himself the time swallowed up by endless commute.

Such a property cost money. More than he could afford at present. When they finished the new orders and added a few more, perhaps he might be able to make the transition. But that couldn't happen for months. Perhaps years.

Priscilla awoke with a start. Through the opening of the window she could see the moon flickering bright, still dominating the night sky. She lay open-eyed, trying to discern what had wakened her. Benyamin's loud snores in the next room were punctuated by Lollia's softer ones in the workshop. Aquila slept on beside her, undisturbed. Nothing seemed out of place.

Then she heard Ferox sniffing under the closed door of their chamber, where he was not allowed to enter at night. He did this sometimes, when he wanted to demonstrate his dissatisfaction with the arrangement. But something about the soft insistence of the dog made Priscilla get up and open the door. She had expected him to scramble inside. Instead, at the sight of her, he wheeled in the opposite direction and walked toward the workshop. She grabbed the oil lamp they left burning on a stand through the night and followed him. He pawed the gate that led to the road, as if desperate to go out. It was an unusual request. Once settled in his bed, Ferox did not like to leave it until the morning.

Priscilla lifted the bar quietly and let the dog out. He headed in the direction of the shed at the side of the house where they kept wood for cooking. Lately, they had begun to store larger pieces of leather there, which they needed for making tents. More a shack than a shed, the structure did not offer a watertight shelter. If not for the fact that they intended to use the leather quickly, they could never have left their expensive supplies there.

Ferox sat outside the shed and gave a tiny whimper. "What do you have there, boy?" Priscilla asked. The dog whimpered again and sniffed at the door.

He had probably cornered a rabbit. She had left her warm bed chasing after a silly animal taking shelter for the night. Ferox's behavior gave her pause, however. Ferox on the hunt was usually excited, his tail wagging, his barks loud with delight. Tonight he remained persistent but quiet. Intent. Curious, Priscilla pulled the door open and held the lamp aloft.

Something stirred in one dark corner where they had stacked a tall pile of leather. Something definitely larger than a rabbit. Priscilla drew a sharp breath. A shape ran into the light directly toward her.

Several things became apparent to her at once. The occupant of the shed was a child. A boy no older than eight or nine. Startled by Priscilla's sudden appearance, the child began to run toward the door. Run with admirable speed, headed directly for where Priscilla's body unintentionally barred the only exit. At the last moment, Ferox sprang into the mix.

"Oomph!" Priscilla gasped as she went sprawling on the floor. Arms and legs tangled for an indefinable moment. By instinct, she snaked out a hand and, before the boy could gain his feet, grasped him firmly around the arm. "Hold a minute." She exhaled, trying to calm her racing heart.

The child pulled as hard as he could, panting. "Hold, I said," Priscilla commanded, getting to her feet and pulling him up with her. "I won't harm you." She righted the lamp, which still burned in spite of landing on its side during her tumble.

Priscilla took a firmer grip on the child and studied him in the weak light. His bones stuck out from his thin frame, matted hair falling over a pair of haunted brown eyes. He was filthy, head to foot covered in dirt, his tunic an indistinguishable color under layers of mud and grime. Bug bites covered his arms and legs in a pitiful array of bumps, some scratched into raw scabs.

Her eyes rounded. "I know you! You fetched me water in the Forum. What are you called?"

He stared at her defiantly, refusing to answer.

She tried another tack. "Are you hungry?" To her relief, he stopped squirming. "I have leftover bread from dinner. Fresh cheese too. And a juicy apple. Do you want me to make you a plate?"

The boy nodded once.

"Come in, then, while I get you the food." The arm under her fingers grew rigid, and he dragged his body back, attempting to free himself.

"Calm down. You don't want to come in? Very well. Sit down and I will fetch you a plate." She let him go. "No one is going to hurt you here, boy. Sit, I say. I will be right back."

The boy stood still as if considering if he should run or risk remaining for the food. Ferox drew close enough to lick the boy's hand. He jumped and snatched his fingers away. Then his mouth softened, and he reached out cautiously to pet the dog's head.

Priscilla had the sense that the child was no stranger to dogs. "His name is Ferox," she said. "You want me to leave him with you while I bring your dinner?"

The boy nodded.

"Ferox," she said again. "He likes it when you call him by name."

"Ferox," the boy repeated.

Priscilla smiled at him, pleased. She forced herself to walk away, knowing the child might decide to run as soon as she turned her back. She piled food on a plate and rushed back to the shed to find him on his knees, playing with the dog. As soon as he heard Priscilla approach, her unexpected guest wheeled about like a feral cat, eyes watchful.

When she held the plate out to him, he walked close enough to take it from her. She was touched when he wiped his hands on the sides of his tunic before tearing into the bread. He shoved the food into his mouth and swallowed before he had time to chew.

"Slow down," she cautioned. "You will make yourself sick if you eat too fast."

He tried to obey for a moment, but hunger broke his resolve, and he stuffed an enormous piece of bread into his mouth, shoveling cheese in after. A horse could not have devoured the apple any faster. Ferox, who had observed the child feasting in silence until then, stood on his hind legs and begged brazenly.

"Ferox! Behave yourself," Priscilla chided.

The boy hesitated. To her disbelief, he broke the last piece of cheese in half and held one piece to Ferox. The dog gulped down the morsel and licked his lips.

"That was generous of you," Priscilla said softly. "Wait here. I will bring you more." At the door, she turned her head. "I am Priscilla." She waited expectantly.

Her visitor frowned as if contemplating if he should respond. "Marcus," he said finally.

He had only offered his first name. Most free Roman males had three appellations, the second connecting them to a particular family. Given names were rarely used by strangers, saved only for close friends and family. She doubted this wary child wanted to share his first name as an offer of friendship.

Slaves, on the other hand, only had one name. Priscilla narrowed her eyes. "Who is your master?" she asked brusquely.

The boy gave her a thunderous look. "I am freeborn." The words, colored with pride and a tinge of outrage, rang true. She found his accent more interesting still, which unlike his rough appearance, sounded as refined and educated as her own. Whatever he was, he was no runaway slave.

"I believe you," she said. "Even if you were a slave, you would be safe with us. Tell me, is it by coincidence that you are hiding in my shed, or did you follow me here?"

The boy chewed on dry lips. "I saw you shopping in the Forum yesterday and followed you."

"Why me?"

He shrugged a bony shoulder. "I remembered you from before. You had been kind."

She nodded. "Thank you for telling me the truth. Now wrap yourself in that piece of leather while I fetch you more food. Your arms are covered in gooseflesh from the chill here."

Her mind raced as she gathered another plate for Marcus. It dawned on her that she did not want him to simply vanish into the night after eating his fill. She could not bear the thought of any child running loose in the streets of this callous city. There was a mystery to the boy with his aristocratic accent and starved body. A secret he guarded with a reticence unusual for his age. Something about the desperation she sensed in him, which went beyond physical need, melted her heart. In an instant, she made a decision that would change her life forever.

Aquila grinned lazily as he opened his eyes. His wife's face was bent over his, her long, feather-soft hair trailing on his shoulders. He smelled cinnamon and honey on her skin, and something more feminine and flowery, which turned his mind from the concerns of the coming day to something entirely more thrilling.

"We need to talk," she said, her expression serious.

He blinked the sleep from his eyes and wistfully put away thoughts of a leisurely start to his morning.

"We have a guest."

Aquila sat up. "What kind of guest?"

"An unexpected one." She settled on the bed next to him. "Do you remember that day in the Forum when you fought the thief?"

Aquila tensed. There had been no more attacks on Priscilla since that day, thank the Lord. It appeared as though whoever had meant her harm might have given up. He could not rest easy, however, having never solved the mystery of the matter. Who had wanted her dead, and what had driven them to give up? At the mention of the incident that still haunted his dreams, he jumped to the worst conclusion. "Don't tell me you have seen that brute loitering around our house?" he rasped.

"Not him," she said breezily, unaware of the fear that had gripped him. "That same day a boy offered to carry my basket. Do you recall?"

Aquila expelled a relieved breath. He had a vague recollection of a ragged child. "I think so."

"His name is Marcus. He is eight."

Aquila frowned. "He is here?"

"You are about to meet him. He has been living on the streets for some time now. I found him in our shed late last night."

"Hold a moment." Aquila rubbed a hand over his face, trying to rouse his tired mind. He had a feeling that he was lagging way behind his wife about something. "What is he? A runaway slave?"

"He claims not, and I believe him."

"I see."

"I would like him to stay." His wife looked at him with unwavering eyes.

"For breakfast?"

"For as long as he likes."

"What? No! Priscilla, you can't just bring a strange child into our home."

"Why not? You brought Ferox, and you knew nothing about *him*."

"Ferox is a *dog*. Who is this child? *What* is he? For all we know, he might be a thief. Or worse."

"He is eight."

"I've seen younger pickpockets."

"He's not a thief. He would be more well-fed if he were."

"Priscilla, be reasonable. We can't just add a strange child to our household. We barely have room for ourselves as it is."

She rose to her feet. "Come and meet him."

Aquila saw the trap at once. She knew that when he saw the child, he would be moved by pity and allow compassion to overcome his good sense. The woman was shrewd. But he knew how to deal with her. "Feed him and send him on his way. I have a mountain of work to do."

To his surprise, she turned her back and left the room without a single objection. He breathed a sigh of relief. That had proven easier than he expected. He washed, combed his hair, cleaned his teeth, and dressed in a wool tunic. Pulling out his rolls of papyrus, he spent some time studying the upcoming orders, prioritizing tasks, and planning the dates he needed to start each item for a timely delivery.

He wondered if enough time had passed for the urchin to have finished eating. Some extraordinary aromas were wafting out of the front chamber. The smell of soft cheese and honey mingled with that of flour and cinnamon frying in oil. His mouth watered and his belly grumbled.

Aquila had learned from experience that Priscilla could create culinary magic on the modest charcoal brazier they kept on a shelf beside the door. He decided that he need not deprive himself of his wife's heavenly cooking. Even if the boy had lingered in the house, Aquila knew himself to be immovable on the subject. In fact, best to address the matter as soon as possible.

He stepped out, his mind made up. He discovered the child occupying a stool, the plate on his lap mounded with various kinds of pastry and honeyed eggs. Lollia and Priscilla, still busy cooking, were adding a new offering to the pile as Aquila watched. Like most modest houses in Rome, they did not own a proper clay oven capable of producing bread. But someone had already walked over to the local bakery to buy a fresh loaf of *quadratus* and cut a thick wedge for their guest.

He studied the boy. His face and hands had been washed recently, judging by his clean skin and wet hair. The rest of his painfully thin body was covered by a crust of dirt, liberally pocked with scabs and bug bites, and probably crawling with vermin.

"Aquila, this is our guest, Marcus," Priscilla said without turning her head away from the pan. To the boy she said, "This is my husband."

The child spared him a brief nod. Aquila nodded back, hardening his resolve.

Priscilla tasted batter from a bowl. "I will have sweet cheese pastry ready for you in a few moments, Husband."

"You can have one of mine," Marcus said. "You don't have to wait." The child held out his plate.

"I . . ." Aquila found himself lost for words. He had tasted his wife's *libum*, a Roman pastry made with honey and soft cheese. He was not sure he would be willing to share his with anyone. Yet this stray, who by the look of him had eaten little food in the past month, was giving his away. He swallowed hard. "Thank you," he said, reaching out to take the offering.

"They are the best I have ever eaten," Marcus said with a nod.

"Me too," Aquila agreed.

Something about the boy nagged at him. He had dark eyes, almost black, too serious for a child of eight. Aquila was willing to bet those eyes had seen things children had no business seeing. His features were comely and typically Latin, with full lips and an aquiline nose that still had the unfinished look typical of a growing child.

It came to Aquila in a rush, the incongruity of the boy's confident manner and highborn speech. Give him a decent haircut, a clean tunic, a vigorous bath, and he could fit in perfectly in a villa in the Esquiline. The paradox tugged at his curiosity as strongly as the boy awakened his pity. He determined to resist both.

Aquila ate in silence, wondering how long before he could politely suggest that their guest be on his way. Benyamin, who must have been awake for some time, came into the room, a garment folded over his arm. "Peace, Aquila," he said cheerfully. "I thought you were never going to come out of your chamber." He turned to the boy. "Here. Try this. It will hang on you, but it's the smallest tunic I own."

Their guest took the gray robe. "My thanks," he said. Carefully he set the garment down on a shelf. "I am filthy. I don't want to ruin your clothes."

"Would you like to go to the baths?" Benyamin asked. "There is a large one near here. I would be happy to accompany you."

Aquila stared at his uncle, openmouthed. It was a conspiracy, he realized. And the old man, like Lollia, had thrown in his lot with Priscilla.

The boy's face solidified into a mask of horror. "No! I don't want to go."

Aquila did not know what had made Marcus so anxious at the mere mention of the place. But he couldn't bear to see the child so haunted by terror. "You don't need to go to the public baths," he said, coming to his feet. "Priscilla and Lollia can heat some water for you. They'll help you wash in the back room."

The boy's shoulders relaxed. "They are girls," he said after contemplating the offer.

"That is true. Would you rather I gave you a hand?"

"I'll take the pretty one," Marcus said, lifting his chin and pointing to Priscilla.

The boy was no fool, Aquila had to concede. "You will take Lollia and be grateful. I am keeping the pretty one for myself."

How he began to discuss arrangements for where the child

would sleep that night, Aquila never knew. But before the hour was up, they had all agreed that Marcus would sleep in the workshop with Lollia. The next morning, Aquila found himself volunteering to teach Marcus the leather trade. By that evening, when he tucked the boy into his makeshift bed, Aquila had already forgotten his intention of asking him to leave.

Eighteen

PRISCILLA DISCOVERED that Marcus knew how to read and write Latin with the facility of a much older child. In time, she came to the conclusion that he must have received rigorous tuition from a capable teacher at some point, though he slithered away from studying with the agility of an eel in water.

He preferred physical activity to almost anything. Give him a wooden sword, and he could spend hours in imaginary battle. Aquila, who still remembered some of the training he had received as a boy, sometimes engaged Marcus in a sparring match, teaching him the basics of sword craft and wrestling. Those were the moments the boy sparked to life.

The previous week, Aquila had taught him a new maneuver. Marcus had practiced it for hours until there were blisters on his fingers. Yesterday he had finally mastered the move. As soon as the family finished eating supper, he had pulled Aquila outside to demonstrate.

Priscilla watched them, boy and man dancing about each other in a tight circle, their concentration intense. When Marcus had performed the maneuver, Aquila had thrown his toy sword in the air before catching it with a flourish and whooping with excitement. "That was well done, boy!" he cried, ruffling Marcus's dark hair, every bit as taken up with the success of the drill as his pupil.

And then it happened. Marcus *smiled.* For the first time since she had met him, that boy stretched his lips and grinned with genuine happiness. Priscilla's belly twisted at the memory.

Thanks to their care, Marcus's body had recovered from the months of living without proper shelter. He had filled out, growing healthy, gaining strength. But some dark weight still pressed him.

He seemed leery of strangers and avoided the workshop if customers were visiting. The wealthier the patron, the more quickly he made himself scarce. He refused to share his full name with them. Refused to tell them the reason a boy of his affluent background should have ended up on the streets. Whatever his secret, Marcus guarded it closely. Priscilla was determined to extricate the boy's story from him. She knew he would never be whole until he confided in someone.

Her hands worked mindlessly on a tent as her thoughts whirled, Aquila stitching in companionable silence across from her. The hour had grown late and her back had started to ache. She stretched and set the leather aside. "Bedtime for me," she said.

Aquila nodded. "I will join you as soon as I finish this section. It won't be long."

She circled past him to where Marcus lay on his mattress, his breathing quiet as if his dreams harbored no monsters.

During the day, Marcus's clever tongue and general air of wary independence fooled one into forgetting how shockingly young he was. In repose, he looked his age. Just a little boy.

Carefully Priscilla bent to give him a light kiss on his forehead.

If he had been awake, he would not have allowed the liberty. She had tried to hug him once. He had submitted to her show of affection, standing like a wooden stick in her arms, too polite to push her away. She had received the unspoken message and learned to curtail any demonstrations of tenderness. She felt surprised by how often she had to quash the urge to kiss or hold this child. He had wormed his way deep into her heart.

She sighed and retreated to her own bed. A few minutes later, Aquila crawled in next to her. "Are we visiting Pudens tomorrow night?" he whispered.

"We are. Pudentiana told me this morning that he has some news for us."

"What news?"

"She would not say."

Aquila turned on his side and huddled up close to kiss her full on the mouth. Drawing back, she wrinkled her nose. "You smell like the inside of a sheep's belly."

He grinned. "I was at the tanner's earlier, looking at leather samples. I will go to the baths in the morning." He was quiet for a moment. "Marcus still refuses to accompany me there. It's as if he is afraid of the place."

Priscilla nodded in agreement. "He doesn't mind washing with a bucket."

"His cleanliness is not the issue. No self-respecting Roman can hold up his head if he is terrorized by the very mention of the baths. He will be mocked by friends and associates alike. We can't keep him sheltered for the rest of his life. He must learn to face this fear."

Priscilla rubbed her forehead. "That is no easy task. He breaks out into a cold sweat if I even mention the matter."

"And yet, the more we delay, the harder it may be to help him."

Priscilla bit her lip. It wasn't that she disagreed with her husband in principle. But the thought of what that little boy would have to go through in order to find freedom made something in her chest tighten.

In the morning Priscilla sent Marcus to buy bread for breakfast while she prepared a thick porridge. Benyamin and Aquila had departed early to deliver a couple of awnings, leaving an indignant Marcus behind so that he could have his Greek lesson with Priscilla. He lingered over the food as long as he could, wiping the bottom of his bowl with a piece of crust.

Not for the first time, she wondered how he had survived months of homelessness. "What did you eat when you lived on the streets?" she asked, wondering if he would avoid answering the question.

It was *this* or study Greek verbs, however. For once, he deigned to explain. "Sometimes I found things in the garbage outside the taverns. Eventually I learned that the best way to obtain food was to help the local sellers. The ones who set up their stalls for the day and leave in the evening.

"If you offer to move their baskets in the evenings, when they are packing up and tired, they may give you a bruised fruit or a bit of old bread in appreciation. I could not lift as much as the bigger kids, but the women liked me. I knew how to sweet-talk them."

Priscilla grinned. "I can imagine."

His eyes twinkled. "You would not have lasted half a day selling food on the streets, Priscilla. As soon as someone like me came along, you would have given away all your food and gone hungry yourself."

She nodded in agreement. Her smile vanished as a thought occurred to her. "Were the sellers ever mean to you?"

"Plenty. Sometimes they would curse you and scream obscenities. Others let you do lots of hard work and gave you nothing in return. Those were the times I collected my pay without permission."

"You stole?

He shrugged. His eyes went dark and flat. He had done what he could to survive. But survival had come at a price. A price he was not proud of.

"Where did you sleep at night?"

"Often I did not. Nights were dangerous. So I kept moving, staying in busy streets, especially near the warehouses. Those remain open at night while workers load wares on carts. If I could find a private little shed like yours, I would sneak a few hours of sleep. But mostly I slept during the day. I took naps near fountains, bridges, or aqueducts, where crowds lingered.

"I could never stay asleep for very long. After an hour, I would have to move and find a new place. Bad things happened to kids who slept too long and forgot to watch their backs."

"Marcus." She had to clear her throat and start again. "Marcus, you will never have to stay awake again because you are afraid to close your eyes. Not as long as I breathe."

A slow flush started at the boy's neck and worked its way up to his cheeks. He dropped his head and swallowed. When he lifted his face, the old guarded look had returned. "Does that mean I don't have to practice Greek?"

"It means you have to practice more. Now that I know how clever you are, we are moving on to bigger verbs."

Marcus rolled his eyes, then leaned over to examine the contents of the pot. Priscilla assumed he wanted more porridge and was about to serve him the leftovers. Instead he said, "I know where a couple of younger boys go, late in the mornings. Could we take them the rest of the porridge, do you think? After we are finished with your dreadful verbs, of course?"

She reached a finger and gently brushed his hair away from his forehead. Her own son, had he lived, would have been five years old by now. Perhaps she, too, would be living on the streets today if her brother had discovered her condition. Her little boy could have been one of the hungry children who did not dare to sleep at night for fear of unspeakable violence. She squeezed her eyes shut, warding off that painful image.

"Every day, Marcus," she promised. "We can bring them food every day."

"I want you to look at a house on the Aventine," Pudens told them the next evening after Priscilla and Aquila finished their teaching. He knew Aquila planned to move to a more suitable residence as soon as he had saved enough.

"The Aventine? I doubt I can afford it, Senator," Aquila said with a frown.

When a tragic fire had consumed some of the more densely populated areas of the Aventine twelve years earlier, large portions of the neighborhoods had been gobbled up by wealthy residents. Luxurious villas had been built in place of the ordinary homes that had once occupied the area. The northern border of the Aventine sat next to the Circus Maximus. Some of the residents could lounge on their expansive roofs and watch the chariot races in comfort. Several could even see Caesar's palace and gardens.

Although now occupied by consuls, legates, and famous attorneys, parts of the Aventine remained populated by common folk.

Such homes were hard to come by and still too expensive for Aquila. He sighed. The location would have been ideal. A hop over the bridge to Rufus's home and much closer to the Pudens residence.

"I think you can afford this one," the senator said, taking a sip of his wine. "It needs a lot of work." He named the asking price for the property. It was at the outer limits of what Aquila and his uncle could manage. But it might be doable once he received payment for the great heap of orders that had come his way.

"Come and see it with me in the morning," his host offered. "First, we have to establish whether it suits your needs. Then we can work out the practicalities."

They were interrupted by a whoop from Praxedis, Pudens's youngest daughter, who was currently engaged in chasing Marcus around the perimeter of the chamber.

It had taken Priscilla hours of coaxing to convince Marcus to attend a prayer meeting at the senator's house. The first night he had come, he had sat in one corner, hidden in the shadows, saying nothing. Praxedis and Pudentiana had teased, prodded, and poked at the boy until he had emerged out of his shell enough to answer a question or two. Eight weeks later, he seemed at home here. While at the synagogue he often fell asleep during the distinctly Jewish service, at the senator's house, he listened to their teachings with sharp interest.

Pudens frowned thoughtfully, his gaze following the boy. "He seems familiar, somehow, now that he has filled out." He shrugged. "I suppose I have reached the age when all children start looking alike to me. He still refuses to reveal where he comes from?"

Aquila nodded. "I think he is afraid to tell us."

"Afraid of what, exactly?"

"If I knew the answer to that, Senator, I would be able to help the boy."

"You have already helped him. The first time I saw him, he was a scrawny, pale little thing who jumped at every sound. Now look at him."

Aquila studied the child. He had the sturdy gait and speed of a natural athlete. His skin glowed with health, the multiple scratches he had earned on the streets long healed. He still kept himself too aloof from them; still viewed the world with a watchfulness that was unnatural in a child. But the senator had the right of it. Marcus had blossomed in his time with them. Aquila smiled softly, his heart thrumming with satisfaction.

"It's perfect," Aquila said as he emerged from the tiny kitchen. An actual kitchen, where his wife would have enough space to cook without bumping into samples of leather and knocking over awls and needles. The house to which Pudens had brought him could accommodate a shop on the street level, while providing plenty of living space on the second floor. A long chamber had ample room for their prayer gatherings. The building was arranged around a modest, roofless courtyard where Priscilla could grow herbs and vegetables. He could even plant a few rosebushes for her.

Of course, some of the walls were crumbling, the plaster had chipped and cracked, the floors were a mix of shattered stones and bare dirt, and no few birds and mice had made use of the chambers for the inevitable purpose. The place looked a ruin. Aquila loved it on sight.

"Will they wait a couple of months until I can put sufficient coin together?"

"No," Pudens said. "This property will be gone before the end of the week." He put his hand on Aquila's shoulder. "I wish to front you the money; repay me when you can."

Aquila shook his head. "Thank you, Senator. But—"

Before Aquila could finish his objection, the senator held up a hand. "Hear me out. You have been a gift to my family, you and Priscilla. You have been our patrons in God's Kingdom. Allow me, now, to become your patron here on earth. Not as the Romans understand the word, which would bind you to me in obligation. But as Christ would define it, bound together with friendship and charity. My patronage would lay no burdens upon you. Only let me repay to you some of the goodness you have shown us."

"You owe us no debt, Senator. You are dear to us. Everything we do, we do for the sake of love."

The senator's eyes grew wet with emotion. "What we have received from you and Priscilla has no price. The Lord returned my wife to me. Because of your guidance, my whole household is being transformed. We have never known such kindness from our slaves and servants. It's as if they work with affection rather than from compulsion. There are fewer disagreements among them. Our home has become a place of peace.

"Now, let me use my wealth and influence to do *your* family a good turn. Even if you had the funds to buy this place today, you would still need more to repair it. Concrete, plaster, paint, wood, furnishings, not to mention workmen. They all require coin. I will loan you what you need so you can move in as soon as possible. I know you are a man of honor, Aquila. I trust you to repay me.

"Besides, you have bags under your eyes from lack of sleep. You cannot continue coming to our house for our gatherings in the evenings and staying up half the night to complete your work. We need a different arrangement. But if I am to come to *your* lodgings, I want a decent dining room where I can eat a pleasant meal in comfort. Don't subject me to a dark hole on the Via Appia, where I will have to bear with the incessant noise of wagons headed to the outer reaches of the empire."

Aquila laughed. It seemed possible that he was about to buy his first house, thanks to the senator's desire for an agreeable meal and a convenient chamber in which to eat it.

Aquila and Benyamin hired professional masons for the heavy labor. It took the workmen a week to repair the broken concrete bricks on the outer walls of their new home and another to restore the leaky roof. Determined to spend as little as possible, Aquila resolved to do the rest of the repairs himself.

To save even more money, the family had agreed to give up their rented lodgings near the Via Appia and move to the new house as soon as the masons were finished with their work. Priscilla had spent most of the morning packing and piling their belongings onto two wagons. Now she stood in her own house, the first place she could truly call hers. She gulped, surveying the mountain of work that awaited them.

Some rooms were littered with mounds of rubble, the wreckage of years of neglect that had to be discarded. Most of the walls needed plastering, floors needed to be laid, shelves installed, doors constructed, curtains stitched, cushions made. Everything was filthy and needed scrubbing. She felt overwhelmed merely thinking of the list.

For today, she only had to focus on making one chamber habitable enough for them to sleep in. They chose the dining room because of its large size and the fact that it had sustained less damage than the other chambers. She and Lollia swept and washed the floor, where most of the original stones remained intact, including a rectangle of mosaics with a simple green leaf design in the center of the room. They cleaned the thick layers of spiderwebs and dust and other unmentionable deposits.

Benyamin and Aquila started transferring their belongings from the wagons, storing them in tidy piles in one corner of the chamber. Marcus helped them, insisting on carrying large handfuls, determined to show off how strong he was.

Ferox ran from room to room, sniffing everything, barking with happiness at the sudden expansion of his world. After a long absence, he returned to Priscilla, looking dusty. Tail wagging with fierce excitement, he dropped something carefully at her feet. Priscilla cried out in alarm as she identified his offering. A dead rodent.

"It's only a mouse," Marcus said sagely, squatting down to examine the animal more closely. He petted Ferox with approval. "Good boy. Go hunt down some more."

Priscilla made a strained sound in her throat, the closest she could come to affirming the dog's actions. She knew Marcus was right. If the creatures were inhabiting the house, they had to be found and expelled. But did Ferox have to drop them at her feet?

Marcus sniffed. "Don't worry Priscilla. I'll get rid of it. *I'm* not afraid." To her astonishment, the boy picked the dead rodent up by the tail and walked to the door, Ferox shadowing his steps.

Priscilla shivered, caught between pride in the boy's pluck and the disgust she felt for all rodents, be they living or expired.

When all signs of their little visitor had been cleared, she let out a relieved breath and turned to Lollia. "We can sleep here tonight.

It's clean enough. Do you want to make dinner while I help Aquila next door? He and Benyamin have started on the plaster."

Lollia nodded and flashed an ecstatic smile. "A real atrium, finally! Do you think he'll let me make my *garum* now?"

Garum was a salty fish sauce made with aromatic herbs and dead fish parts. Romans loved their *garum* and put it in almost every dish, even sweet ones. Many families had their own special recipe, which they guarded jealously. The first time Lollia had tried to make a batch in the Via Appia lodgings, Aquila had turned pale. Fish parts had to sit in the sun, curing with salt for many days before they were considered ready.

"You will run off my customers, Lollia," he had said, eyes watering. "You have to get rid of it."

While the finished product had a subtle aroma, Priscilla supposed that to someone not born in Rome, like Aquila, the stench produced during the process of preparation must seem unbearable. In fairness, even Romans drew the line when it came to their beloved sauce, demanding that the costly commercial *garum* factories move outside the city walls.

"I am not sure even a proper atrium is going to convince my husband to become a fan of our fish sauce, my dear," Priscilla said, unable to hide her smile. "An open courtyard is no match for that particular aroma."

As she made her way to the other side of the house, her lighthearted mood sank beneath the sobering sight of the tasks that awaited them. She had so little time to spare once her routine chores were accomplished that she could not imagine how she might also help transform this place into a home.

She spent the daylight hours working on their leather orders and Marcus's lessons, while also helping Lollia shop, cook, and keep house. She studied the Scriptures daily, trying to nourish her own soul, as well as meet the needs of their growing flock of Gentile believers and seekers. That left only the late evenings to help transform their crumbling house into a home. Though she already loved every brick in it, Priscilla felt unequal to the task that lay before her.

She was on her knees scrubbing the floor when Rufus and Mary arrived. Rufus turned in a circle and whistled. "It's delightful. But you are going to need help, my friend," he said.

Aquila grinned. "I was hoping you would offer."

"Give me a sheep and I'll make you a hide fit for a king." He scratched his beard. "Tiles and mortar, I am not sure about."

Aquila handed him a trowel and pointed him to a stone tub filled with wet plaster. "Try this. I have already prepared this section of the wall. You merely have to apply it." He watched Rufus at work before taking the trowel back and handing him a hammer and a length of wood. "We need a shelf here," he said, pointing to a corner.

Mary and Priscilla giggled when the shelf emerged crooked.

"You could put a taller stack on this side and a shorter one on the other. That will make it look even," Rufus said.

Wordlessly, Aquila took back the hammer and gave Rufus a sponge and a bucket filled with whitewash. "You can do this. I believe in you."

"By which you mean any fool could accomplish it."

Hours later, after Rufus and Mary had returned home, Priscilla realized that all of their sweat-drenched labor had hardly made a dent in even one chamber. And she still had to find their linens among the piles of their possessions and make everyone's beds. Her feet dragged as she went to the dining room, where they would all be sleeping for the foreseeable future. At the door she froze.

Marcus was putting the finishing touches to their bed, straightening the pillows. Noticing her, he stood very straight and pushed out his chest. He had laid out everyone's pallets, covering them with sheets and blankets. The beds had the look of an eight-year-old's touch, a bit wrinkled in places, with uneven edges.

They were the most beautiful sight Priscilla had ever seen.

The fact that she could crawl under her sheets and sleep without having to worry about one more chore left her weak with gratitude. To her embarrassment, she started to cry.

"Thank . . . you, Marcus," she sniffed.

The boy reached out a tentative hand to pat her on the forearm. "It's all right, Priscilla. Everything is going to be all right."

She fell to her knees and drew him into her arms. "You are a heaven-sent gift," she said against his cheek. His arms rose up and for the briefest moment they wrapped around her, holding her tightly. Priscilla's heart stopped.

As if caught off guard by his own actions, Marcus took a hasty step back. "Where do you poop around here?" he said, tucking his hands under his arms. "I've been meaning to ask all night."

Priscilla gave a watery grin. He had reverted back to being an eight-year-old boy faster than an Olympic runner could finish the short race. Then again, she wouldn't have it any other way.

Nineteen

IT FELT TO PRISCILLA as if she had barely laid her head on the pillow when she was awakened by an odd noise at dawn. "What is that?" she croaked, forcing her eyes open.

"It sounds like singing," Aquila said. "I know that song! It's Hebrew." Tossing the blankets aside, he dashed to the window.

Priscilla joined him. The whole of the synagogue at Campi seemed to have descended upon their doorstep. They had come, tools in hand, armed with chisels, shovels, brooms, one saw, and a few objects she could not name.

Rufus stood at the head of the crowd, a cheerful smile flashing through his dark beard. "I took one look at this place yesterday and knew you needed free labor, and lots of it."

Priscilla could not believe how many of the members from the synagogue had shown up. Even Sara had come, toting an ancient rag. Elizabeth had brought her son, who had started walking several weeks ago and toddled around at breakneck speeds.

Pudentiana chased after him while Elizabeth swept energetically. Sabinella had sent two of her slaves, both of whom had substantial building experience. Mary and a few of the other women had come bearing platters of hard-boiled eggs, cheese, bread, beans, and vegetables. No one would go hungry today.

"I can't believe all these people!" Priscilla said to Mary, her mouth agape.

"I can. See that man? You nursed his wife when she was ill. And that one? You looked after their baby for a whole week when he was thrown in jail and his wife had to go to the magistrates to try and free him. Recognize the woman with the white hair? That's Jerusha. You brought her food when her son was sick and could not work. They would have gone hungry except for you."

Priscilla swallowed the lump in her throat. She had never considered her minor acts of charity worthy of note. A little food here, a bit of help there. "What have I done to deserve their generosity? It's not as if I saved anyone's life," she murmured, thinking aloud.

Mary brushed away a stray curl from Priscilla's cheek. "You have spent yourself in places that gain you no great name on earth. But the effect you have on those around you is incalculable. The growing good of the world is partly dependent on unhistoric acts such as yours. My dear girl, the fact that things are not so ill with these folks and with my own heart as they might have been—" she took Priscilla's hand in her own and patted it—"is half owing to you for living faithfully a hidden life. A quiet life of sacrifice. So many of these people have come because they have tasted of your kindness. The rest appreciate what you have done for others."

Aquila, who had been busy giving directions, extricated himself from a group of men and came to her. Without a word, he took her into his arms. They held each other, her head on his shoulder, his hands encircling her waist.

"They have robbed me of words," Aquila said, his lips hot on her temple.

"And me."

They clung to each other, their hearts full, savoring the astounding joy of receiving so much.

Every day for a week, members of the synagogue came to help with the new house. Some arrived at dawn; others could only come later in the afternoons once they had finished laboring at their own jobs. In six days, they accomplished what Priscilla and Aquila could not have done in six months on their own.

By the time they finished, every room in the house sparkled. Walls were plastered and whitewashed, doors repaired, shelves installed for the shop, fresh stones laid on the ground and polished. The water tank in the floor beneath the atrium had been cleaned, repaired, and filled with clean water from the aqueduct, and the fireplace there, which heated the floors above in the winter months, reconstructed. Their small kitchen had been gutted and completely refurbished with a small clay oven and a long stretch of countertop where Priscilla and Lollia would have room to work side by side.

That final afternoon, when everyone had left, Priscilla visited the baths to wash away the sweat and grime of hard work, allowing the hot water in the steamy *caldarium* to loosen her sore muscles. She dipped her head under, holding her breath, eyes closed as warmth seeped under her skin and radiated into her bones.

The world became quiet underwater, sounds distilling into

faint vibrations. Sunk under that wet and still dome, she heard the beat of her own heart, and with every beat, she uttered a silent song of thanksgiving, a holy hallelujah for what God had accomplished on their behalf.

She broke the surface, engulfing a deep, hungry breath, lungs filling with life, the weight of the past weeks falling away with the dirt.

She returned home, her steps light. Home! For the first time, she and Aquila would have a private chamber, one they did not have to share with other people or with leather samples and bulky work paraphernalia. She entered their room softly, inhaling the scent of roses, which someone had left in a vase on a table next to their bed.

She was combing her hair when Aquila opened the door. "How did we come to own such a beautiful place?" he asked, his voice hushed with wonder. "It should have been impossible. We cannot afford this!"

Priscilla laughed. "Nothing is impossible with God." She shivered as the cool air found its way into the damp patches of her tunic where her wet hair clung to the linen in sinuous tendrils.

Aquila took a sharp breath. With a flex of his foot, he snapped the door shut behind him. Covering the distance between them in two long strides, he drew her against him. His kisses were butterflies against her neck. "I've missed you," he said.

She felt the familiar warmth that turned her bones into water as his kisses became bolder, his touch more urgent. Somehow, she found herself on the bed, a large muscular thigh straddling her side, arms supporting her shoulders and head. Aquila's touch grew wilder, more intimate.

At first she returned his passion, felt dizzy with it. Felt herself on the crest of some intangible delight. Then without warning, the feverish wanting dimmed and came to a halt. What had been a union, a twining of two into one, became instead a moment of disconcerting separation. Aquila, caught up in his own tide of desire, nevertheless sensed it in her, sensed the moment she closed like a submersed oyster.

Afterward as he lay next to her, his skin glistening with perspiration, his eyes narrowed with a frown he could not hide. "Is it me?" he asked softly in the darkness.

"What?" Priscilla's heart plummeted like a stone to the bottom of a deep well.

"I have noticed you . . . withdraw in the midst of our intimate times. And I am wondering if I am doing something wrong."

"No!" She pivoted toward him, dragging the sheets to cover herself. "You are perfect. Everything you do is perfect."

"Then what is it?"

She shook her head. "I do not know. I don't really understand it myself."

Aquila grew silent, considering her words. He laced her fingers with his and bent to kiss her very gently on the mouth. "We will have to be patient, then. Let your mind and body catch up with each other."

"Do you think they ever will?" she asked, sounding small.

He cradled her against him. "Someone wise told me that nothing is impossible with God."

She clung to that promise. Clung to the thought that one day, the shame that seemed to still inhabit the subterranean hollows of her heart would be overcome. That her body would discover the natural joy God had intended between man and wife. But somewhere in her mind she heard an echo, an accusing voice that declared God's promise would hold true for everyone but her.

Aquila had not told Priscilla, but for the past few weeks, worry had gnawed at the edges of his happiness. Worry that he might not be able to provide for his family the way he wished. That he might have let them down by allowing himself to buy a house that seemed more fantasy than good sense. Worry that his father's accusations would prove true after all.

A wave of gratitude washed through him as he thought of their home on the Aventine. The fangs of anxiety which had sunk deep into him the moment he had purchased the house finally loosened. Seeing with his own eyes what God had accomplished, Aquila began to realize that he need not agonize about meeting the financial responsibilities that still lay before him. The Lord had provided this far. Aquila had to learn to trust that God would continue to provide.

This is God's *house!* he thought with sudden comprehension. *His to use as he wishes. We are merely stewards of it.*

As if to confirm that conclusion, Rufus visited them on the same evening, carrying a large box. Inside, he had nestled a tall stack of plates and bowls made from red-glazed pottery. "If you are going to host God's church in your home, you need more plates than the five you currently own."

Priscilla laughed. "These are lovely," she said.

Aquila relieved Rufus of the heavy burden, warmed by his words even more than his generosity. "Thank you, friend."

"Your grace knows no bounds," Priscilla added.

"Before you two go on with your praises, let me tell you what I have been thinking." Rufus settled himself on the couch, another gift, this one from Sabinella, who claimed she had too many of them crowding her villa.

Rufus picked up the colorful pillow resting next to him, his fingers plumping feathers that needed no plumping. "Watching our friends labor side by side here, I realized something. We cannot keep silent anymore. It's time to tell the whole congregation about Yeshua. The prophecies of old have been fulfilled. They need to know!"

Aquila paused. "I feel it too, the need to share our good news with them. But surely such a public step will break that precious unity we witnessed in this house. We have been making inroads. You have over a dozen Jews meeting in your house. Priscilla and I have twice as many among the Gentiles. Wouldn't it be better to continue slowly? Otherwise, the synagogue may split, and friend turn against friend."

From the loose folds of his belt, Rufus withdrew a roll of papyrus, its cream-and-ivory striations marked with dark ink.

Without opening it, Rufus said, "Before we came to Rome last year, my mother and I stopped at Antioch. While visiting the church there, we befriended a man named Paul who comes from Tarsus. You will hear that name again, mark my words. Like his fathers, Paul was trained as a rabbi, whip-sharp and knowledgeable, a firebrand of faith. He and one of the leaders of the church named Barnabas had just been appointed by the Holy Spirit to travel through the region and share the gospel. He has recently returned from that journey." Rufus tapped the papyrus on his knee. "Today I received this letter in which he writes about his experiences."

Aquila felt a frisson of excitement. "What does he say?"

"They began by speaking in the synagogue at Antioch of Pisidia. At first, the people proved receptive, asking Paul and Barnabas to return and speak the following week. Many Gentiles became believers, Aquila! But some of the Jewish members of the synagogue provoked the leaders of the city and they incited a mob against Paul and Barnabas and ran them out of town."

Aquila ran an agitated hand through his hair. "This is precisely why I think we should wait."

"I know. I felt the same until I read this letter." Rufus shook the rolled papyrus in his hand for emphasis. "They stirred up trouble, I grant you. But God used them powerfully. Because of Paul and Barnabas, the Lord's message has advanced throughout that region. It spreads like an unstoppable flame. They gain followers for Jesus by the dozens. Hundreds, even.

"They suffer for it wherever they go. Danger surrounds them, and yet they press on. When they went to Iconium, Paul and Barnabas barely escaped a mob that wanted to stone them. But everywhere they preached, people came to faith, and they made many disciples."

"You mean it is worth the price," Priscilla said. "Even if preaching the gospel openly should mean we cause dissent in the synagogue or encounter resistance."

Rufus nodded. "Likely we will encounter far worse than mere resistance. It is no easy thing I ask.

"The crowds stoned Paul in Lystra. *Stoned* him! Then they dragged him out of town and left him for dead. He writes—" Rufus unfurled his letter and scanned the page before starting to read. "'I opened my eyes to a ring of faces. They were getting ready to bury me, I think. I told them not to be hasty, rose to my feet, and returned to town. The next day, we traveled to Derbe, where many more put their trust in the Lord.'"

Aquila inhaled sharply. A miracle that the man had survived a stoning. Most would have abandoned their purpose following such an experience. Returned home after paying so steep a price. And yet this Paul of Tarsus had picked himself up, wounded and bloody as he must have been, and continued on.

He had willingly risked another stoning, more suffering, in order that some may receive the message that had the power of life.

He stared at his hands, steepled between his knees. The way to wisdom was paved with caution. But when caution itself became the destination, a man's heart could become irresolute. And miss the call of destiny. He turned to Priscilla. "What do you think?"

She twined her fingers into his. "I think it is time we see this house bursting with new believers."

Priscilla watched her husband with pride. On the Sabbath, he had read from the prophet Isaiah in the synagogue, and after closing the scroll, he had fearlessly, and with aching conviction, told his brothers and sisters about Yeshua. A storm had broken loose after his final declaration: "Everyone who believes in him is made right in God's sight."

The walls of the small synagogue had reverberated with a thousand questions. Bitter objections had clashed against hopeful inquiries. Two hours later, the clamor of screeching voices had drawn a couple members of the urban cohorts to investigate the source of the commotion. The members of the synagogue had finally calmed down then and apologized for disturbing the neighborhood, mollifying the cohorts with the promise not to cause such a tumult again.

Almost half the synagogue had wanted to know more about Yeshua after that quarrelsome beginning. Fifty of them had gathered at Priscilla's home tonight, seeking answers. Seeking fresh hope.

Aquila cleared his voice as he stood in the midst of the gathering, every eye trained on him. "Most of you have heard of Jonah, the reluctant prophet who ran away. We may not be prophets, but many of us know something about running away. We run away from duty, from sacrifice, from love. We run away from God when what he wants costs too much.

"Today I want to tell you about one who did not run away from God's difficult call." He stopped for a moment as if to collect his thoughts. "Like Jonah, we are pursued by storms and monsters. By temptations and sins and death itself. And they swallow us whole, as Jonah's fish swallowed him. There is no running from death. One day it shall consume our flesh. No one has the power to overcome its hideous appetite. Except for God himself.

"And that is what he did. His Son spent three days in the belly of the greatest monster of all, three days in a tomb, three days dead, his body rotting. On the third day, he rose from death. He willingly faced the monster that swallows us all in order to win the victory for *us*. Death and sin cannot rule us any longer, because Yeshua conquered them on the cross.

"Now, instead of death, it is God himself who pursues us, pursues us like a shepherd seeks his lambs. Like a father pursues sons and daughters who are lost. Like a bridegroom pursues his beloved bride. We can choose Yeshua and find forgiveness for our offenses. We can find healing for our wounds, mercy for our mistakes."

One of the God fearers, Julia, a freedwoman who had once

served as slave in a patrician family, asked, "Is this Yeshua like Orpheus, who followed his wife, Eurydice, into the underworld after she died of snakebite?"

Aquila turned to Priscilla. "I believe my wife can answer you better than I, Julia."

Priscilla smiled. "There are some similarities. In a way, Orpheus overcame death. He saved Eurydice by singing so sweetly that Hades, the god of the underworld, allowed him to take her back to the world of the living."

All the Gentiles, familiar with the story, nodded their heads.

"Orpheus's story is an anomaly, however. Death always wins, and the pagan gods cannot gainsay it. Hades does not give up its residents. In Eurydice's case, we see a singular exception where love overcomes death. An exception that demonstrates the power of love. In this, the story of Orpheus is accurate. But it is only a story.

"Jesus is the Truth. Within him resides perfect love and cosmic power, the divine and human comingled, blood and spirit married in pure union, so that he alone can conquer death. Not as an exception, but as a promise that shall not fail any who follow him."

They talked late into the evening after that, husband and wife taking turns to answer their guests' many questions.

Priscilla knew how to instruct the Gentiles. She had taught the household of Pudens before that night. But that had felt different. She had been sharing with friends, not teaching a newborn church. The first night the members of the synagogue at Campi gathered in her home, Priscilla rose up to lead alongside her husband. They became more than man and wife. They became ministers of the gospel together. They had not talked about this shift beforehand. Her new role in the church came not so much from planning and discussion as from a natural response to need, a flowering of the gift God had planted within her.

She went to sleep that night, the words of the prophet Isaiah resounding in her mind. *"To do his work, his strange work, and perform his task, his alien task."*

Yeshua had entrusted her with a strange work. An alien task. What Roman woman even dreamed of becoming a spiritual leader? This peculiar divine mission both terrified and thrilled her. She might not have been able to fulfill such an unusual calling without Aquila's encouragement. He proved her staunchest supporter, urging her to use her training and natural talent for the glory of God.

Even with Aquila's unbroken support, every time she spoke either to a crowd or to an individual, something inside her learned afresh that without Yeshua himself, she could not accomplish what was asked of her. In the ebb of her weakness, she felt the flow of God, pouring in, filling her more, turning her weakness into his strength.

Twice a week, she and Aquila hosted the gathering of new believers and seekers in their home. One night for the members of the synagogue at Campi and another for Senator Pudens and his household.

With each passing week, more believers joined their numbers. Benyamin, Aquila, and Rufus took turns spreading the gospel among the other synagogues as well, and soon their numbers multiplied.

They began to witness baptisms, at first sporadically, and then on a weekly basis. Though Senator Pudens declared himself not yet ready for such a leap, he never missed a gathering unless the responsibilities of the senate prevented him from coming. And along with him, a small trickle of other Roman noblemen and -women started to attend their weekly gatherings.

In the passing of months, the Word of God spread across Rome, finding a home among prince and pauper, free and slave, male and female. And God used Priscilla as his instrument every bit as much as he used her husband.

Twenty

"WE ARE GOING to the baths today, Marcus," Aquila said. He had cornered the boy in the atrium, where he lay sprawled on his belly, soaking up the sun, practicing his writing on a wax-covered wooden tablet.

Marcus shifted. "I am too busy studying. Besides, I already washed with the bucket."

"Regardless, we are going to the baths."

Marcus sprang to his feet and began taking backward steps. "I need to work on the leather squares Benyamin asked me to stitch."

Knowing from experience how slippery the boy could be, Aquila flashed out a hand and grabbed his collar. "Baths. Now."

"I don't want to go!" the boy shouted.

"I had noticed."

Marcus began struggling in earnest. "You're not my father! You can't tell me what to do."

Aquila stilled. "Who *is* your father?"

The boy stared back mute.

"Exactly. You live with us. That means you abide by our rules."

"I don't belong to you! I can leave anytime I want."

Aquila inhaled a sharp breath. "You can, Marcus. But I hope you will not because I have grown to love you. All of us have. Very much." He knelt before the boy so they were eye to eye. "Like a son."

The rebellious mask crumbled. The boy's lips trembled. "I don't want to leave you."

"Good."

"But I don't want to go to the baths."

"Can you explain why?"

Marcus shrugged. "I just don't."

"Marcus, let me tell you the difference between love and indulgence. It would be easier for me to give in to you. To let you have what you want. Easier for me not to waste my time reasoning with you. So much easier to have your friendship than your resentment. If I do the easy thing now, then I would be giving you indulgence."

"Excellent!" Marcus cried. "That's what I want. Go ahead. Give it to me."

Aquila ignored the outburst. "You would feel a momentary relief by having your way now. But in the long run, indulgence will harm you."

"No. It won't. I promise."

"Yes, it will. You need to learn to overcome. To face your fears. Indulgence cannot give you strength to face the challenges of life. Love can. Love rarely indulges. Instead, it requires you to make the difficult choices. The right ones. The ones that heal and restore."

"Love sounds really hard."

"It can be. But this is what I promise: We will go together. I will not leave your side. Not for one moment. You will not have to face this fear alone. Love never leaves. Never abandons. I want you to learn the difference, Marcus. Because all your life, you will have to choose. Choose between love or indulgence."

"Then I would like to choose indulge . . . indulgement today."

"No, Marcus. You have been making that choice for too long. Yeshua *loves*. So you must learn to choose love. Sometimes, when you are weary and overwhelmed, God will indulge you. But never as a way of life. If you don't learn with me, with us, how to be loved, then for the rest of your life you will tilt toward indulgence. Hunger to have what you want in the moment to satisfy the demands of fear.

"So I am asking you, Son. Will you trust me? Come with me to the baths? Let us face this terror together."

Marcus swallowed. "I . . . Can't you indulge me one more day? You can love me tomorrow."

"I can't. It will not be any easier tomorrow."

A whimper escaped the child. He clutched his belly as if it ached. Then his chin moved in a sudden downward motion, giving assent.

Aquila laid his hand on one slight shoulder and tapped it with approval. He let his hand remain there, warm and strong, a tether of safety, as they walked outside and made their way to the baths. Their house, though large and in many ways luxurious, was not extensive enough to contain its own bathing facility. Aquila chose a smaller, private establishment, which would not be as crowded as a municipal bath.

At the entrance, he paid a fee that allowed them to store their clothes with the attendant. They headed for the tepidarium, a great hall with vaulted ceilings, which housed the warm pool. He felt the boy shiver under his hand as they approached the bath.

"Shall we go in together?"

Marcus sucked the tip of his thumb. "Can we sit at the edge and dangle our feet in the water first?"

"We can."

Aquila sat close to the child. He was shaking violently now, though the room was comfortably warm. Part of Aquila felt tempted to call a halt. To cry, *Enough*. They had come far enough. Then he hardened his resolve. The next time would only grow more dreadful for the boy.

"Shall we go in? I will go first, and then you follow."

Marcus nodded. His lips had turned a strange shade of blue, as though the very breath had left him. They trembled so much, he could hardly form words. Aquila dropped into the water, careful to keep his hand on the boy's leg as he did.

"Now you."

Marcus slithered closer. His fingers clutched the edge of the pool so hard, they turned white.

"You can do it, Marcus. Ask Yeshua for strength. I am here. I won't leave you."

Marcus gritted his teeth, winced as if in pain, and jumped. Aquila caught him and held him for a long, comforting moment before releasing him in the water. Marcus clung to him like a barnacle. Aquila took a step away from the side, bringing Marcus with him deeper into the pool. Then another step.

The boy's teeth were chattering, his eyes squeezed shut.

"Marcus. Open your eyes."

Brown eyes opened with reluctance.

"You did it, Marcus! You did it!"

The child looked around him quickly, then brought his gaze back to Aquila. Without warning, he broke down, large silent tears coursing down his cheeks. His chest heaved as he took great shuddering breaths.

In the months since he had lived with them, Aquila had not seen him cry. Not once. This silent wailing did not resemble the tears of a child so much as the dammed-up strain of deep anguish.

"I saw him! I saw him drown," he gasped.

As quickly as he could manage, Aquila picked up the boy and carried him out of the pool. "You saw who drown?"

"My father."

In a blur of motion, Aquila grabbed their clothes, wrapped Marcus in his own cloak, and herded him to a sheltered corner of the gardens where the sun could warm his chilled flesh. "Your father drowned?" he asked gently, his hand still on the boy's back, a shield from this storm of memory.

"In the pool at home."

"You saw this?"

The dark eyes widened in memory. "My father and I were bathing together. He had sent the slave to bring wine, but the slave never returned. I climbed out of the pool to fetch a sword I had carved myself. I wanted to show it to him. We did not spend much time together. Father always seemed so busy.

"I was in the alcove searching through my pile when I heard voices. I thought the slave had returned. Then the voices became louder as if in quarrel. Surprised, I stuck my head out of the alcove to see why the slave dared to raise his voice when speaking to my father. But it was not the slave. It was my uncle."

"Your uncle?"

"My father's younger brother. They did not get along. My uncle was always in trouble. He shouted, 'You can't do this. He is not of age!'

"My father shouted back, 'I can do whatever I want. You are no heir of mine. I am ashamed of you. I aim to make the boy my sole heir.'"

Marcus started to weep again, his little body shaking, straining to capture a lungful of air. "Father started to climb out of the water. His back was to my uncle. My uncle moved so fast, I almost missed it. He struck my father from behind. Struck him in the head with the hilt of his dagger. I *saw* him do it!"

Marcus folded in on himself, fists clamped around the fabric of Aquila's cloak. "Father lost his footing and fell to his knees in the pool. My uncle grabbed him by the hair and shoved him underwater."

"Oh, Marcus!" Aquila stared at the child in horror. No wonder he was afraid of going to the baths.

"I ran out of the alcove and told him to stop. I had found my wooden sword, and I tried to beat him with it. To save my father. But I did not know what I was doing and he knocked it out of my hand."

The boy went silent. His next words emerged hushed. Raw. "My father drowned before my eyes and I could not stop it. When his body floated to the top, I knew he was gone."

"That's why you ran away?"

"Not then. I could not escape my uncle when he grabbed me. He is a large man. Larger even than you. 'I am master of this house now,' he said. And he was! My father had not had a chance to make me his heir yet."

"Your mother?"

"Died birthing me. My uncle was now the paterfamilias, the new head of the household, and had the power to do with me what he wished. I was only eight. I had no right to deny him."

Aquila felt his mouth turn dry. "Merciful God. What did he do?"

"He gave me to a servant of his and charged him to sell me as a slave in the cinnabar mines. On the way to the traders, I acted like a helpless baby, whimpering and crying, begging the servant for mercy. When he relaxed his guard, thinking me beaten, I ran away and lost him in the market crowds."

Aquila shook his head in wonder. "You are an amazing boy!" He caressed the child's head. "What did you do after that?"

"I tried to sneak back home. I thought I could ask one of our old servants to help me. But then I overheard two of my uncle's men talking together. He had set a reward on me. Ten thousand silver denarii, alive or dead."

Aquila whistled. That was almost twice as much as a Praetorian Guard earned annually, and they earned more than most. "You are worth a lot."

Marcus went rigid. It took Aquila a moment to understand the boy's discomfort. "That's why you never confided your name to us? You were afraid we would betray you for the reward?"

Marcus flushed. "You said yourself, I am worth a lot."

Aquila nodded. "I understand your caution. But, Son, the hand of the Lord has guided you to safety. All these months you have lived with us, you must know by now. There are not denarii enough in this world to tempt me to give you up."

Marcus stared at him for a moment. The air leaked out of his narrow chest in a great heave. Then, so swiftly Aquila was caught off guard, he launched himself into the man's arms and clung to him, fingers clutching with ferocious strength born of trust and need and hope. Aquila's eyes filled. His hands wrapped around the boy, gripping him just as tightly, holding him in the haven of his arms.

When Marcus had first come to them, Aquila had not wanted to keep him. He had thought the child would cause too much disruption and bring all manner of trouble upon them. Now, as he held him, he was struck by the depths of love he had for the boy. Made speechless with it. In a way, he had been proven right, for Marcus had brought a baggage full of heavy troubles. His uncle might well prove a fatal enemy. Not for a moment did Aquila regret the cost of sheltering him. Having discovered his history only made him love the child more. He would fight tooth and nail to protect him.

"Marcus Laurentinus Jovian." Priscilla said the name slowly. "The son of Vibius Laurentinus."

"You knew him?" Aquila asked.

"I knew *of* him. A regular visitor to the palace and a personal friend of Claudius, by all accounts. A man of influence and no small wealth. His death came as a shock. They fished his body out of the Tiber. Everyone assumed he had fallen afoul of thieves."

"Not according to Marcus."

Priscilla clutched her chest. "To think of that child witnessing such a thing. Vibius's younger brother, Aulus, has been in one scandal after another since youth. But to murder his own brother!"

"And Marcus is the sole witness." Aquila paced, long legs carrying him from one wall to the other in the confines of their chamber, where they had retreated for this private exchange. "That child's life remains in grave danger because he can identify his uncle as the murderer. Aulus will not feel safe until he is rid of Marcus. I finally understand why the boy runs aground every time a wealthy patron visits the shop. He is afraid he will be recognized. And betrayed."

"Aquila." Priscilla clutched her tunic with hands slippery from perspiration. "I must go to Claudius. I must tell him what we know. We have to try and find justice for the boy, protect him from Aulus, and return his inheritance to him."

Aquila nodded. "Will he receive you? He is Caesar, after all, with a world to run. Will he even listen to you? Bother to take action on behalf of a child?"

Priscilla remembered her brief meeting with Claudius almost two years ago. The sharp, clear gaze of the old man in whose hands rested the fate of an empire. "If I can manage to gain an audience, I think he will prove receptive. He has a reputation for fairness. I think he will not endure such an outrage against a member of the aristocracy, not to mention a friend, if the gossip be true. But we must bring Marcus before him so he can give his testimony."

"Therein lies the danger. I have no doubt Aulus will have his men stationed near the palace for this very eventuality. They could seize Marcus before we have a chance to set foot inside the Palatine, and we would have no power to stop them. We have no legal right to the child. He belongs to his uncle."

She nodded slowly. "I must approach the emperor alone. Explain the situation. If he is convinced by my account, he can send the Praetorian Guard to fetch Marcus. Then he will hear Marcus's testimony from his own lips."

Twenty-One

PRISCILLA DECIDED TO TAKE a covered litter to the Palatine, a necessary expense if she wanted to make a good impression. Rome's streets had turned into rivers of mud since an unceasing deluge had started three days previously. Arriving in the palace with filth caking the hem of her tunic would hardly inspire the officials on duty to think her worthy of an audience with the emperor.

The men carrying her litter were of uneven height, causing the litter to pitch forward as they bumped along the busy streets. Priscilla clung to the pole, wondering if she would have bruises by the end of her ride.

She straightened her tunic and palla when she disembarked, feeling like her internal organs might have shifted to different parts of her body. Murmuring a short prayer under her breath, she entered the Palatine. Even this far from the inner sanctum of Claudius's residence, Praetorian Guards stood at strategic spots, keeping the activity in the outer courts of the palace under sharp scrutiny.

Priscilla approached a man sitting behind a desk. He was dressed in a sleeveless Greek tunic and wore his thin hair long. Likely an imperial slave, she guessed, a highly educated man who, in spite of his enslaved status, carried a good deal of authority.

She stood before the desk, waiting for him to look up. He did not. "Your business," he said as he continued writing, his ink-stained hands moving with furious speed.

"I wish to see the emperor."

"You and half the empire. Business?"

"It's private."

The man glanced up briefly. "State your business or shove off."

If her father had been alive, she would have been granted an audience within moments. As an unknown woman, she carried little influence.

"I am the daughter of General Priscus. I demand to see Caesar on an urgent matter. Now, if you please."

The official gave a protracted sigh and set his pen aside. "Everyone has an urgent matter."

Priscilla lifted her chin in annoyance. How was she to get past this pesky official?

Her eyes narrowed as her gaze fell on a familiar figure across the wide, marble-covered hall. Dressed in a tunic made from rarest heliotrope silk, an extravagance that could have purchased as many as twelve slaves, the woman presented the epitome of elegance. Antonia! As the emperor's favored niece, she had free access to Claudius, no doubt.

Antonia caught sight of Priscilla almost at the same moment. She considered her coolly, then turned on her heels and approached.

"What are *you* doing here?" she asked.

Priscilla adjusted her plain green palla. Antonia always had a way of making her feel inferior. "I am trying to gain an audience with the emperor."

"For what purpose?"

Priscilla felt the blood rushing to her face. She could not speak Marcus's name in this public place. Nor did she trust Antonia with such a perilous secret. "On a private matter."

"I see." Antonia flicked the ostrich feather fan she held in one hand. "Wait here. I'll see whether he will deign to accommodate you."

"My thanks!" Priscilla exclaimed to Antonia's retreating back, her words drowned out by the clicking of her bejeweled shoes.

She waited a long time, watching the shadows lengthen on the sundial outside. To her surprise, rather than sending a servant, Antonia returned in person.

"He does not wish to see you."

Priscilla's heart sank. "He is busy today? I could return tomorrow."

"My uncle does not wish to see you at any time. At all. It is better that you cease to pester him before you irk him in earnest." She tapped a restless foot on the marble. "Well? Why are you still standing here? Clear out."

"Why would Claudius refuse you so utterly?" Aquila asked, his forehead furrowed. "Is there some enmity between you?"

Priscilla dropped her palla to her drooping shoulders. "He hardly knows me. We only met the once, and he seemed pleasant enough then."

"Could Antonia have poisoned him against you?"

Priscilla thought of their history, of the secret she knew that could destroy the young woman. Antonia would never be able to look at Priscilla without remembering that day. Priscilla's very presence was an indictment. "I fear she could."

"For what purpose?"

She felt herself flush. Though they had no secrets, she still found it hard to speak of that day. "I saw Antonia in the physician's house. When I . . . when I was with child."

It took Aquila a moment to comprehend her meaning. "Did she . . . ?"

"She did."

"And she holds that against you?"

"It seems likely. No woman wants a witness to her worst indiscretion."

Aquila drew her into his arms. "No matter. We will try again. Seek another audience with Caesar. Perhaps I can ask Senator Pudens for his aid."

Priscilla nodded. It seemed like a sound plan. Pudens would be willing to help them, especially once they explained Marcus's situation. But she could not dispel an underlying sense of dread that had settled on her like a millstone.

The synagogue at Campi had turned into a cauldron of bubbling trouble. Those who opposed Yeshua had turned against those who were drawn to him. Every Sabbath spiraled into a drawn-out argument with raised voices hurling accusations. Rufus and Benyamin did what they could to calm those in the congregation who denied Yeshua as the promised Messiah. They might as well have tried to put out a house fire with a cup of water.

On the Sabbath following her visit to the Palatine, Priscilla and her family arrived at the synagogue early so they could pray before the services began. She smiled when she spotted Rufus and Mary ambling down the road toward them.

As the others filed inside, she lingered to speak with Rufus. She wanted to hear how the group gathering at his house was progressing. Since they were all Jewish, they were under greater pressure from the rest of the congregations.

Priscilla noticed a man walking directly toward them and turned to smile, thinking he might be a member of the synagogue. She did not recognize his face, which was round and pockmarked, dominated by a bulbous nose and thin lips. He stared at her boldly, his eyes a strange pale hazel that reminded her of a wild tiger. Her smile faltered. The man continued to approach them with purposeful steps.

"Watch out!" Rufus cried with sudden alarm as the man withdrew a short sword from the folds of his cloak.

Not again, Priscilla thought.

She could not remember screaming, though the sound reverberated in the narrow street. Rufus lunged in front of her just as the man slashed the sword in a fierce arc.

The blade descended into Rufus's chest.

Rufus's sudden leap forward had made his gait unsteady and he pitched backward, crashing into Priscilla. The deadly edge of steel found its mark on Rufus's flesh, and he gasped as his tunic parted in a sharp, diagonal line. Blood bloomed on the fabric covering his chest.

But the assailant's aim proved short. Having been directed at Rufus's original position, the sword slash lacked the power to gut him as he had intended and merely wounded him. Ruthlessly, the assailant shoved Rufus's sagging form out of the way and, raising his bloodied sword, turned on Priscilla.

"Time to die," he said.

The world turned hazy and sluggish, making Priscilla feel as if she were moving through an eerie landscape of molten wax. Every sense grew more acute, the air carrying with each inhalation the iron tang of Rufus's blood, mingling with the salt of her own sweat. Fear had a taste, she discovered. It tasted bitter and briny and sulfurous. She could not get it out of her mouth.

Its stinging bite sharpened her responses, giving Priscilla the power to move. In desperation, she threw her palla at the assassin, blinding him for an instant. She dropped to the ground and, before he could adjust his stance to her new position, rocked back on her bottom and kicked him in the knees as hard as she could, using both feet. He hissed and staggered. Regaining his balance, he raised the deadly steel, aiming it at Priscilla's neck.

Without warning, a small projectile hit the man on the temple. His head recoiled from the impact, blood spurting into his eye and cheek. He swore and grabbed his head. Priscilla saw Aquila running toward them, barely slowing to pick up another stone from the ground and taking aim. Rufus, who had managed to regain his feet, tottered toward them from the opposite direction.

Unwilling to give up when his prey lay so close and helpless, the assailant aimed the sword straight at Priscilla's throat and slashed down with all his might. The blood running into his eyes made his aim sloppy, and the metal's edge scraped against the wall as it descended toward Priscilla. The tip, hot from the sun, sank into Priscilla's skin where her neck joined her shoulder. She felt a sharp, shallow pain and held her breath, expecting the agony of torn muscles and broken bones to follow. But the pain never came.

Another projectile had found the man, making him reel with pain, slackening his momentum behind the short sword. He roared with frustration, withdrew the weapon back to his side, and ran.

Aquila fell to one knee. "You are bleeding!"

Priscilla touched the wound and winced. Her fingers came away with a thin smear of blood. "He barely cut me, thanks to you. I am all right."

Aquila hauled her into his arms. "You have to stop this! You have to stop trying to get killed."

Priscilla huffed, weak laughter mingling with heaving breaths that hardly seemed to fill her lungs. With a gasp, she pulled away. "Rufus!" she said, her mind starting to work again. "He's injured."

"Rufus?" Aquila turned.

Their friend was leaning against the wall, hand on his lacerated chest, his skin unnaturally pale. "You owe me a new tunic," he said before sinking to the ground in a dead faint.

They brought Rufus into the synagogue and laid him carefully on the ground. Mary, noting the stain on her son's chest, dropped by his side. "Mercy, Lord! Is he dead?"

Rufus stirred. "I am not. Don't order any graveclothes."

Benyamin, who had been examining the cut, straightened and laid a comforting hand on Mary's shoulder. "Even though there is copious blood, it's a superficial wound. He just fainted from the shock, I think. He'll be on his feet in no time at all."

Rufus lifted his head and examined his torso. "It may not be deep, but it is long. No need to make me sound delicate because I lost consciousness."

"Indeed. Rufus saved my life at peril to his own," Priscilla said.

"You see? I am a hero." Rufus grinned.

Priscilla was relieved to see his color returning. Aquila insisted on pulling her aside and washing her own small wound, binding it with clean cloths that kept slipping, thanks to his unsteady fingers.

The other members of the congregation had started to trickle in. Someone called the urban cohorts, reporting the attack. By the time the soldiers arrived, there was another heated argument in progress. Somehow, several of those present had arrived at the conclusion that the onslaught had happened as a direct consequence of their teachings on Yeshua.

"This is what happens when you spread lies!" a man named Ezra yelled. "This is what comes of all this nonsense about Christus," he added, using the Latin term for the Christ.

Priscilla, still shaken by the incomprehensible events of that morning, watched in horror as several men came to blows right in front of the members of the urban cohorts.

The soldiers had their hands full calming the heated altercation.

"Who is this Christus?" a Roman soldier asked lazily.

"He is the leader of these people. They are Chrestians," Ezra said, mispronouncing the name.

The soldier picked his teeth with the tip of his blade. "Where is this fellow, Christus? Can he not speak for himself?"

"As a matter of fact, he can't. He was last seen at the top of a Roman cross. He is a criminal. And these people follow him."

"He is not a criminal!" Elizabeth shouted. "And he was last seen alive and well by hundreds of people."

"You see?" Ezra said. "What did I tell you? You should arrest them all. They cause no end of trouble."

The cohort soldier twirled his dagger between dexterous

fingers. "You are all troublemakers, as far as I am concerned. Your neighbors have been complaining about you and the unrest you have been causing the past few months. And if that isn't enough, this is the second synagogue that has broken out into fighting over the past week. I will have to make a report of this business."

"And Festus does not like writing reports," the second soldier said, shoving a finger into Ezra's thin chest and pushing him back. "Not one bit."

Twenty-Two

LIKE A LOOSE THREAD in an unfinished weaving, Priscilla's well-ordered world unraveled by virtue of one capricious judgment. Following the attack at the synagogue and the report from the urban cohorts, Claudius issued a vicious and comprehensive edict that would change many lives forever. With a speed that left them reeling, he banished all Jews who were not citizens of Rome.

His harsh backlash made no sense, for though an annoyance, the Jewish disturbance had hardly merited such a punishment. Hitherto, Claudius had shown himself lenient with the people of Israel. In fact, upon ascending the throne, he had reverted Caligula's insistence that there be a statue of the emperor in the Temple of Jerusalem and permitted the Jews to observe their religious laws freely in all parts of the empire.

Why such a small problem in the synagogues even found its way before the emperor remained a mystery. But once it did, it elicited an immediate and implacable response.

The emperor's edict did not affect the majority of Jews living in the city since most were Roman citizens. Descendants of slaves, many of them had been emancipated by Caesar Augustus over sixty years earlier. But those of Jewish descent who had no Roman citizenship, like Aquila, were required to leave Rome within forty-eight hours.

Priscilla and Aquila approached Pudens as soon as they heard the news. Though concerned, Priscilla did not truly believe that such a decree could affect them personally. Aquila was married to the daughter of a celebrated Roman general, after all. Surely Claudius could be reasoned with to make an exception in their case.

The senator could do nothing until morning, when he would seek an audience with Claudius. Husband and wife returned home, praying that by the next day their troubles would be resolved.

As soon as the sun rose, Aquila and Benyamin left to deliver a tent, taking Marcus with them. Priscilla was surprised when Pudens arrived at her door two hours later, covered in sweat, holding the reins of his horse.

"I have bad news," he said by way of greeting. "Your name and Aquila's are on the emperor's manifest as noted troublemakers. You are to be expelled from Rome."

Priscilla's legs gave way, and she folded down onto the nearest couch. "But why? What crime have we committed that we should turn Caesar against us?"

"He received your names from a source he trusts, accusing you of rabble-rousing and worse. That same source brought the disturbance in the synagogues to his attention in the first place."

"Who?" Priscilla said, her voice a whisper. But she already knew.

"His niece, Antonia. Claudius has a tendency to be fooled by women. I told you Antonia was trouble. But he trusts her. Why has she turned on you?"

Priscilla rested her forehead on a shaking hand. "I know something about her that would ruin her standing with Claudius. She probably believes that I plan to betray her."

"I am sorry, my dear." Pudens shook his head. "You must leave Rome. Leave by tomorrow evening, or Claudius will set his hounds on you. In time, his anger may cool. For now, he grows irritated at the very mention of the name of Christus. I did not dare tell him that I myself follow the man, or he would no doubt have turned his wrath on me as well."

Priscilla flinched. "I understand. It is no longer safe for you." She felt as if the ground beneath her feet had turned to sea, and she was sinking under the swelling waves. Trying to press past the confusion, she asked, "What happens to our house? Will it be confiscated?"

"No. Caesar's mandate only demands banishment. It mentions nothing about property. You will remain owners here. Do not worry about this place. I will take care of it, I promise you," the senator vowed.

Priscilla ran a tired hand over her eyes. "Will you have to sell it?" The question felt like a razor on her tongue. She did not wish to lose her home.

"Not unless you want me to. Aquila has discharged all his debts to me. You need not worry on that score. God knows, the boy worked his fingers to the bone to pay me off.

"I suggest we rent the house while you are gone. That way, when you return, it will be waiting for you. Houses like this are rare in the Aventine. I'll send you the rent I collect so you can pay for new lodgings. Where will you go? Will you return to Pontus?"

"I doubt it. In truth, I have no idea where we are headed." Priscilla slumped forward. "It has not been a year since we settled here. Now we must begin afresh."

Pudens patted her hand. "You must be strong. For Aquila and Marcus. They need you."

Priscilla gulped down her tears and nodded. After Pudens left, she fell to her knees. She felt paralyzed by the enormity of what faced her. Leave their friends. Abandon the growing church. Walk away from their home. Desert those she felt called to help. Aquila had to forsake his growing business. They would have no means of finding justice for Marcus now, though at least, away from Rome, he would be safe from his uncle's deadly plots.

Oh, Yeshua, I am overcome. We are homeless! Where shall we go? I feel crushed between the sorrow of this hour and the dread that hangs over our future.

Aquila arrived an hour later from Trastevere. Priscilla, already packing, rose up and, without a word, ran to him.

He wrapped her in his arms. "Bad, is it?"

She told him Pudens's news, trying to hold her tears at bay. Aquila ran a soothing hand through her hair. Down her arm. Then he grew very still. "How did Antonia know about the disturbance at the synagogue? How was she able to report that incident to Caesar? I wonder . . ."

"What?" She pulled away to stare at him.

"The attempts on your life. Did they not start shortly after the first time you ran into Antonia and the emperor?"

"You think she tried to have me killed?"

Aquila nodded. "She tried a few times, I believe, starting with the attack at your brother's house, followed by the wagon that almost ran you over."

Priscilla's eyes rounded. "And then there was the man at the Forum. But, Aquila, there have been no incidents for months. If this is true, why did she stop? For that matter, why begin anew by sending another of her men after me at the synagogue? It makes no sense."

"It makes perfect sense. She was shaken when she saw you that first time at Quintus's feast and made her first attempts. How vexed she must have been when her assassins returned empty-handed, unable to overcome one helpless woman. Once we made sure you were never left alone, she ran out of easy opportunities. As time passed and you did nothing to threaten her, her fears must have been allayed. That's why she left you alone. Then she saw you again."

"At the palace." Priscilla groaned. "Seeking an audience with Claudius."

"Precisely. Of course, she assumed you were there to destroy her reputation."

"But why? I meant her no harm! I would never have betrayed her trust."

"She has no way of knowing that, my love. When you have dangerous secrets, they affect how you perceive everything. You see people and their motives through the lens of your guilt. And if, like Antonia, you are ruthless, you will act to protect yourself by any means you deem necessary. Failing to kill you at the synagogue, she chose the next best thing."

"She ensured our banishment."

"Her assassin must have hung around long enough near the synagogue to witness the events that took place after the arrival of the urban cohorts. His report would have given her the perfect weapon to use against us. Our expulsion from Rome means you will have no possible access to Claudius. It means she is safe." He exhaled and stepped away. "There is nothing we can do to clear our names."

Priscilla felt a shot of white-hot anger. "Antonia has robbed us of all we have! We are losing everything. Everyone!"

Aquila stared at her as if trying to decide how to answer. Without a word, he pulled her back into his arms. She struggled for a moment, writhing with indignation. The smoldering tide of outrage felt so much better than the grief that had nearly swallowed her whole.

"For now," he whispered against her brow, "we need to press on. Endure this. Carry our family safely out of Rome."

She shuddered hard, and a small whimper escaped her throat. Aquila caressed the nape of her neck, her cheek, her knotted jaw. He lowered his head and pressed his lips to hers, a feathery touch, quieting her, muting the noise of anger.

Lifting his head, he ran a thumb over her lips in a soothing gesture. "Hold on to Yeshua, my love," he said.

"I don't know how." Her voice emerged broken, like her heart.

"Think of his merit. He is worth this loss. This pain. He is worth the hours we will spend sleepless and weeping. He is worth our good-byes and the friends we have to leave behind. Every sacrifice we make for his sake is worthy of the One who will accompany us every step of this journey.

"Don't let fear fool you. I promise, Yeshua has already chosen a house for us in another city. Claimed a place for us among new friends. Carved a new ministry and church.

"We are not alone. We have each other. But most importantly, Priscilla, we have *him*. And he is worthy of every tear we shed now."

For years, Priscilla had felt a stranger, a castaway among her own kin. She had had no place she could truly call her own. Finally God had settled her in a family. He had established her in a home and given her precious friendships. She realized why her grief went so deep. It seemed to her that Antonia had robbed all that God had wrought. Like a sleeper coming awake, Priscilla was reminded again that the Father who had given her so much could give just as generously once more.

Aquila gazed at her as if he could read her thoughts, his eyes steady, unwavering. "He, too, wept when he lived among us, you know? He understands our tears. And he is with us now. He will see us through today, and he will see us through tomorrow. He hasn't abandoned us, my love. He has only called us to a new home."

"I quite liked this one."

He smiled. "On this long road, God will portion out what we need each hour. He will see us through what comes."

Priscilla exhaled. A thread of hope began to undergird the ache of loss. It wove through her grief, lifting its weight until she could breathe.

They had little time to choose a destination. Rufus and Mary arrived in the afternoon, and everyone stopped the work of packing and cleaning to pray together, seeking God's direction. They had twenty-four hours to decide the course of their future. After praying for some time, Rufus abruptly shot to his feet. "I think I know where you are to go."

Benyamin gave him an arch look. "I wished you would tell us."

"I saw a familiar face as we prayed: Stephanas of Corinth. He was an associate of my father's and owns several warehouses in Corinth. Our family has worked with him for over a decade." Rufus rocked on his feet, unable to hold still in his excitement. "He is a man of influence and wealth. A good-hearted man. He will be able to help you when you arrive. Even refer new custom for your business and find the right lodgings." He grinned. "Besides, I have prayed for that man for years! Now I send you to him as an ambassador for Christ!"

Aquila turned to his family. "What do you all think?"

"Corinth provides a good base for the leather business," Benyamin said. "As one of the richest cities in the empire, it maintains a substantial array of shops and stalls, which translates into a constant need for tents and awnings."

Priscilla clasped Aquila's hand. "Wherever Yeshua leads, I will follow."

Aquila straightened his back. "Corinth it is, then."

Rufus wrote a short letter of introduction to Stephanas and sealed it for good measure. By the evening, members of their small church started arriving at their door. A few of them who were not citizens would also have to leave Rome, though most were going to stay with relatives in different parts of the empire.

The friends kept a vigil of prayer through the night, singing psalms to keep themselves alert when eyes started to droop with exhaustion. Some helped with packing; others were entrusted with last-minute errands the following day.

Senator Pudens and his family arrived early the next morning. After settling practical matters regarding the house, they spent a little time reminiscing, lingering over cherished memories of the past months. The women shed no few tears and begged for frequent news. Aquila admonished the new believers to remain true to the faith and not depart from the paths of righteousness.

Benyamin oversaw the stowing of their baggage onto one cart and settled Marcus and Lollia into another. Priscilla must have embraced Pudentiana and Sabinella a dozen times before she could finally bring herself to climb into the covered cart that would carry them to the port of Ostia. The senator, in his usual methodical manner, had arranged passage for them the previous evening.

As the wheels rolled forward, Priscilla pushed aside the tattered curtains so that she could cling to the sight of her friends until they disappeared from view, hidden by a high embankment. At the city gates, the cart swayed violently when one of the wheels dropped into a yawning pothole, and Priscilla heard some piece of pottery, not packed well enough, crash and break at the bottom of one of the baskets.

Shattered pieces of clay jingled a jarring note in her ears as she rode out of Rome. In the eighth year of Claudius's reign, Priscilla bid farewell to the city of her birth, not knowing if she would ever pass through those gates again.

Twenty-Three

CLAUDIUS'S EDICT CAME in late fall, days before ill weather would make sea travel impossible for several months. It should have taken them under nine days to arrive in Corinth. Instead, they needed twelve, anchoring at two different ports on the way to avoid the surging swell of bad storms. Priscilla's belly seemed to rise and fall with the waves, keeping time with the movement of the Mediterranean.

They journeyed most of the way on a narrow trireme, a Roman galley carrying wine from Hispania. Of them all, Ferox proved the best sailor, settling himself near the bulwarks of the ship for hours at a time, face lifted to the wind, tongue lolling, his mouth open in a happy smile that nothing could dislodge.

In the days that they enjoyed fair weather, the ship ate up the distance with negligent grace and finally dropped them off along the western coast of the Peloponnese. There, they transferred their baggage onto a *raeda*, a cloth-top carriage with noisy, iron-shod wheels pulled by four donkeys. The wooden slat where Priscilla sat wedged between Marcus and Lollia proved hard and splintery and more unstable than sea waves.

"I never realized how much I like solid ground," she said with a gasp when, half a day later, they came within sight of Corinth and she knew her torment was finally going to end.

Built on a great hill, Corinth demanded that her visitors scale her heights before they could enter her walls. The way in was steep. Partway up the road, the passengers had to dismount the carriage, as the mules could not manage to carry both them and their baggage over the heavy incline.

Priscilla's legs began to burn, and her aching, swollen feet blistered in their sandals. Above them, the dusky mount of Acrocorinth crouched over the sprawling city like a lumpy spider, looking malevolent and cold.

They walked past many lush villas, a growing suburbia of new residences built for wealthy patrons. Priscilla, who had lived in ancient Rome all her life, found this excess of newness jarring. She already missed the cracked marbles of home, the beauty of aged terra-cotta and hundred-year-old buildings whose histories shaped every brick.

Copious temples and altars dotted their path, overflowing with enthusiastic crowds and lavish offerings. Corinth was a city filled with abundant idols and ardent worshipers. They ambled past a bathhouse and had to hold Ferox back from attempting to swim in a spectacular fountain.

"What's this?" Marcus asked, bending to examine the mark of a bare foot carved into the sidewalk. The boy scratched his brow and followed the footprint's direction with his eyes. The ancient sign of a house of prostitution, it pointed to a marble-faced white building a few steps away.

"Never you mind, Son," Aquila said, turning Marcus's head back toward the road.

They made their way up a wide, tree-lined avenue that disgorged them at the city's gates. Priscilla's eyes widened as she glimpsed the agora, which appeared larger even than Rome's public square.

"Which way?" she asked Aquila.

"The inn Rufus recommended is southwest of the city, past a row of shops. I will ask directions at the gate."

By the time they arrived at the inn, unloaded their baggage, and settled in their room, evening had fallen. They filled their bellies with the tavern's plain bean stew, which lacked the distinct flavoring of both *passum* and *garum*, tasting too bland to Priscilla's palate. She crawled into bed, dizzy with exhaustion yet unable to sleep. She had barely arrived and she was already homesick.

"Lord, you are worthy of this pain," she prayed under her breath and pulled the blanket over her head.

Aquila shoved irritated fingers through his hair, trying to focus on the accounts before him. They had been in Corinth for sixteen weeks. The New Year had come and gone, and the cold winter was loosening its hold on the world. Spring showed signs of tiptoeing into the city. Perhaps with it, new customers would arrive.

Thanks to Stephanas's help, they had found a house to rent, conveniently situated not far from the agora. Though smaller than their home in Rome and less comfortable, it met their needs.

The two-story house with its vaulted doorways occupied the edge of a busy street. The location made the ground floor perfect for their shop. Priscilla had hung an attractive curtain to separate the workshop from the public part of the store, where the customers visited. Sabinella had given them the curtain as a parting gift, the wide length of ecru wool too great an expense for them to otherwise afford. Pudentiana and Praxedis had spent hours embroidering delicate green-and-pink flowers on the edge of the fabric, a gesture that had brought tears to his wife's eyes when she had unpacked it.

"I meant to give this to you when you first moved into your new home here," Sabinella had said. "But it was not ready in time. It will have to serve as a farewell gift, now, a token of our affection, which follows you wherever you go. You take a piece of our hearts with you, my dears, when you leave for Graecia."

Aquila had caught Priscilla gazing at that curtain with wistful longing more than once since they had hung it up.

He blew out a long breath. This displacement had not been easy on any of them. It had come with a price tag that had shocked even him.

For one thing, Aquila had spent all his savings on the move. Travel did not come cheap. Claudius might have demanded that he and his family leave Rome, but he had provided no funds for the fulfillment of such an order. With a sigh, Aquila rolled the sheet of papyrus shut and put it away.

He had moved before, from his home in Pontus to Rome. But he had been unmarried then, with few responsibilities beyond his own needs. Now he carried the welfare of a family on his shoulders. Since the fever, his uncle Benyamin had slowed down, unable to keep up the youthful pace he had maintained when they first arrived in Rome. The care of his loved ones had fallen largely to Aquila. He felt bowed under that weight. Anxious with the demands of it.

Because of Stephanas's gracious recommendation, they were

starting to build a roster of patrons. But to pay for food and rent, they would need more custom.

Senator Pudens had managed to send them four letters by way of merchants traveling to Corinth, his latest telling them that their property in the Aventine had been safely rented. It would take time before they would receive payment, of course, and any revenues would be subject to deep taxation since Aquila was not a Roman citizen. Meanwhile, he had to meet expenses from one day to the next, with no cushion of savings to carry him through should an unexpected need arise.

He spread a fresh length of leather on his lap and adjusted the wick in the clay lamp to help him see better. He worked too many hours. The trade left little time for his wife, for Marcus, for his uncle.

Priscilla had been the one to invite Stephanas and his family to their home for an evening gathering of prayer and teaching, their first in Corinth. She took care of Marcus's needs, ran the household, welcomed customers, saw to the day-to-day running of the shop. He had no idea how he would have managed without her.

Something inside him winced at the thought. Something small and proud. He felt he was letting her down, he supposed. Laying too much on her shoulders. Shame and resentment, like a two-headed dragon, breathed their fire inside him. Shame that he had to rely so much on his wife and, ironically, resentment that after so much work, he should still feel like he had failed her.

It was no fault of hers. Priscilla never demanded anything from him. This conflagration of painful emotions issued from his own mind. And yet he could not quite overcome it.

In the meantime, he had to finish two travel cloaks and try to drum up more business. He closed his eyes to rest them from the strain of working in shadows. His wife would have to wait, as would the condition of his own heart.

Priscilla tried not to cry. The cramping low in her belly made her grind her teeth in discomfort. But the reason for her tears lay in a deeper well than physical pain. She had been married nigh unto two years, and still her cycles came uninterrupted. Anxiety had twined deep roots into her thoughts, curling tendrils that wrapped around her dreams and choked them every time she remembered how deeply she longed for a child.

She had only been with Appius three times—three miserable, shameful tumbles that had barely lasted beyond the time it took for her to cry out his name. But it had been enough for her to conceive. Somehow, she had expected that with Aquila she would conceive with the same ease. More, even, given the love she bore him. Given his tenderness with her. Instead, month after month, her body had betrayed her desires. Her womb had remained stubbornly empty.

Since her betrothal, she had always felt that she could share anything with Aquila. Tell him of every struggle. But Corinth had changed that.

From the day they had arrived, Aquila had drawn away, coiling into himself like a neatly stored leather whip. An unending deluge of work kept him busy, true enough. Only, Aquila had known the pressure of too much work before. Had known sleepless nights as he labored until dawn and began his day anew. None of that had ever made him withdraw from her before.

This time, she sensed the distance between them, like a pit of fire that she could not bridge. She had grown so accustomed to his presence, so reliant on his listening ear and encouraging companionship, that his sudden absence became like an olive grind, crushing her. She discovered, in a whole new way, that loneliness could eat at her soul with the voracious hunger of a beast of prey. She could not even remember the last time he had kissed her. Reached for her in the night. Sometimes she felt as if he looked through her. She had become invisible to her husband.

This Aquila did not invite confidences. He did not make her feel secure enough to express her fears to him. Worse. She suspected that her barrenness might be the very reason for his detachment. What was the use of a wife who closed up when you touched her and failed to even bear you a child?

She took a shivery breath and pushed away the thoughts that tormented her. She had no one in whom she could confide. No one to whom she could disclose her greatest fear: that she had no babe at her breast because God wanted to punish her for her sins.

Returning to the workshop, she lifted a brown piece of leather, which Benyamin had prepared beforehand, and began the stitching for the tent. These days, timely delivery was more important than ever. The rate of new custom remained steady, but not nearly as copious as it had been in Rome. They had not yet had enough time to establish a name in Corinth. Delivering the existing orders on time meant satisfied customers who would recommend them to others.

Close to noon, Aquila returned from the agora, where he had gone to introduce himself and their business to the traders. The sun had yet to reach its zenith in the sky, but there were already dark circles under his eyes. He had lost weight, she realized. Too little sleep. Too little food. Without thinking, she reached for his hand. "Is all well, my dear?"

He did not look at her. "Of course." He loosened his hand from her hold and reached for the leather. "Back to work."

Priscilla bit her lip, racking her brain for some topic that might draw her husband in. "At least they speak Latin in Corinth. It won't be as hard for Marcus to adjust. He still struggles with Greek."

"Hmm."

She sensed his need for quiet and pressed her mouth shut. A weight settled on her like a gravestone that would not be rolled away. Silently she rose to help Lollia with lunch. Porridge and lentils again. She knew their finances worried Aquila and was trying to economize every way she knew.

When she served him the meal, he tasted the small, homemade roll and frowned. "Does this have honey?"

She smiled, pleased he had noticed. "It does."

"That's expensive, Priscilla. We can't afford that right now."

"It's from a jar Mary gave us as a parting present. I did not pay for it."

"Better save it for a special occasion rather than fritter it away on daily use. I don't know when next we shall be able to buy such luxuries."

Something in her shriveled at the criticism. She had used the honey for his sake, to tempt his appetite. He had not noticed her careful parsimony over the past few weeks. Her prudent thriftiness made their coin spread further. Instead, he had only noted her supposed extravagance.

They consumed the rest of their meal in silence before Aquila returned to the workshop. Priscilla began to clean the dishes, her hands knowing what to do from long habit, her thoughts far away.

Her own transgression had led to this painful banishment and financial strain. If not for her sin, she would never have run into Antonia in the physician's house. And they would not find themselves in a strange city now, strapped for income, barely surviving from one day to the next.

On the third day of the week, just before Priscilla was preparing to shut the door and bar it for the evening, a short, wiry man with large, dark eyes walked into the shop. She had the impression of an ordinary face with forgettable features and a thick beard.

"Good evening," he said. "I look for Aquila of Pontus. Am I in the right shop?"

He spoke Greek rather than Latin, with perfect fluency, though tinged with an unfamiliar accent she could not quite identify. "My husband is away making a delivery. May I help you?"

"I am Paul of Tarsus," he said. "I had heard you work in leather. As do I, it so happens."

Priscilla felt her legs wobble and sat awkwardly on the narrow bench they kept for customers. "I have heard of you," she said.

The laugh lines in the corners of his eyes deepened. His gaze sharpened with interest. "I must be a better tentmaker than I thought."

"I know nothing of your work with leather, sir. I was told you are a rabbi. And more to the point, you love Yeshua."

Her guest went still. Something with the force of a storm seemed to gather behind his eyes. With a sudden jolt she became aware of the illusion wrought by his ordinary features; there was nothing ordinary about this man. He stared at her for a moment, his body emanating leashed energy. The room seemed to lose some of its air.

"You know of Yeshua?" He smiled slowly. "I thought I was sent here by Stephanas. Now I see God directed my steps."

She motioned for him to sit across from her. They stared at one another in silence. Priscilla tried to swallow past the dryness in her throat. A few months ago, stories of this man's exploits had encouraged them to plant the church in Rome despite the threat of persecution. Now he sat, ankles crossed in comfort, at his ease under her roof.

"Do you know Stephanas well?" she asked, trying to follow the thread that had led him to their door.

"I met him briefly for the first time today." He shrugged. "I went to fetch a parcel from Stephanas's warehouse in the port of Cenchreae. I happened upon him on my way inside and we began a conversation. When he found out that I am a Jew and that I am looking for employment with a leatherworker, he gave me Aquila's name."

"We know Stephanas through Rufus of Cyrene. I believe you are acquainted."

Paul chuckled. "How perfectly the Lord guides our steps. Is my friend Rufus well?"

"Very well. Shepherding a growing flock in Rome. We would be with him now, but for Claudius's edict."

"You were fellow workers with Rufus?"

Priscilla nodded. "Aquila and I hosted gatherings of Gentile believers at our home, while Rufus and his mother taught the Jewish followers at their house. He is a Roman citizen and safe from the recent decree. But we, along with other Jews who held no citizenship, were expelled from Rome. We had to leave the disciples behind." Her tone grew pensive and she dropped her head.

Paul lowered his brows. "I believe Yeshua brought you here,

just as he brought me." He rubbed his hands together and grinned like a fox. "Don't worry. He will take care of the church in Rome. In the meantime, he has plans for Corinth."

A shadow fell across the door, drawing their attention. Aquila and Benyamin walked in, fatigue etched on their features.

Priscilla sprang to her feet. "My dears, we have a special visitor."

Aquila's lips stretched in a smile that did not quite reach his tired eyes. "How may I help you?"

"This is Paul of Tarsus, Husband. The man of whom Rufus spoke."

Aquila froze. *"Paul?"*

Paul rose to his feet.

For the first time in weeks, a spark of excitement brought a slow flush to Aquila's cheeks. "My brother in Christ!" he cried, and enveloped Paul in his arms. Paul, no less enthusiastic, returned the embrace and laughed, a booming sound that wrapped about Priscilla like a blanket.

"This is a warm welcome," the man of Tarsus murmured after he had greeted a beaming Benyamin.

"You do not understand," Aquila explained. "Your letter to Rufus changed our lives. Because of you, we began to speak openly of our faith in the synagogues. You gave us courage to be bold. And many pursued the Lord as a result."

"And now look at you. Booted out of Rome and in exile." Their guest slapped Aquila on the shoulder. "And with me by your side, a load of fresh trouble will be heading your way." He grinned. "To God be the glory!"

Priscilla pulled her palla higher over her hair. "In that case, I better see to dinner. It's never a good idea to face trouble on an empty stomach."

Twenty-Four

"I CAME TO LOOK FOR YOU because I need work." Paul wiped his mouth on his napkin. "I do not want to place the burden of my keep upon our brothers and sisters throughout Asia. I am an experienced leatherworker and intend to earn my living while doing the work of our Lord. My needs are modest. I do not require a large income."

Aquila dropped his gaze. He wanted to help Paul so badly, it felt like an ache in his chest. But he simply could not afford it. "I would hire you today if I could. But we ourselves are recent arrivals to Corinth and have yet to amass a large enough clientele to afford extra hands."

Paul nodded. "I understand. If the Lord wills it, he will provide the increase you need. Shall we pray on it?"

"Of course. In the meantime, you must be our guest. Stay with us and allow us to help you by any means we can."

That evening, Aquila retired to his chamber earlier than he had in weeks. "Can you believe Paul showed up at our doorstep?" he asked Priscilla as he splashed water on his face and scrubbed his hands.

"I can't believe he is sleeping under our roof," she said softly.

Her face looked pale in the lamplight, gray shadows rimming her eyes. She worked too hard. The thought smote him, a living ember to his cringing conscience. He stripped off his tunic and crawled into bed.

Priscilla gave him a weak smile and closed her eyes. He lifted a hand toward her and let it hover in the air above her shoulder. It had been a long time since he had touched her. He had been weary for so long, both inclination and strength for anything beyond a few hours of precious sleep at night had been sapped out of his bones.

On the few occasions he did manage to break through the haze of exhaustion, she avoided his gaze and turned away before he could reach for her. There was a haunted look that rarely left her face these days, a lingering sorrow he did not understand. In truth, he did not *want* to understand. He assumed she felt dismayed with him for letting her down. For dragging her from hardship to hardship.

He preferred silence to *that* conversation. His hand dropped back to his side.

She did not want him. So be it. A little more sleep wouldn't hurt him. Aquila turned his back, pulled the blankets higher around his neck and slammed his eyes closed, missing the longing look his wife sent his rigid back.

The next morning, soon after they had opened the door of the shop for business, a balding man walked in, wrapped in the linen toga of a Roman citizen. "Are you the owner of this shop?"

Aquila gave a slight bow of his head. "Aquila of Pontus, at your service."

"You are familiar with the Isthmian Games, I presume?" the man asked.

"Of course." One of four celebrated Panhellenic festivals, the Isthmian Games were esteemed almost as highly as the famed Olympics. "Every other year, the people of Graecia gather here in Corinth to celebrate athletes and musicians of rare talent."

"All the *world* gathers for the Isthmian Games, sir. All the world." The balding man's voice rang with pride.

"I look forward to attending them next spring," Aquila responded. "I fear we arrived here too late to partake of the previous games."

The man nodded. He lifted an arm in an affected gesture, as if an orator about to make a public presentation. "I am Iuventius Proclus. I served as president of the games last year. Next spring, I shall be president again."

Aquila, who had worked for Roman senators, consuls, and praetors, hid his smile. "Welcome, Proclus."

The visitor dropped his arm and bent his chin in condescension. "For one hundred and ten uninterrupted years, we have hosted the Isthmian Games in Corinth, not to mention the ancient history of the games in this place, and each year we gain popularity.

"The number of visitors who descend upon us for the duration of the games has been steadily growing. Last year, we almost burst at the seams. There are not enough inns and taverns in Corinth to handle the swelling numbers of our visitors. Folks set up tents along the streets for days, and even those become overcrowded.

"I am determined to be better prepared for next year's games. We plan to have more tents for travelers and additional awnings for street sellers. Which is why I am here. I wish to commission you to make those tents and awnings." Proclus adjusted his toga. "Shall we discuss the price?"

Aquila remembered to shut his mouth. He realized Proclus was about to place a significant order. Even so, he was not prepared for the extent of merchandise Proclus needed. After they had agreed upon the fee and the date of delivery, Proclus handed Aquila a bag of coins as deposit.

"Do you not wish to see a sample of our work before you pay me?"

Proclus shrugged. "I saw one already and found it satisfactory."

"May I ask where?"

"I ran into an acquaintance last night, just after sunset. The man had ordered a tent from you. Couldn't speak highly enough of your workmanship. I confess I was headed for another leather-worker, a longtime resident of Corinth. But my acquaintance assured me that your labor is superior. When I saw the tent, I had to agree."

Aquila thanked the man and saw him out in a daze. *"Just after sunset,"* Proclus had said. Last night, they had prayed for an increase in their business as the sun had started to set!

Rushing out of the shop, he climbed the narrow stairs that led to their private chambers. He found Paul speaking quietly with Benyamin in the dining room.

"You are hired!" Aquila cried, holding up the purse of coins. "When would you like to start?"

That Sabbath, Paul accompanied them to the synagogue. Priscilla and Aquila introduced him to Titius Justus, a Gentile worshiper of

God who lived next door to the assembly hall and often attended services, followed by Crispus, the ruler of the synagogue. Crispus welcomed their guest with a warm show of hospitality and invited him to speak to the congregation, as was customary when a learned teacher visited.

After the Scriptures were read, Paul took his place before the congregation and began to tell his own story, starting with the day a young man named Stephen had been dragged outside Jerusalem's walls and stoned to death by an enraged crowd.

"I was present that day," Paul said, holding the crowd spellbound with his deep voice. "I stood guarding the garments of those who threw the stones. I shouted my approval as Stephen fell to his knees, his face covered by rivulets of blood. I screamed my vitriol as he cried out with a loud voice, 'Lord, do not hold this sin against them.'"

A collective gasp broke the silence in the synagogue. This story had taken an unexpected turn.

"That day, the heavens opened to take home a precious man, one whose faith could make the angels smile," Paul continued. People began to shift in their seats. Spiritual leaders who persecuted, even killed a man, were not in the habit of praising their victims. They stared at Paul, bewildered. Who was the good man, here? Paul or Stephen?

Paul went on to tell the rest of his story, describing his avid persecution of those he despised, followed by his utter regret for having done so. As he spoke, the assembly hall grew increasingly hushed, silenced with an odd mixture of confusion and fascination.

"I have met Yeshua for myself," he continued. "Only once, on the road to Damascus."

A whirlwind in the guise of man, a tempest of faith encased

in flesh, Paul told the tale of his miraculous encounter with one whom he had persecuted.

"I will tell you, my friends, if ever you see him, your knees will fold, and your tongue will confess him Lord.

"On the road to Damascus, my God struck me blind. In truth, that was the moment I gained my sight for the first time in my young, self-satisfied life."

As his story unfolded, some faces began to express awe. Others, rage. Undeterred, he went on. "The Christ has come," he said. "But you don't have to believe my story to be convinced. I can show you the truth of it from Scripture."

Then he began to teach in earnest, like a surgeon with a knife, cutting open and revealing ancient truths, showing how Yeshua fulfilled the many prophecies about the promised Messiah. When he finished teaching, the synagogue exploded, voices erupting, the noise deafening.

Crispus jumped to his feet and motioned for silence. "Brothers, sisters, I urge you to maintain order. If you have questions, raise your hands, and Paul will answer you one at a time."

The place sank into uneasy silence. Paul answered question after question with the facility of one well trained in Scriptures. With expert ease, he cut the ground out of every objection. Sensing the growing agitation of some in the crowd, he halted his instruction.

"Let us stop for now. Draw breath and rest. I am staying with Aquila and Priscilla. If any wish to know more, come to their house tomorrow evening. I will await you there."

Dozens of eyes turned accusing glares at Priscilla and Aquila. Priscilla had felt the weight of enough censure in Rome not to be thrown by it. She smiled sweetly and followed her husband and their controversial guest out of the synagogue.

Priscilla was unsurprised when Titius Justus arrived at her home in time for supper the following night. He had sat on the edge of his seat, drinking in Paul's every word on the Sabbath. But she almost toppled off her stool when Crispus arrived, his wife in tow. The ruler of the synagogue had come either to try to put an end to Paul's teaching, or because he felt genuinely drawn to Yeshua.

Stephanas attended too, bringing his wife, son, and two grown daughters. His eldest daughter, Chara, a golden-haired beauty Priscilla had met once before, brought her cithara.

After they finished an early dinner, Priscilla invited Chara to play a song of her choosing. The girl settled the box-shaped instrument on her lap and inclined it toward her torso. When she began to pluck the strings, Priscilla forgot to breathe. Chara had the rare gift of a true master.

Paul approached the young musician when she had completed her flawless performance. His hand indicated the instrument held loosely in her arms. "I see your cithara is damaged." He pointed to a large chip at the edge of the frame.

Chara tipped her head to examine the wood. "My brother dropped it by accident."

Paul nodded. "Still, you made it sound like a heavenly chorus. We, too, are like this cithara. Imperfect and broken, every one of us. Damaged. Yet if we are yielded to God, utterly given to his purpose, leaning on him as securely as this cithara leaned against Chara, then he can make our lives reflect the beauty for which we were created. Jew or Gentile, it is of no consequence to God. Turn to him in trust, and he will become the anchor of your soul."

When Paul finished speaking that evening, Stephanas sprang

up. "I want to give my life to Yeshua. I want to be yielded to him, guided by him. What do I have to do?"

Chara stood up next. "I want the same."

His wife, son, and younger daughter came to their feet at the same time. "You may as well count all of us in," his wife said. "What must we do to join the household of faith?"

"It so happens," Paul said, "that I can arrange that."

Priscilla penned a letter to Rufus and Mary that same night, knowing their delight would match her own.

Your prayers have been answered. Tomorrow Paul is baptizing Stephanas and his whole household in the waters of the Aegean Sea. They will be the first to come to faith in all Corinth.

They would not be the last.

Twenty-Five

THE HEAVENS REMAINED in the grip of darkest night when Priscilla and Lollia began to prepare breakfast. Twilight had crept into the horizon by the time they served warm wheat pancakes with dates. Ferox climbed on the couch next to Marcus, stretching his legs as he had seen the humans do, laying his head on Marcus's lap. Marcus laughed and petted the dog.

"Don't encourage him," Priscilla said. She pointed to the ground and looked at Ferox sternly. The dog dropped his muzzle and jumped off. He gave a sad whimper, then climbed down the stairs obediently, back to his own dish on the ground floor, which Lollia had filled with fresh food and water.

"Maybe you should try teaching *him* Greek verbs," Marcus said. "He is smarter than most people."

Priscilla rolled her eyes. "He has enough trouble obeying Latin."

"That's exactly how I feel!" Marcus cried and everyone laughed.

Benyamin was meeting with Stephanas that morning and left directly after breakfast. Aquila accompanied Marcus to the baths, which were less crowded in the early morning. Over the passing months, the boy had grown accustomed to these visits, and although he still experienced a shivering discomfort every time he dipped underwater, he no longer felt terrorized by the experience. Instead, now, when he emerged from the bath, he beamed like a conqueror, knowing he had vanquished the power his father's murder had once held over him.

After cleaning the breakfast dishes and tending the fire, Priscilla joined Paul in the workshop, where they began working on an awning for a felter's stall. They sat near one another, fingers busy in silent labor. Priscilla was thinking of her friends in Rome, whom she missed with an almost physical ache. Mary's motherly kindness, Sabinella's protective wisdom, Pudentiana's companionship. Her friends would have been a comfort as she contended with her empty womb, wondering if it would ever be full again.

Preoccupied with her thoughts, Priscilla's hand bumped into Paul's arm, making him drop his needle.

"Your pardon!" she cried.

He sighed and laid aside the thick hide spread on his knees. "Tell me what weighs so heavy on you, child."

Priscilla stared. "What do you mean?"

"For weeks I have lived in your house, eaten your bread, tasted of your hospitality. I have watched you teach with the expert reasoning of an old rabbi and nurture our people with the tenderness of a mother. That you love God, I have no doubt. That you would lay down your life for your family is evident to all.

"But in all this time, Priscilla, I have sensed a shadow in you.

You are like a fish squirming in a net, caught in something that pains you. Tell me what it is. Perhaps I can help. I can certainly intercede with God."

Priscilla gulped. She had prayed and prayed that Yeshua would send her a friend in whom she could confide. Someone who would help lift the burden of loneliness from her.

But *Paul*?

Did she want to open her heart to this man whom they called an apostle? Share her fears and, inevitably, her shame?

In truth, Paul had a right to know her past. She could not minister alongside him, remain under his tuition and spiritual guidance, without revealing her scars.

She remembered the day she had exposed her sins to Rufus and Mary and Benyamin. Remembered the grace they had shown her. Remembered how free she had felt afterward, knowing they accepted her in spite of her sins. She could only hope Paul would offer a similar mercy. Even if he did not, she had to face this revelation and leave the outcome to God.

She dropped her head. "I long for a babe, you see. But I fear I am barren. And it is my own fault." Bit by bit, in broken scraps, she told her story. She confessed the guilt she had thought washed clean by the Lord. Yet it had risen again in recent months, that shame, blowing its fetid breath, claiming her once more. How many times must she repent of this sin before she could be free of it? How many layers did she have to peel before she could unshackle herself from the chains of her past?

"I cannot help but feel that God himself is punishing me." Her voice cracked. "Withholding a child from me because I am unworthy to be a mother. Why else would my womb be empty?"

Paul pulled on his beard, his brow creased in thought. In prayer. "Not every storm is of God's making," he said. "Not every unfulfilled dream is his punishment. We live in a fallen world where our enemy runs wild. His talons gouge every heart he can reach, and that is many.

"God can use such things for good. That does not mean he instigates them.

"I do not know if it is in God's plan that you should ever conceive again. But I do know it *is* in his plan that you should be a mother. For he has already given you a son. What is Marcus to you if not your own child? You love him as a mother. And that boy! Every time he looks at you, his heart is in his eyes. No son is more devoted to his natural mother than he is to you.

"You are worthy of being a mother, Prisca. To deny it is to concur with the lie the enemy whispers in your ear. You are colluding with him against yourself. Against Christ's plans for your life.

"Here is the truth: if you were unworthy, God would not have entrusted Marcus to your care."

Priscilla exhaled. She did love Marcus as her own. That love had grown so quietly, spread through her veins so furtively, she had barely acknowledged the depths of it. She had called him a heaven-sent gift, this brilliant child. A treasure. Would God have given away the care of this boy lightly?

She had never thought of the significance of that choice—of God committing this prodigious child into *her* keeping. He had given Marcus to her because he considered her worthy of the blessing of motherhood.

God had blessed her, and she had missed it. She had focused on the misery of her barrenness instead. And lost in that pain, she had overlooked his gift.

"The shame you feel is not of God," Paul said. "You must repent of wallowing in it."

"But Aquila does not feel the same," she burst out.

"She said *what*?" Aquila cried.

"That you blame her for being barren." Paul settled himself more comfortably on the couch.

The women had left earlier to shop for dinner, and Benyamin had taken Marcus to the palaestra for some exercise. Paul and Aquila were alone in the house, which at least afforded Aquila privacy, if not understanding.

"Why would she think such a thing?" he said, his ire growing. "I never accused her of it."

Paul made a calming gesture. "She never said you did."

"You just said—"

"This is how she *feels*. The conclusion of her heart, regardless of what you may have said or left unsaid." He leaned into the cushions. "Tell me, Aquila. Why do you think she never spoke to you about her struggles with conceiving?"

Aquila ground his teeth. "I cannot imagine. We are not in the habit of keeping secrets from each other."

"Precisely. So why this time? Has something changed between you?"

"Not on my part."

"Are you certain of that?"

Aquila reddened. "I have been busy putting bread on our table. Perhaps I have not been as attentive as I should."

Paul nodded. "That is understandable. No woman can expect her husband to dance attendance upon her every whim."

"Priscilla is not that kind of woman. She is not selfish or demanding." Aquila frowned.

"No."

Aquila's stomach turned a somersault inside him. His wife had been drowning for months. Drowning in guilt. Yet she had not dared come to him because she thought he blamed *her*.

She had interpreted his distance as an indictment. In the void he had created with his silence, his continuous absence in heart, if not in body, she had sought and found her own explanation. The wrong one, as it happened.

Just as he, fool that he was, had interpreted her lingering sadness a result of her disappointment with *him*. He, too, had arrived at the wrong conclusions.

Glad for the support of the couch beneath his legs, he dropped his head in his hands. "I should never have allowed such a wall to spring up between us," he said. "In my weariness, I felt I had little to give. But I ought not to have drawn away from her as I did."

Paul placed a strong hand on Aquila's shoulder. Something passed through the press of those warm fingers into Aquila's flesh, like a tiny bolt of lightning, making him snap out of his painful speculations.

"Do you remember the story of Elijah?" Paul said. "In the famine, when exhausted and hungry, the prophet asked the widow in Zarephath to make him some bread."

Aquila gave a weak nod. "Though she had barely enough flour and oil left to cook one final meal for herself and her son, she baked bread for Elijah."

"She did! And that jug of oil never ran dry, nor did the jar of flour empty. Day after day, those few drops stretched and proved enough to feed the prophet as well as the widow and her family.

"I have learned that we can be like that bottle. Almost empty, but always enough. Because, my young friend, it does not matter how empty the vessel is. What matters is who wields it.

"Your problem, Aquila, was that you set your gaze on the emptiness in your bottle. On how little you had to offer your wife. You forgot to keep your eyes on the God who provides. The one who can stretch the few drops and make them sufficient. So *you* felt insufficient."

Aquila looked up. "I abandoned her, even though I remained by her side."

Paul heaved a sigh. "Nothing you have done is irreversible. This breach can be repaired because you love Priscilla, and because, God help her, she loves you."

Aquila smiled weakly. "I do love her."

"So listen well." Paul lifted a finger as if in warning. "You must guard your heart. Guard it harder in the arduous seasons when the lies of the evil one ring loudest."

Aquila's throat became dry. He had, by virtue of neglect and pride, invited a twisted deceit to take root in his mind and allowed his marriage to be weakened.

He thought of Priscilla and all that she was to him as his wife: His trusty comrade, friend, shipmate, fellow soldier. His lover, but at the same time all that any male friend had ever been to him.

He remembered the soaring and iridescent joy of being with her in every sense. How could he have pushed aside the very best part of his life? He had become a mere fragment of himself as a result.

He would be more vigilant henceforth. He would shield the precious gift God had bestowed upon him.

Twenty-Six

PRISCILLA HURRIED DOWN the warren-like narrow street, jostling against the press of bodies, trying to sidestep the unpleasant detritus of an overgrown metropolis. She had sent Lollia back home to start preparing lunch but had lingered to purchase bread from her favorite bakery, which was a fair distance from their house.

She could have bought the loaves from shops more conveniently located. But none of them rivaled the quality of Otho's creations. He used a light mix of different flours that made the *quadratus* crusty on the outside and springy-soft on the inside. Rivaling the best in Rome, Otho's bakery merited the longer trip.

But she had to hurry. Priscilla had promised Marcus that if he learned a particularly difficult list of Greek vocabulary, she would make him fresh *libum* with honey. Since Proclus had placed his substantial order, their finances had become less strained. Better yet, Pudens had forwarded money from the rental of their home, so they could once again afford small luxuries like honey and *libum*.

She knew Marcus would have returned home from the palaestra

by now, hungry from exercise. He would be waiting for her, impatient to show off new accomplishments and more impatient to devour a plate of her sweet cheese pastries.

A rickety cart barreled down the road on the opposite side, forcing a pedestrian to take a hasty sidestep, plowing into Priscilla. She stumbled, her foot kicking something soft, before she regained her balance. A truncated groan rose from the vicinity of her ankle and Priscilla looked down. A body lay curled at her feet, arms tucked about its middle as if in pain, toes peeking from under the ragged cloth of her tunic.

"Pardon!" Priscilla gasped and bent down to help the pathetic coil of humanity that lay helpless on the ground.

Oily, dark hair tangled into a nest of knots around the woman's face. The liberal dirt on her cheeks could not hide the pustulating sore that disfigured her visage. More sores ran along the naked arms.

Vague recognition tugged at Priscilla. She knew this poor creature from somewhere. Then it came to her, at once, in a rush of shocked realization. The eyes, the distinctive nose. *"Antonia!"* she gasped.

The world became silent and distant as Priscilla stared, stupefaction rendering her speechless. Antonia seemed no more inclined to words. A flash of defiance sparked to life in the brown orbs and died quickly, giving in to despair.

Rage plowed into Priscilla with the force of a concrete wall, and she staggered back. Here lay the woman who had usurped her home and friends, the woman responsible for robbing her of the life she loved. Priscilla straightened and, turning her back, began to walk away. One step, two, three. Twenty. The rage began to dissipate, pushed out by plain curiosity.

She felt the press of questions rattling her resolve to leave. What in heaven was Antonia doing in Corinth? And what circumstance had reduced her to such a state? She saw the dirty face again, disfigured by that weeping sore, and the lesions that marred her arms like mold blooming on a damp wall. Priscilla stopped abruptly.

People cursed and pushed past her where she blocked the way. She remained oblivious to their exasperation. Instead, she waged a quiet war within, trying to reconcile the pathetic creature lying in her own filth with the silk-clad woman she had once known. Anger battled against pity, rioted its displeasure at the very thought of offering this woman any measure of compassion. Reluctantly Priscilla turned around and trudged back the way she had come. A few steps away from the huddled bundle on the ground, she hesitated.

Years ago, while living under the callous rule of her brother, she had learned to look beyond his cruelty into the wound that had shaped him and made him stone hard. Knowing his pain had helped her to forgive him time and again, when her heart had cried for revenge. That old lesson rose up to aid her now.

She remembered the haughty woman in the physician's house, proud as a queen. The niece of an emperor whose veins flowed with the blood of heroes and conquerors must have been rejected by somebody to have found her way into that particular den. And every day after that, she had had to live with the fear of discovery.

Priscilla knew the burden of such a secret. And though that burden had shaped her differently, had driven her to generosity and grace instead of the venom of savagery, she found in herself the morsel of compassion she needed to act as Yeshua willed.

She knelt by the woman and placed a gentle hand under her arm. "Come. My home is not far. We will care for you there."

If Antonia had any fight left in her, she did not show it. She gave in soundlessly to Priscilla's ministrations and hobbled barefoot alongside her without demur.

As Priscilla walked, her pace slow to accommodate her ailing companion, she wondered again at the calamity that had reduced the elegant aristocrat to such a state. For the length of a heartbeat, temptation sat at her door and called. Temptation to feel pleased by the woman's condition. To savor the justice of it. Antonia had sought to end her life more than once. She had been the cause of her expulsion from Rome. Everything they'd lost had been because of her.

And now she suffered.

Priscilla stood at the precipice of that realization and the allure it held. To revel in the bleakness of Antonia's circumstances. To find satisfaction in her undeniable pain.

She pushed the thought aside, refusing to give in to its enticement. She had received too much mercy from God to choose to be judge today.

Before they had reached the door of the house, Marcus ran out to meet them and came to an abrupt stop when he saw her companion. "Who is that?" he asked.

"Her name is Antonia. She is not well. We need to help her. Can you fetch her some food?"

The boy nodded. "I will bring a plate of stew with bread."

"Good. And some well-watered wine with honey, please, Marcus."

Priscilla wondered if those shuffling feet could manage to climb the stairs to their private quarters above. She did her best to support the weight, which had folded against her. Whatever strength had held Antonia together in the past had broken. She leaned into Priscilla, frail, helpless.

They made it to the upper floor, and Priscilla helped the woman to a couch. She lay down on her side, knees pulled up to her chest, arms wrapped about her legs, and shivered. Fetching a blanket, Priscilla covered her as softly as she could, avoiding the bleeding sores. She placed a pillow under the tangled hair.

Lollia barreled in, chest heaving from running up the stairs. "Marcus said you brought . . ." Her words drifted. "Good heavens above, Priscilla. Is that—?"

"Antonia. Yes. She will need a bath," she said. "And a physician. Can you prepare the one and send for the other?"

"For *her*?"

"For her."

Lollia sucked her lips as if tasting an unripe persimmon. "You certain you want to nurse that viper?"

A fair question. Did she want to commit to this path? Priscilla stood motionless for a beat. She studied the pitiful rags and bones huddled on the narrow couch, knowing she could not welcome Antonia to this house without first settling their accounts in some measure. This required more than passing pity. It required an act of heaven. It required a move of will that might well prove beyond her.

She thought of her own offense, then, which had driven her to the physician's door, and her desperate quest for forgiveness since. Taking a deep breath, she made a decision. She chose to extend to Antonia the compassion she had learned from Yeshua. As if the mere choice had shifted something, she felt a peculiar sense of freedom, a chain she had not known she bore loosening and breaking. No sooner had she allowed this narrow crack in her armor, than she sensed the light of Christ thrust in, widening the gap until it shattered, and with the wonder of a child speaking its first words, Priscilla realized that she could forgive Antonia, and indeed had already begun the process.

"I am certain," she said.

Lollia jerked her head down once and headed for the stairs. Marcus arrived shortly afterward, bearing a full platter in a two-handed grip. "I'll bring the cup next. Didn't want to slosh it all over the stairs."

"Good idea," Priscilla murmured, relieving him of the clay plate. She sat on her haunches before their unexpected guest. "Antonia. You need to eat."

"Leave me be," the woman snarled.

Priscilla stared helplessly, not knowing what to do. Marcus approached their guest, his steps sure, unafraid. He lifted a hand and patted her vermin-infested head. "You don't need to be angry. You're safe here. We'll take care of you."

He broke off a small piece of bread and held it against the woman's closed lips. "I know you are tired. Just open your mouth and chew."

To Priscilla's amazement, the woman obeyed.

Marcus dipped the bread into the stew next. Priscilla watched with awe as, bit by bit, Marcus fed Antonia until the bread was gone.

"Thirsty," Antonia whispered.

"I will fetch you a drink," Marcus said, and left.

Priscilla set the plate aside and readjusted the blanket around the inert form. Marcus arrived, having run all the way.

"She fell asleep," Priscilla said.

The boy set the cup on the floor next to the couch and studied Antonia's face.

"Marcus, where did you learn to take care of someone like that?" Priscilla asked.

Marcus turned to her. "Don't you know? I learned from you."

Priscilla felt the air knocked out of her. "I never did for you what you did for her."

He shrugged. "I lived on the streets. I know what it's like to be too tired to eat. To move. But I learned from you how to be kind."

Priscilla's throat clogged. She had not realized how closely Marcus had watched her over the months, how her simple actions had left an impression on him. She had been teaching him more than Greek verbs and she had not known it.

Antonia moaned and opened her eyes. "Here," Marcus said in his matter-of-fact way. "I brought you sweet wine. Lots and lots of honey. You'll like it." He pressed the cup to her mouth and she drank obediently. Some of it trickled down her chin. Priscilla wiped the drippling wine with a cloth. A bit of skin showed through the dirt, pale and feminine, a reminder of what this woman had once been. A reminder of her humanity.

Lollia came huffing back in. "Bath is ready. Sent Benyamin for a physician."

Priscilla nodded her thanks. "Antonia, would you like a warm bath? It's only a tub, I'm afraid. We don't own a proper pool."

The woman shrugged.

"Lollia gives good baths," Marcus assured her. He tugged on Antonia's hand, and she rose to follow him. In Priscilla's chamber, Lollia had set up the wooden tub they used for washing clothes.

Marcus let go of Antonia's hand at the door. "This is for girls only. I'll see you after." He scooted out, not waiting for a response.

Lollia and Priscilla set to removing Antonia's clothing. Crawling with lice and encrusted with dirt, it would all have to be burned. Lollia gathered the lot, holding the bundle as far away from her as her short arms allowed. Priscilla helped Antonia into the tub. Her legs crowded against her torso in the cramped space. She expelled a deep sigh.

Priscilla let her soak for a long while before she began to rub her skin with scented oil and, using a strigil, scrape the dirt off methodically. They had to keep changing the water, refilling the tub as the contents became too dirty to be of use. Her body cleaned, they turned their attention to her head. Even wet and oiled, her hair remained stubbornly tangled, defeating the comb.

"Just cut it off," Antonia snapped. "Shave the whole thing. The vermin are driving me insane."

Priscilla did not argue. It was the sensible choice, though she cringed as she fetched the implements. Using a large pair of leather shears, she cut off Antonia's hair and then, borrowing Aquila's razor, shaved the hair close to the scalp, which was red and swollen from countless bites.

By the time Antonia emerged from the bath, she was shuddering with exhaustion. Priscilla and Lollia wrapped her in a sheet and led her to the bed. The physician arrived, made a cursory examination of the near-unconscious woman in the bed, and left them with a large jar of ointment and a larger fee before taking himself off.

Aquila had barely entered the house when Marcus told him about their guest, the boy's story embellished by acidic interjections from Lollia.

"You left my wife alone with *her*?" Aquila hissed at Lollia. He had gone on a short delivery run while Priscilla was still out shopping for food. All the way on the return trip, he had imagined finally being alone with his wife. Imagined the joy of their reunion.

Instead, he had come home to the news that Antonia had taken shelter under his roof.

"Priscilla told me to leave," Lollia said. "What could I do? Besides, that lioness is asleep like a lamb."

Asleep or not, the thought of that particular woman in the same chamber as Priscilla made Aquila's blood run cold. He dashed along the courtyard, taking the stairs two at a time without bothering to remove his muddy shoes. His forehead was drenched in uneasy sweat by the time he skidded to a stop at the doorway to their bedchamber.

The person responsible for almost unraveling his life lay asleep in *his* bed, covered in *his* sheets and blankets, with his wife sitting vigil at her side. Without a word, he grabbed Priscilla about the waist and pulled her into his arms and held her there for a long time, until the beat of his heart slowed and he stopped feeling like his entrails would burst out of his throat.

He took a short step away, keeping his hands on Priscilla's arms, wanting to assure himself of her continued safety. "What is that woman doing here?" he choked.

Priscilla gave him one of those heart-melting smiles that still managed to hit him in the gut like a gladiator's fist, stealing his breath.

"You can never tell who Yeshua will lead to your doorstep." She took his hand and led him out of the chamber and into the dining room, where they could speak alone.

"She could have harmed you, Priscilla! Goodness knows she has tried often enough."

Priscilla laid a calming palm on his chest. "She is too weak to hurt anyone, Husband, and in desperate need of help."

Aquila inhaled slowly. "How did she come to be here, in Corinth? And in this condition?"

"She has not told me."

"Was she robbed, do you think?"

"Perhaps. But there is more to this story than mere theft. She has been living on the streets for some time, judging by the state of her body. The niece of Claudius would be able to find assistance in any city in the empire long before this. She never demanded that I send for the proconsul when I found her."

Aquila raised a brow. "She has fallen into disfavor with the emperor."

"It is the only explanation for her plight. And if that is true, she no longer poses a threat to us. She has no reason to protect her reputation from me. Clearly it has already been sullied."

"I do not understand why you brought her *here*."

The blue eyes softened. If Aquila had been present the day Yeshua healed the lepers who came to him for help, he thought he might have caught a similar look in his Savior's eyes. "She has nowhere to go," Priscilla whispered.

Something in him melted, something hard and crusted. He stared at his wife with awe.

"He is worth this sacrifice, beloved," she said.

He pulled her into his arms again, wanting to feel her next to him, to feel this woman who could nurse her enemy with her own hands. He kissed those hands now, rattled by the hurricane of emotion that clogged his throat.

When he had managed to calm a little, he rubbed the back of his neck. "It is unfair to quote my own words at me. She can stay. But did you have to put her on my side of the bed?"

Priscilla flashed him another smile. "It was closer, and she had grown heavy. Although I do have a confession." She fetched his razor and handed it to him. "I am afraid I used this on her head. For the vermin."

He winced and ran a hand against his cheek. "I was thinking of growing a beard."

"Don't you dare," she said. "You are too handsome to cover your face."

He felt his cheeks warm. "You think I'm handsome?"

"Undeniably, unmistakably, exceptionally handsome."

"Well," he muttered under his breath, "we could put Antonia on a pallet in Lollia's room right now."

Priscilla bit her lip. "I will not tell Lollia you made that suggestion."

"I suppose she must remain in our bed for the present."

He leaned toward her. His body remembered, with sudden vigor, all that it had been missing for weeks. He felt strained, as if awakening from a long dream and realizing he had misplaced something valuable.

His head bent forward a fraction without a conscious decision from him, and he kissed her. The shock of sensation went through his lips all the way down to his bones. The kiss became deep and heated, filled with longing. She gasped and burrowed closer to him.

"This is intolerable," he mumbled. "We have nowhere to go in our own house."

She laid her cheek against his shoulder. He could feel her smile against his chest. His shoulders drooped. "In any case, we need to talk."

Twenty-Seven

AQUILA SETTLED ON THE COUCH, drawing Priscilla next to him. He took a few moments to gather his thoughts. Seeing Antonia sleeping in their bed had wrecked his concentration and put his well-prepared speech straight out of his mind. He swallowed through a dry throat and plowed ahead. "I must ask your forgiveness."

She shook her head as if to deny this confession. He did not even consider taking the easy way, slithering out of the door of grace she had opened. Leaving things unsaid, though far more painless in the present, would ultimately lead to more misunderstandings.

"I do need to ask it, Priscilla." He looked down, his eyes catching the muck that still clung to the shoes he had not removed in his haste. "I know I have been cold and withdrawn. You have been the best of wives, and I have acted like a blind fool.

"You must understand, Priscilla, this is not your doing. I was starting to feel insufficient as a husband. As a man. Our finances had dwindled alarmingly, and I saw it as a personal failure. I started to think it was up to me to provide for us. I forgot to trust the Lord."

She reached for his hand. "I forgive you, Husband. You must forgive me, also. If not for my sin, we would never have had to abandon our home in the first place."

He caressed her cheek. "That is a lie. We are not here because of your sin, but because of the will of God. The Lord used Antonia's scheme to fulfill his own purpose. He has need of us in Corinth. Besides, for all we know, God saved Marcus's life by removing him from Rome.

"We cannot understand the twists and turns of God's plans. But we can trust them. Remain in them. No more blame and condemnation, beloved. Not for you. Not for me.

"I know you have been lonely, and that is my fault. I am here now. Tell me. What is this sorrow that haunts you?"

Priscilla dropped her head. He wondered if she might be unable to trust him now, after his neglect. That possibility shook him—the thought that he might have bruised that precious, fragile trust which she had bestowed upon him.

Her throat worked, but no sound emerged. *O God! Please!* He prayed. "What is it, beloved? Won't you tell me?"

So low he almost missed the words, she whispered, "I fear I may be barren, Aquila." A tear slid down her chin, followed by another.

Aquila smoothed away the soft tendrils of hair that clung to her damp skin. "I think it too soon to jump to such conclusions. Couples sometimes have to wait for years before a child comes along. Think of Zechariah and Elizabeth. They were old when they had John."

"That necessitated a miracle, Aquila!"

He smiled. "God hasn't run out of those."

"But what if I never conceive?"

"Then we will grieve together and love one another through

the pain. We have Marcus. To me, he is like a son. I cannot adopt him—"

"Why not?" a small voice said from the doorway.

"Marcus!" Aquila took in the boy's pale visage and bid him come into the room.

"I wasn't eavesdropping. I overheard what you said."

"I know, Son. Come here."

Marcus came closer, until he stood in front of them, knee to knee. His lips had turned into a rigid line. "Why *can't* you adopt me? If you want me?"

Aquila looked from the boy to his wife, who was practically sitting on her hands to keep herself from smothering him in an embrace. "If I adopt you, you will lose your right to Roman citizenship. Lose your inheritance. Lose the name of Laurentinus. You will become the son of a Jew."

"What if I don't care about any of that?" Marcus said, back stiff.

"If you want us to adopt you, Priscilla and I will. With all our hearts. We feel that you belong to us already. But we cannot do it yet, Marcus. Not until you are old enough to understand what you are losing. I never want you to regret anything because of us."

Marcus stood very still. "You want me to belong to you?"

"More than anything," Priscilla said softly. She pulled him against her chest. He had grown too tall to fit in her lap properly. She did not seem to care. She kept pulling until his body lost its stiffness, and he let go, yielded right into her, and she cradled him against her.

He squeezed his eyes shut. When he opened them again, they were welled up with a lifetime of tears, making spikes of his long eyelashes.

Staring at Priscilla, he said, “I love you.” His voice broke.

It was the first time he had ever said those words in their hearing.

Priscilla started to laugh and cry at the same time, as if she could not quite decide which direction her body should take and tipped both ways. She caressed Marcus’s hair with shaking fingers, repeating the words to him, her voice hoarse.

Aquila watched, mouth dry. He had always known the boy adored Priscilla. He felt a burst of joy for her sake, knowing how deeply she had longed for this tender moment.

At the same time, he could not help feeling left out. Marcus had never had a mother, but he remembered his father well. Aquila could never fill those shoes.

Then to his astonishment, Marcus reached a strong hand, fisted it about Aquila’s neckline and pulled him until he collapsed against his wife and half flattened Marcus. The boy giggled through tears. “I love you, too,” he said to Aquila, looking straight into his eyes.

Aquila felt his heart melt. “Son. My son,” he croaked, though he meant to say so much more. To give assurances, blessings, praises. To make commitments. But all he could manage were those two words: *My son.*

And even those two miserly words dried up when the boy sat up and said to Priscilla, “Can I call you Mother?”

Before she could assure him that she would like nothing better, Marcus turned to face Aquila with unblinking eyes. “Can I call you Father? Even if you don’t adopt me?”

Priscilla made up a pallet for Antonia in a small alcove off the dining room, and hanging a sheet as a makeshift curtain in front of the tiny nook, she managed to create a modest place which their guest could call her own. "It is not much," she told Antonia. "But it is yours, if you want it."

A few months ago, this woman had enjoyed unimaginable luxuries, including, no doubt, a palatial chamber of her own. In her current circumstances, however, the claustrophobic alcove Priscilla and Aquila offered must seem a veritable haven compared to the horrors of living on the streets.

Antonia stared at the pallet with its pile of rough blankets. Without comment, she stepped inside and drew the curtain in Priscilla's facc.

Priscilla ground her teeth. She was hard to love, this woman.

That afternoon, guests started trickling in, the wealthy who led leisurely lives arriving early. Others came later, as their jobs allowed. In fair weather, they would have gathered in the courtyard with its open rooftop, which allowed a refreshing breeze. But the day had grown cloudy, and spring rains pelted the ground in sudden bursts, driving the guests into the shelter of the dining room instead.

The guests found seats wherever they could, pressed tight against one another in the confines of the triclinium. They had grown friendly enough over the past few weeks not to mind the cramped arrangement.

Priscilla had invited Antonia to join them. Not surprisingly, the emperor's niece declined. However, given the location of her alcove, with nothing but a thin sheet separating her from the gathering company, she could hardly avoid listening to the teaching and prayers. Priscilla tried to suppress a satisfied grin without success. God had provided the only arrangement that would convince Antonia to listen to the gospel.

Some of the guests had brought their own cushions to sit on. Others brought jugs of wine, platters of bread, cheese, olives, and dried fruits to share. Before they began to eat, Paul celebrated the Lord's Supper, and their first bite was of spiritual food.

Afterward, when they served supper, Priscilla saw to it that the poor received generous portions. Some of the people under her roof would not eat another good meal until they visited there again.

Crispus and his family arrived last, when the sun had set and the heavens wrapped his arrival in a cloak of darkness. Paul's teaching in the synagogue had stirred many to anger. A man named Sosthenes, who wielded substantial influence among the people, had grown especially adept at stoking the fires of animosity. Crispus found himself caught in a painful vise, between his growing attraction to Yeshua and increasing pressure from members of his congregation to pronounce Paul a heretic.

For now, he managed to walk a fine line, committing to neither one nor the other. He came to their home in secret lest he be banished from the society of his people. But he came.

Stephanas's daughter Chara had learned several psalms from Paul, and they began the evening with a song while she accompanied them on her cithara.

You are a hiding place for me;
 you preserve me from trouble;
 you surround me with shouts of deliverance.

After praying, Paul began to teach them, and for a while, Priscilla forgot to worry about Antonia or Crispus or the convoluted problems they faced in the synagogue.

The moon was high in the night sky when a loud knock sounded at their door. Priscilla jumped, startled by the unexpected noise.

"I will get it," Aquila said, motioning her to remain.

They could hear the murmur of voices belowstairs. When Aquila returned, he was followed by two smiling men. Priscilla did not recognize them. But Paul sprang to his feet and wove his way through the crowd as fast as he could.

"Silas! Timothy! About time you arrived in Corinth. I have a mountain of work for you to do!"

The older of the two rolled his eyes. "I missed you, too."

The other, a young lion of a man, wrapped muscular arms around Paul's wiry frame and embraced him with comfortable familiarity. "Macedonia proved boring without you."

Paul's eyes sparkled. "You will find plenty of excitement here, Timothy."

The other man, who Priscilla assumed must be Silas, held up a hand. "Has anyone beaten you up yet?"

Paul shrugged. "It's early days. Give me time."

"Not much time," Crispus growled. "He stirs the world around him like a cook with a pot."

In the morning a new letter arrived from Senator Pudens. The papyrus on which he had written looked crumpled, and one side had torn off completely. Water stains smudged the ink, rendering some paragraphs illegible.

"Shipwreck," the man carrying it explained. "I had tucked that in my belt. It's a miracle either of us survived. But it's been delayed by a couple of months. Took me a while to make my way here after the ship went down."

Priscilla thanked the sailor and fed him a hearty meal before settling down to read the letter to her family. The senator's greetings and opening remarks had been streaked by seawater. She began to read the first legible sentence.

> *"Rome is abuzz with fresh scandal, which involves someone who has had no small bearing on your own lives. Claudius's niece Antonia has been banished from Rome."*

"Well!" Aquila smirked. "For once, we are ahead of the senator."

Benyamin waved a hand in a dampening motion. "Let us hear the senator's account. Perhaps he can help us solve this mystery. Carry on, Priscilla."

She nodded and began to read once more.

> *"Claudius sent Antonia away not long after you yourselves departed for Corinth. But the story is only now reaching public notice.*
>
> *"If rumor is to be believed, Antonia has been involved in an affair with a married man. What with the emergence of the New Woman, Antonia's indiscretion would hardly seem worthy of mention."*

"What is a New Woman?" Benyamin asked. "I haven't even begun to understand the old one."

A huff of laughter escaped Priscilla. "An increasingly large number of aristocratic Roman wives are balking at the old-fashioned constraints of marriage," she explained. "They call themselves the New Woman, though there is considerable diversity in how they understand that term. Some merely shed their veils in public as a sign of their growing independence." She felt her cheeks redden. "Others go much further and consider themselves free of all marital bounds. Their veil-free status becomes a symbol of a myriad of liberties. They cavort with other women's husbands, live in open infidelity, and consider such behavior their right."

"That's a new woman?" Benyamin whistled. "I think I liked the old kind better."

"This is why Paul insists that married women cover their hair during worship," Aquila pointed out. "He does not wish the freedom of Christ to be confused with immorality."

Benyamin nodded. "I see. So Antonia is a New Woman who preferred someone else's husband. Is that why Claudius banished her?"

"I suspect there is more to her story." Priscilla read the next legible section in the letter:

> *"Dissatisfied with a mere affair, Antonia pressured her lover to divorce his wife and marry her. But the man refused her demands. Unwilling to let the matter lie, Antonia hired some brute to pay the wife a visit and convince her to divorce her husband."*

"Ah. That sounds more like dear Antonia." Aquila arched a brow. "What does *convince her* mean, exactly? Beat her? Blackmail her? Worse?"

Priscilla sighed. "The senator does not say. He writes that the plot was discovered and the outraged husband himself approached the emperor about the matter. Antonia denied these charges passionately, of course. But Claudius was inclined to believe the husband. Since the debacle with his former wife Messalina two years ago, the emperor's patience has worn thin when it comes to scheming women."

"What happened with Messalina?" Benyamin asked.

"She cheated on Claudius," Priscilla explained.

"With numerous people," Aquila clarified.

"And she married another man," Priscilla added. "While she was still married to Claudius." She made a face. "Not a wise choice, as it turned out."

"No. I can see that would be a problem."

Priscilla perused the rest of the letter. "According to Senator Pudens, Claudius renounced his niece in short order once the offended husband approached him. After confiscating her property and wealth, the emperor banished Antonia from Rome, putting her on the first ship bound out of Ostia. She must have arrived in Corinth with the clothes on her back and not much else. Which means she is destitute and friendless. No one with any ambition will raise a hand to help her, lest they displease the emperor."

Aquila stretched. "And those are the only people she ever associated with."

Benyamin sat upright. "Hold a moment. Does this mean we can return to Rome?"

Priscilla looked over Pudens's letter and shook her head. "The senator tried to raise the subject of the banishment of the Jews with the emperor. Claudius did not want to hear of it. With a new wife and the endless political maneuvering that surrounds him, no doubt he finds himself too busy to revisit old decisions."

Aquila turned toward her. "What now?"

She gave him a small smile. "This solves the enigma of how she came to be in Corinth. But it changes nothing. We will take care of her."

Aquila regarded her in silence, eyes turning molten green. Reaching for her hand, he lifted it to his lips. "I am proud to have you as my wife."

Twenty-Eight

AFTER ALMOST THREE WEEKS, Antonia had lost the sickly look of one who sat not far from death's door. She had gained weight, and the ulcerating pustules on her face and body had healed, leaving behind faint scars.

Once again Priscilla invited her to attend their prayer gatherings. "We would welcome your company," she assured her sullen guest.

"I prefer not to," Antonia said, grabbing the curtain, ready to pull it shut.

Priscilla's hand flashed out, holding the fabric in place. "As you wish. But from now on, if you want to eat, you must join us."

Priscilla had begun to grow weary of carrying plates back and forth to the woman now that she had regained the strength to move with ease. Besides, she could not hide in this cramped alcove for the rest of her life. High time she faced the world.

Antonia took a step back and bumped against the wall. "You expect me to show myself in public like this?" She pointed at her head. Her hair had started growing in like new grass, straight and shiny. And shorter than a man's.

"I will give you a palla."

"And a new tunic. This one is a disgusting color."

Priscilla studied the brown tunic she had given Antonia. She crossed her arms. "What color would you prefer?"

"Something that does not remind me of cow dung."

A huff of laughter escaped Priscilla. "It is rather a nauseating shade, I grant you. I will see what I can find. But my choices are limited."

"Why are you so cordial to me?" Antonia scowled. "I suppose you want a favor?"

Priscilla's gaze softened. She realized that her guest had no way of knowing that they had already discovered her fall from grace. She assumed they were helping her in hopes of a reward. "No, Antonia. I want no favors."

Priscilla fetched a pale turquoise–colored tunic and palla from her room. The old Antonia would have scorned anything so plain. But the woman who had lain in her own waste by the side of the street took the clothing and held them against her chest.

"Thank you," she whispered before shoving the curtain closed in Priscilla's face. Priscilla did a little dance before walking down the stairs in perfect decorum. Antonia had *thanked* her.

In the evening, they welcomed a new arrival: a young man named Theo, who needed a place to stay. He had a hollow look about him, as though some part of his soul had been gouged out. Handsome, with classic features that could easily have served as model for a statue of Apollo, Theo came in like a wraith, silent and haunted. Paul did not expound on his situation, only that the young man had suffered a broken heart.

When Marcus discovered that Theo had won the famed chariot race at the previous Isthmian Games and that he was considered a venerated champion in Corinth, he became a barnacle at the side of the young man. Priscilla tried to pry him off their guest more than once.

"You must not bother Theo, Marcus," she said one afternoon when her son pelted the young man with questions about horses.

"He is no bother," Theo assured her. He studied the mosaics under his feet, a stylized pattern of swirling waves. "I have my own share of questions," he said.

"If it is about horses, I cannot help you," Priscilla said.

Theo shook his head. "They hold no mysteries for me. But your God is a different matter."

Theo had attended their gatherings with silent but intense attention every night. He had kept his questions to himself thus far. Yet she knew that many preferred private conversations about God to public discourse.

"Ask, and I will try to answer if I can," she said.

"You say your God loves us. And yet he allows our hopes to be crushed. You say he has a purpose for us. Yet he does not seem to care when our dreams are destroyed. How can love be so uncaring?"

"The answer to that question is not an intellectual thesis. Even if I were able to give you such, it would not matter, because you ask a question that belongs to the heart, not reason.

"I can tell you that my own dreams have been crushed more than once. But when I condemned myself, God extended forgiveness to me. When I felt broken, he gave me strength. When I thought the future held nothing but pain, he gave me joy. Those are the actions of love.

"Look to the cross of Christ, Theo. Because on that cross you will not find an uncaring face. You will find unbroken love. And his plans are better than yours."

When Antonia sauntered into the dining room and joined the family for lunch, Priscilla almost choked on her vegetable stew. Their guest did not deign to say a single word. Instead, she wiped her mouth daintily on her napkin after finishing her salad, then rose to retire in her nook without offering any help. After that, she attended meals regularly, though she never came for breakfast, which proved too early for the hours she preferred to keep.

Once in a while, if the topic of conversation turned to fashion, jewelry, gladiatorial games, or chariot races, she even offered a few words. Since these were not common topics in Priscilla's home, however, she spoke rarely. The rest of the time, she continued to hide in her alcove with the curtain drawn, especially when the church gathered.

One evening, Aquila quoted a verse from the prophet Isaiah:

"See, I am doing a new thing!
    Now it springs up; do you not perceive it?
I am making a way in the wilderness
    and streams in the wasteland."

To Priscilla's astonishment, the curtain moved, as though disturbed by a figure leaning into its folds. When Aquila started to speak about God's desire to stir new beginnings and release fresh starts in every life, the drape of fabric parted and Antonia stepped into the room. Avoiding eye contact, she found a narrow spot on the floor, settled herself there, and did not move until the last prayers were offered and the guests started to depart.

Priscilla picked up a large platter, now empty save for bread crumbs, to be washed belowstairs when she found her path blocked by Antonia. "I have no money to give you," Antonia said abruptly.

Priscilla nodded. "I am aware of that."

"I can't help you find favor with the emperor, either."

"I am aware of that, also."

"I don't understand."

"We expect nothing from you, Antonia."

The woman rubbed the bridge of her nose. The palla fell onto her shoulders, exposing her shorn head. She seemed utterly vulnerable in that moment. Powerless. How shocking that realization must have been to her, Priscilla thought. The knowledge that she could not buy or manipulate or bully her way out of this trouble.

"It was my fault," she said, her voice thin. Strained.

Priscilla's breath hitched. "What was your fault?"

"Your expulsion from Rome. That was *my* doing. I lied to Claudius. Told him that you and Aquila were roiling up dissention among the Jews, creating trouble for Rome."

"I know."

The lowered head snapped up. Antonia stared in amazement. "You *know*? How?"

"A friend told us when we were still in Rome. He tried to intervene on our behalf, to no avail."

"You knew back in *Rome*?" The full lips began to tremble. "Then why did you help me? Why not leave me in the street to rot?"

Priscilla set the platter down and wiped her hands on the towel she had tucked at her waist. "Antonia, have you been listening night after night in your alcove as we teach?"

The woman nodded, a short, awkward movement of her head. There was nothing regal about her now.

"Then *you* tell me. Why do you think I have harbored you in my home?"

Fingers wrapped into one another in tortured twists. "I don't know."

"Think about it," Priscilla said and bent to retrieve the platter.

"Wait."

Priscilla abandoned the dish.

"This new beginning Aquila spoke about. Can I have it?"

"That depends on what you mean by a new beginning. If you wish to return to the life you once led, a life solely focused on yourself and your desires, then no. God does not promise to give us a fresh chance at *that* life. Because, as you may have discovered by now, it leads to no good. It does not satisfy.

"God's fresh start begins here." Priscilla touched her chest. "It requires a transformed heart. You can begin a new life, Antonia—a fulfilling life, which no emperor can take away. But you will need God first."

"Is that what you have?" Antonia's fingers bunched her palla. "You have few of the things I always valued. Power. A wealthy husband. Land. Pretty jewels and expensive clothes. You don't have many servants or crowds of people staring at you in admiration, jealous of all you possess. And yet you always seem content.

"I used to think you were too stupid to realize you should want more. Now I don't know. You have married a Jew with no land, no renown. Not even a citizen! Yet he expresses more love for you with one look than I ever received from the caresses of . . . any man."

Priscilla leaned against the wall. "I know what it is to settle for unworthy things. I know that ache. I have learned that God offers so much more, and now I won't settle for anything less."

"I used to hate you," Antonia said abruptly.

"Because I saw you in the physician's house."

"I suppose Aquila does not know? He is such a devout prude."

"He *is* devout, though I would not call him a prude. He knows all my secrets."

The brown eyes widened. "Yet he married you."

"It took him a while to ask."

Antonia laughed. "Gods. Men are stupid."

"They are broken, as we are. Yet the astounding, wonderous truth which never ceases to amaze me is that like us, they are made in the image of God."

Antonia's throat worked as if she could not quite swallow. "When I say I hated you, I mean . . ." She adjusted the palla over her head, covering the pathetic stubble.

"That you tried to have me killed? More than once. I know."

She gasped. "What are you? A witch?"

Priscilla smiled. "No. You are just not as clever as you think."

"I think we have proven that." The thick lashes swept up. "Priscilla. Why do you help me, knowing what I have done?"

"Well, I might not have been as forgiving about it if you had actually succeeded in killing me."

"Please. Don't jest." Antonia looked beseechingly at the woman she had once hated venomously. Murderously.

Priscilla reached for her hands, cracked and rough from her weeks of sleeping in the streets. "I am helping you because you are worth another chance. A fresh start. Because Yeshua can give you a new life. Just as he did me."

Antonia's eyes began to shimmer. "I am grateful you are not dead," she said. High praise, considering the source.

Twenty-Nine

FOR THE THIRD TIME in as many hours, Aquila stuck his nose into Priscilla's hair and inhaled deeply, as if she were sweet pastry. "You smell so good!"

She grinned. Theo had presented Priscilla with a basket full of fist-size spheres, which he called soap. He and his foster father, Galenos, had begun a new business venture producing hair pomade and hoping to export it to other ports of the empire. Infused with rose oil, it had left her hair cleaner than she had ever thought possible. Given Aquila's enthusiastic response, she planned to become Theo's most ardent customer.

For a few days after Theo joined them, Priscilla had worried that Antonia might set her sights on him. He had the kind of thoughtless charm and beauty that could unknowingly break hearts. Antonia's affections would have been wasted effort. Priscilla suspected Theo had no heart to offer anyone. He had left it in someone else's keeping. Someday, perhaps, he might outgrow whatever love bound him. But that day remained a long way off.

Thankfully, Antonia must have come to the same conclusion since she stopped simpering and fluttering her lashes in his vicinity.

With the passing of the month of June, their diminutive home had to stretch its walls to accommodate one more guest, this time a woman named Claudia. Though wealthy, she had escaped the cruelties of a wicked husband, arriving in the middle of the night with nothing save the clothes she wore. Well, those and the gleaming jewels that covered her from head to foot.

Antonia almost swooned when she first set eyes on the sparkling woman. "You can share my alcove," she declared to the new arrival.

Priscilla whipped her head in astonishment. It was the first time she had seen the emperor's niece act unselfishly.

Antonia caught her gaping look and shrugged. "Your house is full, and there are few places that offer privacy."

Claudia told them that she needed to remain in hiding for several weeks before returning to her father's house. She hoped that her tempestuous husband would eventually be convinced to leave Corinth and give up any claims on her.

Priscilla saw, at once, the potential for friendship between the two women. They had far more in common with one another than they did with Priscilla, since both loved the luxuries that wealth could afford them. They were also broken women who had lost everything, though Claudia had walked away from her marriage with a sizable bundle of expensive baubles. But they had both learned what it was to be humbled. To fail. To fall short of their dreams for fame and importance.

Their friendship could have tugged them back into the world that had once so charmed them. Instead, it gave them the strength to begin a wary exploration of God together. Because these women had been astounded by the actions of those who had helped them in God's name, they now turned to Yeshua to discover for themselves how a humble carpenter could inspire so much grace.

They shared a budding hope, a growing longing, which for once tilted not toward men or wealth or success, but to something altogether more, and they spurred one another in faith, though they did so one tiptoe at a time.

They never turned to Priscilla as an equal. Her faith, with its ocean-depth of generosity and trust, daunted them. She found it hard not to feel hurt by this exclusion. The part of her that had lived through years of loneliness in her girlhood and tasted the bitter bread of being an outsider now relived the pain of that old rejection. Once again, Priscilla became aware that Rome had managed to chase her all the way to Corinth, the good and the bad years casting their shadows on her new life. She consoled the bruised young girl who still lived somewhere within her, trying to remember that Christ had found her worthy of pursuit. He had called her friend even if her guests refused to do so.

One evening, Antonia and Claudia arrived first at the prayer gathering and, as was their habit, secured the best spot on one of the comfortable couches. Paul approached them, accompanied by an ancient slave woman whose back had been bent by the ravages of time and years of strenuous work.

"Good evening," he said politely. "May I introduce our sister Alba?"

Claudia and Antonia stared at Paul without comprehension. Priscilla could guess their thoughts. What did the Jewish teacher want them to do? Greet the slave as if she were an equal?

Priscilla smothered a laugh, knowing Paul wanted *more*. He stared down at the young women stretched indolently on the couch, his brown eyes narrowing, slowly gathering a thunderbolt of displeasure.

Antonia squirmed and sat up straight. "Ah. Hail, Alba," she offered.

Alba was pulling on Paul's arm, trying to draw him away, whispering urgently something Priscilla could not hear. Paul ignored her. He had a habit of going deaf when someone's request did not agree with his plans.

"Alba suffers from a painful back condition." Paul glared pointedly at the couch.

Finally Antonia caught on. With an imperious hand, she readjusted her palla and opened her mouth. Priscilla winced, expecting a caustic speech, dismissing Alba and Paul in one breath. Before speaking, Antonia turned her head a fraction. Her gaze collided with Priscilla's.

Priscilla smiled and patted a cushion that remained empty next to her on the floor. Antonia swallowed hard. She turned to face the slave.

"Please take my seat, Alba," she said, and then removing herself in short order, came to settle next to Priscilla.

"That was well done," Priscilla whispered.

"You are extremely annoying, you do realize?" the emperor's niece said. But slowly her lips twitched and widened in a grin.

"I imagine Claudia is not accustomed to sharing her couch with an old slave."

Antonia's grin turned into a chuckle.

On the Sabbath, Aquila accompanied Paul and his friends to the synagogue. A large group began screaming insults at the former Pharisee as soon as he began to speak. Several of the members threatened him with arrest or bodily harm if he continued to insist that the man of Nazareth was the promised Messiah. Aquila watched Crispus try in vain to calm his congregation. The crowd's rage had grown explosive.

Aquila grabbed Paul by the arm and tried to haul him out of the building before the situation devolved into violence. The wiry man pulled himself free from his grasp and returned to face the congregation.

"Remember the warning of the prophet," he shouted. "'He will be a stone that causes people to stumble and a rock that makes them fall.' You are stumbling upon the Lord himself—stumbling upon the name of Yeshua."

The insults grew louder and more threatening.

"Leave this place. Pack your lies and go. No one wants you here!" Sosthenes screeched. Other voices joined his.

Paul's voice drowned them. "Your blood be on your own heads!" he cried. "I am innocent. From now on, I will go to the Gentiles."

"Good riddance!" Sosthenes cried. "Stay there and don't return."

Paul stormed out, Aquila and Priscilla on one side, Benyamin on the other, Timothy and Silas following, expressions grim. Titius Justus the Gentile God fearer also followed. No one else came.

"Paul!" Aquila halted when they had gained some distance from the building. "You of all people must understand how hard it is for the sons and daughters of Abraham to receive our message. You who persecuted the followers of Yeshua."

Paul inhaled sharply. "I *do* understand. It breaks my heart to see them deny the treasure we offer."

Aquila nodded. "We must be patient."

"Patient?" Paul pointed the way they had come. "Do you see anyone else following?"

No sooner had the words left his mouth than the silhouette

of a single man appeared in the doorway of the synagogue. Then another form appeared behind him, followed by another. As they drew closer, Aquila recognized Crispus, along with his wife and the rest of his household. He grinned.

They waited in silence for the stragglers to catch up. "It seems I am no longer the ruler of the synagogue," Crispus said when he was close enough to speak. "Sosthenes has that honor."

"What happened?" Aquila asked.

"My heart is certain that Yeshua is all you claim him to be. I can deny him no longer. I told the congregation so, and they showed me the door."

"I am sorry. I know it is a great loss to you."

Crispus pulled his cloak tighter about him. "For the first time in weeks, I am not at war with myself." His chest expanded as he gulped a great mouthful of air. "As soon as I made the decision to follow the Christ, I felt peace replace the storm of uncertainty and fear that has dogged my steps since I heard Paul speak of him. It is good to be free."

That very day Paul baptized Crispus and his whole family in the waters of the Aegean Sea.

Priscilla's house was bursting at the seams. Paul shared Benyamin's chamber; Theo, Timothy, and Silas slept in the workshop; and Antonia and Claudia occupied the nook off the dining room. It made for a tight fit.

Paul noticed the problem. "You are running out of space," he said as they worked together.

She shrugged. "We will manage."

Paul pulled on his beard. "Titius Justus has invited me to move to his house. I will accept the invitation."

Priscilla gasped. "You are leaving us?"

"I will still come to the workshop. But I will lodge at Justus's house. The believers are growing in number. You and Aquila can continue to host gatherings in your home, while I begin new ones. Timothy and Silas can help us both. It will double our outreach while solving your space problem."

Priscilla felt a hollow in the pit of her stomach at Paul's news. She had come to look upon him as a father more than a teacher. She loved having him in her home, loved being able to turn to him at whim, asking for guidance. Sometimes she felt stronger, safer, merely sitting in his presence. He was not a soft man. More fire than breath, really. Yet something about the solidity of his faith made the ground under her feet feel firmer.

"I will miss you," she said, recognizing the sense in his decision. Then her brows lowered. "Titius Justus lives next door to the synagogue."

Paul grinned. "Isn't that fortunate?"

Priscilla shook her head. "They will be forced to watch as Yeshua's following grows. They will not be well pleased. I don't know whether to admire you or despair of you."

"I would prefer that you pray for me."

One evening, Theo returned home looking like a mere shell of himself. Priscilla had thought him a broken man before that night. But now, he looked like he had seen the terrors of hell. She had no idea what had happened to him. She only knew that Theo had been gouged, like the victim of a lion's ferocious attack.

Sensing he could not face a conversation, she sent Ferox to him. The dog, quiet and watchful, plumped himself into Theo's lap. Theo held on to the animal with trembling hands, dropped his head as if the weight of it had grown too much for the muscular neck, and wept. Priscilla closed the door of the workshop quietly and left, knowing that sometimes a man needed to wrestle his monsters alone.

In the morning, when the family had gathered for breakfast, still sleepy from the early hour, Theo joined them, eyes looking large, framed by purple shadows. "Will you baptize me?" he said to Aquila.

Aquila sprang to his feet. "It would be my honor. But are you certain? It is no small decision."

Theo nodded. "When you are drowning, life becomes simple. You know you need a Savior. It is only a matter of choosing who or what you reach out for as the waves crash over you. I am a drowning man. In this house, I have had a glimpse of your God. I have seen Yeshua's face on that cross, and you are right. It is the face of love. I have sensed his hand stretching out to me. I choose to take it."

His eyes shimmered. "One thing I am certain of. I need a father besides the one I have been given. I will take Yeshua's Father for my own."

When Priscilla shared the news with Paul, his forehead crimped as if in pain. "Pray for him," Paul said. "That man has been burned by a fire few would survive. But the Lord has set aside a future and a hope for him."

Aquila settled back against his chair and looked over at Marcus. They had established a pattern, studying the Scriptures together in the mornings before Aquila began work. He owned a copy of the Torah in Greek and had set Marcus to studying the story of Joseph.

Surrounded by giants of faith like Paul, Silas, and Timothy every day, their conversations rich with God's truths, his son had inevitably been growing in the Spirit. He still preferred play to study, however.

"Could we practice swords, Father?" Marcus asked.

"After you memorize a verse of your choice."

Marcus fidgeted some more. Aquila furled the portion of Genesis he was studying and set it aside. "What have you read about the story of Joseph so far?"

"He is a boaster. After he has a nice little dream, he rubs his brothers' noses in it."

"What then?"

"That's all I've read."

"Son, you were supposed to finish it today."

Marcus sighed dramatically. "But it's boring! There are no sword fights, no chariots, no soldiers. It's good for women, I suppose. All this dream business."

Aquila tried not to laugh. "Let me tell you a little more of his story. Joseph's brothers, jealous of the favor he curried with their father and tired of his dreams, decided to kill him when he came upon them in the pasture one day."

Marcus sat up a little straighter. "Those ruffians!"

"One of the brothers, Reuben, interceded with the rest. So instead of murdering him, they threw Joseph into an empty pit. When a caravan of Midianite traders passed their way, they sold Joseph to them as a slave."

Marcus went still. "Like my uncle wanted to do to me."

"Very much like that."

"What happened to Joseph?"

"You will have to read for yourself, won't you?"

"I will. I promise. Can you share a little more, Father? Please?"

Aquila tousled his son's hair. "Joseph became a slave in Egypt. He had many difficult adventures. But in the end, he rose up to be a great man. A powerful leader. And he helped save many lives by his wisdom."

"That's a good story," Marcus admitted. He fretted the hilt of his wooden sword, his nails scraping off the dirt stuck in the grain.

Aquila cupped his hand over the moving fingers, stilling them. "I know you want to be proficient with your sword so that you will never again have to watch helplessly as someone you love is harmed." He sighed, not sure how to make Marcus understand. "You cannot take charge of the world in your own strength, Son. You cannot drain it of all pain or danger. This sword will not make you safe."

The boy's eyes glittered. "I will revenge my father and redress the wrong done to me. Isn't that what Joseph did to his brothers?"

"No. Joseph chose to forgive them."

Marcus chewed on his lips. "I don't know if I can forgive my uncle."

"Forgiveness does not mean there will be no consequences. Your mother and I will try our best to pursue justice for you. Your uncle is a dangerous man. You and your father are likely not the only people he has harmed. He needs to be stopped. That does not mean that your heart has to be chained to thoughts of vengeance. God will deal with Aulus."

"How am I supposed to forgive him after what he did?" the boy cried.

Aquila laid the flat of his palm on the unfurled papyrus. "Start with this."

Marcus looked from his sword to the ragged papyrus on the table. It was clear which held his interest more.

"Marcus, your uncle may have robbed you of your inheritance. But there is another treasure that belongs to you. One that no one can rob."

Marcus frowned. "What treasure?"

Aquila tapped the open roll in front of the boy. "Here is one. This Scripture is part of your inheritance. The spiritual treasures that belong to you are vast, Son. The ability to speak to Yeshua. To hear from him. To help others through your prayers. To love rightly. To find joy in God's presence. To live a life of contentment. A fruitful life. To have the gift of eternity. The list is so long, no one knows the full contents! An endless trove of worthy treasures has been set aside for you. It waits for you. Don't give any of it away cheaply."

He put his elbows on the table and leaned forward. "Unlike your earthly inheritance, your spiritual birthright cannot be stolen from you. But you do have the power to waste it. You can fritter your time away on swordplay and wrestling. On thoughts of revenge. On plans of your own making."

He tapped the papyrus again. "Hold on to this, Marcus. Study it. Set your mind on it. And let God determine the paths of your life."

"But what if God calls me to be a soldier, not a scholar?"

Aquila smiled. "Then you will become a soldier. First, though, you have to draw so close to God that you will hear his voice and learn to distinguish it from your own."

For a while, Marcus remained quiet, contemplating Aquila's words. He started reading Joseph's story again, this time finishing the account. Then he rolled the papyrus closed, his touch careful on the delicate scroll.

He cleared his throat. "When you baptize Theo, will you baptize me too?"

Thirty

HAVING LIVED IN ROME, Aquila had not thought it possible to ever see architecture that might rival its grandeur. The agora in Corinth came close. The imposing marketplace housed the administrative center of the city, including the council chamber and several sanctuaries, both ancient and modern, which boasted gold-covered statues ornamented with bold colors. An inn and tavern just off the southwest corner of the agora offered a luxurious shelter to cosmopolitan visitors, and to the east, an elegant basilica was decorated with statues of the imperial family.

Many of Aquila's deliveries took place in the agora, and he had quickly become familiar with its crowded layout. Having finished a particularly bulky tent made of goatskin, he asked Paul to help him deliver it to the impatient customer, who had a bakery near the marketplace. They were still some distance from the *bema*, the outdoor court with its exquisite cream-and-blue marble, when a group of shouting men led by Sosthenes accosted them.

Aquila recognized their faces from the synagogue. They grabbed hold of Paul with rough hands and dragged him toward the tribunal. It all happened so quickly—their unexpected arrival, their boiling rage, their attack on Paul as they pushed and shoved him along—that Aquila barely had time to offer any objections. Offer them, he did, receiving a few blows for his pains. He bent over, the ache in his gut momentarily paralyzing him.

The commotion attracted the crowds, who left off their shopping to gape. Storekeepers, irritated by this disruption to their business, followed behind the men from the synagogue as they marched to the tribunal.

Paul motioned Aquila to silence. In truth, as a Roman citizen, the apostle would be safer before Corinth's proconsul, Gallio, than he would in the hands of his own enraged countrymen.

Lucius Junius Gallio, a thin man with veiny legs, scowled at the large crowd gathering before him. "What's this? What's this? You are giving me a headache with your noise. Silence!"

To Aquila's relief, the mob obliged. Sosthenes stepped forward. "Proconsul Gallio, if you please. I represent this delegation of the Jews of Corinth. We bring a complaint against this man." He poked a finger in Paul's back. "He is persuading people to worship God contrary to the Law."

Paul opened his mouth to respond. Gallio raised a bony hand and motioned him to remain quiet. "Let me understand. You are complaining about some infraction of your religious Law?"

Sosthenes nodded vigorously. "He is disrupting our worship."

Gallio rolled his eyes. "This is not a matter of civil wrongdoing or crime," he barked. "If this man had robbed or killed someone, then I would be the appropriate official to delve into the problem. But by your own admission, this concerns your Law. You must see to it yourselves. I refuse to judge this affair."

He rose to his feet. "And in the future do not disturb the agora with your imaginary charges. Do you not hear the crowds? They are mad as hornets, and I can't blame them. You have disrupted their business for no good reason at all." He made a motion with his hand, and before Sosthenes could object, a couple of burly members of the urban cohorts shoved him and his friends out of the tribunal.

Paul and Aquila slid out quietly after them.

Aquila took his first easy breath since being accosted by his compatriots. "Thanks be to God! I was beside myself with worry. I thought I would see you whipped," he said to Paul.

"You will see a beating today. But not mine." Paul pointed his chin toward the agora. The Corinthian crowds had surrounded the members of the synagogue, looking more threatening with every passing moment.

"We are sick of people like you interrupting our business by bringing ill-founded accusations to the tribunal," one man, wearing a butcher's apron, shouted. "Every time a crowd shows up frothing at the mouth, I lose half a day of trade."

Others yelled their agreement. Someone grabbed Sosthenes. "You are their ringleader. I saw you earlier."

Sosthenes tried to appease them. "No, friends. I am not at fault. The true culprit stands over—" He never finished what he meant to say. An elbow landed in his mouth.

Aquila bounded forward. "We must try to stop them!" But before he could make his way into the thick knot of people, the crowds started to disperse, bored with beating their wailing victim. He could see Sosthenes was not seriously hurt in spite of the blood that spurt out of his nose and the limp in his leg as he began to walk away, supported by his companions.

"He will have a bruise or two. Nothing serious. Trust me. I

know a few things about being beaten," Paul said dryly. "Sosthenes meant to harm us, but God has used his scheme for our good. After watching him in the hands of that angry mob, the members of the synagogue will think twice before bringing charges against me again. Bless the misguided fellow. Because of him, we will be left in peace to preach the gospel."

Aquila tried to smile. But he could not banish the memory of Sosthenes's face as he turned to stare at Paul, his features distorted with loathing.

The church in Corinth grew and spread by dint of its leaders' toil. Priscilla and Aquila opened their home to men and women who were greedy, immoral, drunkards, slanderers, and swindlers until Yeshua grabbed hold of them. The free mixed with the slave, the poor with the rich, the honest with the thief. There were no boring days at the church in Corinth.

Priscilla had learned that God's straight paths sometimes took twisted turns on earth. She had lost her home because of a betrayal. Ironically, in Corinth, the betrayer found a home.

Priscilla knew that Antonia needed a fresh start. A life beyond their tiny nook, especially when Claudia would return to her father's home in a couple of weeks. Antonia would wake up to the fact that her new friend had moved on. Moved forward, while she remained stuck in a dead-end existence that led nowhere.

When Priscilla had first met Berenice in Stephanas's house, she had realized that the lavishly dressed woman with thinning white hair might prove an answer to her prayers for Antonia. The widow of an olive merchant, Berenice's husband had been a shrewd man of business, a commoner who had gone on to amass a considerable fortune before his death.

Thanks to Stephanas, Priscilla had discovered that Berenice had an insatiable curiosity about the Roman aristocracy. Her longing to learn everything about patrician life was matched only by her passion for gossip on the subject. Priscilla made certain that the widow knew about the very aristocratic guest living under her roof.

"Antonia has been received at the palace in Rome many times," she said to Berenice. "She has met most of the senators in person."

The exuberantly applied powder on Berenice's cheeks could not mask the rising color in her face. "Has she actually met the emperor?" she gasped.

"Many times." Priscilla presented her blandest expression. "Would you like Antonia herself to tell you some of her stories of life in Rome?"

Berenice almost tripped in her haste to accept Priscilla's invitation to her home.

When she introduced the widow to Claudius's niece, Berenice appeared utterly overwhelmed. Even with her humble clothing and growing faith, Antonia still had a way of making others feel only slightly above an insect beneath her feet. After leaving the two women alone to speak for a while, Priscilla drew the widow away.

"Did you enjoy your conversation with Antonia?"

"Oh, my dear! She is very refined. Very refined, indeed. And the people she knows! Why, I could listen to her speak for hours."

"It must be difficult for you to live alone," Priscilla said.

"I am not quite alone, you know." The old woman adjusted her embroidered tunic. "My slaves and servants are always about."

"Of course. But it's not the same as having a companion, is it? A true friend? One with equal interests. Now that your husband is gone, I mean."

"True. True. I do miss Lucius. Though he was never one to converse a great deal."

"Not like Antonia."

"Oh, well. That is different, my dear. She is patrician through and through. Good manners and speech are in her blood."

"She has recently experienced a painful tragedy, sadly, and cannot return to Rome."

Berenice's eyes widened. "How terrible! What happened?"

"It is not for me to speak of. But her ill fortune might be regarded as a blessing when seen in the right light. She could use a friend like you, Berenice."

"Work?" Antonia stared at Priscilla as if she had shot her with a poisoned arrow.

"Not with your hands," Priscilla clarified hastily. "Something suitable to your talents."

Antonia crossed her arms. "Such as what, for example?"

"Berenice is willing to welcome you as a companion. She is aging and has no children. She grows lonely. She has servants to take care of her needs. What she desires is a friend. A friend who can speak to her of Rome. Of life in the palace."

Antonia made a face. "That old woman?"

Priscilla said nothing. Antonia flushed, the weight of Priscilla's unspoken censure making her squirm. "Does she know I have been exiled by Claudius?"

"Not from me. I thought you might wish to tell her yourself. I believe, in her eyes, your aristocratic lineage will take precedence over any indiscretion you may be guilty of."

Priscilla leaned forward. "Antonia, it is the perfect position for you. Berenice will adore you. She will practically worship the ground you walk on."

"That sounds . . . acceptable."

"She has agreed to furnish you with clothes."

Antonia's head whipped up. "What kind of clothes?"

"Better than what you are wearing now."

"That's not hard. You have horrible taste in clothing."

"I have insufficient funds for clothing. And Berenice plans to give you a beautiful chamber of your own. In fact, she is going to refurbish everything from floor to ceiling. She told me it would take her over a month to prepare it to a standard worthy of you."

"Finally! Someone with some sense."

"And did I mention Berenice will also pay you a wage? A generous one. She was concerned that you might be offended if she offered. I assured her you would be amenable should the amount prove appropriate. In return, you merely have to offer her companionship. Tell her stories of your life in Rome. Perhaps you might even find it possible to explain how empty that life proved in the end. Help her understand that God alone can offer peace."

Antonia smirked. "You are hopeless. Everything ends in God with you."

"Thank you."

Antonia grew silent. Her head drooped. "I know you are younger than I am," she whispered, "but in a strange way, you have been like a mother to me." Her voice grew thin, like a child's. "I will miss you if I leave here."

Priscilla wrapped her arm about the young woman's shoulders. "Antonia, I will miss *you*! And if that is not proof of God, then I can't imagine what is."

The two women dissolved into laughter and could not stop.

The sound reverberated around the house, drawing Aquila. "What is so humorous?"

"Priscilla will miss me," Antonia said, convulsed with gasps between each word.

Aquila grinned. "Now that *is* funny."

Thirty-One

PRISCILLA HAD SKIPPED BREAKFAST that morning, and her belly grumbled with hunger as she worked next to Aquila. Lunch would not be ready for hours yet. She was dreaming of warm bread and soft cheese when the door to the workshop slammed open and Theo raced in. "Paul is in trouble," he said.

Priscilla sprang to her feet at the same moment as Aquila.

"What's happened?" Aquila asked, already pulling on his cloak and grabbing a bag of coins.

"I left early this morning to meet with a merchant. I was walking down a quiet lane when, ahead of me in the distance, I noticed Paul. He was speaking with Sosthenes. Out of nowhere, four armed men descended upon them."

Priscilla gasped. "Thieves?"

"That's what I thought at first," Theo said. "But they attacked Paul and left Sosthenes alone. The fellow just stood there smirking as they manhandled Paul." Theo's eyes narrowed. "I know one of those men. He belongs to the urban cohorts."

Priscilla's heart sank. "They arrested Paul?"

"No. This was no official arrest. Those men were not in uniform, and they did not charge Paul with anything."

"Sosthenes has hired mercenaries!" Aquila said.

"That's my guess. I hid behind a tree while I considered my options. The place was deserted, with no help to be found. I did not think I could take down all four attackers. They had the look of professional soldiers. But I decided to take a chance and charge them. Just before I revealed myself, they began dragging Paul away, and I realized they did not intend to beat or kill him. At least not in that alley. They intended to hole him up somewhere."

"Do you know where?"

Theo gave a narrow smile with more edges than a dagger. It dawned on Priscilla that behind the amiable facade of Theo's features ran a wide vein of deep-rooted strength. "I know exactly where. They took him to an empty warehouse."

Aquila exhaled. "You followed them. Well done." He considered for a moment. "We cannot seek help from the urban cohorts. If one of them is part of this plot, then more may be involved. Going to them might make matters worse. We need to handle this ourselves."

Theo's smile widened. "I hoped you would say that." He cracked his knuckles. "We better hurry before they move him. Or worse."

Priscilla stared at the men, aghast. Her belly had turned into a turbulent sea. Then the faint glimmer of a plan began to form in her mind.

"I will return as soon as I can," Aquila told her, striding toward the door.

Priscilla held up a hand. "I am coming with you."

"No. Absolutely not. This is no place for you."

She pulled up her palla and donned her shoes. "I have an idea. I will explain as we go. If you don't like it, I will return home."

The warehouse, a two-story, dilapidated building on an isolated lane, had no windows on the ground floor. The only gate was closed. When they crept around the back, they saw a smaller door, also closed. They had no way of knowing where Paul was imprisoned within the building. Or whether he still lived.

Aquila pondered his options. The windows were too high up to be of use. They could try the back door. Then again, that might lose them the element of surprise.

Without bothering to discuss his intentions, Theo began to climb the side of the building, finding holds in the old concrete where it had cracked. Aquila's eyes widened in disbelief. Theo scaled the wall with the easy grace of a man climbing a ladder. In moments, his fingers caught the edge of an upper-story window, and he pulled himself all the way up, resting his knees on the narrow ledge.

The wooden slats on the shutter were closed. But when Theo pulled on them softly, they gave way. Aquila could not see beyond into the chamber where Theo clambered. He could only hope the young man had not landed in the midst of a company of guards.

After a moment, Theo reappeared, signaling all was well, and Aquila expelled a relieved breath. His relief proved short-lived, however, when Theo bent out of the open window, not only at the waist as any normal man might have done, but all the way out, until gasping, Aquila thought the man would tumble out and crash on his head.

Instead, Theo hung upside down, his hands free and swinging in the air. Aquila blinked. Then he realized Theo had wedged his feet against the window, allowing them to bear the full weight of his body. He had known, of course, that Theo was a celebrated athlete. But this was beyond athletics. It seemed a feat of magic.

Theo clapped his hands and beckoned Aquila forward. Approaching him, he whispered, "What?"

"Grab my hands and climb," Theo instructed.

"Climb? Climb what?"

"Me."

"Are you insane? You will fall!"

"No. Trust me. And hurry."

Aquila shook his head. How had he landed himself in this lunacy? But what alternative did he have? He could not climb the wall as Theo had. And every moment of delay placed Paul in greater peril. Shaking his head at the absurdity of his situation, he leapt into the air and grabbed hold of Theo's wrists. The man held fast, his body taut and unyielding, bearing the pressure of the new weight now hanging from him. As fast as he could, Aquilla clambered upward, using Theo's body as a rope, until he reached the window and hauled himself into the dark chamber beyond.

With a limber flexing of supple muscles, Theo bent upward, grasped hold of the ledge, and loosened his feet until his body's position had reversed, legs dangling down. "Until later," he whispered. Then, as if unaware of the distance between him and the ground, he leapt. No sooner had his feet reached safety than he began to creep toward the alley, which ran across the front of the warehouse.

Aquila huddled in a corner of the empty chamber and waited for the signal. A few moments later, he heard the voice of his wife rising from the alley. She would now be standing squarely in front of the warehouse, in plain view of the scoundrels inside. *Madness,* Aquila thought. Madness to bring Priscilla into this dangerous venture. But he had to admit that her idea had merit. It offered a safer alternative to a direct attack. Sweat drenched his body as he thought of her, vulnerable and exposed, standing out there.

Priscilla's screeching bellow emerged in a nasal Greek, utterly unlike her usual cultured Latin, seasoned with words lewd enough to make a sailor blush. He had not known his wife had such an expansive glossary of colorful words.

"How dare you dally with that tramp Doris?" she screamed. "I forbid it."

"I can dally with Doris if I want," Theo screamed back. "I can dally with her sister, Daphne, too. You don't own me!"

Priscilla swore. "See if I pay for your haircut and fancy tunic again!"

"You call *this* fancy?" Theo spat. "I can find better wool on the back of a donkey."

"It *is* on the back of a donkey, you ass!" This would be where she would try to slap Theo and miss, a choreographed move they had discussed beforehand. She cursed again, this time using the word that was their signal, indicating that she had seen someone move on the upper floor. At least one of Paul's captors, if not all, had grown distracted by the unfolding drama on the street below.

Aquila could hear his wife's screeches growing more hysterical. The muffled sound of laughter echoed from the chamber on the opposite side of the house, overlooking the street. By the sound of it, Priscilla and Theo had managed to keep three of the guards distracted.

He hoped he would not come upon the fourth at Paul's side.

He found the narrow stairs leading to the ground floor without running into unwanted company and crept below, intending to make a systematic search of every room. The first chamber proved empty save for dust. The second contained dilapidated baskets, but no Paul. The third also appeared empty, except for some broken furniture. He was about to turn away when a faint sound caught his ear. He went back inside and looked carefully.

A pair of feet were sticking out from behind a shabby couch. They were tied roughly with rope. "God be thanked!" Aquila exclaimed and fell on his knees next to the bound man.

Paul lay on his side, face bloody and already bruising, hands tethered by rope to an iron hook wedged in the wall.

"Aquila?" Paul mumbled through swollen lips.

Aquila cut Paul's bonds with his dagger. "Can you walk?"

"Can try."

Aquila hefted his friend to his feet, allowing Paul to lean heavily on him as they limped out. If he could only make it to the back door without being spotted, they might have a clean getaway. Five steps. Ten. Fifteen, and he was there! A heavy wooden slat barred the door. Aquila gently settled Paul against the wall and grabbed the beam in a two-handed grip and pried it loose. To his straining ears, the sharp, cracking noise of wood grinding against wood seemed as loud as a thunderbolt. He winced and placed the bar on the floor, then dragged the narrow door toward him. The hinge, long neglected, moaned like a hurricane.

Abruptly the noise he had been dreading echoed above his head. The sound of racing feet pounding toward them.

"Run," he hissed, then half pulled, half dragged Paul's body with him.

One of Paul's attackers shouted a curse behind them. "You are dead men!"

They had determined their escape route in advance, which made their progress faster as they cut through one alley into the next. In the third street, a door opened, and before their pursuers were close enough to observe, Aquila and Paul slid inside and the door promptly shut behind them.

Aquila heard the pounding of feet pass by outside, growing faint as their pursuers continued on without slowing. They had managed it. They had escaped with their lives.

"Thank you," he mumbled to Galenos, Theo's foster father, in whose house they had sought refuge, before collapsing on the floor, lungs on fire.

Paul gave him a lopsided grin, teeth red with blood. "You should have told me you can run so fast. I would have sent you on more errands."

"What did they want from you?" Priscilla asked, placing a bowl of hot broth into Paul's hands. She and Theo had abandoned the scene of their charade when they realized they no longer had an audience. She had not known until she caught up with Aquila and Paul an hour later, that they were unharmed. That Aquila was safe.

She still shivered thinking of it.

"They thought if they beat me hard enough, I would grow too frightened to preach about Yeshua anymore."

"What did you do?"

"I preached to them about Yeshua, of course. They seemed to need it very badly."

Priscilla shook her head. "You lack sense, sometimes, Apostle. What were you doing with Sosthenes on that desolate road?"

He shrugged and winced with pain. He was covered in bruises, and she suspected that he had broken a rib or two. He took a sip of his broth. "He told me he wished to make amends. We met in a crowded street. I paid no attention as we began to walk and did not realize until it was too late that he had led me to a trap." He closed his eyes. "Thanks be to God none of you was hurt on my account. How *did* you manage to free me?"

Aquila pointed to Priscilla. "Sometimes I forget my wife is the daughter of a Roman general. She can certainly strategize like one. She came up with a way to distract your jailers. And Theo climbed up the wall like an ape."

Theo grimaced. "I seem to come off badly in this telling. How is it that she is a general and I am a monkey?" He rubbed a reddened cheek. "Not to mention the fact that Prisca slapped me."

She cringed. "Your pardon, Theo. You were supposed to duck."

"I ducked three times as we had planned. The fourth blow came as a surprise."

"I grew distracted and lost count." Priscilla's smile faded. "We almost lost you today, Paul."

The apostle became quiet. "There came a moment, all alone in that place, when I despaired of life. But then I remembered that Yeshua has delivered me from such deadly peril before, and he will deliver me again. On him I have set my hope." His gaze turned to Priscilla and Aquila, an ocean of love in the bloodshot eyes. "You have been my true companions. And now you have saved my life."

Priscilla's throat clogged. A fist squeezed around her heart, a foreshadowing of things to come. Paul lived a dangerous life, one foot always poised over a precipice of death. She knew in that moment that they would have to part from the apostle, sooner perhaps than she had thought.

"You are not safe yet," she pointed out. "We have to make certain Sosthenes does not try this again."

"I know a friend who will help us," Theo said.

By that very afternoon, Sosthenes found himself the recipient of a letter addressed to him from the office of Proconsul Gallio.

The missive informed him that an honored Corinthian had witnessed his involvement in the kidnapping of a Roman citizen named Paul of Tarsus. They also knew the identity of a certain member of the urban cohorts who had aided in the attack. But since the victim of this unfortunate incident had no wish to press charges against Sosthenes, they were willing to let the matter drop.

If there should be another attempt against the man, however, from Sosthenes or members of the synagogue he led, then Sosthenes would find himself chained in the pit of Corinth's jail, awaiting a protracted trial.

The same evening, Sosthenes returned a message assuring the office of the proconsul that he would never harm a hair on Paul's head. Priscilla believed his promise. Under the man's bilious bluster lay a pitiful coward who would not dare further outrage now that he had been caught.

The apostle remained at Priscilla and Aquila's house for a few days to recuperate from his injuries. Priscilla tried to convince him to rest. Paul had kept an overwhelming pace for months, often going without sleep, tentmaking in the early hours to generate an income and doing the work of God in the afternoons and evenings. His body had grown weary, and the wounds from his recent beating did not help.

Antonia volunteered to carry a tray of food to the apostle every day while he convalesced. Priscilla, who had never seen the woman perform any form of physical labor, gaped at her the first time she calmly began to fill up a bowl.

"What?" she said. "He is hurt." She shrugged. "I remember how it felt to have someone help me when I was hurting."

Thirty-Two

ONCE AGAIN PRISCILLA HAD FAILED to conceive. Another month of barrenness. She dropped her head in her palms. Palms that had never held a babe of her own. Grief had become a peculiar companion, coming at odd moments, twisting its bitter knife when least expected. Sometimes it arrived alone. Sometimes it came with its favorite companion, reproach, and tried to haunt her not only with the pain of loss, but also the added sting of blame.

An old battle. One she had fought over and over again, sometimes winning. But after every victory, there seemed another battle yet to win. Another round of striving with guilt. She wondered if she would ever truly be free.

Marcus skipped into the room, his mere presence tugging at the joy that lay curled, hidden beneath the weight of grief. *"Ave, mi carissime mater!"* he said in jovial tones. He always spoke floral Latin when in a good mood. Switching to Greek, which she insisted he practice, he repeated his words. "Hail, my dearest mother. You have a letter from the senator."

She raised an eyebrow. They had received a letter from Pudens the week before and had not expected another for several weeks. She broke the seal and began to read. Her face paled as she took in the short missive.

Greetings, my beloved friends. I have news. The emperor is willing to receive Priscilla. But only Priscilla. I was with him yesterday when a slave girl served us wine. She had red hair, the same lovely shade as yours. It put him to mind of you. When he asked after you, I told him of your circumstances and reminded him of your father's valiant service to our empire.

For the general's sake, he has agreed to meet with you and hear Marcus's case. But he refused to countenance Aquila's return. He seems adamant regarding the expulsion of the Jews and will make no exception.

Now it is up to you. If you wish to come and bring Marcus, you can. You will, of course, stay with us. Perhaps together we can find the boy a measure of justice.

Aquila seemed at a loss when he heard the news. "Send you and Marcus to Rome alone, with no protection? How can you ask it, Priscilla! If the boy's uncle finds out, he will come after you. Both of you."

Priscilla reached for his hand. "We have no choice," she said. "This might be the only opportunity we have to secure our son's future."

Aquila stepped away from her. His hand shook as he pushed a

tuft of dark hair out of his eyes. "Is that future worth your safety? Your lives? He is happy as our son. Why not let it be?"

"He is happy now. But how will he feel when he discovers that we could have pursued justice for him, for his father, and did not? We must face this danger, beloved. For his peace. For his heart." She swallowed. "I know something about the pain of guilt, and that boy carries a load. I know it is unreasonable. He was just a child when his uncle murdered his father. Still, he feels he ought to have done something. If we do not help him stand up to his uncle now, he will carry that burden for the rest of his life. We owe him this opportunity to cleanse his conscience. Even if it places us at risk."

Aquila spun around, turning his back to her. "I couldn't bear to lose you. Lose you both."

She wrapped her arms around his back and held tight, her face buried in his neck. She wanted to promise that no evil would come upon her or Marcus. Promise they would return to him safely. But she had no such assurance. Instead, she held him and waited in silence until the tension drained out of him. Until he arrived at the only conclusion open to them.

He turned around and drew her close against him. "When do you want to leave?"

"As soon as we can arrange passage. We need to come before the emperor while his promise is still fresh in his mind."

Antonia came to help Priscilla pack. Or at least her version of help, which consisted of sitting on the bed and ordering Priscilla about. "What are you going to wear for your audience with Claudius?"

Priscilla showed her the pale-green tunic she had set aside. Antonia shook her head. "Don't wear that. His last wife, Messalina, had a preference for green, and now Claudius abhors the sight of it. Do you have anything in dark blue? That's his favorite."

Priscilla sighed. "I only have four tunics. Two for work, which only leaves the green or this." She held up a shabby brown tunic which bore the marks of many repairs over the years. She forbore to mention that she had given Antonia the closest thing to a blue tunic she had possessed.

"Wait here," Antonia demanded. She returned with a piece of fabric folded over her arm. "Berenice sent me three new outfits this afternoon. You can have this one." She tossed the garment to Priscilla, who managed to catch it midair. Made of wool so soft it felt like a caress, the short-sleeved tunic had been dyed a dark blue, the color of deepest ocean, and decorated with delicate golden buttons on the shoulders.

Priscilla whistled. "This is glorious. But I can't take your beautiful tunic from you, Antonia."

"Of course you can." She shrugged. "Don't make a fuss about it. I took your tunic, didn't I? And you can't come before the emperor in *that*. Now, do you have a palla that is remotely suitable?"

Priscilla rummaged through her chest. "This belonged to my mother. It's in reasonably good shape. Will it do?"

Antonia examined the light-blue fabric with its delicate needlework flowers. "Merciful heavens! I must be dreaming. This is almost pretty." She tossed it back to Priscilla. "Pack this one. Claudius will appreciate your modesty. He's had enough of flashy women. And be sure to seek his audience before noon. Last I saw him, he had grown accustomed to drinking heavily. By noon, he was often befuddled. If you need him clearheaded, approach him earlier in the day."

On impulse, Priscilla reached out and gave the woman's hand a grateful squeeze. To her astonishment, Antonia clung to her hand for a moment and gave a regal nod before untangling her fingers.

Priscilla and Marcus arrived at the port of Ostia and disembarked to the warm welcome of a gaggle of friends. Pudens and his family stood alongside Mary and Rufus. At the sight of them, the exhaustion of the journey evaporated, and Priscilla ran into her friends' arms, the ache of months of separation dissolving in a moment.

They spent hours sharing stories, catching up on the precious details of life that could never fit in a letter. Priscilla had not written about Antonia, fearing that the letter might fall into the wrong hands. Now, they stared wide-eyed with shock as she told them the story of finding Claudius's niece curled up on a sidewalk and how the woman who had once been her nemesis was slowly finding her way to the Lord. Midnight had come and gone when they finally decided to retire to bed.

The following morning, Priscilla, Marcus, and the senator sat in the courtyard of his villa, the sun shining down through the opening in the roof, warming their tired bones. The gangly olive trees had grown fuller, and the patch of rosemary and thyme she remembered now overflowed their stone ledge.

"Marcus's biggest problem is one of identity," the senator said, sipping from his cup. "He can't merely charge in and demand justice. He could be anyone. He needs to prove that he is his father's son."

"How do I do that?" Marcus asked, fidgeting awkwardly in his chair. His body had shot up over the past year, and he had not become accustomed to the extra length yet.

"Is there anyone who could recognize you? Vouch that you are, indeed, Marcus Laurentinus Jovian?"

Marcus thought. "There were a few slaves I was close to."

Pudens made a slashing gesture. "Their testimony won't count."

Marcus's shoulders sank. "My father's steward would know me. He was a citizen. But my uncle had already sent him away by the time I left the house. I have no idea how to locate him."

"What is his name?" the senator asked. "I will do my best to find the man."

Marcus slumped in his chair. "He could be anywhere in the empire. He could be dead."

Priscilla patted his shoulder. "Nothing is impossible with God, my boy."

Marcus turned to her, seeking assurance without words. The time she had spent alone with him on the ship from Corinth to Ostia had solidified their bond in a fresh way. Until now, she had felt that she had hardly been a true mother to this child. She had not nursed him at night or sung lullabies to him when he could not sleep. She had not taught him to speak or held his hand as he toddled.

Something had shifted between them during this journey. With his future hanging in the balance, Marcus had turned to Priscilla with a child's clinging need for reassurance. For nurture. And hungry to give reassurance and nurture, Priscilla poured her heart into the boy. For the first time, she began to know, deep in her bones, the treasure of being a mother and of belonging to the boy whom God had brought her.

"We cannot locate your steward," Pudens said. "My men have searched everywhere. But there is no sign of him, I'm afraid."

Marcus slumped against Priscilla's side. "It's hopeless, then. Claudius will never believe me."

"It's never hopeless," Priscilla said. "Let us think through this. What do you recall about this man?

"He was always kind to me. My father trusted him. Called him clever and honest."

Priscilla nodded encouragingly. "Did he have family?"

"Not that I know." Marcus twisted the corner of his tunic with agitated fingers. "He was an ordinary man. Nothing remarkable. Well, except for his speech."

"His speech?" Priscilla prompted.

"He had an odd accent. Not from Rome. But a touch of the countryside."

Priscilla's focus sharpened. "Have you ever heard anyone else with that accent?"

Marcus narrowed his eyes. "I have. Somewhere . . . I know! The senator's gardener! The one with the bald head."

"Constantius?" the senator asked.

"That's the one," Marcus nodded.

They sent for the man. He arrived within moments, looking alarmed. The poor man was probably unaccustomed to being rushed into the senator's presence. "What's amiss, master?"

"Nothing is amiss, Constantius. Be at your ease. I have a question for you. Were you born in Rome?"

The man scratched his shining pate. "Me? Gods no, master. I wouldn't know nothing about gardens if I had been."

Pudens gazed at Marcus. "Does his speech sound familiar?"

Marcus nodded excitedly.

"Where were you born, Constantius? Where did you grow up?"

"Why, I was born in a village near Aternum."

Aternum! A city that sat at the mouth of the river Aternus, on the eastern border of Italia, a day's journey from Rome. Priscilla had never been there. But she had heard of it.

"Thank you, Constantius. That will be all," the senator murmured. When the befuddled gardener made his way back to his precious flowers, Pudens said, "I will seek for him in Aternum. If he has returned there, we will find him."

The days passed slowly as they waited, hope stretching thin with each passing hour. On the fifth day, Pudens called them into his tablinum. "Found your man," he said as soon as they entered. "Working in a warehouse in Aternum. You were right, Marcus. Festus was born there, and he returned home when your uncle dismissed him."

Marcus gave Priscilla a wide-eyed stare. "We will go right away," she assured him.

Festus, they discovered, had charge of a small warehouse in Aternum, which they found without trouble.

They spotted him unpacking plates under a bright window. Marcus whispered his name, and the man turned with a pleasant smile. His jaw sagged when he saw the child. Nerveless fingers dropped the plate they were holding, and the red clay smashed on the floor, scattering around their feet.

"Master Marcus?"

Marcus nodded, his throat bobbing. "It's me."

"Praise the gods!" The man leapt forward and grabbed Marcus's hand. "I thought you were dead! Or moldering in a cinnabar mine."

Marcus laughed. "That was my uncle's plan. But it did not suit me." He hesitated. "Have you seen him?"

"Your uncle? Not since he took over the household."

"I have a favor to ask of you," Marcus said. "Will you swear before a magistrate that I am my father's son?"

"Of course. But it will do you no good. Your father never had the chance to change his will. He meant to change it in your favor, you know? But he died before he could."

"Except that I saw my uncle kill my father."

Festus's eyes grew round. "I knew it! I knew his death was suspicious. Your father was much too careful to allow himself to be captured by thieves."

Marcus's mouth tightened. "There was no thief. Just a wicked brother."

He turned and pointed to Priscilla. "This is Prisca, daughter of General Priscus and wife to Aquila of Pontus. They took me in. They have been my mother and father. Now they are helping me to seek justice against my uncle. That's why I need your help. I need you to confirm my rightful identity. Are you willing to give me aid, Festus? It may prove dangerous, especially if the courts do not rule in our favor. My uncle is not a good man to cross, as I well know."

Festus squared his shoulders. "I will help you, Master Marcus."

After over a year of silence, Aulus must have considered himself safe from his nephew and impervious to the sword of justice. Likely he assumed Marcus dead. His brashness worked in their favor. Without bothering with subterfuge, they walked into their meeting with the emperor in broad daylight. By the time Aulus would hear of this audience, it would be too late.

Claudius turned to Priscilla, giving her a benign politician's smile. His years as emperor sat heavily upon him, creasing his narrow face with too many lines for a man of his age. "I knew Laurentinus personally, though I never met his son. I will give the boy a fair hearing. We cannot have brother murdering brother in Rome as if we were savages. If the boy's testimony proves convincing, I will ensure that Aulus receives just punishment."

Next he addressed Marcus, treating the boy not as a child but with the dignity he would have offered an adult. "You claim to be the son of Vibius Laurentinus?"

"I do, Caesar."

Priscilla looked approvingly at her son, his bearing erect, his voice confident.

"Do you have proof?"

"I offer this man's testimony."

Festus stepped forward and introduced himself, stammering before this potentate who ruled the world.

"Can you prove that you served Laurentinus?"

"Yes, my lord." Festus offered a sheaf of papers to the emperor. "I kept copies of many of my master's dealings, including letters of instruction he wrote me in matters of business."

Claudius took his time studying the papers. "It is clear that this man was Laurentinus's steward and trusted by him," he said aloud for the benefit of his secretary and several other officials who were present. "And you personally know this youth?" he asked Festus.

"I do, my lord. He is the son of Vibius Laurentinus, Marcus Laurentinus Jovian."

"You are certain?"

"I have no doubt, my lord. Furthermore, two days before his death, his father confided in me that he was about to change his will in his son's favor in spite of Marcus's young age. He felt that his brother should no longer be considered a viable heir."

Claudius frowned. "Does the will reflect such a change?"

"It does not, my lord. Vibius Laurentinus died before he could alter it."

The emperor nodded to Marcus. "Now that we have established your identity, what is your case?"

"I witnessed the murder of my father at the hands of my uncle." Eyes bright with tears he refused to shed, Marcus told his story. Priscilla watched Claudius's face as he listened, brow furrowed in concentration.

Marcus chose every word with care, his emotions held in check, evident only in the deep flush of his face and the faint trembling of his fingers. Claudius nodded in approval once, pleased by Marcus's speech. He swore when Marcus described the murder, then made the boy demonstrate Aulus's strike, the angle of the sword, his father's location, meticulously examining every detail for lies.

Finding none, he said, "Why did you not seek justice before now?"

Marcus explained their failed attempt to reach Claudius, though he did not make mention of Antonia's treachery. "I only survived because these good people took me into their home and raised me as their own. Remaining with them meant that I had to leave Rome when they did. For all I know, it saved my life. My uncle had put a price on my head."

When the emperor heard the amount, he swore again. "That treacherous water snake." He sent several members of the Praetorian Guard to arrest Aulus. To Priscilla's surprise, he limped over to Marcus and took the boy's hand in his. "I know your uncle. He cheated me at dice once, when I was younger and considered a nobody. It will be my pleasure to give you back what is rightfully yours. And to make him pay for the blood he shed."

When Aulus arrived, hemmed in by two Praetorians, he appeared shaken. At first, he did not notice Marcus or the emperor. "What is the meaning of this?" he shouted and cursed the guard who dragged him forward roughly.

"Keep a civil tongue before your emperor," Claudius drawled. "You have a visitor," he added calmly and stepped aside so Aulus could see his nephew.

It took him a moment to recognize the boy. Then he paled. "That miscreant is still under *my* rule. He has not reached the age of majority," he hissed.

"That miscreant has an interesting story to tell."

"He lies!" Aulus lunged toward Marcus. One of the guards grabbed him by the back of his tunic and pulled him away.

Claudius crossed his arms. "You haven't even heard it."

There was a commotion at the door and another Praetorian Guard walked in with a wide-shouldered man with scarred arms in tow. He saluted the emperor. "Found one, Caesar. Didn't have to look very hard," he said.

Priscilla threw Pudens a questioning glance. The senator shrugged.

"What is this?" Aulus's voice shook.

"This," Claudius said, "is your funeral." He turned to the new arrival and, pointing at Aulus, asked, "Did this man tell you that he would pay you a sum of money if you were to find his nephew? Alive or dead?"

The scarred man bowed his head. “He told a lot of us, sire. Never found the kid, though.”

“I have the right of life or death over a child in my own household. He was only five or six.”

“I was eight,” Marcus said. “And you did not have the right of life or death over my father.”

“He has a point there,” Claudius said.

Aulus pulled himself up and straightened his tunic. “Who are you going to believe? That skinny boy or a nobleman of Rome?”

“Definitely the skinny boy,” Claudius said. “You killed his father because he threatened to dispossess you. When the boy witnessed the crime, you sent your assassins after him lest your murder be discovered. You have left a trail of sloppy evidence behind you, Aulus. And I am going to see to it that you pay for your crime.” He crooked a finger to Marcus. “Boy!”

Marcus approached the emperor. “Caesar!”

“I henceforth restore to you all your father’s property. Where is that steward who gave testimony on your behalf?”

“Here, my lord,” Festus said.

“You will manage Vibius Laurentinus’s lands and income until Marcus is of age. I suspect that is what Vibius intended before his brother cut his life short. Your salary shall remain the same as you received under your old master. Do you agree?”

Festus grinned. “With pleasure, Caesar.”

“And you, Marcus?”

The boy slammed a fist to his heart in perfect imitation of a grown man and bowed his head. “Hail Caesar!” He then turned to Aulus, his eyes never wavering from the face that had haunted his dreams for months. “I want you to know, Uncle, that I pity you.

You could have had a brother's love. You could have had a nephew's affection. Our loyalty and support could have been yours forever. These are greater treasures than the land and money you killed for. You lost the best in life the moment you murdered my father."

Claudius looked from him to Priscilla. "Kings and princes could learn a few lessons from that boy."

"Yes, Caesar," Priscilla whispered, in awe of this boy who once could not face dipping into a bath and now confronted his enemy with dignity and strength. His next words robbed her of breath.

"I forgive you, Uncle. One greater than I will judge you one day. I will pray for you, that you may be able to stand before him."

Thirty-Three

"PRISCILLA, I AM SORRY, my dear. Your brother is ill," Sabinella said when Priscilla returned to the house. "His steward came to our home while you were at the palace."

In the years since her marriage, Priscilla had not heard from Volero. She lowered herself slowly next to the older woman. "Is it serious?"

"I am afraid so."

"What is wrong with him?"

"He is a leper, Priscilla."

Priscilla rocked back. "A *leper*? How? Is there an outbreak here in Rome?"

Sabinella shook her head, her brown eyes brimming with sympathy. "Some years ago, Volero Priscus purchased a beautiful Egyptian slave girl—Merneith, I believe the steward called her. Do you remember her?"

"Not well. She worked mostly in the main house and I rarely saw her."

"Apparently Priscus took quite a shine to her. Made her his mistress. She was leprous, though they did not know it at the time. He seems to have caught the disease from her. From what the steward said, he has had symptoms for some years, though he has managed to hide them. But the disease has progressed. He is disfigured now, no longer able to keep his condition secret."

Priscilla thought of her proud brother, always desperate for admiration, struck down with so brutal a malady. "Lord have mercy."

"Once, you had told him to come to my husband if he sought news of you. That is why the steward came to us today. Volero is gravely ill, Priscilla. And he is quite alone. His wife left him when she realized the nature of his disease. The slaves have either run away or refuse to serve him."

"Lord, have mercy," she said again, unable to think of anything beyond the mercy of God that could bring relief to Volero.

"He started to drink heavily when the disease grew rampant, and it has taken its toll."

Priscilla blinked. "He is dying?"

"Yes."

It felt like someone had punched her in the solar plexus. Priscilla sagged. Though the relationship between them had always been troubled, she had never ceased to think of Volero as her brother. Her father's son. Forever tied to her by the unbreakable bonds of blood.

She dropped her head, trying to come to terms with the shock of this news. Trying to decide what to do next. Everything in her longed to go to her brother. To offer him some relief. But she could not endanger the well-being of her husband and son, not to mention her friends, by rushing to his aid. What if she should catch this contagion? What if she should bring it back with her to taint those she loved?

She wept silently, torn. Unable to decide the right course. With wrenching abruptness, the hurricane of uncertainty whipping around her mind came to a stop. She could not explain how, but she knew with sudden and undeniable certainty that she was to go to her brother. Yeshua would take care of her.

Straightening, she came to her feet. "I will go to Volero. I will take care of my brother."

"I thought you might say that. Our carriage is waiting for you."

Priscilla changed into a plain brown tunic; folding Antonia's garment carefully, she put it away. She hugged Marcus and told him again how proud she felt to be his mother, then strode out of the house and into the waiting carriage.

Volero did not recognize her. He stared at her with fever-bright eyes and whispered, "Wine. I die of thirst. Give me wine."

His appearance shocked her. The thick brows and lashes were gone. The aquiline nose she remembered was a thing of horrors now, half-eaten away. Marred by nodules and blisters, his cheeks hardly resembled human flesh anymore. There were lesions on his arms, which had lost all color, as if the man were turning into a ghost bit by tiny bit. Little more than bones, his skin sallow, eyes sunken, ankles unnaturally swollen, her once-meticulous brother lay in his bed, reeking of vomit and sweat and decay.

Priscilla could barely swallow her tears. Dropping her palla about her shoulders, she fetched a cup and filled it with water. As she held it to his lips, his eyes widened with recognition.

"It's you," he croaked.

"I came to care for you."

He started to weep.

"You are not alone anymore," she said, eyes overflowing.

Silence hung between them. Priscilla poured the broth Sabinella had sent with her into another cup and sweetened it liberally with raisin wine to tempt his appetite. Volero took a sip and turned his face away.

"Why did you come for me?"

"You are my brother." She spoke the simple truth, one she had always known and he had never accepted. How different their lives might have been if he had.

"I never treated you as if you were my sister," he said, expression empty.

"That did not stop me from being one."

He moved restlessly and she adjusted his pillow. "I am glad our father did not live to see me like this."

She reached for his hand. He avoided her touch by shoving his hand under the blankets. "Get away from me. I don't want you to sicken on my account."

"The Lord will protect me." She tried to speak to him of Yeshua. But he said he would rather die alone than spend his last hours listening to stories about a foreign God.

The day had turned fair, with a gentle breeze that prevented the sun from growing too hot. She opened the window so he could enjoy the fresh air. He fretted the edge of his sheet. "You have pretty hair, like your mother," he said, his voice hoarse. "I am sorry I teased you about it."

She pressed his hand over the blankets. "I forgive you, Volero. For that, and for everything else. I forgive you."

He stared at her. "Why?"

"I have been forgiven much. It makes it easier to do the same."

"Your babe, you mean?"

Priscilla's heart stopped. *"What?"*

"I knew. One of the slaves discovered your secret and reported it to me."

She gaped at him. "I thought you would murder me if you found out."

"I considered it."

"Why didn't you?"

He shrugged. "You lost the child before I got around to it." He turned to look through the window at the cerulean sky. "Your God has forgiven your indiscretion?"

Her throat ached. "He has."

"I am glad for you."

"You can have forgiveness too, Volero! And peace. Yeshua—"

"Don't give me a headache."

Priscilla bit down her words. He was no more hungry for her God than he was for her food.

"Are you happy? With that Jew of yours?"

"Aquila. Yes. We are very happy."

"He treats you well?"

"Like a queen."

He gave a faint smile. "That's something, at least. I knew when he came here in search of you that he loved you. Loved you for yourself, not for what you could give him. I was a little jealous, to tell the truth. No one has ever loved me like that."

"I never wanted anything from you, Volero."

"I know that, now. But it's too late." He turned to the wall.

"Maybe this counts for something. You and me, together. Holding on to each other in this dark hour."

His smile was bitter. "The most honest moment of my life as I lie dying. All the people who said they were my friends were just hangers-on, as I myself hung on to men greater than myself. The only one to bide with me is the sister I never wanted."

"I am sorry."

His chest rattled as he tried to draw air into his lungs. "I regret it, you know. Regret mistreating you. Regret not being a part of your life."

Her throat clogged. "I understand why you couldn't. I always did."

"But it's still my loss."

The week had not drawn to a close when Volero died. Though he refused to listen to any talk about the Lord, his last words to Priscilla were about him. "Tell your God to remember me with mercy."

Standing at his funeral pyre, she wept for the life he had wasted. His life had been, as Solomon had once bemoaned, a chasing after the wind. He had frittered his days away on meaningless things and regretted them all in the end.

Once again, she had to take leave of precious friends. This time, she left not as a victim of calumnious scheming but as a willing traveler, walking down a road chosen for her by God.

"Tell that apostle of yours that I will wait on him to be baptized," the senator said, wagging his finger. He had been enraptured by tales of Paul's brazen ministry, as well as the power of his prayer. "Tell him to get himself to Rome without delay."

Priscilla laughed. "You will have to fight me for him. I am not yet ready to let him go." But she knew Paul's times were not in her keeping, nor even in his own. One day, he would come to Rome, whether she wished it or not.

With one arm she held tight to Marcus as the ship left the harbor, waving at her friends with the other until it ached. Marcus leaned his head on her arm. He had gained something since his audience with Claudius: a vague mantle of maturity, a covering of peace. "Are you sad to leave, Mother?"

"I suppose I leave a piece of my heart in their keeping. This is the price of love, Marcus. A part of you remains with the one who cannot stay near you."

Thirty-Four

AQUILA KISSED PRISCILLA so thoroughly when she disembarked from her ship at the port of Cenchreae that the sailors started catcalling. "The house was empty without you," he declared with a long sigh.

"Try to behave, you two," Marcus said, rolling his eyes. Aquila took the boy in his strong arms and held him, squirming and complaining, until both dissolved in laughter.

"I want every detail," he said. "Don't leave out anything."

And they did not. Between them, they covered every moment of their journey to Rome, reminding each other of minor details one might have forgotten. Aquila drank up their words, looking gratifyingly impressed, horrified, proud, and sad at all the right moments. They were a family, and they shared their lives as people do when they belong to each other.

"I thought you said the house was empty," Priscilla said when she came home and found a crowd gathered around Paul in the dining room. Bodies stuffed every nook.

"So you made it back," Antonia drawled before Aquila could respond.

Priscilla grinned. "It's good to see you too, Antonia. I brought your tunic back in one piece."

"Thank the Lord. Did Claudius admire it?"

"Well, he didn't banish me while I was wearing it. I suppose that is a good sign."

"And," Marcus added, "I am rich now."

Antonia studied the boy. "Too young," she declared. "Come back and tell me that in ten years."

Priscilla laughed. "Good to know some things never change."

"Some things do. I am leaving for Berenice's house tomorrow."

"Oh, Antonia!"

"The old girl is lonely. Besides, my chamber is ready."

"It was ready ten days ago," Aquila clarified.

"I didn't like the color." She crossed her arms and returned to her cushion on the floor to listen to Paul's teaching.

"I think she just used that as an excuse," Aquila whispered in Priscilla's ear. "She didn't want to leave before you returned. I believe she wanted to say good-bye."

Priscilla's eyes softened. "I'll still see her when she moves to Berenice's. The villa isn't that far away."

"It won't be the same as living here. And she realizes that we may not remain in Corinth forever."

"I've grown fond of that girl. I really have."

"And that," Aquila said, poking her in the ribs, "is one of the reasons I love you."

They lingered in the dining room for a few moments to listen to Paul. Priscilla sensed a deeper anointing on their friend, a spark of greater power.

"Last week, he prayed for a man who had broken his arm after falling from the roof," Aquila said. "The bone healed in front of our eyes as Paul interceded for him. Since then, more people come to listen to him, whether he speaks at Justus's house or here."

Priscilla wanted to remain and listen to the apostle preach, but her eyes were drooping, and leaning on Aquila's arm, she allowed herself to be led to their chamber.

A faint sound awoke Priscilla in the darkest hour of the night. She lay in bed, her limbs tangled with her husband's, her mind still in a fog of dreams. The sound came again, indistinct. Distressed. Softly she moved so as not to waken Aquila, donning her tunic and grabbing the single lamp that burned with a faint, sputtering glow.

She followed the sound, the gasping cry of someone weeping into a pillow, trying to suffocate sobs. Tracing the muted whimpers, she came to Antonia's alcove. Priscilla rested the back of her head against the wall for a moment, trying to decide what to do. If she went in now, she would violate Antonia's dignity, her treasured pride.

But no one ever found solace in loneliness.

Priscilla whipped the curtain aside. She knelt down in the tight space and laid a hand on the trembling back.

"Go away," Antonia gasped.

Priscilla did not argue. Instead, she left her hand where it was, allowed her eyes to drift closed, and began to pray silently.

The weeping ceased after a long while. Antonia sat up, her face ravaged, looking much older than her twenty-five years. She bit her lip, where a trickle of blood had pooled already. "Do you ever think . . . ? Do you sometimes wonder . . . ?"

Priscilla was not certain how she knew. Nothing in the words themselves hinted at what Antonia meant. Yet she understood, without doubt, that the woman was speaking of her babe. "I think of him every day," she said.

Antonia shook her head. "I never thought of mine. For years. When I first came out of that place, I felt only relief. I never shed a tear. Never wasted a thought for that child.

"Then, a few months ago, the man I loved had a child. His wife bore him a son. And it came to me like a flood, after the passing of so many years, an avalanche of regret. Of loss. Sometimes I wake up in the middle of the night, quivering with rage, and I can't even say who I am angry with. Him for abandoning me, or myself for what I chose, or the world for forcing me into such a decision.

"Sometimes the sorrow chokes me until I can't breathe." She flopped on her back, eyes unseeing. "I long, so badly, to hold that child in my arms that I ache. It's as if someone has dug a hole inside me, a crater that nothing will ever fill.

"Some days, I feel well. I think that I have overcome this madness. Then it hits me again. Regret chokes me in wave after wave, and I sink."

Priscilla reached a hand and caressed the woman's short hair, soothingly, gently, as if she were a lost child. Antonia tensed for a moment, and Priscilla feared she might buck like a wild horse, too proud to receive comfort. Then the bloody lips trembled, and with a broken wail, she melted against Priscilla and allowed herself to be consoled.

"Has God forgiven you?" Antonia asked, curled up against Priscilla's side.

Priscilla hesitated. It had not been long since she had asked that question of herself. Accused herself again. She had repented of her doubts as Paul had bid her. But a tiny root of guilt still lingered, weak and inconsequential now, but waiting for the opportunity to gain strength and rise up against her once more. "I hope so," she said.

Antonia's head bobbed up and down, tugging on Priscilla's tunic. "You should be forgiven. You are so good."

"I am not forgiven because of *my* goodness. I am forgiven because of *God's* goodness. When we talk about Yeshua suffering, dying, this is what we mean. He bears our burdens. He dies our deaths. He carries our punishments. We are washed clean in love. His love. There are some things you cannot undo on this earth, Antonia. You will never have your babe back. But know that he is safe. He lives. He lives more fully than you and I because his life is now lived in the fullness of eternity."

"I always thought her a girl. My daughter."

Priscilla smoothed away a tear from Antonia's cheek. "Then you are probably right."

Antonia lifted her head. "Is she happy?"

"Happier than we can comprehend."

"Does she hate me? For what I did to her?"

"Heaven has no room for hatred, or it would not be heaven. No, Antonia. Your child does not hate you."

"God will never forgive me."

The lamp cast a long shadow over Antonia, its dim light revealing a young woman, utterly broken, guilty, sin sick, hopeless. Looking at her, Priscilla knew the answer. Knew it without doubt. The vastness of God's mercy crept inside that humble alcove, filled it, overflowed through it.

Even this, thought Priscilla. *Even this is not too much for you.*

And then she felt the words whispered into her own heart, into the tiny root of guilt that never seemed to go away completely. She felt it, like a breath on a living thing, the power of grace, the truth of it. *Even this.* Her own sin. Her own failure was no match for Yeshua's love.

She was washed clean, utterly. Utterly. She felt the root wither. Die.

It was her turn to weep.

"Antonia. Yeshua will forgive you, even as he has forgiven me. Reach for his hand. He is waiting for you."

Antonia, though she saw nothing but shadows, extended her hand into the dark.

Aquila kissed his wife one last time, his body shuddering against hers. "What just happened?" he asked, still dazed with shock and a satiation that felt a little like drowning.

He had been half-asleep when she had slipped beneath the sheets, her skin cool. Her skin. Her *naked* skin. The sensation had chased the cobwebs of sleep right out of his head. His wife never came to bed without some covering. Not even in the heat of summer.

He had sat up so fast his head had hit the bedside table. Without explanation, she had reached for him. Kissed him. A wholly unfamiliar sensation, having his wife initiate this kind of touch.

"What just happened?" he said again, disoriented and ridiculously elated at the same time.

"I just wanted to be with my husband," she said, a teasing note in her voice.

"Mercy, Priscilla. You can be with your husband anytime you like!"

She giggled, pulled him down, and snuggled into his warm body. And he knew, then, that God had blessed him with a taste of heaven on earth.

They continued to host multiple gatherings in their home each week. Friends ate and prayed together, shared their troubles, devoted themselves to following Yeshua more wholeheartedly, and celebrated the Lord's Supper. They gave to the poor and nursed the sick, asking for nothing in return. They watched as invalids were healed, demons were cast out, cynics were converted, and Corinth began to change. They had lived there under two years. But they made inroads for God that would last for generations.

When Paul asked them to accompany him to Ephesus, they did not mourn the loss of one more home. They simply packed and followed the guidance of Yeshua, who led them into unexpected paths.

Standing on the bow of another ship, bound for another city not home, Priscilla locked arms with her husband on one side, her son on the other, Benyamin and Lollia keeping company with Ferox nearby.

Closing her eyes for a moment, she lifted her face to the wind, supported by the arms of those she loved, knowing herself safe. Aquila lay his cheek on top of her head. "My beloved," he whispered.

Her smile spilled over as her tears had not.

"We will return to our home on the Aventine one day," Aquila assured her. "You will settle in Rome again and eat your stinky *garum* by the bucketful."

She knew her friends would be waiting in Rome, each bringing their own brand of treasure. Rufus would offer his prayers; Mary, a mother's love; Pudentiana, warm embraces; Sabinella, a mounting tray of food and words of love.

Ferox flopped by her side and licked her toes before settling his large head on her feet to warm them. She caressed his bristly fur.

Years ago, she had walked into a wilderness, grown lost in its winding paths, only to find a door of hope. Over and over again, that door had opened for her, leading her to a fullness of life she could never have imagined.

She had been born a daughter of Rome. But she had become the daughter of the Most High God. Now, home was where he led. Home was the arms of her loved ones, the company of her family, and the world that spread before her, desperate to be conquered by Love.

ALSO BY TESSA AFSHAR

TURN THE PAGE FOR AN EXCITING PREVIEW

"Afshar again shows her amazing talent for packing action and intrigue into the biblical setting for modern readers."

—PUBLISHERS WEEKLY—

Join the conversation at crazy4fiction.com

TYNDALE FICTION

www.tyndalefiction.com CP1221

Prologue

YOU ASKED ME ONCE how a woman like me could become a thief. How could I, having everything—a father's love, a lavish home, an athlete's accolades—turn to lawlessness and crime?

Were I in a flippant mood, I could blame it on sleeplessness. That fateful night, when I abandoned my bed in search of a warm tincture of valerian root to help me rest and found instead my father slithering out the side door into the dark alley beyond.

He was a man of secrets, my father, and that night I resolved to discover the mystery that surrounded him. A mystery so cumbersome, its weight had shattered my parents' marriage.

Snagging an old cloak in the courtyard, I wrapped myself in its thick folds and followed him along a circuitous path that soon had me confused. The moon sat stifled under a cover of clouds that night, shielding my presence as I pursued him.

Finally Father came to a stop. The clouds were dispersing and there was now enough light to make out the outline of the buildings around me. We had arrived at an affluent neighborhood.

During the day, we Corinthians left our doors open as a sign of hospitality. At night, we shut and latched them, both for safety and to indicate that the time for visitation had passed and the occupants were in bed. As one would expect, the door of this villa had long since been barred.

I hunkered down behind a bush, wondering what Father meant to do. Rouse the household with his knocking? He fumbled with something in his belt and proceeded to cover his face with a mask.

I gasped. Was he playing a jest on the owner of the house? Did he have a forbidden assignation with a lady within? He was an unmarried man, still handsome for his age. I had never considered his private life and felt a twinge of distaste thinking of him with a woman. Now was perhaps a good time for me to beat a hasty retreat. But something kept me rooted to the spot.

My father approached the south wall of the villa and nimbly climbed a willow tree that grew near. I had to admire his agility when he jumped from the tree to the wall. Deftly, he grabbed hold of the branches of another tree growing within the garden and swung himself into its foliage. I lost sight of him then.

I sat and considered the evidence before me. Father's stealthy movements in the middle of the night. The mask. The furtive entry into the villa. The answer stared me in the face. But I refused to believe it.

As I waited, I found it hard to gauge the time. How long since he had scrambled into the villa? An hour? Less? No alarm had been raised . . . yet. I began to fret. What was he doing in there? What if someone caught him? I left my hiding place and, slinking my way toward the villa, made a quick exploration of the area. The place seemed deserted. Tucking my tunic and cloak out of the way, I climbed the same willow my father had and nestled in its branches. Still I could discern nothing.

I laid my forehead against a thick branch. What should I do? Wait? Go in search of him? Then I heard a noise. Feet running through bushes. More than one pair of feet.

A man cried, "Halt! You there! Stop at once!"

My hold on the branch slipped. I thought a guard had seen me, and I prepared to leap back into the street. What I saw next made my blood turn to ice.

Father was running toward me with a large man in close pursuit, his hand clutching a drawn sword. The man bearing the weapon was quickly gaining on my father. I estimated Father's distance from the wall, the time he would need to climb up the tree on one side, and then back down the other. He would never make it in time.

He was about to be caught. Killed, as I watched helplessly from my perch of branches.

Well. You know the rest of that story.

I suppose I could accuse my father of leading me astray that night, of setting the example that ruined my best intentions, for had he not tried to rob that house, I would not have turned to thieving myself.

But the choices that lead us into broken paths often have their beginnings in more convoluted places.

Places like the thousand words spoken mercilessly by my grandfather when I lived in his house—barbed and ruthless words; or a thousand phrases never spoken by my mother, soft and nurturing expressions that would have healed my wounded soul. I could blame the years in Athens, when I became invisible to my family, a girl child in a world meant for men.

Yet the final blame, as you and I know, dear Paul, rests with me.

It was I who chose as I did. I could have taken the wounds of my early life and turned them to healing. Instead, they became my excuse to do as I wished.

Until you taught me love.

I write you this letter while I sit waiting by a funeral pyre, memories assailing me. The fires blaze and burn the bones of one I failed to love. The smell of ashes fills my nostrils as I remember your words: *"Love never fails."* And even in the shadow of this conflagration that swallows up its human burden with such hunger, I am comforted to know that there is a love that shall never fail us. A love that covers the many gaps I have left in my wake.

Chapter 1

THE FIRST TIME I climbed through a window and crept about secretly through a house, the moon sat high in the sky and I was running away from home. *Home* is perhaps an exaggeration. Unlike my brother Dionysius, I never thought of my grandfather's villa in Athens as home. For eight miserable years that upright bastion of Greek tradition had been my prison, a trap I could not escape, a madhouse where too much philosophy and ancient principles had rotted its residents' brains. But it was never my home.

Home was my father's villa in Corinth.

I was determined, on that moon-bright evening, to convey myself there no matter what impediments I faced. A girl of sixteen, clambering from a second-story window in the belly of night without enough sense to entertain a single fear. Before me lay Corinth and my father and freedom. As always, waiting for me faithfully in uncomplaining silence, was Theodotus, my foster brother. Regardless of how harebrained and dangerous my schemes might be, Theo never left my side.

He stood in the courtyard, keeping watch, as I made my way down the slippery balustrade outside my room, my feet dangling for a moment into the nothingness of shadows and air. I slithered one finger at a time to the side, until my feet found the branches of the laurel tree, and ignoring the scratches on my skin, I let go and took a leap into the aromatic leaves. I had often climbed the smooth limbs, unusually tall for a laurel. But that had been in the light of day and from the bottom up. Now I jumped into the tree from the top, hoping it would catch me, or that I could cling to some part of it before I fell to the ground and crushed my bones against Grandfather's ancient marble tiles.

My fingers seemed fashioned for this perilous capering, and by an instinct of their own, they found a sturdy branch and clung, breaking the momentum of my fall. I felt my way down and made short work of the tree. My mother would have been horrified. The thought made me smile.

"You could have broken your neck," Theo whispered, his jaw clenched. He was my age but seemed a decade older. I boiled like water, easily riled into anger. He remained immovable like stone, my steady rock through the capricious shifts of fortune.

The tight knots in my shoulders relaxed at the sight of him, and I grinned. "I didn't." Reaching for the bundle he had packed for me, I grabbed it. "The gate?"

He shook his head. "Agis seemed determined to stay sober tonight." We both looked over to the figure of the slave, huddled on his pallet across the front door, his loud snores competing with the sound of the cicadas.

"I am afraid there's more climbing in your future if you really intend to go to Corinth," Theo said, his voice hushed. He took a step closer so that I could see the vague outline of his long face. "Nothing will be the same, you know, if you do this thing, Ariadne. Whether you fail or succeed. It's not too late to change your mind."

In answer, I turned and made my way to the high wall that surrounded the house like an uncompromising sentinel. Grandfather had made it impossible for me to remain. I should have escaped this place long ago.

I studied the daunting height of the wall and realized I would need a boost to climb it. By the fountain in the middle of the courtyard, the slaves had left a massive stone mortar that stood as high as my waist. It would do for a stepping-stone. The mortar proved heavier than we expected. Since dragging it would have made too great a clamor, we had to lift it completely off the ground. The muscles in my arms shook with the effort of carrying my burden. Halfway to our destination, I lost my hold on the slippery stone. With a loud clatter, it fell on the marble pavement.

Agis stirred, then sat up. Theo and I dropped to the ground, hiding in the shadow of the mortar. "Who goes there?" Agis mumbled.

He rose from his pallet and looked about, then took a few steps in our direction. His foot came within a hand's breadth of my shoulder. One more step and he would discover me. Blood hammered in my ears. My lungs grew paralyzed, forgetting how to pulse air out of my chest.

This was my only chance to break away. If Agis raised the alarm and I were apprehended, my grandfather would see to it that I remained locked up in the women's quarters under guard until I capitulated to his demands. He held the perfect weapon against me. Should I refuse to marry that madman, Draco, my grandfather would hurt Theo. I knew this was no empty threat. Grandfather had a brilliant mind, sharp as steel's edge, and a heart to match. It would not trouble his conscience in the least to torment an innocent in order to get his own way. He would beat Theo and blame every lash on me for refusing to obey his command.

The fates sent me an unlikely liberator. Herodotus the cat came to my rescue. Though feral, it hung about Grandfather's property because Theo and I had secretly adopted it and fed the poor beast when we could. My mother had forbidden this act of mercy, but since the cat had an appetite for mice and other vermin, the slaves turned a blind eye to our disobedience.

Just when Agis was about to take another step leading to my discovery, Herodotus ran across his foot.

"Agh," he cried and jumped back. "Stupid animal! Next time you wake me, I will gut you and feed you to the crows." Grumbling, the slave went back to bed. Theo and I remained immobile and silent until we heard his snores split the peaceful night again.

This time, we carried our burden with even more attentive care and managed to place it next to the wall without mishap.

I threw my bundle over the wall and stepped cautiously into the center of the mortar, then balanced my feet on the opposite edges of the bowl. We held our breath as the stone groaned and wobbled. Agis, to my relief, continued to snore.

The brick lining the top of the wall scraped my palm as I held tight and pulled. I made my way up, arms burning, back straining, my toes finding holds in the rough, aged brick. One last scramble and I was sitting on the edge.

Theo climbed into the mortar next, his leather-shod feet silent on the stone. I leaned down and offered my hand to him. Without hesitation, he grasped my wrist and allowed me to help him climb until he, too, straddled the wall. We sat grinning as we faced each other, basking in the small victory before looking down into the street.

"Too far to jump," he observed.

On the street, next to the main entrance of the house, sat a squat pillar bearing a dainty statue of Athena, Grandfather's nod to his precious city and its divine patron. At the base of the marble figurine the slaves had left a small lamp, which burned through the night. I crawled on the narrow, uneven border of bricks twelve feet above ground until I sat directly above the pillar.

As I dangled down the outer wall, I took care not to knock Athena over, partly because I knew the noise would rouse Agis, and partly because I was scared of the goddess's wrath. Dionysius no longer believed in the gods, not as true beings who meddled in the fate of mortals. He said they were mere symbols, useful for teaching us how to live worthy lives. I wasn't so sure. In any case, I preferred not to take any chances. Should there really be an Athena, I would rather not draw her displeasure down on me right before starting the greatest adventure of my life. She was, after all, the patron of heroic endeavor.

"Excuse me, goddess. I intend no disrespect," I whispered as I placed my feet carefully on either side of her, balancing my weight before jumping cleanly on the street.

Being considerably taller, Theo managed the pillar better. His foot caught on the goddess's head at the last moment, though, and smashed it into the wall. I dove fast enough to save her from an ignoble tumble onto the ground. But her crash into the plaster-covered bricks had extracted a price. Poor Athena had lost an arm.

"Now you've done it," I said.

Theo retrieved the severed arm from the dust and placed it next to the statue on the pillar. "Forgive me, goddess," he said and gave an awkward pat to the marble. "You're still pretty." I caught his eye and we started to laugh, half mad with the relief of our escape, and half terrified that the goddess would materialize in person and punish us for our disrespect.

"What are you doing?" a voice asked from the darkness, sharp like the crack of a whip.

I jumped, almost knocking Athena over again. "Who is there?" I said, trembling like a cornered fawn.

The speaker stepped forward until the diminutive lamp at Athena's feet revealed his face.

My back melted against the wall as I made out Dionysius's familiar face. "You scared the heart out of me," I accused.

"What are you doing?" he asked again, his gaze taking in our bundles and my unusual garments—his own cloak wrapped loosely about my figure, hiding my gender.

I swallowed hard, struck mute. I was running away from my mother and grandfather. But in escaping, I was leaving behind a beloved brother. Dionysius was Grandfather's pet, the son he had never had. I think the old man truly loved him. He certainly treated him with a tenderness he had never once demonstrated toward Theo or me. Grandfather would not stand for Dionysius leaving. He would follow us like a hound into the bowels of Hades to get him back.

My escape could only work if my brother remained behind.

I told myself Dionysius loved Athens. He fit perfectly into the mold of the old city with its rigorous intellectual pursuits and appreciation for philosophy. Athens suited Dionysius much better than the wildness of Corinth. I was like a scribe who added one and one and tallied three. I lied to myself, twisting the truth into something I could bear.

Dionysius had a more brilliant mind even than my grandfather, a mind that prospered in the academic atmosphere of Athens. But he had inherited our father's soft heart. The abrupt separation from Father had wounded him. To lose Theo and me as well would cut him in ways I could not bear to think about. Not all the glories of Athens or Grandfather's affection could make up for such a void.

I had not told him of my plan to run away, convincing myself that Dionysius might cave and betray us to the old man. In truth, I was too much of a coward to bear the look on his face once I confessed I meant to leave him behind. The look he was giving me now.

Theo stepped forward. "She has to leave, Dionysius. You know that. Or the old wolf will force her to marry Draco."

My brother shifted from one foot to the other. "He is angry. He will cool."

I ground my teeth. Where Grandfather was concerned, Dionysius was blind. He could not see the evil that coiled through the old man. "He threatened to have Theo flogged if I refuse to marry the weasel. One stripe for every hour I refuse."

"What?" Theo and Dionysius said together. I had not even told Theo, worried that he might think I was running away for his sake more than my own, and refuse to help me.

"He has no scruples when it comes to Theo. Or me."

"Mother—"

"Will take his side as she always does. When has she ever defended me?"

I rubbed the side of my face, where the imprint of her hand had left a faint bruise, and winced as I remembered her iron-hard expression as she hit me.

Two days ago, Draco and his father, Evandos, had come to visit Grandfather. After drinking buckets of strong wine, the men had crawled to bed. The wind had pelted the city hard that evening, screaming through the trees, making the house groan in protest. The rains came then, sudden and violent.

I had risen from my pallet and slid softly into the courtyard. I loved storms, the unfettered deluge that washed the world clean. Within moments, I stood soaked through and grinning with exultation, enjoying the rare moment of freedom.

An odd sound caught my attention. At first I dismissed it as the noise of the wind. It came again, making me go still. The hair on my arms rose when it came a third time, a tortured wail, broken and sharp. No storm made that sound. My heart pounded as I followed that unearthly wail to a narrow shed on the other side of the courtyard. I slammed the door open.

He had brought a lamp with him, and it burned in the confines of the shed, casting its yellowish light into every corner. My eyes were drawn to the whimpering form on the dirt floor, lying spread-eagle. In the lamplight, blood glimmered, slick like oil, staining her thighs, her face, her stomach.

"Alcmena?" I gasped, barely recognizing the slave girl.

"Mistress!" She coughed. "Help me. Help me, I beg!"

I turned to the man standing over the slave, his face devoid of expression. "You did this?"

He smiled as if I had paid him a compliment. "A foretaste for you, beautiful Ariadne. I look forward to teaching you many lessons when you are my wife."

"Your *wife*? Get out of here, you madman!"

"Your grandfather promised me your hand in marriage. We drank on it earlier this evening." He stepped toward me. His gait was long and the space narrow. In a moment, Draco towered over me. He twined his fingers into my loose hair and pulled me toward him. The smell of the blood covering his knuckles made me gag. Without thinking, I fisted my hand and shoved it into his face. To my satisfaction, he staggered and screeched like a delicate woman. "My nose!"

"I beg your pardon, Draco. I was aiming for your mouth."

He rushed at me, hands clenched. I screamed as I stepped to the side, missing his bulk with ease. I had good lungs, and my voice carried with eerie clarity above the howling gale.

He faltered. "Shut your mouth."

I screamed louder.

The muscles in his neck corded as he hesitated for a moment. Then he lunged again, and I braced myself for a shattering assault. It never came.

Dionysius and Theo burst through the door, causing Draco to skid to a stop. My brothers seemed frozen with shock as they surveyed the state of Alcmena. Relief washed through me at the sight of them, and I sank to my knees next to the slave.

"What have you done?" my brother rasped, staring at the broken girl who could not even sit up in spite of my arm behind her back. "You brutal maggot. You've almost killed her."

Theo placed a warm hand on my shoulder. "Are you all right?"

I nodded, crossing my arms and trying to hide how badly my fingers shook.

Grandfather sauntered in, my mother in tow. "What is all this yelling? Can't a man sleep in peace?" He wiped his bristly jaw.

"Draco hurt Alcmena," I said.

My mother had the grace to gasp when she saw the slave girl, though she said nothing.

"He asked my permission to take the girl, and I gave it." Grandfather tightened his mouth when Alcmena doubled over and retched painfully. "You must have drunk too much, boy. Go back to your father."

Draco bowed his head and left without offering an explanation.

"He is crazed," I said. "He claims he will marry me. That you made an agreement with him earlier this evening."

"What of it?" Grandfather said, his voice hardening.

I expelled a wheezing breath. "You can't be serious! Look at what he did to the girl."

"The boy is a little hotheaded. Too much wine. Things got out of hand. Nothing to do with you. I have made the arrangement with my friend Evandos. It is done."

"Grandfather!" Dionysius cleared his throat. "I think we should ask Draco to leave the house."

"We shall do no such thing. If an honored guest wants to abuse your furniture, you must allow him," Grandfather said. "She is my slave, and the damage is to my property. I say it is of no consequence."

"She's hardly a woman. Younger than I am," I cried. "What do you think Draco will do to me if he gets his hands on me? You should be ashamed of yourself for even entertaining the notion of my marriage to such a man."

Calmly, my mother raised her arm and slapped me with the flat of her hand, putting the strength of her shoulder into that strike. I tottered backward and would have fallen if Theo had not caught me.

"Don't be rude to your grandfather. Now go to bed."

Furniture. That's what the poor girl amounted to in the old man's estimation. And I was not far above her in his classification of the world. In the morning, Grandfather insisted that my betrothal to Draco would stand. He expected me to honor his precious word by marrying Evandos's brutal son. My mother watched this tirade, eyes flat, as her father bullied me. She expected me to obey without demur as any good Athenian girl would.

With effort, I pushed away the memories and returned my attention to my brother. "Mother informed me yesterday afternoon that she had started to work on my wedding garments."

Dionysius blinked. In the flickering light of the lamp his eyes began to shimmer as they welled with tears. I knew, then, that he would not hinder us. Knew he would cover our departure for as long as he could, regardless of the pain it caused him.

I encircled my arms around him. Grief shivered out of us as we tried to make the moment last, make it count for endless days when we wouldn't have each other to hold. I stepped away, mindful of time slipping, mindful that we were far from safe. Theo and Dionysius bid a hurried farewell, locking forearms and slamming chests in manly embraces that could not hide their trembling lips.

Grabbing my bundle, I threw one last agonized glance over my shoulder at my brother. He stood alone, blanketed by shadows save for a luminous halo of lamplight that brought his face into high relief. I swallowed something that tasted bitter and salty and entirely too large for my throat and stumbled forward.

A NOTE FROM THE AUTHOR

WHO WERE PRISCILLA AND AQUILA? We don't know much about this extraordinary couple who saved Paul's life, set up house churches in three different cities, and became influential spiritual leaders through some of the most harrowing years of the church's history. The fact that Priscilla served alongside her husband cannot be disputed. The unusual mention of her name *before* his in several passages suggests that, indeed, on certain occasions, she might have been considered the more knowledgeable teacher and a respected leader in her own right.

Priscilla is a diminutive for Prisca, a name that might give us a clue to this remarkable woman's identity. The male version of Prisca's name, Priscus, was a well-known Roman appellation, belonging to a noble Roman family. Prominent Roman households had a habit of naming their slaves after the patriarch. As such, Prisca (female for Priscus) could be a slave name. However, Priscilla was married, which means that she could not have been a slave, as slaves were not allowed to marry. Hence, she was either a member of the Priscus family or a freed slave. The latter option is not likely since the Romans rarely freed their female slaves. To me, the most plausible option points to Priscilla being a scion of the Priscus family. The story line deals with this heritage.

According to the book of Acts, Emperor Claudius commanded "all the Jews to leave Rome" (Acts 18:2). Such a wholesale banishment of the Jewish population seems problematic to most scholars. At the time, Rome had a substantial Jewish population, and the sudden expulsion of such a great number of the citizenry would have been noted in several archives—something we lack. However, most of the Jews in Rome were citizens. This made me think that perhaps all the Jews who were not citizens had been expelled. The Bible is rarely interested in mentioning such distinctions, and the generalized comment in Acts would make sense since its only purpose is to explain Aquila and Priscilla's presence in Corinth, not to give an exact historical recitation. Hence, I believe "all the Jews" in the passage refers to all the Jews who were not citizens, an explanation which perfectly aligns the historical and biblical accounts.

Aquila, a Jew, was originally from Pontus (Acts 18:2). We know that the church had been well established in Pontus by the early 60s (1 Peter 1:1-2), about ten years after the events in *Daughter of Rome*. Certainly during this period, there would have been Christians in Pontus. Yet even with Priscilla and Aquila's extensive travels, Pontus is never mentioned as one of their destinations. The plot takes this curious absence into account.

How, precisely, did our indomitable couple risk their necks to save Paul's life (Romans 16:4)? This remains another unsolved biblical mystery, which makes for fun fiction. Some scholars believe the occasion is related to the events in Corinth; others feel that it might have occurred later, in Ephesus. In either case, we only know that the apostle felt that he owed his life to Priscilla and Aquila.

Some of the descriptions of the synagogue in Rome, which has not survived the ravages of time, are based on the third-century synagogue discovered in Dura Europos, where men and women sat together during worship.

The Hill of Amphorae, made entirely of broken pottery shards, would have been more of a molehill in this period and not fully developed for another ninety years. However, I was so enchanted by the concept that I cheated on the timeline and included it in the novel.

Besides Priscilla, Aquila, and Paul, several other characters in *Daughter of Rome* are based on historical figures. Rufus and his mother are mentioned in Romans 16:13 among those whom Paul greets with affection. We know that Simon of Cyrene (present-day Libya) had two sons, one of whom was named Rufus (Mark 15:21). It is not unlikely that these are one and the same man. Pudens is mentioned in 2 Timothy 4:21. According to church tradition, Pudens was a senator in Rome who welcomed Peter and Paul into his house and was baptized by one of them. Later he was martyred under Nero. Both his daughters went on to be recognized as saints of the church, opening their homes for the work of God and ministering to the needs of the poor. Stephanas was a respected member of the church at Corinth, whose family became the first converts in Greece (1 Corinthians 16:15-18). He and his household were among those few that Paul baptized personally (1 Corinthians 1:16). Other biblical figures in the novel include Justus (Acts 18:7), Crispus (Acts 18:8); and Sosthenes (Acts 18:17).

Antonia is a fictional character. But the Emperor Claudius's tendency to be fooled by women of a certain character is well documented by history.

As usual, I used a few quotes in the context of the book for the sheer fun of it. Aquila's words at the end of chapter 8, "The only way to peace is by learning to accept, day by day, the circumstances and tests permitted by God. By the repeated laying down of our own will and the accepting of his as it is presented in the things which happen to us" are a paraphrase based on the preface to *Hinds' Feet on High Places* by Hannah Hurnard. Mary's words to Priscilla in chapter 19, "The growing good of the world is partly dependent on unhistoric acts such as yours. That things are not so ill with these folks as they might have been . . . is half-owing to you for living faithfully a hidden life" are a paraphrase of the closing scene in George Eliot's *Middlemarch*. At the end of chapter 25, Aquila describes what Priscilla means to him, borrowing several phrases from C. S. Lewis's description of his own wife, Joy, in *A Grief Observed*. The minor adjustments I made to these quotes were in order to make the flow more seamless.

The more I studied this couple, the more they amazed and inspired me. They were iconoclasts, intrepid warriors for the Kingdom of God who broke the rules and helped change the world. Their marriage must have been an incredible partnership. Priscilla, especially, sheds some light on the crucial and extraordinary role of women in the early church.

As always, no novel can begin to capture the sheer depth of the Word of God. The best way to study the Scriptures is not through a work of fiction, but simply by reading the original. This story can in no way replace the transformative power that the reader will encounter in the Bible. To learn more about Priscilla and Aquila, please refer to Acts 18:1-28; 1 Corinthians 16:19; Romans 16:3-5; and 2 Timothy 4:19.

ACKNOWLEDGMENTS

THANKS, FIRST OF ALL, to my husband, my greatest strength, my deepest blessing. I don't know how I used to write books without your help! Seriously! How did I?

What a marvelous treasure I found in my agent, Wendy Lawton, who continues to bless me with her friendship, her protective vigilance, and her vast knowledge.

I remain profoundly thankful for the incredible fiction team at Tyndale, who have become like a beloved writing family. They even sent me chicken soup and cookies when I most needed a touch of comfort. What more can a girl ask? What a joy to work with Stephanie Broene and Kathy Olson again: their astute insights and patient counsel has transformed *Daughter of Rome* into one of my favorite books. Karen Watson, Jan Stob (thanks for the extra time you spent with me in Charleston), the precious sales team, and the hardworking marketing experts—I owe every one of you so much thanks. And chocolate. Tons of chocolate.

Inexpressible thanks to Rebecca Rhee for her priceless friendship and her insightful edit of this story, which helped to create a much better read. Thanks also to Kim Hill, whose encouragement, prayers, and sheer belief in my calling helped me keep going. I remain indebted to Lucinda Secrest McDowell, who read the early chapters of the story and told me it was good before I had figured out what the story was really going to be about. Now that's enthusiasm.

I have to dedicate a whole sentence to my mama here, who without fail, genuinely feels I am the best writer in the world. Can't ask for a more loving or committed fan.

A special thanks to my super assistant, Amanda Geaney, who graciously puts up with me, helps me in countless ways, and leaves me free to actually write a little.

I owe a special debt to Peter Habyarimana, who candidly shared his memories of life as a street kid in Uganda. Some of Marcus's experiences as a homeless child in Rome were based on Peter's true-life stories. A staff member at World Vision today, Peter's harrowing childhood accounts made me laugh and cry and wonder at the incandescent soul that could survive so much neglect and go on to love with such abundance.

To every single one of my readers who keeps coming back for more stories and shares in these amazing adventures: thank you. You are the very best any writer could ask for. It is an incredible privilege to write for you. Keep those letters and emails coming! They are fuel during the weary, brain-dead hours.

And finally, words fail when I think of God's grace. Gratitude hardly seems enough.

I will open my mouth in a parable;
    I will utter dark sayings from of old,
things that we have heard and known,
    that our fathers have told us.

We will not hide them from their children,
    but tell to the coming generation
the glorious deeds of the Lord, and his might,
    and the wonders that he has done. . . .
That the next generation might know them,
    the children yet unborn,
and arise and tell them to their children,
    so that they should set their hope in God
and not forget the works of God,
    but keep his commandments.

PSALM 78:2-4, 6-7

DAUGHTER OF ROME DISCUSSION QUESTIONS

1. This type of novel is called "biblical fiction," a genre that sets stories during the time of the Old or New Testament and incorporates people we know from the Bible (in this case, Priscilla, Aquila, and the apostle Paul). Do you enjoy reading biblical fiction? What are its benefits for contemporary readers? What are its drawbacks?
2. Did you enjoy the historical information about the city of Rome and its customs? In what ways does it add to or detract from the story?
3. Who are your favorite characters in the book? Why?
4. How well were you able to identify with Priscilla? Have you personally experienced any of her struggles, such as having a hard time accepting God's forgiveness for something in your past? How have you dealt with such challenges?
5. Priscilla faces a huge test of her faith—and faithfulness—when she has the opportunity to help Antonia, a person who has intentionally set out to harm Priscilla. How did her response to Antonia challenge your own faith? How did it encourage you?

6. What was Aquila's core struggle? Can you relate to him?
7. Did you enjoy the subplot about Marcus? How did it add to Priscilla and Aquila's story?
8. As in previous books by the author, the apostle Paul makes an appearance. How do you feel about her portrayal of this early Christian leader? In what ways is the character in these pages like the man we read about in Scripture? Are there ways in which he is different?
9. Did you find the portrayal of the early church in this book appealing? What can we learn from the lives of these early Christians? How can their struggles and victories inform our twenty-first-century worship and church life?
10. If you have read *Thief of Corinth*, did you enjoy seeing Galenos and Theo again? Do you like it when authors bring back previous characters in new books?

ABOUT THE AUTHOR

TESSA AFSHAR is the award-winning author of several works of historical fiction. Her most recent novel, *Thief of Corinth*, was an Inspy Award finalist in the historical romance category. *Land of Silence* won an Inspy Award in the general fiction category and was voted by *Library Journal* as one of the top five Christian fiction titles of 2016. *Harvest of Gold* won the prestigious Christy Award in the historical romance category, and *Harvest of Rubies* was a finalist for the 2013 ECPA Christian Book Award for fiction. In 2011, after publishing her first novel, *Pearl in the Sand*, Tessa was named New Author of the Year by the FamilyFiction-sponsored Reader's Choice Awards.

Tessa was born in Iran and lived there for the first fourteen years of her life. She then moved to England, where she survived boarding school for girls and fell in love with Jane Austen and Charlotte Brontë, before moving to the United States permanently. Her conversion to Christianity in her twenties changed the course of her life forever. Tessa holds a master's of divinity from Yale, where she was cochair of the Evangelical Fellowship. She served in ministry for nearly twenty years before becoming a full-time writer and speaker.

Visit her online at www.tessaafshar.com.